LAIRD OF ROGUES

ALSO BY SUSAN KING

The Whisky Lairds Series

Laird of Twilight

Laird of Secrets

Laird of Rogues

The Border Rogues Series

The Raven's Wish

The Raven's Moon

The Heather Moon

The Celtic Nights Series

The Stone Maiden

The Swan Maiden

The Sword Maiden

Laird of the Wind

The Scottish Lairds Series

Taming the Heiress

Waking the Princess

Kissing the Countess

The Celtic Lairds Series

The Angel Knight

Lady Miracle

LAIRD OF ROGUES

THE WHISKY LAIRDS SERIES
BOOK THREE

SUSAN KING

ePublishingWorks!
love what you read.

Book and cover design by eBook Prep
www.ebookprep.com

June 2023
ISBN: 978-1-64457-608-3

ePublishing Works!
644 Shrewsbury Commons Ave
Ste 249
Shrewsbury PA 17361
United States of America

www.epublishingworks.com
Phone: 866-846-5123

For my amazing, wonderful, patient family.

*"Oh, what a tangled web we weave
When first we practice to deceive..."*

— SIR WALTER SCOTT, *MARMION*, 1808

PROLOGUE

*M*oonlight and mist gleamed over cobblestones as Ronan MacGregor approached the tavern, wary as he went, boots echoing. The old town of Culross, known for coal and salt exports through its harbor, favored smuggling traffic too. Free traders swept down from the hills to move clandestine goods swiftly out the harbor of a night.

Though he had numbered briefly among those rascals, it was time he returned to life as laird, lawyer, and distiller of whisky. New-minted viscount as well, dare he claim it. But that could bring more trouble; some might claim he wanted the property that much. What he wanted was justice.

Tonight, traveling north to Perthshire from Edinburgh, he meant to meet friends waiting for him in the tavern yonder. What he had heard in the city made it imperative to find them.

Stepping inside the tavern, he entered a haze of smoke, noise, and lamplight. His Highland gear—belted plaid, old jacket, tartan waistcoat— stood him in good stead here. In the city, he preferred neatly tailored clothing of dark superfine; the Courts of Session and Justiciary would look askance at a lawyer in Highland kit. Even so, he wore his hair longer than most and kept to the stubborn note of a tartan waistcoat. If a Whig eyebrow twitched here or there, so be it.

Moving through the main room, he was watchful, part of the habit he had formed in the dragoons and later in smuggling. The patrons looked ordinary enough; old men in plaids and bonnets sharing ale and playing cards, likely down from the hills for the cattle market; a weary family eating supper. No excise officers here. Good, then.

He pushed through a curtain into a smaller room to see two Highlanders at a table, one lean and fair, the other brawny and dark. They looked up.

"Glenbrae, here at last," said the tall blond fellow, speaking Gaelic.

"Greetings, Stewart. MacInnes." He sat. The table held glasses, a squat brown crockery jug, and a plate with leftover crumbles of cheese and oatcakes.

Iain MacInnes poured from the jug and handed a glass to him. "How was the city?"

"Grand and busy. Filled with rumors of the king's visit this summer."

"That has been dangled and canceled for a year." Arthur, Viscount Linhope—Mr. Stewart here—broke off a bit of cheese. "I wonder if he will come at all."

"They say August."

MacInnes raised his glass, amber liquid gleaming. "To King Geordie, may he learn to love the Scots, which he does not at present. How was court?"

"A verdict of not proven for my client, so he is free. The lad never should have been arrested. Remember," he added low. "John R. MacGregor, advocate, was never here, nor were his friends, the doctor and the engineer. Just three reprobates."

MacInnes lifted his glass. "To rogues and reprobates."

Linhope saluted as well. "To Will and Darrach, who began this sore adventure."

Ronan drew a breath against the power of the names and the tug in his heart. His brother. His cousin. He took a sip.

MacInnes indicated the glass. "So? Tell us what you think."

Ronan swirled the liquid. "It is not Glenbrae whisky, I know that."

"Glenbrae has no equal," Linhope laughed.

Ronan tasted again. Malt, heather, peat, a subtle hint of earth and stone through the water source, he decided. He cupped it on his tongue to find an elusive taste—ah, grass and wild garlic. He swallowed the sweet burn of it.

"Pitlinnie," he declared. "Over three years in the keg."

Iain butted Linhope with an elbow. "No one can tell the whisky like the laird of Glenbrae."

"Pitlinnie does not trim the burnside that runs past his still, so his whisky tastes of what grows there. But this is good." Ronan turned the jug to read the handwritten label. *Pitlinnie. Fine Highland Whisky.* "It will sell."

"He is shipping a quantity of it tonight. The English pay well for Highland whisky," Linhope said. "Northern whiskies made with good barley malt are heaven's nectar compared to Lowland liquor made from cheap grains. Pitlinnie will profit."

"But we are not here to talk about Pitlinnie," Iain said. "Ronan, what news? Did you learn more about the Darrach estate?"

"It remains unresolved and will proceed to the courts since my cousin died intestate."

"Go to Darrach Castle and look for the papers yourself," MacInnes suggested.

"Mairi Brodie told me the housekeeper stayed there to wait for a new lord. She wrote to me," Linhope added, "wanting advice in treating a tenant's bad cough."

"Ah." Ronan had made his peace with Mairi Brodie, yet felt guarded. A deeper love he would never find, though she had married his brother instead. He shrugged. "I have something else on my mind. We must retire our concern. It is time, lads."

"We knew the risks in taking this on when your kinsmen were killed,"

Linhope said. "We agreed to finish their work to honor their memories. It has gone well."

"And I am grateful to you both."

"We could hardly abandon you to danger." Iain grinned.

"You both enjoy suchlike," Linhope said. "Not me. If we are done, then good."

Iain huffed. "What then of the Wild Whisky Lairds?"

"The name makes us seem like heroes. We are not," Ronan said. "We provide a service, moving goods about, collecting funds promised to our kinsmen, sharing it with their families. That is all."

MacInnes shrugged his big shoulders. "It is an honor to be called 'Whisky Lairds' by Sir Walter Scott himself."

"He christened Will and Darrach that for their escapades, not knowing their true names," Ronan pointed out. "Highland heroes in plaid defending their people and saving the ancient Celtic brew. It could all go black as the Earl o' Hell's waistcoat for us."

"But Pitlinnie wants a new arrangement," MacInnes said. "Very lucrative."

"He wants what only benefits him. We already refused him."

"And he is not pleased to be moving his lot on his own," MacInnes said.

"We must turn to other matters now—doctoring, building, lawyering," Ronan said, gesturing to each. "And making whisky. The Glenbrae distillery is doing well. Join me in that. We can build our whisky business. Let the Whisky Lairds be forgotten."

Linhope nodded. "We finished what Will and Darrach began. We all wish those two brave fools were here now. But they are not. It is time to end it, as Ronan says."

"Listen," Ronan said. "The laws will change in January, they say. Highlanders will no longer benefit from free trade. Licensed distilleries will profit. We are gentlemen, not thieves. My grandfather forfeited his lands and title for his loyalty to Prince Charlie, and the family came to poverty. But my father brought up his family to have manners and education. I intend to build that legacy, not destroy it."

"You are not just a fine lawyer, but a war hero, and never ran from danger," Linhope said. "We trust your opinion, aye, Iain?" The other nodded.

Some memories Ronan would rather forget. "Just be wary. More excise officers and more arrests and penalties will come. We did what we promised."

"Aye, then," MacInnes nodded reluctantly.

"Good. We will talk later." Ronan stood, leaving coins on the table. Heading for the door, he felt a prickle on his neck, dread in his gut. "Go. *Now,*" he growled.

He stepped outside first, wariness strong. Empty tavern steps, a moonlit street, dark buildings—but down the way, two carts. Horses. Something was not right.

Footsteps, shadows, the glint of pistols as men swarmed out of the darkness. "Stop!" a man called. "His Majesty's excise officers. Which of you is Glenbrae?"

Whirling, Ronan felt a pistol poke hard in his back. He spun away, but tough, meaty hands grabbed, yanked, held him. A shot rang out and whizzed past his head. He jutted out an elbow to strike a jaw and ducked to evade a clubbing. Nearby, Linhope and Iain took and gave blows as a fierce brawl escalated on the tavern steps.

"Stand fast!" Two men had MacInnes by the arms, the big man nearly wrenching free. Others knocked Linhope to his knees. Feeling cold steel press against his temple, Ronan went still. His arms were wrenched from behind.

"MacGregor of Glenbrae," one man growled. "We have you now."

"Where is your warrant?" Ronan demanded. "Standing on the steps of this establishment, you need permission to invade its boundary or threaten its patrons."

"Talking like a long-robe? Hah! The Whisky Lairds, found at last!" The man spit. "MacGregor of Glenbrae. Stewart and MacInnes. We are excise, taking you for your crimes this night."

Held fast, breathing hard, Ronan recognized Peter Dawson, an excise officer who had nearly caught them before. Ronan's brother had believed

Dawson was in the pay of others intent on taking down the Whisky Lairds. Suspecting Dawson was responsible for the deaths of his brother and cousin, Ronan felt even more sure now.

"You witnessed no crime of ours this evening," Ronan said.

"We had word you three are moving illicit parcels tonight. A load o' peat reek just left by secret transport. Take 'em," Dawson ordered.

Linhope was shoved forward. MacInnes bellowed, caught fast. Then Ronan felt a slam to his head, cobbles lurching toward him. Blackness.

CHAPTER 1

The stone steps leading down to the dungeon vaults beneath Edinburgh Castle were so steep and timeworn that Ellison Graham proceeded carefully in thin slippers. In one gloved hand, she held the skirt of her gown, lavender muslin trimmed in black ribbon; with the other, she steadied Lady Strathniven's arm as they descended toward the old wooden door where a red-coated guard waited.

Just ahead, Adam Corbie, secretary to Ellison's father and nephew to the viscountess, waved a folded letter. "Sergeant! This letter is signed by Sir Hector Graham, Deputy Lord Provost of Edinburgh, allowing us entry."

"My gracious, it is hot today," Lady Strathniven remarked, her dimpled cheeks flushed, the color creeping upward to the iron-gray curls neatly framing her face. She fluttered a silken fan and peered from under the rim of her straw bonnet. "I hope this proves worth the trouble."

"I hope so too," Ellison agreed. The viscountess smiled, brown eyes twinkling. Lady Strathniven's beauty and impishness had endured, though she was older than Ellison's father, her longtime friend. But Sir Hector had become even more stodgy and grumpy with time.

Though Ellison hoped his sour demeanor was not all her fault, she knew it might be. If he discovered she went to the dungeons today, he would be furious.

"They will let us in now," Adam Corbie said as they joined him. The sentry beckoned them into the dark interior, where a second guard met them. Both wore the scarlet coats, white cross-bands, dark plaid trousers, and black tricorns of the soldiers of the Regiment of Foot assigned to Edinburgh Castle. And both looked displeased to see the visitors.

"This is not the usual entrance, sir," one sentry told Corbie. "Visitors wishing to see these prisoners must purchase a ticket from the office of the Governor of the Castle and enter through the castle above."

"This letter exempts us," Corbie said stiffly. "These ladies need not wait with the public. This is Miss Graham, the daughter of the deputy lord provost, who is also chief of the constabulary. And Lady Strathniven, my aunt. They wish to see the famous prisoners."

While the guards conferred, Corbie glanced at the women. "I am glad I was able to facilitate this for you today."

"Two widowed ladies need no escort, Adam," his aunt said, "but we appreciate your help. I am curious to see these fellows the whole city is talking about."

"You should not have to wait with the common crowd. And I feel it is incumbent upon me to ensure your safety."

Ellison gave him a cool smile. She had known him nearly all her life, for Lady Strathniven had been her mother's best friend. But lately, Corbie showed a deeper interest in her that she tactfully overlooked. Familiar with his arrogance and need for praise, she felt more comfortable keeping him at arm's length.

Yet she was grateful he used her maiden name in public; she preferred it now. "Mrs. Graham-Leslie" seemed like another person—a foolish girl released from a calamitous marriage by tragedy. For her father's sake after the scandal, she strived to be complacent and subdued, and she hoped to start over, if only in his eyes.

Life had become dull, but she had allowed it. Nor had she quite given up mourning, clinging to the grays and lavenders that reflected her life. Today, however, she risked a little disobedience and adventure, as she used to do.

"But sir, viewing hours have not begun today," one of the guards was saying.

"Did you read this?" Corbie flapped the letter. "We have permission to privately view these Whisky Lairds. Ridiculous name," he muttered.

"Very well." The guard beckoned them to follow.

As they went, Ellison glanced around in fascination at the subterranean maze beneath Edinburgh Castle. Walls and arched ceilings of rough stone caught the eerie light of flaming sconces. The long corridors and shadowy cells were dim and cool, hewn centuries earlier from the living rock of the castle cliff.

She absorbed every detail she could, intending to describe the warren of passages and dungeon cells in the novel she was writing. Today's opportunity to see the dungeons—and real Highland smugglers!—could greatly enhance her story.

But she kept that to herself. While her family believed she dabbled in poetry, she had not written verse since her husband's death. The viscountess said her poetry should be published, and even Papa admitted the lines had some quality. But Ellison wanted to write adventurous tales of old Scotland like Miss Jane Porter's *Scottish Chiefs*.

For now, she would guard her passion fiercely and silently. Her father would disapprove, thinking novel writing just another unfortunate impulse on her part. And Lady Strathniven, whom she adored, struggled to keep the smallest secret.

As they passed cells with iron-barred doors, she glimpsed lantern light, men moving about, and heard murmured voices; she could smell meals cooking that masked less pleasant odors. Taking the viscountess's arm, she hurried after the guards.

"Are the whisky criminals here?" Lady Strathniven asked.

"Further along, madam," one sentry replied. "These are foreign prisoners. Some were captured after Waterloo and a few have been here much longer."

"Will they be released?" Ellison asked.

"The government will decide, Miss Graham. We house prisoners of state here. Most others go to the jail on Calton Hill. But the Lord Provost ordered the whisky smugglers placed here temporarily. They will be sent up to Calton soon."

"They are here because they generate income for the city," Corbie said.

"We do sell a good number of tickets to see them, sir," the guard agreed.

"They are scoundrels, but the city can use the extra revenue with the king expected this summer. Our office is organizing it," Corbie boasted.

"Aye, sir. This way, around this corner."

"These fellows are quite the sensation this summer," Lady Strathniven said. "A Highland man is always a sight to admire, do you not agree, Ellison?"

"So interesting," she replied, not wanting to seem too enthusiastic.

"I do not share the sentiment," Corbie remarked with a sniff.

"The newspaper accounts are thrilling. I so enjoy hearing Ellison read the articles aloud. Dangerous rascals, *The Courant* called them."

"This whole matter is absurd," Corbie said.

"We are grateful for your company, Adam, but do try to be more pleasant."

"Pardon me, Aunt. But they should be in Calton jail, not lauded by the public."

"Just along here." The guard gestured to a secondary passageway.

Ellison's heartbeat quickened. Reports of the Whisky Lairds had fired her imagination for months. Now she would see them at last. No one knew that she devoted long hours to studying Scottish history and writing in secret. Caution had made her life too quiet, but she could find adventure in writing stories.

When the notorious Whisky Lairds had been captured, she read avidly about them in the news journals. The Lord Provost's decision to allow visitors to see them for the benefit of a fee sparked her interest and anticipation.

"Miss Ellison, you are wool-gathering." Corbie offered his elbow. She took it. "We must hurry so that we can depart before public hours begin."

"Everyone is mad for a peek at these fellows," Lady Strathniven said as they moved ahead. "This is the most interesting thing the city has seen for a while."

"Until the king's visit in August," Corbie said.

"True. It does not give the city much time to prepare, though," his aunt said.

"We have been planning for months on the chance, but our office will be busy."

"I thought Sir Walter Scott headed the organizing committee," Ellison said.

"He does, and he has plenty of ideas—revues, receptions, balls, dinners, and so on—but our office must make the arrangements. His requests can be outrageous."

"But it will be such an exciting time! Adam, you promised that Ellison and I would have invitations to the royal events."

"I will do my best, my lady aunt."

As they walked, Ellison heard a plaintive melody. "Fiddle music!"

"That will be one o' them playing," the guard said. "No harm in it."

At the end of the corridor stem, two sentries sat at a small table beside a cave-like cell. The door was a wide iron grate set into the rock frame. Inside, Ellison saw three Highland men, one standing, two seated. Thin sunlight streamed through an aperture high in the rock wall, illuminating their forms and faces.

Transfixed by the music and compelled by the sight, she walked forward. The cell's interior was simple—straw-covered floor, bench, small table, three narrow cots. The fiddle player, tall and fair-haired, stood. Two Highlanders sat on a bench. Ellison drifted closer.

The fiddler was a master, the tune a favorite of hers, played at dances and soirees. His gilded hair swept over his brow, his fingers were deft and nimble. He had a fine face, she thought; gentle and kind. One of the seated men held a book in his hands; big and brawny, he had a swarthy dark beard and unruly black curls. The third Highlander seemed asleep, chin dropped, arms crossed, long legs extended. A scruff of beard and long dark hair framed a face with handsomely shaped features, dark brows, and thick eyelashes.

All three wore belted plaids of various patterns, crumpled shirts, shabby waistcoats, stockings, worn leather shoes. Unkempt from head to foot, they looked strong and healthy, and younger than Ellison expected, perhaps thirty years or so.

Highlanders of a rough sort, just as the newspapers claimed. The accounts said they spoke only Gaelic and lacked manners and education. Yet the fiddler played with skill, the black-haired brute was absorbed in reading, and the third fellow possessed a banked power. He was sharp and aware, tilting an eyebrow at the slight sound of her shoes scuffing the stone floor outside the cell.

"Highland scoundrels," Corbie said.

Startled, Ellison turned. "I find them intriguing."

"Oh my," said Lady Strathniven, flapping her fan. "They are rather stunning."

Watching them, Ellison felt a wrench of compassion. She had spent her childhood in the Highlands until her mother's death; life had been so happy there. She had developed an affection and respect for the Highland people, finding nobility in their character, traditions, and beautiful language, and sensing strength in the face of their plight, with many cast from their homes, the life they knew vanishing.

Perhaps these men had been brought low by English laws that were not always fair to Scots. She knew something of the smuggling trade from her father's conversations. Highlanders producing whisky and other goods felt forced to find clever ways to slip past English authorities and avoid heavy taxation, thus helping their families survive. Surely these men had families, wives, children, reasons for their actions.

The poignant fiddle music filled her heart, brought tears to her eyes.

"Savages," Corbie said. "Do not fear them, Miss Ellison. I am here to protect you." He touched her elbow briefly.

"I am not afraid. It just seems wrong to intrude on their privacy."

"Criminals give up the right to such privileges."

"Oh, my," Lady Strathniven breathed again. "These are hardly savages. Why, with a barber, decent clothing, and better circumstances, they would pass for Highland gentlemen. Can you not see them as noble clan chieftains with velvet jackets and feathered bonnets?"

"No," Corbie said.

"They do look heroic," Ellison agreed. "As if they stepped out of one of Sir Walter Scott's epic Highland poems."

"I agree! I am glad we had this chance to see them." Lady Strathniven gave Ellison's arm an affectionate pat.

The viscountess had adopted a maternal role toward Ellison and her two sisters after their mother's death ten years before. Since then, Lady Strathniven had lost her husband and grew even closer to the Grahams. Ellison loved her dearly, appreciating the lady's salty and generous nature, refreshing and kind.

"We must go," Corbie said, as the fiddler began a slow, sad melody.

"Soon. I want to listen to the music," the viscountess replied.

As the music flowed outward, Ellison felt a sense of dignity and intelligence in the three handsome Highlanders. Each one had a wildness and grace about him. She had a strong feeling that none of them belonged in prison.

The black-bearded man set down his book, flexing his big hands, and glanced up. Seeing Ellison, he smiled shyly. His size gave him a beast-like appearance, but his eyes and expression were gentle. Returning his gaze, she felt a swirl of compassion.

The sleeping man—or was he merely bored, she wondered—stirred, broad shoulders pressed against rock. He murmured something in Gaelic to the large man.

Aingeal, answered the black-haired beast. The two spoke softly.

Understanding some of it, Ellison gasped softly.

Gaelic had been the language of the servants and her nurse, attuning her ear and tongue early to that lilting language. Later, she studied with a tutor in Edinburgh. For all his grousing, Papa had encouraged education for his daughters and was pleased when Ellison used her knowledge of Gaelic by joining an Edinburgh ladies' society. With them, she occasionally traveled into the Highlands to help Gaelic-speaking crofting families.

Iain, why are you smiling? the bored one asked.

An angel is visiting today, his friend answered. *Open your eyes, lad.*

Aingeal. Ellison felt her cheeks burn.

"Ruffians," Corbie muttered. "This is no place for ladies. We have seen enough."

The bored Highlander flashed his eyes open with a glare like a blue arrow.

"Oh!" Lady Strathniven breathed, flapping her fan.

His gaze found Ellison. She met it, held it, caught like a moth to that blue flame.

He had the rare beauty some men possess, his face an elegant blend of angle and curve, strength and tenderness. Long-lidded eyes under dark brows, squared jaw, and firm rounded lips were framed by waves of dark hair and a darker beard.

More, he had a gaze like a lightning strike. Meeting his gaze, she felt a chill run through her, crown to foot. Here was the hero of the adventure novel she was writing; here was the Highland rogue she imagined: noble, strong, beautiful.

"Fascinating," Lady Strathniven murmured.

"Oh aye," Ellison whispered.

"Rude," Corbie muttered.

Then the Highlander closed his eyes, shutting away that burning blue. He leaned back. His burly friend yawned. The fiddler set down the instrument.

"The one fiddles a decent Irish tune, I suppose," Corbie admitted.

"He played Scottish tunes," Ellison pointed out.

"No matter. They will go to trial soon and the city will be quit of them. Tried, sentenced, hanged. Shall we go, ladies?"

"Mr. Corbie, you seem determined to condemn them."

"They are reprehensible rogues, not the noble Highlanders of Mr. Scott's poems, Miss Ellison. I urge you to set aside your lofty ideals."

"Ideals are essential. They ennoble us."

In answer, Corbie made a scoffing sound.

Ellison glanced toward the cell. The fiddler spoke in Gaelic and the others answered quietly. The big brawny one shrugged, half-laughed.

"Likely plotting their escape, though it is impossible," Corbie grumbled.

"They are saying," Ellison replied, "that they feel like animals in a zoo."

The bored Highlander snapped his eyes open and looked straight at her.

"A zoo indeed," Iain said.

"And you a wretched bear," Linhope said. Iain shrugged, chuckled.

Narrowing his eyes, Ronan watched the young woman in lavender, watching them from under her straw bonnet. She understood Gaelic. He was certain of it.

"Careful," he warned. "Your angel knows what we are saying."

"Oh!" said the angel, confirming it.

"What is it, dear?" The older lady, plump and handsome, turned. The angel's mother? "Did they say something wicked?"

Rosy color spread into the girl's cheeks. "They mentioned an angel."

"You do look quite pretty today, Ellison."

Ellison. He liked the name. Feminine, with a tenor of strength. He was curious that she understood Gaelic; few of the privileged class in the city bothered to learn Gaelic these days. He frowned.

And Iain, the beast, had a poet's heart; the lass was indeed angelic, even enchanting. Willowy, petite, with golden hair wisping from under the bonnet, she was all creamy skin and easy blushes, with large grayish eyes and lush rosy lips. Despite that china-doll prettiness, her gaze was winsome and intelligent.

Pity she was just another who paid a fee to gape at the Highland prisoners.

She returned his gaze, direct and alert. He tilted his head to acknowledge it. Her lips quirked in a smile as she turned away. Though he felt a tug of attraction, he would not let himself show interest in a haughty society girl.

An uncomfortable thought struck. Had he met her at some occasion in the city? He would have remembered her, he thought. Generally he avoided such events, but as a lawyer, chieftain's son, cousin to a clan chief —and available bachelor—John MacGregor, advocate, had value in social circles. Perhaps he had met both women. The older one looked distinctly familiar.

The girl turned to the others. "Mr. Corbie, Lady Strathniven. Shall we leave?"

"Immediately," the gentleman replied.

Strathniven. Ronan had met the viscountess, he realized. Several years ago, he and his cousin, the new Viscount Darrach, had visited their solicitor's office and had entered a heated discussion with Lord Strathniven over land rights to that property. As they explained their family's legal, moral, longstanding claim to the land, Ronan had nearly snapped at the lady's husband. That truculent older gentleman, a Crown-awarded viscount, had spouted the letter of English law in claiming the property to which Ronan and his kinsman had full right by Scottish law. But Strathniven had prevailed. Ronan recalled the lady's kindness and embarrassment at her husband's insistent and rude behavior.

Dipping his head, he hoped his outward aspect as a possible criminal, bearded, unkempt, of scant importance, would hide his identity in case any of the visitors had seen him before.

"I suppose we should go." Lady Strathniven fanned herself. "But I would like to see these Whisky Lairds again."

"We should not return, my lady," Corbie said. "And best call them what they are—scoundrels, ruffians, savages, Highland devils."

"That is excessive even from you, Adam," she retorted.

"But accurate. Miss Ellison, do you feel well? You have gone pale."

"We must not stand here staring at them so. It is rude."

True, Ronan thought. Gawking at prisoners could only amuse for so long.

Standing, he went to the iron grate. The viscountess saw him and smiled. No spark of recognition, just curiosity. Good. Lifting a hand, he waggled his fingers. She fluttered her fan and nearly giggled.

"My lady, come away from that rascal," said Corbie.

"Oh bother, Adam. They have nice manners and are no threat."

"My lady." Miss Graham took the woman's arm. Her glance met Ronan's.

"*Slàraich, mo aingeal,*" he murmured. *Farewell, my angel.*

She blinked, gasped, eyes wide.

"*Ah, tha i a' tuigsinn,*" he murmured. *She understands.*

She whirled away. The man called Corbie took both their arms.

"Miss Ellison, did he insult you? I will have a word with him!"

"He was polite. Let us go."

Ronan stepped back. He would never see the girl again. Within weeks, he and his friends would be sentenced, imprisoned or sent away in servitude, even hanged. Only a miracle would save them. He knew the law and their poor chances.

An angel might have visited, but a miracle was unlikely.

CHAPTER 2

"'*P*eople visit the Castle dungeons just to see the prisoners, while ladies brave enough to venture in seem alarmed, fanning themselves madly, distressed to see these dangerous Highland rogues—'"

Ellison paused, reading aloud from that day's edition of *The Edinburgh Observer,* her attention caught by the illustration of the smugglers in the Castle dungeon. Three bearded men in plaid amid a haze of inky shadow. However, this article provided names.

Stewart. MacInnes. MacGregor of Glenbrae. But which man was which?

"Do read on," Lady Strathniven said. Ellison glanced up at the viscountess and Adam Corbie, waiting expectantly.

They sat together at breakfast in the dining room of the Graham home on George Street. Despite the morning downpour, Corbie had arrived early as usual to assist Sir Hector. Lady Strathniven had arrived soon after, eager to escape the noise of renovation work in her home on Charlotte Square.

"Go on," Corbie picked up his cup of coffee. "Distressed ladies, etcetera."

"We were not distressed, seeing those poor fellows," his aunt commented. "We were quite interested, were we not, Ellison?"

Corbie made a huffing sound and rose from the table to refresh his coffee at the sideboard and heap sausages onto a plate. He returned.

"Miss Ellison, I nearly forgot," he said. "Your father wishes to speak with you this morning. I saw him earlier as he was entering his study."

"Thank you." Her stomach clenched. Did Papa know about yesterday's visit to the Castle, or had he discovered the novel she was writing? She kept her manuscript locked away, and her father rarely ventured into his daughter's territory.

"He seemed displeased," Corbie added.

"Your father hardly ever looks pleased these days," Lady Strathniven added blithely. "Do finish reading before you go, dear."

She resumed. "'Despite being rough and uneducated, the Whisky Lairds are strong, healthy, and pleasing in visage,'" she read.

"And so polite," Lady Strathniven said, then nibbled at her toast.

She read on while Corbie demolished his sausages and rain sluiced against the windows, draining the sunny cheerfulness of pale Chinese wallpaper and golden damask curtains chosen by her mother. For a moment Ellison wondered what Lady Graham would think of her visiting the dungeon. Likely she would have approved and would have sweetly overridden her husband's opinion. But she was gone.

"Yes, yes, they fiddle, read, play cards," Corbie droned. "But they are thieves. The noble Highlander is a myth."

"Every Highlander I have ever met is polite and intelligent," Ellison returned.

"Then you have not met enough of them, Miss Ellison."

"I spent my childhood in the Highlands and we go there often, you know that. They are considerate and kind. I am sorry you have a different opinion."

"She is correct, Adam. Read," Lady Strathniven urged.

"'Visiting the dungeon to see the prisoners is a popular outing this summer. Even notable citizens appear. Recently seen were—" Ellison stopped. "Oh!"

Corbie reached over to pluck the page from Ellison's hands. "Aha! 'Lady Strathniven and Miss Graham, seen in the company of a young gentleman, were admitted privately—'"

"Oh, my," the viscountess said. "Does Sir Hector know?"

"He might. In my defense, I was hounded by two lovely harridans."

"We asked nicely, and you agreed," Ellison said. Surely her father had seen the newspaper by now. Her stomach sank. "But how did *The Observer* know?"

"Journalists are busy, curious, and very interested in our sort," Corbie said.

"Our sort? Papa is of some interest due to his position, but we are not."

"We had every right to go," the viscountess said. "Widowed ladies may do as they please. It is a privilege of our sad station in life. I encourage Ellison to enjoy what little independence this offers her now."

"My lady, my mother would have been grateful to you for all you have done for my sisters and me these years," Ellison murmured.

"Thank you, dear. I have tried to do my best."

Corbie snapped the paper and began to read aloud. "Listen. 'The Highland criminals may display a noble spirit, but poor actions invite poor circumstances—'"

"Yes, noble! I can imagine them as clan chiefs," Lady Strathniven said dreamily.

"And I imagine this entire debacle will end soon," said a deep voice.

Ellison looked around as her father entered the dining room. Tall and imposing with iron-gray hair, his broad torso encased in black with a brown damask waistcoat, Sir Hector Graham was a fine-looking man even in his sixties. But the deep lines framing his mouth replaced the smiles Ellison remembered.

As he entered, a little dog trotted in on his heels. Sir Hector narrowly avoided stepping on the long-haired terrier, who sat to look up at him.

"Ellison, your pup is always underfoot," Sir Hector muttered.

"Here, Balor," she called, as the dog came to her. She broke off a bit of bacon to feed him quickly.

Sir Hector went to the sideboard and peered at the silver samovar as if it might magically produce coffee. Ellison rose and filled a cup, adding cream for him.

"Good morning," he said to all, taking a seat. "How goes the work at your house, Marjorie?"

"Nearly done, Hector," the viscountess said; they had used familiar names as childhood friends. "Though I am planning to head to the Highlands for the summer as usual. Will you and Ellison come up to visit?"

"This summer will be too busy, I am afraid." He took up a newspaper from the stack and snapped its pages open.

Ellison let out a breath. "Would you like sausages and eggs, Papa?"

"I breakfasted very early. Coffee will fortify me until luncheon. I see the *Observer* has a new piece about the Highlanders," he murmured, turning a page. "And there was a bit in *The Courant* as well. I would prefer none of my family see them, but it seems I am too late." He peeked past the page.

Ellison hunched her shoulders a little. "Please do not be cross, Papa."

"We quite enjoyed our outing, to be honest," Lady Strathniven said.

"A widow of your standing may do as she pleases, my lady. But—"

"Your daughter has the right too, as a widow now."

"I am sorry, Papa," Ellison blurted. "We did not want to trouble you."

He lowered the paper. "Mr. Corbie could have troubled me. I thought the letter of permission I signed was just for you, sir. Harangued, were you?"

"In a word," Corbie said.

"It is my fault, Hector. I asked Ellison to come with me, and Adam to escort us."

"So you indulged in a common spectacle." He lowered bushy eyebrows over gray eyes. "Ellison, I hope it was a lesson in the consequences of poor decisions."

"She is hardly planning a life of crime," Lady Strathniven said.

"No matter. We have a greater problem regarding these whisky runners now. Mr. Corbie, I need you to compose a reply to the royal secretary. A letter was delivered to me last night."

"Yes, sir."

"And Ellison, I will see you in half an hour in my study."

"Yes, Papa. I have a question," she ventured. "What if these men are wrongly accused? Everyone seems to assume their guilt."

"Leave the matter to the Court of Justiciary, Miss Ellison," Corbie said.

"True, sometimes men are unfairly accused," her father replied. "But our legal system manages to discover such things. Though some Highlanders experience hardships that drive them to crime, we must pursue and punish those who break our laws, whether the writ is Scottish or English. My dear, the government is not so mean an institution as you think."

"I fear the Whisky Lairds have caught your daughter's fancy, sir," Corbie said.

"Ellison is not easily dissuaded of dreams and ideals," Sir Hector agreed.

Not eager to hear an analysis of her faults, Ellison stood. "Excuse me. I have some correspondence to finish."

Balor trotted along behind her as she left the room. Somehow she always managed to displease her father as the disobedient young daughter. Her older sisters led idyllic lives with their husbands now, and although they had all endured challenges, Papa found them generally charming and faultless. Ellison had made a romantic but impulsive mistake that her father could neither forget nor forgive.

As she closed the door, she heard Lady Strathniven.

"Hector, let her be. She has been through enough at twenty-five. She is a compassionate girl and has a fine talent for writing, all to her credit."

"Her poetry is good. But her dreamy nature will be her undoing. I hope she marries again someday, but her impulsive, idealistic character works against her."

"Sir—and my lady aunt—if I may speak," Corbie said. "You probably suspect that I would like to court Miss Ellison. I wonder if you both approve."

"Oh," said Lady Strathniven. "I wonder."

"We will discuss it later, Adam. I must go back to my work."

Ellison hurried to her room, fighting anger and tears. If her father decided she should marry stiff-necked Adam Corbie, who had no imagination and a lofty opinion of himself, he would press hard for it. Corbie was heir to the Strathniven estate, which could be enough to decide the matter for everyone except her.

She had earned the right to manage her own life through tragedy. Her brief marriage to a viscount's son, romantic but hasty, had ended with his fatal fall from a horse. Despite his daughter's grief, Sir Hector could not seem to overlook her lapse in judgment. She might never recover his good opinion.

So be it, she decided then. This summer she would enjoy her independence, especially if her life might change. She would ask to accompany the viscountess to the Highlands. At Strathniven, she had freedom. She could write—and she could reclaim her lost spirit before it was too late.

The thought gave her a sense of determination. Of hope.

Minutes later, she was seated at her desk, taking her manuscript from its locked drawer. She wanted to shape her hero, an ancient Highland lord, to resemble the Highlander she had just seen.

Smoothing a fresh sheet of paper, she dipped a pen in ink and began to write.

The Highlander's eyes, the rich blue of a lochan in the twilight, went soft and sad as he remembered once more the hurt that had torn into his heart like the sharpest sword blade. To see Lady Isabella again after five years was a blow to his very soul. He had guarded his heart against her charms after she had dealt him a deep and unseen wound the day that Isabella Grant had chosen the Earl of Strathearn over Alasdair MacAlpin of Garslie.

Small laird by sunlight, poet by candlelight, cattle thief by moonlight—yet Garslie's strength, cleverness, and devotion could not compare to wealth and treachery. He scrabbled a living on rocky land, scratched heartfelt words on parchment, borrowed cattle when it was merited, and loved a lass who looked away.

She crossed out a word, scribbled a change, wrote on.

~

"That's a mournful tune, lad," Iain said. "Brings the ghosts out the very walls." He flipped cards while astride the bench facing Ronan. The prisoners had acquired the fiddle, a few books, cards, even a chess set from the castle governor, who thought to make the Whisky Lairds more attractive to visitors.

Certainly, it staved off boredom, Ronan thought. He felt slightly irritated by the music and Iain's foot tapping in time. His nerves felt raw that day. Weeks of being trapped here threatened to break his usual reserve.

Arthur was skilled in music and medicine; Iain was content with cards, books, drawing on the wall, and being annoyingly cheerful. Both were making the best of these days in prison. Ronan knew he should take a lesson from them, but today he just needed a good glower. He had no useful talent for whiling away the hours.

He dealt a new hand on the bench. Iain snarled and tossed one to the floor.

"Nine of diamonds! Curse of Scotland, they call it. Bad luck we do not need."

Hearing footsteps and chatter from the visitors outside their cell, Ronan did not look up. People came by almost daily to gawk, but the angel of days ago had not returned. He might show some interest if she had.

Yet that delicate beauty had stared like any onlooker before returning to her privileged existence. He shrugged and sorted the cards in his hand.

Linhope ended the song. "If the ladies enjoy the music, may it stir them to plead for mercy for three captive lads. If their kinsmen are judges, it could help."

"The judges of the justiciary court are stonehearted fellows," Ronan said.

"I wonder when we will hear word of a trial or a transfer," Iain said.

"Fifty-eight days since the night of our arrest, fifty-three since we came to Edinburgh." Ronan set down another card. "I am keeping count."

Sighing, Linhope sat on the straw-littered floor. "Public sentiment favors us. That could help."

"Perhaps a jury of fifteen will include some who enjoyed your music," Ronan drawled. "Still, there could be a way out of this."

"Escape? How?" Iain looked hopeful.

"It was done long ago when a cattle reiver went out a window of a dungeon cell on bed linens and shirts. But escape is punishable by further imprisonment. I meant a legal way out of here."

"Aye?" Linhope asked.

"If I could visit the Advocates Library, I could find the solution. But I cannot get there, even if it is down the High Street."

"If we were in Calton jail, escape might be easier," Iain said.

Ronan huffed. "Be glad we are not there, lad."

"Horrible place," Linhope agreed. "A handsome new building and already a hellish prison. Worse than the old Tolbooth it replaced."

"But a pretty fortress on its high hill, all towers and turrets. A fine design." Iain threw down a couple of cards, and Ronan groaned to see them.

"Says the architect," Linhope commented. "Last winter I visited the Calton infirmary with a colleague, but we could do little for the men there. The guards do not summon medical assistance except in dire cases. The Deputy Lord Provost in charge of the constabulary either does not know the conditions or does not care."

Hearing fading footsteps in the corridor, Ronan glanced up as the crop of visitors walked away. "Someone dropped a news journal."

Linhope went to the door to stretch an arm through the lower part of the grate, grabbing the paper. Returning to study the pages, he huffed a laugh.

"We are mentioned here. Smugglers, ruffians . . . hah, and a sketch of three hairy beasts in plaid."

"A fair description," Ronan said. "What's the date?"

"Thirtieth of June," Linhope said. "Have we been here that long? *Tempus fugit.* Ah. Here it says the king is expected to arrive in August."

Iain huffed. "We will get our best Highland kit ready."

"By God," Linhope said, reading on. "The Duke of Atholl is returning to his Perthshire property to attend a funeral." He glanced up. "Sir John Murray MacGregor has died. Your kinsman, Ronan. I am sorry."

Ronan felt a clench of sadness. "Chief of the Gregorach. My father's cousin. They grew up together. Sir John was tough as old leather but fair. Even as a boy, I wanted his respect." Memories flew past, some happy, some tainted with regret. He scowled against them.

"Sir Evan will be chief of the MacGregor clan now," Iain said.

"My second cousin, aye. A good man. The clan will do well under him."

"Thanks to you. He owes you his life. A hero's stand, they say," Iain said.

Ronan shook his head. "Evan was the hero that day in India, facing the odds bravely. We did our best to save him and each other. Only a few made it out." He recalled kin and friends, courage and grief on a day he would rather forget. Several years ago, he had sailed to India to join his cousin, having exchangd out of a Highland regiment into the dragoons to be at Evan's back. But it had gone sour between them since then.

"Once Darrach is yours, you will be a chieftain in the Gregorach and part of the chief's tail," Linhope said.

"The estate needs sorting first. Nor would Evan approve a kinsman accused of smuggling. But he will be a fine leader." He threw down his cards.

Linhope picked up the fiddle and began another tune. The music seemed to draw the sadness out of the very air, transforming it. Ronan leaned back and closed his eyes. Thoughts of his home in the Highlands flowed past on the melody—the breeze over heathery hills, the cool drench of a stream, the honeyed fire of whisky down the throat. He imagined relaxing in a sunlit meadow, a woman in his arms, soft and warm. Nameless, faceless, yet perhaps someday—

He frowned as the woman in his thoughts became the delectable Miss Ellison Graham. A pointless dream. Just now, his only concern was how to avoid a hanging.

CHAPTER 3

"Ellison," Sir Hector said, "we have a delicate matter to discuss. Mr. Corbie is aware."

"Papa, I have explained and apologized for the visit to the dungeons."

He came around the desk to lean against it, crossing his arms as he scowled down at her. Adam Corbie stood nearby, frowning too. Seated by the desk, Ellison straightened her spine against a sense of intimidation.

"This is more serious. I must ask your assistance in a difficult situation."

Ellison blinked. "My assistance?"

He picked up a letter from his desk, its royal seal broken. "The king's secretary sends requests regarding the king's visit. The Lord Provost insists that the city must do all in its power to satisfy them."

Ellison nodded. "You have been working diligently with Sir Walter Scott and the Celtic Society to prepare for this visit. I would be happy to help with any details."

"The king's arrival has not been publicly confirmed, but we expect him in August. That leaves six weeks before the city turns topsy-turvy. Our office is attending to many of the arrangements. Mr. Corbie has been invaluable in that."

"Thank you, sir."

"We hope all will go well and we can avoid too much pageantry and spectacle. But a new problem has come up." Sir Hector tapped the letter. "King George, it seems, is very fond of Highland whisky."

"I am sure your office can provide him a good supply," she said.

"He takes a dram or two every night, they say, and is devoted to the habit. He is especially fond of a particular Highland whisky."

"Does he know most Highland whisky is illicit, thanks to English laws?" Ellison asked pertly. "What he enjoys may come from kegs smuggled into London."

"He, uh, may not realize that," her father said. "He is especially fond of Glenbrae whisky, according to the royal secretary." Sir Hector cleared his throat. "Trouble is, King George has asked to meet the Glenbrae distiller."

"Trouble? Is Glenbrae illicit rather than licensed?" she asked.

"Licensed, I hope. Mr. Corbie, check this year's listings." In response, Corbie went to a bookshelf to pull a large ledger free, setting it down to flip through it.

"This particular request cannot be handled by the Lord Provost," Sir Hector went on. "As deputy lord provost, I oversee the constabulary and prisons."

"Prisons?" Ellison frowned.

"The Glenbrae distiller is presently incarcerated."

She caught her breath. "The king's favorite dram is produced by a smuggler? Is it—one of the Whisky Lairds? Oh, my!" She nearly laughed.

"It is hardly amusing. MacGregor of Glenbrae is a crofting laird, a tenant of the landowner. He might make the brew, but the landowner is legally the distiller. That presents another complication. Mr. Corbie, do you have it yet?"

"Here." Corbie glanced up from the ledger. "Glenbrae distillery in Perthshire was licensed two years ago to John R. MacGregor of Glenbrae. That would be Viscount Darrach," he added. "Glenbrae is on his estate. It is not far from my aunt's property of Strathniven, sir."

Sir Hector nodded. "This Viscount Darrach—he was a MacGregor?"

"Several MacGregor families live in the glens up there. The land was theirs long ago but was parceled out. They are crofters now. Tenants. Yes."

"I have seen those hills when riding in the countryside near Strathniven," Ellison said. "It is beautiful there."

"And full of smugglers," Corbie said.

"What matters here," Sir Hector said, "is that Viscount Darrach is dead."

"Oh, dear. Then there is no distiller to introduce to the king," Ellison said.

"So it seems," her father agreed. "There is confusion over the inheritance, so no heir has been named. It will go to the courts to decide, from what I understand."

"If you can supply the whisky, would that satisfy the Crown's request?"

"No. The king expects to meet the distiller. He was told the fellow is a peer."

"That is a problem, then," Ellison said.

"What we must determine for now," her father went on, "is if this MacGregor is the distiller. He must tell us where to find his supply of whisky. The excise officers have not found it."

"But how can I help?" Suddenly Ellison knew. "Ah, they speak Gaelic. You need a translator."

"Exactly. The castle governor appointed a sergeant to translate for them, but we must be discreet about this. A brief interview is all that is needed."

Her breath quickened. Here was a chance to see the smugglers again and talk with them. And a chance to please her father. "Of course, Papa."

"You have a good command of the Gaelic language. You spoke it as a child with the servants and have put it to good use in your work with the ladies' society."

"But I do not claim fluency. That would take a lifetime."

"Lady Strathniven tells me you are very proficient."

"I adore her, Papa, but she exaggerates. She thinks I am an expert in languages and an extraordinary poet." She laughed. "And my sisters are the equal of Beethoven and Raphael in art and music. And you, sir, will be Provost one day."

He pursed his lips. "The lady is generous. But we do need your expertise."

"Sir, this is no task for a young lady. Let me talk to the fellow," Corbie said.

"Do you speak the Highland tongue? I did not think so," Sir Hector barked.

"Papa, you said the viscount died? What happened?"

"Shot in a hunting accident. Very unfortunate."

Corbie shut the ledger. "The excise called it murder. Said the viscount came upon smugglers in the hills. The housekeeper at Strathniven said he had just inherited the property and was not well known in the glen."

"Murder, and so near Strathniven!" Ellison shuddered.

"Thieving and smuggling are everywhere in the Highlands, Miss Ellison. Though my lady aunt only keeps legal whisky at Strathniven House. The housekeeper makes sure of it."

"Does she," Sir Hector drawled. "As I recall, the excise officers reported that these so-called Whisky Lairds killed the viscount."

Ellison blinked, astonished. "I cannot imagine them committing murder."

"An innocent's observation," Corbie murmured.

"If a rumor of murder reached the journals, it would go poorly for us. These men are popular in the city, just as we are negotiating the royal visit," her father said.

"Perhaps you can tell the Crown there is no distiller to introduce," Ellison said.

"Lord Arbuthnot insists that the Crown's every request be met. It is imperative to secure the king's goodwill toward Scotland. If he is displeased, he may decide to visit France instead."

"Very well, then I will bring your message to this Mr. MacGregor."

"Just ask a few questions about the whisky, my dear."

"Can I tell him he will be paid for his whisky?"

"He is a prisoner, stripped of all rights," Corbie said.

"It is a reasonable question, sir. Papa?"

"This entire affair is an infernal nuisance," Sir Hector muttered, and sat. "The king cannot be refused. To be blunt, Adam, we will suffer consequences if this does not go smoothly. Every detail of the visit must be successful. Ellison, simply ask the man some questions. Mr. Corbie will accompany you."

"Shall I explain the king's request? It is an honor for Mr. MacGregor."

He shook his head. "The less he knows the better."

"Yes, Papa." She hid her rising excitement. Which one of the prisoners was MacGregor? Immediately she thought of the one with the very blue eyes and resonant voice who had spoken to her directly.

"We could never present a prisoner amid this royal spectacle," Corbie said. "It would make us a laughingstock."

"True, these rough Highlanders cannot be seen," Sir Hector agreed.

Ellison recalled Lady Strathniven's words. *With a barber, decent clothing, and better circumstances, they could be taken for fine Highland gentlemen.*

"Papa," she said, "could you introduce MacGregor to the king as Glenbrae, a laird and the distiller? It could be done quickly."

"Impossible," Corbie said.

"Interesting." Sir Hector looked thoughtful.

"There are strict protocols for any royal introduction," Corbie said. "Proper etiquette, required dress, and so on. The assemblies will be attended by hundreds, nay thousands, of peers and dignitaries, even Highland chiefs. Bringing a prisoner into one of these assemblies is unthinkable, Sir Hector. Surely you see that."

"Mr. MacGregor could dress as a gentleman for the introduction," Ellison said. "Papa, as chief of the constabulary, you could arrange his release for the day."

"That is absurd!" Corbie looked appalled. Sir Hector continued to frown.

LAIRD OF ROGUES | 41

"If he is kin to the deceased viscount, he might be an heir," Ellison suggested.

"Is the fellow presentable?" Sir Hector folded his arms. "Both of you saw him."

"No," Corbie said.

"Yes," Ellison said. "All three could pass for gentlemen in any crowd, given proper clothing and grooming."

Corbie scoffed. "Next he will need lessons in manners."

"Papa!" Ellison sat forward, excitement growing. "He could be tutored to prepare for the introduction."

"Sir, we must inform the Crown that this Glenbrae fellow is dead," Corbie said.

Sir Hector scowled, tapping his fingers. "Adam, find out the status of the Darrach inheritance."

"This is madness," Corbie muttered. "We would be complicit in fraud if we put forth this man as a person of merit."

"Then we would claim that the fellow misled us," her father said.

Ellison looked at him in surprise. Though he might entertain the thought, she realized he would want little to do with it. "Never mind," she said. "I will speak to the man as you request."

"Thank you, my dear."

Something occurred to her. "But—would it be possible to pardon him? If he is not a prisoner, he could be introduced as a laird and distiller in truth."

"Good heavens, no!" Her father held up a hand.

"Sir, your daughter is a perpetual romantic. None of this is helpful."

"Mr. Corbie, if you need my assistance, pray be more gracious," she snapped.

"Ellison," her father warned.

Twisting her fingers in her lap, she smothered impatience. If she could prove helpful, she might win back her father's regard. And she could see the Highland prisoners again, perhaps learn something for her novel. She had been longing for some small adventure, and here it was.

"I will do it, Papa. Whatever you need."

"Thank you, Ellison. We will make the arrangements."

She stood. "Papa, if you decide to introduce Mr. MacGregor, he might still need a translator. I could—"

"A few questions will be enough." He picked up a letter in clear dismissal.

Nodding, Ellison went to the door, opening it as the men quietly conferred.

"Preposterous, sir, and even dangerous," Corbie said.

"Still, we are in a precarious position. The king could cancel altogether. What other business do we have today? Sir Walter sent another request."

"Yes, asking that scaffolding be erected on Castle Hill for the crowds, and blue bunting cloth added as decoration."

"Expensive and excessive," Sir Hector muttered.

They had forgotten her presence. Ellison shut the door behind her.

CHAPTER 4

"Hey," Iain murmured. "The angel is here again."

Ronan looked up from the book he was reading. A guard was opening the iron grate, entering the cell carrying a tea tray, china and silverware rattling, and set it on a rickety table. The things wobbled precariously. "Tea and visitors," he announced.

Then she was there, setting gentle foot on straw-covered stone as if floating into the cell—a vision in lavender and black lace, a little bonnet curving around her head, golden curls escaping. The gentleman who had accompanied her before was back as well. Corbie, he recalled.

Ronan stood, as did Iain and Linhope, in expectant silence.

Ronan was not keen on tepid tea or guests, but seeing her, he was intrigued. They were all weary of this place and the ruse as Highland scoundrels, although their guises protected their identities as well as their kin and glen folk too.

But for now, the ploy must continue. Yet these weeks had made him even more determined, when he was free, to push for greater justice for Highland folk. The proud ancient culture of the Gaels, and their loyalty, their legacy, deserved appreciation and preservation. After this venture, he intended to promote truth for himself and others. But not today.

The young lady entered the cell after her. "I am Mr. Adam Corbie, secretary to the Deputy Lord Provost of Edinburgh," he announced. He was a slight man, sandy and plain in a tailored suit. The curl of his lip matched the slight sneer in his tone.

She translated into Gaelic, unaware it was not needed.

"This is Mrs. Graham-Leslie," Corbie went on. "She will speak with you briefly. You will show decent manners in her presence or I will have the guards on you directly."

She translated only part of that, her cheeks turning pink.

Corbie scowled. "They do not have a word of proper English."

"It is quite possible they understand some. Mr. Corbie, please wait outside. I need just a few minutes." She shooed him away with a gloved hand.

Ronan pinched back a smile. Corbie seemed oblivious to her subtle impatience with him. And, he noted, the young lady had a married name. Interesting.

Graham-Leslie. That was curious. Corbie had announced himself as secretary to the Deputy Lord Provost—Sir Hector Graham. Ronan had met the older man in passing in the courts; he was a stiff and unyielding fellow, chief of the constabulary in addition to his position as deputy lord provost. A kinsman to this young woman? That would explain the visiting privilege.

Stepping outside, Adam Corbie stood by the grating to watch them. Mrs. Graham-Leslie smiled as if she was attending a tea party. As she moved, a floral and vanilla scent wafted lightly over the dungeon's less pleasant odors. She seemed as delicate and divine as a beam of sunlight in these dank shadows.

"*Beannachdan, a dhaoine uaisle,*" she said. "Greetings, gentlemen." Her accent was good, but not native. "You are Mr. MacInnes, Mr. Stewart, Mr. MacGregor?"

Iain bobbed clumsily, while Linhope made a proper bow. "*Fàilte,*" Linhope welcomed her in Gaelic. "It is a pleasure to meet you."

The good doctor stopped short of kissing her hand, Ronan noted sourly. As for his turn, he only nodded in silence.

"I am pleased to meet you." Her smile was impish and yet angelic, with fleeting dimples. Beauty was a devastating contrast in this sorry place, Ronan thought. The girl was petite with lush curves and graceful bones; her sweet air held a thread of steely determination, and her eyes sparkled with intelligence.

The combined effect took him down swiftly, though he stood unmoving.

"May we offer you tea, madam?" Linhope asked in Gaelic.

"Keep your distance, sir," Corbie growled, watching.

"Miss Graham will do. I am widowed and do not use my married name."

Ronan raised a brow at that. Some Scotswomen kept their maiden names; Mairi Brodie had done so too. Yet this girl from an aristocratic family in the city made an unusual choice, as the status of widow reaped some benefit in social circles.

He glanced again toward the disapproving and possessive fellow at the cell door, and wondered if he was courting her.

"Let me pour." She tipped her bonneted head, a golden curl slipping free. Ronan savored that beauty and grace, rare in this dreary under-world. Oddly, she seemed at ease, not the least uncomfortable, almost as if she enjoyed this.

He narrowed his eyes. Why was she here, and what did she want?

She picked up the teapot. "*Am bu toil leat tì?* Do you want tea?" Iain and Linhope each thanked her as she poured into cracked cups.

"*Cha toil leam tì,*" Ronan said. *I do not want tea.* He folded his arms petulantly against the damnable effect she had on him. Her mere presence, this delicate wee widow who tossed her suitor out and faced three accused criminals alone, softened his hard reserve. He liked tea. What he disliked was a breach of his emotional barricade.

Linhope shot him a dark glance. *Behave,* it said.

She poured tea and served cakes as if the cell was a parlor in a fine mansion. The little cakes were studded with currants. Likely stale as a rock, he thought.

Iain and Linhope accepted the refreshment as if they, too, were in a parlor having tea. When the girl offered a cup to Ronan, he took it, declining the cake. Instinct told him to hide his ease with teacups and manners and lovely ladies pouring for gentlemen. He would continue to play the simple crofter.

He glanced at his friends to remind them of that, but they were too besotted to notice. Linhope sipped, Iain slurped, both smiled. Ronan held his cup and scowled.

"Now," Miss Graham said, balancing her teacup in white-gloved hands, "which of you is Glenbrae?"

Startled, Ronan said nothing. Iain pointed. "That one."

"I am *from* Glenbrae," Ronan emphasized in Gaelic, shooting a sight-dagger toward Iain for good measure. The fellow missed it, content as a happy pup.

"Mr. MacGregor—Glenbrae—may I have a word with you?"

"Me?" His surprised retort slipped out.

"If you please," she said in all her angel brightness. She came closer, her head scarcely at his shoulder. He looked down at her. Too close. Stepped back.

"What is it, Miss Graham?"

"It is Mr. Ronan MacGregor? Of Glenbrae? Is that correct?"

He paused. His baptized name was John Ronan MacGregor; as a lawyer, he used John R. MacGregor. Ronan was reserved for kin and friends—and lately, the justiciary court.

"What do you want of me?" he asked stiffly.

"I have your welfare in mind, only good intentions. I was sent by my father."

Ah. There it was. "We do not need saving by heaven's grace. Good-bye, Miss."

"Oh! Not that!" She nearly tilted the cup in her hands. "My father is the Deputy Lord Provost of Edinburgh. Sir Hector Graham. He sent me with a message for you."

Ronan frowned. "Why would any father send his daughter to such a place?"

"He cannot be seen speaking to you himself. And I offered to translate."

"Miss Ellison, are you quite done?" This from Corbie at the grate.

"Not yet," she called, adding in Gaelic to Ronan, "I trust I am perfectly safe?"

He bent slightly. "You are safe, madam," he replied softly. "But do not try to change me with charitable intentions or a churchy mission—or bring me your father's demands, if the man will not face me but sends a slip of a lass instead."

"Change you and convince you?" She looked up. "But Mr. MacGregor, that is precisely what I mean to do."

Her eyes were silvery gray, wide and limpid, her lips full and rosy, her gaze guileless and sparkling with intelligence. In an instant, Ronan felt himself succumb to her candid, whimsical, sensual charm. He stepped back against its subtle force.

"Miss Ellison," said the fellow at the door. "Shall I come in there now?"

"I am fine, Mr. Corbie," she said in English.

Intrigued by the girl and irritated by the fellow, Ronan leaned close. "Call off Sir Hound and tell me your business here. You and I are not acquainted. I would certainly have remembered you. Go on, deliver your father's message."

She looked up at him, face tilted, eyes bright. He was as wary of her innocent appearance as her mysterious mission. "You are the distiller of Glenbrae whisky?"

"I am."

"Miss Graham!" Her pesky escort grabbed the bars. "We have been here too long. Come out, please, or I will fetch you out for your safety."

"One moment, Mr. Corbie." Her gaze stayed with Ronan.

"Is he being discourteous, Miss Graham?" Ronan murmured.

"It is just his nature."

"Since your young man is anxious, I assume that your visit is unofficial and your father's request clandestine."

"Somewhat." She glanced sideways at Corbie.

"Your young man is about to stuff himself between the bars."

She gave a soft laugh. "He is not my young man."

"Does he know that?" He spoke low, only to her.

"You there!" Corbie called. "Move away from the lady. I have my eye on you—"

Ronan thrust out an arm, palm flat, to silence him. All the while he looked down at the girl. Corbie bit off the next word and glared through the bars.

"Why do you ask about the whisky?"

"Is there a supply of it hidden away, Mr. MacGregor? Do you smuggle it?"

"I will not answer those questions. Sir Hector Graham knows better than that."

"Would you reveal where your whisky is located if it was to your advantage?"

"That depends. Why?"

"We must know, you see, because—an important gentleman enjoys your whisky and would like to meet you."

"What nonsense is this?"

"It is not my place to say. You may learn more later."

"I can hardly wait."

She watched him for a moment. "The Whisky Lairds have become folk heroes, did you know?"

"Not heroes. It is a fiction courtesy of Sir Walter Scott. If your important gentleman wants to send me clean clothing, a key, and a horse, I might agree."

A tiny dimple danced beside her mouth as she smiled again. That whimsical little hook drew him in like a lure for a fish. "I am sure you would."

"One favor for another." He shrugged.

"Miss Ellison, I am coming in there," Corbie said. "Guard, open the door."

"I must go." Ellison Graham set down her cup and turned, nodding farewell to MacInnes and Linhope. She glanced back at Ronan. Something flickered in those silvery eyes that he could not quite read. Regret? "I am sorry, Mr. MacGregor. I thought to have a little more time with you."

"Not with your watchdog growling like that. If you want, I can have a word with him concerning his manners."

"Manners!" She laughed, dimple flashing. "I must go. Good day, sir."

"Miss Graham." He inclined his head.

The guard opened the door and she slipped through. Corbie took her arm to squire her away, sending a dark glance toward Ronan, who waggled his fingers in response and turned back toward his friends.

"The deputy lord provost sent her?" Linhope asked. "Why?"

Ronan shrugged. "Some important fellow wants a supply of Glenbrae whisky."

"Who? If he can show us some favor, give it to him," Iain said.

"I suspect she knows little about it and just wanted a bit of adventure."

"A lass with a spirited nature. I like that," Iain said.

So did he. Ronan glanced toward the empty corridor. Her presence lingered along with her soft scent. He breathed in, out, and shook his head against it.

"If anyone knew where our cache is hidden, they would claim it quick," he said.

"Just as well you said nothing. Bonny lass, though," Linhope said. "Pity she will not be back."

CHAPTER 5

"Your scheme is intriguing," Lady Strathniven said a day later, seated at supper in the Graham household. "I am excited to help."

"Scheme?" Ellison looked at her father. "Has something been decided?"

"I had a chance to speak to Lady Strathniven earlier and explained our dilemma. I thought she might be of assistance."

"I am off to Strathniven tomorrow and will return in time for the glorious spectacle in August," the lady explained. "Ellison, I hope you will come with me. I believe Sir Hector's plan will be better accomplished in the north."

"My plan?" Sir Hector frowned.

"Your predicament," the lady amended.

Intrigued, Ellison set fork and knife across her plate, having finished her meal, an informal supper of cold meat, roast vegetables, fresh rolls, and a good French wine. Noticing that her father, the viscountess, and Mr. Corbie were finishing as well, she rang a little silver bell to signal a maidservant that they were ready for the table to be cleared for coffee and pudding. The moment gave her time to think.

"Strathniven? It is a good suggestion, Papa," she said.

"Possibly." He sat back as two maids entered the room to remove supper dishes and bring in a glass bowl containing a trifle of berries, cream, and cake. They served coffee and the trifle and departed as Ellison thanked them.

Corbie leaned forward. "You cannot mean to send MacGregor north!"

"They say," his aunt began, "the only thing King George truly admires about the Scottish is their whisky. You must please the king, yet you cannot trot a prisoner before him, even if he is responsible for the best brew in the Highlands. True?"

"We must not disappoint the king, true," Sir Hector said.

"Thus, a scheme is needed, and I can help. Send the fellow to Strathniven, where we can train him properly and discreetly for a royal introduction."

"But the man is in prison," Corbie protested.

"Let him out. Hector, surely you can arrange that." She waved the little silver spoon in her hand and dipped it into her trifle.

"It is not so easy, my lady," Graham replied. "First, I must ask what you have heard of Glenbrae and Darrach. Did you know either the viscount or this Glenbrae?"

"Many MacGregors are up there," she replied. "But I never met either of these men. Though he did remind me of someone—he is the one who spoke to us, Ellison?" As Ellison nodded, the lady continued. "But I could be mistaken. They are a handsome people, these MacGregors. Such presence."

Indeed, Ellison thought, recalling her brief meeting with Ronan MacGregor, whose presence was so compelling that he had even invaded her dreams since then.

"My lady, do you know aught about this viscount?" her father was asking.

"I never met him. Castle Darrach is nearly a day's ride from Strathniven, but I have seen it. So picturesque! I heard the viscount was a young man, killed while hunting. Very tragic."

"They say a bit more than that," Corbie commented.

"Yes, my housekeeper mentioned talk of murder and smugglers in those hills. It would not be surprising. Ruffians are everywhere in the Highlands, and every glen has hidden stills, so they say. The people are clever at hiding their stills and moving the whisky about secretly. Many do that just to survive," she added crisply.

"They are caught often enough by excise officers," Sir Hector defended.

"It is not my business what they should or should not do, but they have my sympathy. I keep to my estate except when my driver takes me to visit a friend or my sister. Harriet has a country house not far from Strathniven, you know."

"I recall. Mrs. Beaton is a lovely lady," Sir Hector said.

"Some Highlanders still resent the peerage, you know." She pursed her lips. "Years ago, Strathniven was part of a vast estate once held by MacGregors. A forfeited earldom or some such. My late husband's father inherited it, along with a title. The locals were not pleased. Old Jacobite loyalties linger there."

"That trouble may never end, Aunt." Corbie helped himself to more trifle.

"True. In fact, a few MacGregors brought a petition against my husband to regain ancestral land lost in the uprising. There was an uproar over it in our solicitor's office, but my husband had rights through the Crown. I felt sorry for those young men. What a delicious pudding!" She dipped her spoon. "Fresh peaches and strawberries. Wonderful. And how long will MacGregor be a guest at Strathniven?"

"I have not promised that he will," Sir Hector said.

"My lady aunt, please remember he is a criminal," Corbie added.

"Ellison and I saw these men when you did, Adam. What I saw were three proud and vigorous Highland men in difficult circumstances. This Glenbrae is a neighbor of Strathniven, so perhaps I can be of help to him."

"Are you certain, Marjorie?" Sir Hector asked quietly.

"The solution to your predicament seems simple to me. You cannot prepare the fellow for a royal introduction in prison. It must be accomplished elsewhere."

"It is a good idea, and gives us time to properly prepare him," Ellison said.

"This is preposterous," Corbie said. "Sir, you cannot seriously consider this."

"The justiciary court may review their case soon. They could be tried and sentenced just as the king arrives," Sir Hector said. "We must remove them from the public eye soon."

"Remove all three? Where?" Ellison asked.

"Hanged," Corbie barked.

Ellison paused, spoon in hand, to stare at him.

"Removed from Edinburgh Castle," Sir Hector corrected.

"True, King Geordie will want all the attention for himself," Lady Strathniven said. "Otherwise he might throw a royal tantrum, and then what would we do!"

Graham coughed. "We should not express opinions about the king so bluntly."

"I will say what I like in this company."

"It would be horrid to hurry their sentencing just for the king's convenience," Ellison said. "Papa, you must find a way to prevent it."

"They will only get what they deserve," Corbie said.

"Considering the riots over the hangings that occurred in the city two years ago," Sir Hector said, "the courts will not risk a similar incident. Perhaps MacGregor can be transferred into my custody briefly, and the others transferred to Calton."

"Wherever this fellow goes, he must remain under guard," Corbie said.

"I so love our little scheme!" Lady Strathniven exclaimed.

"My lady, this is not amusing," Sir Hector said.

Thinking again of MacGregor, stubborn and keenly intelligent, Ellison leaned forward. "Papa—what if Mr. MacGregor refuses? He may not care to meet the king."

Corbie huffed. "He will have no choice, or face consequences."

"Consequences?" She looked at her father.

"Let me see what can be done," Sir Hector said.

"The man must be proper in every respect. *Comme il faut.* We have our work cut out for us, Ellison dear." Lady Strathniven seemed almost gleeful.

"This is not yet decided," Corbie said.

"That depends on Sir Hector," Lady Strathniven said. "What do you say, sir?"

"Ellison, just prepare the fellow and then we will see," her father said.

"I could tutor him in the etiquette for a royal occasion. Papa, did you say that Sir Walter has written a pamphlet with advice on decorum for the visit?"

"He has. I will give you a copy."

"This Highlander will be a gentleman to make anyone proud. We shall try him in the north first, Ellison. A country dance!" The lady clapped her hands.

"We are not giving this scoundrel a holiday," Sir Hector growled.

"Sir, Miss Ellison should never be alone with this fellow," Corbie said.

"I speak Gaelic and must tutor him," Ellison pointed out.

"He will require good clothing as well as manners," the lady said. "Adam, you must lend him something nice."

"The fellow is too big and would split my tailored coats apart," he retorted.

"Well, we must find something for him. So, it is decided," she replied. "Send the fellow to Strathniven. We will tutor him and introduce him as Lord Darrach."

"What?" Sir Hector asked.

"It makes sense if we are arranging his introduction. Besides, the other fellow is dead," Lady Strathniven said blithely.

Sir Hector put a hand to his head. "I am not convinced that is necessary."

"It is if you want to please the Crown," the lady said. "What harm in it for a moment in the assembly? No one would know otherwise. The other fellow was new to the inheritance. Chances are slim that anyone in society met him."

"Listen to reason," Corbie insisted. "He is a crofter and a thief in plaid rags who speaks no English, has never seen the sharp side of a razor, and would not know a soup spoon from a sugar spoon. More than a frock coat and a few polite English phrases will be needed to civilize him. If this fails, we are all at risk."

"You can be so dreary sometimes, Adam," his aunt said.

"Likely he was educated in a glen school at least," Ellison said. "He seems an intelligent man. He did create a whisky so extraordinary that the king loves it."

"Hector?" the viscountess asked.

"Papa?" Ellison asked, turning expectantly.

Sir Hector threw his napkin on the table. "I see no other solution. I will arrange something. A temporary warrant of release may do for a fortnight."

"Thank you, Papa."

"I insist that this be kept quiet. And Ellison, you must never be alone with him."

"Sir Hector, I should go to Strathniven as well."

"No. I need you here, Mr. Corbie."

"No matter. I will act as chaperone," Lady Strathniven said. "We will teach him proper manners. Dancing too."

"Heaven forfend," Sir Hector muttered.

Standing by a tall window in the library, Ellison watched for the arrival of Lady Strathniven's coach. Her baggage was packed and ready in the foyer, and Balor was curled at her feet, tail tapping the carpet eagerly, as if he knew adventure was afoot.

Sir Hector had promised that MacGregor would have a safe warrant to grant at least a temporary release. Still, she wondered if the Highlander would comply with the scheme—he seemed proud and strong-willed.

She wondered, too, how much her father and Corbie would reveal to him.

Sighing, she knew Corbie was adamant against her tutoring MacGregor. He could be protective, even possessive, despite his apparent fondness for her. Anyone would think him an excellent match for her, with his persistence and his potential for greater responsibility within the government. And he was heir to Strathniven.

But with his habit of criticism and arrogance, she doubted he could grow into a caring husband. Though both Sir Hector and Lady Strathniven might approve a marriage, she knew that Corbie cared most about Corbie.

Ellison would keep a cool distance. All that mattered to her now was a chance to regain her father's respect with this new challenge. Corbie was a doomsayer and her father was skeptical, but she felt a delicious anticipation. MacGregor would make a convincing gentleman, and he could enjoy a little freedom in the north.

She refused to consider what might become of him after the royal visit.

Out in the hallway, she could hear her father and Corbie talking. She turned expectantly, glancing around the library with its high bookshelves, gleaming table, and damask chairs. For her, a beautiful, quiet library was the perfect refuge. She looked forward to weeks at Strathniven House and its two peaceful libraries, where she—

Papa and Corbie entered, dispelling peace with some petty argument.

"I do not want a military translator," Sir Hector said. "Ellison will do that."

"Sir, she cannot travel with this man. I have arranged for a soldier of the Regiment of Foot to accompany MacGregor. A guard is part of the agreement in our request for temporary custody."

"I am looking into a conditional pardon that will relieve me of direct custody. Otherwise, Ellison must be the only translator and tutor for this infernal nonsense. You will arrange all the details."

"He will be taken north in a few days, suitably cautioned. Ah, Miss Ellison, there you are!"

Ellison smiled, hands folded. "Good morning. I am waiting for Lady Strathniven's carriage to arrive."

"I am glad you are here," Corbie said. "I have prepared a list of the tasks to be achieved at Strathniven and would share them with both of you." Corbie took folded pages from a pocket and handed them to each.

Ellison came forward to accept her copy, scanning the list written in Corbie's spiky handwriting.

Barber and a bath, it said. *Burn the plaid and Highland kit etc. Acquire one set of proper clothing and shoes from a man of matching size. Avoid expenses in tailoring and boots.*

Blushing at the quick image of MacGregor at his bath, muscled and gleaming—*stop it,* she told herself—she tried to envision him in a dark coat, snowy cravat, but her mind placed him in Highland plaid looking grand. She cleared her throat.

"Mr. Corbie, we cannot burn a Highlander's plaidie," she said. "It is insulting."

"Fleas," Corbie said curtly.

Ellison read on. *Teach simple English phrases. Give school examination for reading skills.*

"An examination intended for children? I will not do it."

"'Meals are to be taken alone in his room,'" Sir Hector read from the list. "He may be permitted to join an evening meal to practice manners.' This should do."

"It will not do," Ellison protested. "We must give the man his dignity if we expect him to act the gentleman. And I must decide on what lessons are needed."

"The list is only meant to ensure that the process goes smoothly," Corbie said.

"It will. Papa." She turned. "It will take a little time to do this, you know."

"Two or three days ought to do it," Corbie said.

"A fortnight at least, perhaps more, to tutor him. Ensuring that he is outfitted appropriately will take time too. Unless we can present him to the king just as he is."

"A filthy smuggler in rags?" Corbie scoffed.

"A Highlander," she snapped. "There will be many Highland gentlemen at the royal assemblies in full Highland regalia."

"He need not dress like a peacock in plaid. It would attract too much notice."

"Adam," Sir Hector warned. "True, Sir Walter is keen to create a sense of the Celtic heyday of Scotland and encourages Scottish dress. But we cannot risk too much pageantry. Many gentlemen will wear formal attire that is elegant and appropriate in the presence of the king."

"A Highland gentleman dressed authentically is a magnificent sight," Ellison said. "The king will learn to appreciate Scottish culture even more."

Sir Hector waved a hand. "We want to accomplish that in this royal visit, yes. But my dear, you must not idealize Highlanders. Especially this one."

"They are at heart a noble race brought down by—"

"This sort of romanticizing brought you trouble in the past," he interrupted.

"Years ago, Papa, and I paid dearly for it."

"Teach the man his please-and-thank-yous and be done with it," Corbie said. "Sir, I fear your daughter may be infatuated."

"She is not," Ellison retorted.

"Sir, let me repeat that I can go to Strathniven to ensure the man's behavior and Miss Ellison's security."

"And I repeat that you are needed here. Your aunt will chaperone."

"My lady aunt cannot protect Miss Ellison physically. He must have a guard."

"Every military man will be needed to manage the crowds already entering the city. Soon the streets will be packed day and night. They say every bed and broom closet will be rented out as people arrive from all over Scotland."

"I am taking Balor with me," Ellison said. Hearing his name, the terrier stood, wagging his tail. "He is fiercely protective."

Corbie laughed. "That little mop! He snaps at boots and chews carpet."

"That pup is more trouble than he is worth," Sir Hector said.

"He did chew some carpet but grew out of the habit. Lady Strathniven adores him. As for chaperones, she keeps a full staff in summer."

"Then someone at Strathniven can be enlisted to help," Sir Hector said. "Who is that strapping young lad who helps in the stables—Donald or Douglas."

"Donal Brodie," Ellison supplied. "A good lad, and smart. Mr. MacGregor will need a valet, and Donal would do."

"Valet!" Corbie said. "We need someone to watch his every move, not tie his cravat."

"Donal will do. Mention it to Lady Strathniven," Sir Hector told his daughter.

"I will. Papa—is Mr. MacGregor aware of the plan?"

"Not yet, but he will comply," Corbie said.

The undercurrent in his words made her wary. "What do you mean?"

"His conspirators will be transferred to Calton, and MacGregor will find that their safety depends on his cooperation."

"I do not recall ordering that," Sir Hector said.

"I appended it to the petition for safe warrant, sir. You signed the papers, so you surely read it. Busy as you are, you may have forgotten."

Sir Hector frowned. "I would not forget a detail such as that."

"You ordered that the other two would be moved when MacGregor was moved to attract less notice. MacGregor must appreciate that his cooperation is essential."

"Ah. Well, if I ordered it." Sir Hector looked perplexed.

None of this felt right, Ellison thought. "You expect MacGregor to cooperate in return for the safety of his friends? That is hostage for black-mail—it is medieval and despicable! Papa, you cannot allow this."

"Transferring the other two will be sufficient, Mr. Corbie."

"You cannot betray the man when you need his help," Ellison told Corbie.

"We must exercise caution."

"I will not be party to betrayal."

"You are already part of this scheme," Corbie told her.

Without answer, she went to the door, Balor at her heels, and pulled it open.

"Elly." Her father's tone and his use of her childhood name made her pause.

"Papa, I will not be art and part to betrayal."

"All you need do is turn a frog into a prince," Corbie said.

"Pity. I quite like frogs." She left the room, the dog trotting after her.

CHAPTER 6

reedom. He had nearly forgotten the feeling.

Through the window of the rolling carriage, Ronan watched the morning fog lift away from buildings crowding the High Street. Two Regiment of Foot guards had escorted him from his cell to the castle forecourt and a waiting vehicle. Now the coach lurched along the descent so quickly that he tilted on the cracked leather seat, wrists and ankles bound with rope.

Where the devil were they taking him?

The Foot guard seated across from him had said little; Sergeant Bain had translated for Ronan and the others in the dungeon and would do so today, unnecessary though it was.

He breathed in the summer morning with its earthy scents from the cobbled street, the tantalizing smells of bacon and new bread wafting from booths in the Lawnmarket where merchants were setting up for the day. The High Street was crowded with farmers, merchants, women carrying baskets, children running, and a few soldiers from the Castle in their red coats, tartan trews, and tall black hats. Overhead the bells of Saint Giles rang out.

For them, an ordinary morning; for him, extraordinary.

The shabby vehicle was a hired hackney, which he found curious. A cart might have meant he was headed for trial and hanging; a carriage meant a longer trip. Why, and where?

Whatever the day would bring, he would face it. Fortitude was his only choice.

Heading down the long slope, the coach turned into a shadowed close and stopped beside the tall building of the offices of the Constabulary. Ronan frowned.

Through the window, he saw a portly gentleman approaching. Draped over his black coat he wore a wide blue ribbon, gold badge, and silver whistle on a chain. An Edinburgh constable.

"This will be Ronan MacGregor of Glenbrae in Perthshire? Accused of offenses against the Crown, including trafficking of illegal goods? Hmph," he intoned. "Sergeant, a word."

Bain exited the coach to confer with the beefy constable, returning after a few moments. "Mr. MacGregor, there are new orders for you," he said in Gaelic. "You are to be taken out of the city."

"Has some rural court laid claim?"

The soldier leaned forward to speak low. "Listen now, for you are a Gael and a MacGregor, and my mother is a MacGregor, and so I will be honest with you. Best that you comply with the conditions proposed for you."

"What conditions?"

"The constable has a writ signed by the Right Honorable Sir Hector Graham, Deputy Lord Provost. You are to be released."

"Who paid the surety?" he demanded.

"Sir Hector's office, perhaps. You are remanded into his temporary custody. The constable warns that you can be confined again for any offense not subject to the terms of this release."

"If I am free on discharge there should be no condition. But what interest does Graham have in me?"

"I do not know, sir. All I know is that you are to be taken north."

Frowning at that, Ronan recalled Miss Graham mentioning an

important man interested in Glenbrae whisky. The release must be part of that odd request.

Shoulders tight, tension growing, he puzzled over pieces that did not fit. It was unusual for the Provost's office to free a prisoner, even at the request of the chief of the constabulary. Hearing the horses snort and stamp, hearing voices, he looked up as the coach door opened again to admit another man.

Recognizing the man who had accompanied Miss Graham, Ronan felt a warning chill run through him.

"This is Mr. Adam Corbie," Bain explained in Gaelic. "Secretary to the Deputy Lord Provost of Edinburgh. He has some information for you."

"Ask if I am a judicial ward of the provost's office or free on my own accord," Ronan replied. Bain did so.

"Temporary. Conditional," Corbie said vaguely. "Ask MacGregor if he is responsible for Glenbrae whisky and if he smuggles it."

"I need not answer that. He is not an officer of the court," Ronan said.

The translation earned him a flat stare from Corbie. "Tell MacGregor he is liberated temporarily on a minor detail. Sixty-five days have passed since his arrest without trial. That alone entitles him to petition for release. Such requests are rarely granted. He should be grateful."

"Then my friends should be released as well," Ronan said. Bain conveyed it.

"They require separate petitions. There is no time for that," came the reply.

"Ask what the devil he wants," Ronan snapped. Bain did.

"The king is fond of Highland whisky." Corbie sneered as he spoke. "We require a supply of your product as a gift."

"Send word to Glenbrae distillery to purchase the kegs that are needed."

As Bain translated, Corbie flicked his fingers dismissively. "It is more than that. MacGregor will be informed as necessary."

Was King George be the one interested in Glenbrae whisky? It seemed preposterous. Ronan shrugged. "Does the Provost's office want to avoid embarrassment because the Glenbrae distiller is accused of smuggling? Am I released to be taken elsewhere until the king leaves Scotland?"

"MacGregor is heading north," Corbie answered Bain's translation. "That is all he needs to know."

"What of my friends?" Ronan waited for Bain to speak, frustrated by the indirect exchange.

"In Calton by now. Their safety depends on his cooperation," Corbie replied.

"What the devil!" Ronan growled in English, glaring at Corbie.

"So you do speak English," Corbie drawled.

"Some," he bit out.

"Explain to him that he is under the protection of the deputy lord provost until otherwise decided. Comply, or his accomplices will pay the price. And he too will be sent to Calton."

"Tell him I will not comply with blackmail." Bain interpreted.

Corbie lifted a hand. "That is all. Take him north, Sergeant. Ride with him until you meet the second coach at Kinross." He exited the coach, then turned back.

"Make sure he understands," Corbie added low, "that when he sees Mrs. Graham-Leslie, he is to keep a strict distance. Or else," he said, looking hard at Ronan, "I will see him arrested and hanged. Or kill him myself." He walked away.

Bain did not translate.

Silent, Ronan fisted his hands, wrists still bound, as the driver stirred the horses and the vehicle climbed the slope to the High Street, turning to head out of the city to begin the journey north.

"Since you are declared free, there is no need for these." Bain produced a small dirk and leaned forward to slice through the ropes binding wrists and feet.

"Thank you." Ronan rubbed his wrists. "We are headed to Kinross?"

"Aye, to meet another coach. I will return in the hackney while you travel on. I do not know where," Bain added.

Looking out the window as the coach took to the northern route, watching golden fields flow past and give way to hills stretching into the distance, Ronan felt simmering anger fade. He was baffled. Grateful for unexpected freedom, he could not enjoy it, thinking of his friends. Threats, mystery, and betrayal seemed to lace through this situation.

For much of the long day-long journey, though they stopped once to change horses, Bain either shared something of his boyhood in the Highlands or dozed. Ronan could not rest, turning the conundrum over in his mind.

Somehow the delectable Miss Graham was involved in this. *When he sees her*, Corbie had said. Not *if*.

Watching rainclouds gather over distant hills, he wondered if Sir Hector and his secretary knew that they had sent the prisoner home toward friends and opportunity. A small sense of hope dawned.

Smiling a bit, he settled back.

"Aye, Mr. Balor, we will go out in a moment for a good run before supper," Ellison said as she tied the black ribbons of her straw bonnet. As the little terrier jumped about by the door leading out to Strathniven's kitchen garden, she bent to pat his head while Balor, his dark coat nearly brushing the slate floor, waited, his compact little body quivering with excitement.

She smoothed the flounced skirts of her lavender dress and plucked a tartan shawl from a hook to drape it over her shoulders in case of rain. Remembering the boots she kept at Strathniven for traversing the hills, she found them in a corner, slid out of her black slippers, and tugged the boots on, tying the laces.

"Sensible shoes. Good!" Lady Strathniven stepped into the dim corridor. "These hills can be so muddy in rain."

Ellison straightened. "I fell once in slippers on a hill and learned a lesson."

"Yes, you broke an ankle that time. But this visit will be quite different. I am afraid you may not get the rest and respite you hoped to have here."

"Perhaps not, once our guest arrives." Ellison took up the dog's leash.

"But you are the perfect tutor for this task. Oh, that sky looks ominous." Lady Strathniven peered through the window. "Let one of the maids take the pup out."

"I enjoy doing it. Besides, the staff are all busy. Donal Brodie offered earlier today, but I have not seen him since."

"He went to Kinross with Mr. MacNie to pick up the wee man. Sir Ronald."

"Ronan," Ellison said, surprised by the news. "Mr. MacGregor arrives today?"

"Did I not mention? Yes. What should we call him? Lord Darrach, or Sir Ronald—Ronan?"

"Glenbrae or Mr. MacGregor should do. Later in company we may need to call him Lord Darrach, though I don't suppose he will like it."

"We shall see. MacNie is picking up some things while he is in town, including the post. Did you know they leave it at the inn now, rather than bringing it around as before? What is efficient for them is not very efficient for us, since we must fetch it. Hey, Balor," the lady added, bending to pat his head. "Sweet pup!"

"He adores you," Ellison said. "Papa said I should leave him in Edinburgh to save your Turkey carpets."

"I would rather he chewed all my carpets than stayed with that old numpty. What a good lad," she told the dog in a silly voice while he licked her hand.

Ellison laughed. "He does love the freedom here. So do I."

"We may do as we please here, my dear. It is one reason I love the Highlands." She sighed. "Though I wish my nephew appreciated it as much we do. I should leave the estate to him as my heir, but he has become such a sour fellow. I told him he must marry a practical and kind wife if he wants Strathniven. You know he is quite fond of you."

Tugging on her gloves, Ellison frowned. "I wondered."

"I am sure your father would approve," Lady Strathniven ventured, while Ellison suddenly busied herself with the dog's leash. "Though Adam did not inherit much from his father, he has a respectable income and an ambition to succeed."

"I have noticed. Oh look, Balor is very anxious to be off."

"Be back soon, dear. Your Highlander will arrive soon. I know Adam disapproves of him being a guest here," the lady went on, "but Ronald MacGregor must be made to feel like a gentleman if he is to act like one."

"Ronan," Ellison said absently. "My lady, does this ruse trouble you?"

"It seems necessary. With the kerfuffle surrounding King George, no one will even notice another Highland lord. Go on, now." She opened the door.

As Balor half-dragged Ellison down the kitchen path, Ellison guided him firmly toward the lawn and flower gardens, and then quickly beyond the low stone wall toward the meadow that met the slopes behind the house.

On the incline, skirt hems brushing wet heather, she paused to glance back at Strathniven House. Golden sandstone soared on green lawns under gray clouds; its elegant windowed façade and jumble of slate roofs defined the main house, while an old stone tower, all that remained of the medieval structure, capped a far corner. Tucked against the foothills, it looked like a fairytale castle.

She loved every stone, every acre. Someday Adam Corbie would be master here, but for now, she was grateful to be here. She wondered if Corbie truly cared about the estate. Would he protect it, cultivate it, be a fair landlord to the tenants on its vast acres? Lady Strathniven was right. Her nephew would need a capable wife and helpmeet once he inherited the estate.

Much as she loved Strathniven, she could not be that helpmeet.

The hills were steeper now, and pines soared green and strong against rugged slopes misted in purple heather and yellow gorse. Savoring the rough and familiar beauty, glad of the surprising luck that had him rumbling home, Ronan sat up. The tug in his heart felt almost physical.

Yet he did not know what lay ahead. He dared not think of Invermorie Castle, old stone and ivy on a heathery hill, or of Castle Darrach, the L-shaped tower that may or may not be his right. Instead, he puzzled over the curious arrangement that brought him this freedom. He wondered what the lovely Miss Ellison Graham had to do with it. He also doubted King George cared a whit who distilled the whisky in his glass so long as it was abundantly supplied.

But he knew Glenbrae whisky was just that good, especially the casks released earlier this year, aged five years in old casks and exceptionally smooth and rich. If some of that batch had made it to the king's table, he would consider it good news.

The landscape grew increasingly familiar, and soon he saw the church steeple and market cross of the small town of Kinross. He knew every surrounding hill, every path and cave; every castle, croft, and bothy. Here he could find home, kin, friends; enemies too.

The coach drew to a stop in the forecourt of an inn, another place he knew. He drew back, wary of being recognized, but Bain beckoned him outside, stepping out of the hackney himself. Across the yard, he saw a black brougham, old but well-kept, with two stocky horses, black and chestnut. The driver, an older fellow, sat beside a youth. Both pulled plaids and caps against the rain.

"That coachman will be waiting for you," the sergeant said, pointing. "They will take you onward. I wish you *slàn leat, deagh fhortan.*"

"Luck to you as well." Ronan drew the shoulder swath of his plaid over his head against rain and recognition. "If you and the hackney man want a pint and a meal before you go, the fare is good here."

"Hey!" The coachman called and climbed down to approach them.

Jolted—he knew the man—Ronan half turned away.

"Ben MacNie here to meet ye, sir," the man told Bain. He gave Ronan a keen glance. Nodding silently, Ronan glanced at MacNie, whose rough-carved, amiable features were familiar, as were the sharp blue eyes that studied him keenly. The man gave no hint he knew him.

Looking beyond, Ronan felt another sharp tug to see the face of the young man seated on the driver's bench.

His ruse now depended on these two.

"Mr. MacNie, this is Mr. MacGregor. He speaks little English," Bain said.

"Does he now," MacNie drawled. "Come from Edinburgh with a military guard? I thought we were to fetch a gentleman guest."

"He is a guest of Lady Strathniven."

Strathniven! Keeping his head down, Ronan stayed quiet. Why the devil would Sir Hector send him there? He remembered the viscountess had visited the prison, but he could make no sense of this.

"Aye, well. Sir," MacNie told Ronan, "I am steward and factor at Strathniven, and keep the stables too. The MacGregors are a good lot. My stable lad is of that ilk. *Fàilte,*" he added in welcome. "Come this way, sir. Good day, Sergeant."

Thanking Bain, Ronan followed the man across the yard through the rain. No doubt MacNie had guessed, and soon enough young Donal Brodie would too.

CHAPTER 7

"*B*alor!" Ellison called as the terrier scampered ahead, then ran until the leash stopped him. He returned when she called to offer a bit of the oatcake tucked in her pocket.

Keeping pace while the dog explored the hillside, Ellison raised her face to the soft, clean rain, enjoying the freedom she felt in the hills above Strathniven. Here she could think more clearly, feel untethered, and reclaim her spirit.

Balor pulled her along, rounding back when she called, eager for a pat and praise. Following, Ellison glanced down the long slope toward the road that swept up from Kinross to curve around the foothills near Strathniven. MacNie would bring MacGregor along that road, and the lessons would begin. She caught her breath.

Soon the lessons would begin. Only a gentleman would do for the royal request and the scheme, she knew, and she understood that her father must distance himself once he had arranged to relocate the prisoner. But Corbie's veiled threats and his disrespect for MacGregor revealed a colder heart than she had realized.

For all his haughtiness, he was not capable of malice, just conceit. But if her father thought his daughter would agree to marry his secretary, he would be sorely disappointed.

A burst of wind interrupted her thoughts, whipping her skirts and bonnet brim as fat raindrops splattered turf and rocks at her feet. She looked around for the dog.

"Come here, Balor!"

Digging, then running, the dog ignored her, forging ahead through brush and bramble, silently intent on a quest. Holding the taut leash, Ellison followed a rough path between heather, gorse, and rocks as rain now fell in earnest. Time to head back to the house, she thought, calling again. "Balor! Here!"

Thunder rumbled overhead, lightning cracked, and the dog bolted like an arrow, frightened by the storm. The leash pulled, then snapped.

"Balor!" She ran, but he had already vanished among rocks, gorse, and scrub. Spotting his little dark rump beside a spreading golden-flowered gorse bush, she hurried, fearing his coat would pick up the painful spines.

More thunder, another brilliant crash of lightning, and the rain turned to a downpour. Knowing both she and the dog must get off the hill, she ran, heels sliding. She caught herself with a hand splayed on turf already turning muddy. Scrambling to her feet, she hurried, calling out. But the delay of her fall and a loud roll of thunder caused Balor to flee again. Now she could not find him anywhere.

Pausing, spinning, she saw the house in the far distance and realized how far the chase had taken her. The wind and slanting rain grew more forceful as she drew her whipping plaid close about her, then lifted the brim of her bonnet to peer out.

"Balor!"

Desperate, turning again, she saw movement below along the road. The black Strathniven carriage rounded a curve, its red-painted wheels a blur in the rain. Ellison hurried down the hill, waving her arms.

"MacNie! Mr. MacNie! Stop!" Heels slipping again, damp skirts clinging, she reached the bottom of the hill and stepped directly into the road. The carriage pulled to a halt.

"Miss Ellison!" MacNie shouted. "Ye gave me such a fright! What is it, lass?"

"Mr. MacNie! Donal! Balor ran off in the storm!" She hurried toward the carriage as Donal Brodie climbed down to meet her, MacNie following. "I cannot find him—I am so glad to see you! Can you help?" She was breathless, looking like a drowned harpy. Beyond the two men, she saw the coach and a face at the window.

Dark hair, rough-bearded jaw, shoulder pressed to the glass. She felt a leap in her stomach. MacGregor was there. But Balor was all that mattered to her.

"Where did you see the dog last?" Donal asked.

She pointed. "Up there, that direction. He must have found a place to hide. Storms frighten him so." Another roar punched through the clouds. She jumped.

MacNie drew his red plaid, worn overcoat and trews, high over his shoulders and cap against the rain. "The rascal! Donal, wi' me. Wait in the coach, Miss."

"I can help you find him!"

"Ye're soaked through. Her ladyship will have my hide should ye take ill. Inside, now. Dinna mind the young man there. He's all right." He waved her away.

But MacGregor had stepped out of the vehicle, pulling the shoulder swath of his dark plaid over his head against the downpour. "Miss Graham! What is the trouble?"

"My dog is lost on the hill." Distracted, she pointed up the slope.

"We will fetch him," MacNie called. "Lass, into the coach!"

"I am going with you," MacGregor said. With a fleeting touch to her elbow—she felt the tender comfort of it all through her—he hurried away, taking the slope in long strides.

Watching for a moment, she went to the coach and climbed inside. Something tapped at her awareness, but she pushed it away, anxious for the dog's safety. Shaking out her skirts and stamping her muddy boots, she sat on the leather bench and watched the hill. Rain pounded on the roof, thunder rumbled, and lightning cracked. Tugging off her wet gloves, she craned her neck to look up the slope.

High on the crest, the men moved through a haze of rain, shouting, waving arms as if to herd the dog. Had they found him? Cracking open the door, she listened.

"Here—no, there! Over there! Hey! To me, Balor! Och, beastie, here to me!"

"There he goes—over here, you rascal!"

She could make out MacNie in his flat cap, Donal, lanky and fast, and MacGregor, tall and strong, arms extended. When a small dark shape darted across the ridge, MacGregor spun and dove toward the dog.

Then victorious shouts came through the storm as the men headed down the slope toward the road. Seeing MacGregor clutching a squirming bundle inside his plaid, Ellison jumped down from the coach and ran toward them.

He patted the bump tucked in the plaid across his chest and grinned. MacNie spoke, Donal hooted; MacGregor laughed, the sound warm through cool rain.

The man was at ease here, Ellison thought as she approached. No longer wary, he seemed confident, untroubled, a Highlander in his element. And he had rescued her pup. Grateful, she ran forward, tugging her drenched shawl around her.

Suddenly that sense of something forgotten became clear.

They had spoken English on the hill—not a word of Gaelic. MacGregor too.

Then Balor's little black snout poked out of the Highlander's plaid, and Ellison cried out with relief, reaching for him.

"Is this the small one you are wanting?" MacGregor asked in Gaelic.

"Tapadh leat," she said, thanking him quickly, hands open to lift the dog. MacGregor cupped his long fingers gently over the dog's head.

"Hold off. He is excited and may bolt again." This in Gaelic too. "Come into the coach. You are wet and will catch your death." He touched her elbow to guide her.

Another rush of safety and strength in his touch. She stepped away.

"Give me the dog, Mr. MacGregor." She spoke in precise English.

∽

Thunder boomed, lightning snapped, and the dog in his arms yelped. Ronan took the girl's elbow in a firm hand. *"A-steach don charbad, mo nighean."* Into the carriage, my girl.

She glared, eyes stormy gray. He wondered what sparked her temper. Then he knew. What a fool he was to forget his ruse. He had used English naturally while chasing after the dog with the others, reverting to Gaelic with Ellison Graham. She, clever girl, had noticed.

Thunder again. The dog jerked. Ronan led the girl to the carriage and she allowed him to take her hand to assist her inside, her fingers slender and cool. Her attitude was cooler. She sat, smoothing her damp skirts without looking up.

He sat opposite, cradling the pup in one arm, aware she was angry and knowing he deserved it.

"You take the pup and I will do the walking," he offered in Gaelic.

"Then you will be catching your death," she responded in that language.

"If I do not catch it from you first."

She opened her mouth to speak, but the carriage lurched forward and she nearly tumbled from her seat, righting herself and turning indignantly away from him. He noticed that her gown had fared poorly, with soggy flounces at the hem and wet lace at the bodice. When dry, the thing would be fetching; yet she would be fetching in any state, despite the flashing, irate eyes and pursed lips now.

Stroking the quivering dog's head, he waited. Miss Graham fussed at her damp shawl, pushed at her bedraggled bonnet, at wet golden curls straggling free. She glanced at him, cheeks high pink, rain-colored eyes snapping.

"Do you want the pup now?" He used Gaelic just to be stubborn, just to push against the attraction he felt. Tension hung between them. She did not reply.

Wriggling and warm, the dog stretched its snout to lick Ronan's bearded chin. He chuckled, could not help it. The girl melted a bit, reaching out.

"Wee laddie, come here," she cooed, and took the creature to cuddle it, heedless of mud and damp. The love between dog and mistress warmed the dreary carriage interior like sunlight. Warmed Ronan's heart, too, though he folded his arms over his chest, keenly aware of how easily he could fall for this sopping, messy, indignant, beautiful girl and her mucky wee pup.

He needed to stay aloof, needed to mistrust her, her suitor, her father. With his freedom in question, his friends threatened, and this journey of some mysterious benefit to others, he must remain vigilant.

Thunder rolled, loud and startling. The dog barked, the girl squeaked, the carriage hurtled onward. "It is dangerous for MacNie and Donal to be outside in this awful storm," she said in English.

"We will arrive soon. Your man drives like the very devil." He too used English.

"MacNie drives fast no matter the weather." She held the whimpering dog close. The coach rocked, pitching her sideways. Ronan straightened his leg to brace his boot against the opposite seat, a barrier should she tumble again.

"Thank you," she said as she dropped his foot to the floor. She watched him over the dog's head. "So you do have English."

"I do." He felt a bit of the burden lift.

"A good bit, I think." She lifted her chin, a habit he had noticed in her.

"Aye so." He inclined his head.

"Perhaps you used the Gaelic as protection. To keep your privacy?"

"It proved convenient." The girl was quick and perceptive; kind too. But he could not allow kindness, or this drenched, charming, delicate vision, to sway him.

"May we use English between us?" An offer of peace rather than accusation, it said much about her character. He nodded.

"Aye. But the ruse has been helpful."

"Ruse?" Her hands clenched. "Tell me, are you a true Highland man, then? There is more to you than one might guess."

"One could say the same for you, Miss Graham." She was learning him as fast as he was learning her. "I am Highland born and bred and have spoken the Gaelic since my first words. English too. Lately, the native tongue suited best, as you noted."

"I suppose it would be a risk to reveal too much about yourself."

"I can hide little from you, Miss Graham. I am warned."

"I am not your enemy." She looked out the window. "Cha mhòr an sin." Almost there.

Gaelic again. Bless the girl. "Strathniven House?" Looking through a haze of rain, he glimpsed a massive sandstone façade rising just over the next hill.

"Yes." Tugging at her bonnet, she combed her fingers through the honey-colored curls spilling over one shoulder. "I look a fright."

"Not at all." She looked a wee goddess. Not just lovely, but intelligent, forthright, unpretentious, with a touch of whimsy. Such qualities in a woman were his downfall. One such lass had slipped through his grasp years ago, and his uncertain future might not allow finding another. Yet this girl fair glowed with allure and wit, and he felt as if he could fall—

Careful, he thought. This was no time to invest his hopes and dreams.

"You look fine, Miss Graham. Though your wee hat has suffered."

She touched the woebegone flowers. "Your things are soaked as well. Thank you for finding the dog. I appreciate it so much."

"Let me thank you. I enjoyed chasing about in the rain. It has been too long."

"Then thank Balor for running away." She ruffled the dog's head.

"Balor, is it? Chief of the Fomorians in Irish myth—a formidable name for a wee Skye terrier." He reached across the gap to scratch the little head and received a licking of the fingers in return. "Fierce laddie."

She smiled. "Do you have a dog?"

"Two deerhounds, staying with kin while I have been away." He went silent, having eased up caution too soon. The girl broke his focus.

She laughed as the dog licked her chin. Ronan enjoyed the silvery

sound and her impish, fairylike smile. Out of nowhere, a wash of contentment warmed him.

"Regardless of the reason," he said, "it is good to be out in the world
again."

"So you agreed to what was asked of you?"

"I understand the king has a fondness for my whisky. I saw your Mr.
Corbie."

"And he explained the rest?"

"Only that the king wants a supply of Glenbrae whisky, which I am
expected to provide. But that may take some doing."

"You have a few weeks to arrange it."

"He hinted at some difficulty for my friends if I do not comply. With
what, exactly," he murmured, "should I comply?"

"Oh." She worried her teeth against her lower lip. "I thought he told
you."

"About the whisky, aye. I suppose I have been removed from Edinburgh to avoid embarrassment for Scotland, the Glenbrae distiller being a
prisoner."

"That is part of it." She paused. "Do you not know?"

"Know what? If I am missing something here, best say it."

"Mr. Corbie thinks you should be a sort of—hostage."

"Does he," he drawled. "Held in abeyance, my good behavior in
exchange for my friends' safety? Corbie hinted at such. Are you my
custodian?"

"Not me. But there are expectations—truly, did he not explain
more?"

"I have been liberated. What expectations?"

"Liberated?" She tipped her head in surprise. "Free? Not in
custody?"

"A nicety of the law fell in my favor. I hope to extend it permanently.
What is expected of me, Miss Graham? What do you and the others
want?"

Something unsettled flickered in her eyes. "Please understand, Mr.
MacGregor. I am not a threat to you."

"I would quake in my boots if you were. Out with it, Miss."

"The arrangement should have been explained."

"I was told to keep my distance from you. Am I to display excellent manners at your country house? Pretend to be better than I am? I can manage it briefly. It would try me so," he snapped.

She winced, cheeks going pink. "M-manners? Please, you must agree to what is asked." Above the sound of rain and wheel, her voice turned urgent.

"Or have your spiteful wee clerk after me?"

"He is my father's secretary."

"And in love with you, if I am not mistaken."

"I do not know." She looked away.

He did not believe that, but he was after a different truth. "Miss Graham, I sense your gallant Mr. Corbie has left the lady to explain the rest. And he calls himself a gentleman," he muttered.

"Gentleman! Oh." She held the dog tightly against her.

"You will smother that pup. Tell me," he prodded.

"We—we should talk later. We have arrived." She pointed. "Strathniven House."

Now he saw that they were rolling between two stone gates to enter an earthen courtyard edged by pine trees. Ahead, a broad sandstone façade was articulated by rows of gleaming windows, an ancient graystone tower tucked at a rear corner, the whole set amid lawns and edged by gardens. To one side were stables and sheds; beyond soared heathered hills marching into the distance.

He knew this place—the fine house and estate his great-grandfather had lost to punitive forfeit long ago.

Strathniven is no longer ours, his father had told him once. But Glenbrae and Invermorie is ours still, and will be yours after I am gone. Your cousin John will have Darrach. It is all that remains of the ancient estate. You both must guard the land well.

"May we speak of this matter later?" the girl asked.

"What? Aye." The carriage slowed and stopped. "MacNie can leave me at the servants' door."

"You are a guest at Strathniven, Mr. MacGregor. Shall I call you Glenbrae?"

"If you like," he said, distracted.

The carriage door opened, and Donal peered inside, tall and thin, black-haired, with the rounded beauty of a young man who would grow into lean handsomeness. He pulled his cap down against the drizzle. "Miss Ellison," he said, handing her out.

"Donal," she said, "MacGregor of Glenbrae is our guest here. Sir, this is Donal Brodie, one of our grooms. He will serve as your valet."

"Sir." The lad touched his cap. Covering his surprise, Ronan nodded as he stepped down. Donal took the dog from the girl and set the pup on the ground, attaching the broken leash. "I will take Balor to the kitchen, Miss."

"Thank you. Oh, Donal," she added, "Glenbrae does not have much English. Your Gaelic is good enough for conversation, I think?"

The lad's brows lifted under the dark gloss of his hair, and his whisky-brown eyes widened in surprise. "I know a bit."

"Good. That will be a help." She turned for the house. "Mr. MacGregor?"

"A moment," Ronan said in Gaelic, and waited until she was out of earshot. "Donal Brodie," he murmured, "you have sprouted since I saw you last."

"I have. Welcome back to Perthshire, Uncle." Donal grinned.

Ronan's throat tightened. Then he clapped his brother's stepson on the shoulder and walked with him toward the entrance.

CHAPTER 8

"Welcome, Glenbrae! I am pleased you are here!" Lady Strathniven enunciated loudly, her voice echoing in the foyer. Ellison stood by, glad to see Lady Strathniven acting as if she had never seen the man before. But he was not deaf.

MacGregor inclined his head. "My lady, thank you," he replied in English.

"He speaks English?" Lady Strathniven looked at Ellison in surprise.

"A little," she replied as she loosened her soggy bonnet ribbons.

"Thank you for saving the pup today! Mr. MacNie told me all about your rescue!" As the lady continued to shout, the Highlander smiled amiably.

Ellison translated in Gaelic, even knowing it was unnecessary now. Seeing the spark of humor in his blue eyes, she wondered how she had not discerned the truth sooner.

"He seems a nice young man to me." The viscountess spoke to Ellison. "I do not understand the kerfuffle over bringing him here. MacNie says the dog likes him very well. Balor's good opinion is golden to me."

To me as well, Ellison thought. "Oh, dear, I am drenched. I hope we are not tracking mud over the floors."

"Everything can be cleaned. Tell me, did you and Glenbrae have a chance to chat in the carriage?"

"Some." Ellison felt aware of the man standing so tall, so close, so attentive.

"Good! You will want to practice polite conversation with him. It is why we are here." As the lady spoke, Ellison saw the Highlander tilt a brow.

"Practice conversation?" he asked in Gaelic.

"My lady," she said, "our guest will want to rest after his long journey today."

"Yes. Mrs. Barrow prepared a room in the tower for him. Adam wanted him to have a room in the servant quarters. I am afraid I do not take instruction well."

Ellison smiled. "You do not, to be sure." She translated for MacGregor—*your room is in the old tower. It is very private*—while avoiding his steady gaze. Looking down, she saw that his mud-plastered boots were worn and scuffed, his feet long and large. His plaid and other garments were soaked and grimy, and the man had an earthy aroma that was not very gentlemanly.

Corbie's list had included *bath, shave, clothing*. She had to agree.

Now she wondered if the clothing she had asked Donal Brodie to fetch for their expected guest would even fit. The things were stored in a chest in a Strathniven attic and she had thought they would be appropriate.

But she had misjudged. MacGregor was taller, heavier, and more muscular than her late husband. Colin Leslie, tall and lean with a poet's soul and an artist's elegance, had worn closely tailored suits and fashionable boots. Brawny MacGregor could fill a space with his very presence, let alone his powerful build.

"Will Glenbrae join us for supper? I asked Cook to prepare a simple meal."

Turning, Ellison repeated the question in Gaelic.

"An honor, but I must decline." The resonance of his murmur sank through her like whisky. "Please tell the lady I am fatigued and would not be good company."

"Well," Lady Strathniven said, upon hearing the answer, "Mrs. Barrow will see Glenbrae to his room. My dear girl, your things are ruined. A pity you did not bring a maid with you. I will ask my maid Jeanie to help you."

"She is busy enough, but if she could clean my dress, I will make the repairs." Glancing around for Mrs. Barrow, Ellison was reluctant to leave the Highlander with the viscountess in her talkative mood. He might hear too much, too soon. She must find a chance to speak with him privately.

"Adam thinks the man cannot act the gentleman no matter what we do, but—"

"Mrs. Barrow!" Ellison called as she heard approaching footsteps.

"Here is your room," Mrs. Barrow said loudly, taking a lesson from the viscountess. Ronan had followed the bustling gray-haired housekeeper through the house to a stem corridor that connected to the tower, then up three flights of stone spiral steps, where she flung open a door.

"Thank you." Ducking slightly under the old lintel, he followed her inside. "A fine room. A fine house." He spoke simply in English.

The room was pleasant, cozy and antique with whitewashed walls, a beamed ceiling, and Turkey carpets on the planked floor. An old curtained bed with a red coverlet filled much of the space. Near it, a small table and wooden chair sat beneath a mullioned window framing a misty view of hills. The room had an isolated air, situated high in the old tower.

Long ago, a MacGregor ancestor had constructed this medieval tower, and perhaps had slept in this room. He turned. "Thank you, Mrs. Barrow. Very nice."

"You speak English?" she asked loudly.

"Some. Thank you."

"Most keep clear of this old tower, but my lady thought you would like it."

"Yes."

"And Mr. MacNie out in the rain at his age, catching his death to fetch you in Kinross," she muttered half to herself, "and you bringing mud over the carpets and much in need of a bath and a barber. What are we to do with you, I says. Gentleman, the lady says. Glenbrae? It is curious."

"Thank you, Mrs. Barrow." He set a hand on the door.

"Are you kin to the Glenbrae and Invermorie MacGregors? And Darrach too?"

"Kin? Some."

"I didna know the viscount who died, but I knew his father. You have the look of the Glenbrae MacGregors." She squinted. "A dark and handsome folk."

He smiled. "Yes, thank you, Mrs. Barrow."

"*Och*, not a word did he get," she muttered. "Well! Sir, we have a bathing apparatus here. Lord Strathniven had it brought up from London long ago. You may use the bathing apparatus." She enunciated each word distinctly.

Ronan huffed in amusement. "Bathing apparatus. Thank you."

"Down the stairs." She pointed out the door.

"Yes." He wanted a bath desperately. A basin and cloth would do, but he would try the shower machine, though he had encountered the things before and disliked them.

"Clothes." She pointed to the chair and the bed, where items were stacked. "Towels. Soap. Bath," she repeated, and sniffed.

"Very kind."

On the bed were folded white linen towels, a fat ball of soap, and grooming items. The canopied frame was a hefty dark monstrosity with a thick mattress piled high with pillows. It looked tempting after months on straw mats. Beside it, a wooden chair held folded clothing; a pair of polished boots sat on the floor.

He smiled again, nearly gritting his teeth, hoping she would leave so he could bathe, change, and rest.

"Why does a guest arrive without his things, I wonder? But your manservant found things for you to use. Young Donal."

"Yes." Guard more than manservant, but a fortunate choice nonetheless.

"Do you need anything more," she said, enunciating as loudly as before.

"No, thank you, Mrs. Barrow. Kind." He inclined his head.

"Supper? Hungry? I will send a tray up for you. Tomorrow, breakfast is in the main house. That way," she added, pointing. "Breakfast. Dining Room. Understand?"

"Yes. Breakfast. You are kind."

"Hmph," she muttered. "You have more English than anyone knows, I suspect."

He let his eyes twinkle at her. She brightened. "So, Glenbrae, is it? I know some MacGregors hereabouts."

"Aye?" He went wary.

"Most are good folk. But there are smugglers in these hills. Are you with them?"

"I bring no trouble here." Her question deserved an immediate answer.

"Huh. We shall see. Good night." She left the room, closing the door.

He sighed, ran a hand through his disheveled hair, rubbed his beard scruff, and reminded himself again to be cautious at Strathniven.

Exploring the room, he sorted through the clothing—linen shirt and neckcloth, waistcoat of brown damask, coat and trousers of black superfine. He wondered whose they were; the cut seemed suited to a tall man.

But first he wanted to feel clean again. Gathering the things he needed, he went in search of the bathing machine. On each level, he found rooms with furniture draped in sheets. One door opened on a small library crammed with bookshelves, a table, and a few chairs. He hoped to spend a little time there if there was a chance.

On the lowest level, one door revealed a narrow room with a high raftered ceiling. The walls were trimmed in blue Delft tiles, and the room contained just the apparatus he sought.

He eyed the contraption skeptically. A wooden tub fitted with tall iron struts formed a cage-like enclosure supporting an open canopy. Pipes ran up to a metal tank tucked in the rafters above. Water conveyed downward through the pipes, operated by a long cord hung inside the cage; pulling it would draw water down like a fall of rain.

At least, that was the theory behind such things. In Ronan's experience, they spit and shuddered and trickled and could be troublesome. Pipes could leak and refilling the tank required a ladder and two strong men. But the beast was as he expected.

Stripping out of his things, he stepped inside, tugging a lever and a cord. The water spitting downward provided just enough tepid trickle for washing. He hurried through the process, wary of the rickety frame and creaking valves, as he lathered his hair and body with the soap ball that smelled of pine.

Earlier, the downpour on the hillside had given him a natural shower, and the machine completed the task. Rinsing the soap away, pulling the cord to stop the shower, he stepped out and toweled off. Clean was clean, and he was grateful for it.

Using the grooming tools to trim his beard as best he could, he combed his too-long hair, which waved nearly to his shoulders. Because his clothing was too filthy to wear again, he dressed in the borrowed things.

They fit, just; the shirt and waistcoat were snug, the trousers short. The stockings, of soft, fine-spun wool, were good, and the boots, of excellent quality and hardly worn, were tight.

Climbing the stairs back to the guest room, he discovered just how tight. He winced with each step. He would ask Donal to clean his old brogues, hard-worn but comfortable, along with his plaid and other kit.

He would prefer to wear the dignity of good Highland gear rather than things suited to his work in the city. Perhaps Donal could fetch Ronan's things; the lad would know just where to find them.

Supper waited on a covered tray in his room, left in his absence by a servant, or perhaps Donal. Sitting by the window, he tucked into barley soup, crowdie cheese, and an oatcake, washed down with ale from a jug. A squat pottery jug held whisky. Pulling the wax plug free, he sniffed and sampled. Pitlinnie.

He was intrigued to find Pitlinnie whisky at Strathniven. Either Mrs. Barrow purchased it for the household from Sir Neill Pitlinnie, or the fellow gifted an illicit supply to the household to buy silence and loyalty. He suspected the latter.

A folded paper was tucked under the china plate; he picked it up, finding creamy stock creased repeatedly in the style of a secret note. Opening the tiny quarto folds, he saw a note written in a feminine hand.

Mr. MacGregor,
Lady Strathniven requests your company at Breakfast tomorrow morning at Nine o'clock in the Dining Room of the Main House. This evening, please visit the Tower Library at half Eight. A message awaits you there.
E. S. G.

Ellison Graham. Her hand was artistic, though two blots spoke of haste.

Hoping she could add clarity to this odd situation, he sat back, sipping the Pitlinnie. The mantel clock chimed softly; just nine. He had a little time to relax in these quiet surroundings. Grateful for freedom, he thought again of Linhope and MacInnes, likely on Calton Hill by now. Their fate depended on his actions.

Whisky in hand, he sipped and frowned, gazing out at the evening sky, where rainclouds gave way to late twilight. Weariness pulled at him.

Then he roused himself and looked at the clock. Nearly half nine.

~

The door to the small library was ajar, showing lamplight and bookshelves. Opening the door, he saw the young woman standing by the mullioned window, haloed by the glow of an amethyst sky at twilight.

No message, then, but a conversation. Good. Knocking softly, he entered, glancing around at old ceiling beams painted long ago, planked floors, old hefty furniture—and bookshelves crammed with volumes stacked beside vases, globes, and more. The table was flanked by sturdy wooden chairs. An oil lamp shed golden light on books and papers.

Ellison Graham turned. "Mr. MacGregor—Glenbrae. Please come in."

"Miss Graham. Good evening." He too spoke in English.

"Please sit." She indicated two armchairs by the window, upholstered in red brocade. The evening light shone rosy over golden hair caught up with soft curls framing her face. Now she wore a dark blue gown, a prim thing with a high collar and long full sleeves that made her appear small and fragile. She sat, twisting her fingers as if anxious. "I thought we would have some privacy here."

Ronan eyed a red chair warily. The thing looked too slight to support a large male. Instead, he drew one of the wooden chairs closer, angling it toward her.

"The sky is lovely this evening now that the rain has lifted," she said.

"Beautiful, aye." The sky, his freedom. The girl.

"In the city, the Whisky Lairds won over public imagination, I think."

"We have Sir Walter Scott to thank for the name, I hear."

"Indeed. My father said he mentioned it at a dinner party, speaking of a group of Highlanders who efficiently moved whisky in great amounts and used the profits to help crofters in dire conditions. He called them Whisky Lairds and compared them to Robin Hood and his men."

"A romantic notion rather different than the truth, to be honest."

"Sometimes Highlanders must smuggle goods to protect their families. Good intentions cause good men to break laws. There is some nobility in that."

"An interesting observation from the daughter of a government official."

"I have great respect for Highlanders. I have seen the difficulties they face."

"They do." Best not pursue the subject of what Highlanders lacked under English governance, he thought. Instead, he glanced around the room. "A fine library. This tower is very old."

"Not as modern as in the main house, true, but I prefer it. If you would like a different room, I will tell Mrs. Barrow."

"It is very nice. I appreciate the hospitality and the loan of excellent clothing, too." He brushed at the coat sleeves.

"There was some clothing in storage here." She tipped her head. "If I may, sir, I wonder if the fit is comfortable."

"These seem to have been tailored for a slighter gentleman."

"He was tall, but not as—robust. We will have your things cleaned."

Curious whose suit this had been, he did not ask. "A Highland plaid is most comfortable but may not be proper here." He sat straighter, praying the coat seams would hold.

"Tartan is proper anywhere in Scotland nowadays. Fashionable, even. And Lady Strathniven approves, I assure you."

He nodded. "So, Miss Graham?"

"You are owed an explanation."

"I am listening." Something troubled her; beneath that calm, lovely exterior he sensed tensile energy and vulnerability. Her fingers folded, then opened like a lotus.

"We need your help, Mr. MacGregor."

"I will provide the whisky, given some time."

"Yes. And you—" she paused. "You will be introduced to the king at one of the assemblies," she blurted. "It was the king's personal request."

Of all the possibilities, he had not expected that. "That is absurd."

"He asked to meet the distiller of Glenbrae whisky. And he expects to meet a gentleman. But—" She paused.

The pieces came together swiftly. "But the distiller is a smuggler, worse, a prisoner, and yet the Provost's office cannot refuse the king. What to do?" His voice had an edge. "Hide the scoundrel away, or clean him up and trot him past the king. Is that it?"

"Something like that. The introduction will be arranged."

"It is not necessary."

"My father's office is obliged to fulfill the king's every request."

"Even this one?"

"Even this." She watched him steadily.

"What a fuss for Scotland this visit is. The last English king to visit Scotland was Charles the Second, I believe—that is, outside those intent on defeating us."

She smiled. "You must have had a good education in the village school. My father will be pleased to know it."

Good Lord, he thought; this Highland savage act had gone too far. "I can read and write and count on my fingers. After the glen school, I attended the public academy in Perth." He was sore tempted to add he had studied law in Edinburgh, apprenticed in an uncle's law office in Perth, and practiced there still. "Tell Sir Hector the Highlander can also quote the Greeks and Romans, spool on about history, philosophy, and maths, and even discuss points of law." He had said too much, but he was indignant. And though he regretted every ruse, his friends needed protection. He breathed, cooled.

Color rose in her cheeks. "Either way, sir, the introduction will be arranged."

"No doubt a fast audience where I bow and say something proper before being whisked away to meet my punitive fate."

"Not quite so dire as that, I hope."

He huffed. "And your role in this travesty, Miss Graham?"

"I am to tutor you in protocol and appropriate manners."

"I am hardly a savage." He took quick offense—tired, perplexed.

She lifted her chin. "I know that. The situation is complicated."

"I dread to ask."

"As I mentioned, the king expects the distiller to be a gentleman of some rank. A peer, in fact."

"I see." More pieces clicked into place, beads on an abacus. "The prisoner is to be scrubbed and trained. I will do the scrubbing, you the tutoring. But—a peer?"

Her cheeks burned deep pink; she seemed to hold her temper even as he did. "I am also here to translate for you, but that is unnecessary now. Clearly, you do not need much tutoring either. But for your sake, my father and Mr. Corbie should not know that yet."

Ironic, he thought, trading one ruse for another. "I can behave cordially enough if I do this."

"Will you?"

"I seem to have little choice. 'What a tangled web we weave, when first we practice to deceive,'" he quoted.

She blinked. "Scott."

"It seems appropriate."

"Another reason for this plan involves the license for your whisky."

Startled, he masked it. "It is licensed. Ah, the landowner is legally considered the distiller no matter who makes it."

"Yes. Viscount Darrach. Did you know him?"

He shrugged casually. "Somewhat. He died last year. Surely you do not expect me to pose as Viscount Darrach," he added.

"As I said, it is complicated."

"Simplify it," he clipped.

"The viscount was not well known, and the inheritance is still undecided, from what I understand." She frowned, glanced away.

He knew the inheritance matter would be decided by the court soon, and he had a solid claim as next of kin. Yet he could not reveal that. "If an heir is found, this scheme will crumble. It would not be pleasant for any of us."

She blushed furiously at that, and Ronan saw how very transparent her thoughts and feelings could be. That vulnerability stirred a protective urge. He folded his arms against it.

"The royal assemblies will be attended by thousands," she said. "An heir to a small estate would hardly be noticed. It will all happen quickly."

"Whether a minute or a lifetime, impersonating a peer is punishable by prison or exile. If this is discovered, and worse, viewed as an insult to the king, we could all be charged with conspiracy. Even you."

"You know something of the law."

"A bit."

"There are risks." Her brow furrowed, eyes shadowed. She was not just aware, he thought; she was frightened. Her hands fluttered, folded.

"So you will train me up, run me past the king, and hope no one notices."

"Do you need a tutor at all?" she snapped.

"Yes," he bit out. "If I set one foot wrong and ruin this lunatic scheme, my friends will suffer. I can manage to be polite for an hour or two." He spoke bitterly, though she did not deserve his anger. Her father and his secretary did.

Ellison Graham wove her fingers in and out, thinking, frowning. He wanted to reach out and calm her hands—calm her. She looked delicate as porcelain in the twilight, yet beneath her nervousness, he sensed strength—regret too, and sadness. He had secrets and sadness as well. Something inside him succumbed.

"I apologize. You may be as caught in this as I am," he said.

"Do you agree to see this through?"

The rogue they meant to train was more a gentleman than they knew. But he would hide that for the sake of his friends. "I will."

"Thank you." She breathed out as if relieved.

"So. What sort of lessons do you have in mind?"

"Polite conversation, how to address nobility and royalty, certain aspects of gentlemanly behavior, proper costume, and so on. Perhaps a dancing lesson." As she spoke, her fingers fluttered gracefully, like pale butterflies. He sensed she was forced into this, as he was.

"Using the wrong fork is a serious matter, is it? Tie a cravat properly or someone will die?" He raised a brow. "A dangerous wee game, this. And afterward?"

She ducked her head. "I am not sure."

"Polite chatter and a little dancing are preferable to hanging, I suppose."

Her earnest nod was almost endearing. That was dangerous too. He stood. "We have been alone too long. Best practice propriety, you and I."

She stood too, just at the height of his shoulder. He felt very tall, strong, and protective. Going to the door, he held it open.

"Miss Graham," he murmured. "Whatever happens to me is my concern. Do not fret over it. You did a brave thing tonight."

"Brave?" Her eyes were dark gray, sincere. His breath stirred a soft curl at her brow. Aware he should lean back, he did not, nor did she.

"You delivered a message that two men were too cowardly to give. Just who needs lessons in manners?"

She smiled. "Tutoring you should prove easy enough."

"See how quickly I learned English tonight. What shall we do next?"

"Do whatever you think is best, sir."

"I always do," he murmured, reaching over her head to open the door.

CHAPTER 9

"Glenbrae, is the coffee to your liking this morning?" Lady Strathniven asked at breakfast. "Cook was pleased to prepare breakfast this morning for a man with a healthy appetite."

"Everything is excellent, my lady." He stirred cream into the cup as he stood beside the sideboard. "Thank you again for your hospitality."

As Ellison glanced up at the Highlander, she could not help but recall their meeting in the old library last night. Dressed again in the black suit that so closely fitted his tall, muscular figure, and with his dark hair swept back and beard all but gone—just a shadow this morning—he was not just handsome. He was perfectly distracting, a powerful masculine contrast in the pink and cream sunlit dining room.

He added some fruit and rolls to a small plate and resumed his seat opposite hers at the table, glancing at her quickly, silently.

"All we usually take is tea and toast or porridge, isn't that so, Ellison?" Lady Strathniven said. "But anything would be better than prison fare, I trust. What did you eat there? Moldy bread and old beer?"

"My lady!" Ellison said, not sure whether to laugh or scold.

MacGregor only chuckled. "Bread, cheese, thin ale, weak tea. Porridge. Soup. Occasionally meat."

"We shall feed you very well here, I promise." The viscountess tipped her head. "I must say, sir, your English has improved overnight."

Ellison began to speak, about to translate into Gaelic. Catching her eye, MacGregor shook his head.

"Lady Strathniven, I have a confession."

"That you speak excellent English after all, and do not require an interpreter?"

"I speak both English and Gaelic fluently."

"My lady, Mr. MacGregor found Gaelic more useful in his previous situation," Ellison explained. "Papa and Mr. Corbie only assumed he needed a translator."

"Good! It will make your conversations easier. Oh—is he aware of the arrangements? Did I speak out of turn?"

"I am aware, my lady." MacGregor inclined his head politely.

"Since you speak like a gentleman, may we assume you also require less tutoring than expected?"

"My mother taught her children excellent manners, and our parents ensured that we had education, regardless of diminished fortune."

"Diminished?"

"Like many after Culloden, my great-grandfather lost land and a title."

"How unfortunate. I am sorry," Lady Strathniven said.

"Nevertheless, I would benefit from instruction. I have not met royalty before."

"Most of us in Scotland have not," the lady replied. "But Sir Walter has written a book of advice for us to follow. For example, ladies are to wear gowns with trains several feet long, with nine ostrich feathers in their headdresses. And there are useful phrases when speaking to royalty that we can all learn. Elly," she added, "we should study his etiquette guide carefully."

"We will," Ellison agreed. "Papa gave us copies of the pamphlet," she told MacGregor. "It is written by an 'anonymous citizen,' but Scott is the author."

"He does enjoy anonymity," MacGregor agreed. "He denies being the author of the Waverley novels and insists he is just a poet."

"But some think novel writing is not as respectable as poetry," Lady Strathniven said. "Ellison writes lovely poems. Though I do love a good novel."

"Poetry?" MacGregor quirked a brow, looking at Ellison.

"Some." And the novel she was secretly writing. She felt a fierce blush growing.

"I too prefer a good novel." He sipped his coffee.

He was much more educated than he let on, Ellison thought. No ordinary Highland smuggler, he had his secrets. She only hoped nothing would complicate this lunatic scheme, as he had called it.

"The pageant master will help us prepare for the visit," the viscountess said.

"Pageant master?" MacGregor asked.

"She means Sir Walter. It is not meant in a flattering way, dear," Ellison clarified for her.

"Well, his little book will be useful. Glenbrae, please borrow my copy to read. Then you can tell me what it says. It seems too dull to me to read. I will leave my copy in the library for you."

"The little library in the tower?" he asked.

"The large one just along the corridor here. My late husband's library. Not the musty old library in the tower. But feel free to explore both collections. My husband took great pride in his books and was pleased to share them. You enjoy reading and scholarship, I think?"

"I do," he murmured.

"Ellison, your task will be an easy one." She smiled. "Sir Hector and Adam will see the progress when they arrive to judge for themselves."

Sipping her tea, Ellison sputtered a little. "They are too busy to come north."

"True, though Adam may come up to be sure we are all prepared."

Her stomach sank. "We will be ready."

"Glenbrae." Lady Strathniven turned. "I have confidence in you and your excellent tutor. But let us be honest between us."

"Madam?"

"This venture is chancy, but it is the best solution."

"I wonder for whom it is best, my lady, if we are being frank."

"I see no reason for them to know that you speak English as well as anyone and already comport yourself as if born to the peerage. Let them be pleased with Ellison's work, and with you."

"I agree, my lady." His eyes sparkled with amusement. He was enjoying this too much, Ellison thought. "Do excuse me, ladies. I thought to find Donal Brodie this morning to see if we could ride out. I would very much like some air and exercise."

"Donal is at your disposal, and you may use horses or a carriage, whatever you like to explore the estate. I hope you will be back in time for luncheon."

"I will do my best. My lady, Miss Graham." He stood.

"Sir, I thought to begin lessons later today," Ellison said. Nodding his understanding, he left the room.

Lady Strathniven smiled. "My dear, your work is done before it has begun."

"He does have the makings of a gentleman," she agreed faintly.

"How are your mother and Sir Ludovic?" Ronan asked Donal as they walked toward the stables, pausing in the shade of a cluster of birches.

"Aye, good. Mother is busy making her herbal concoctions and helping those who come to her—she is still much needed in the glens as a healer, especially with Linhope gone. And Grandda Ludo helps keep the garden."

"Is he still writing his history of the clans?"

"The thing is enormous now. He hopes to publish it someday, though Mother says he will never finish. He just keeps adding more."

"Good to know they are well." Ronan clapped a hand on Donal's shoulder. At sixteen, the lad was tall, black-haired and handsome, with his mother's warm brown eyes. He was Mairi's only child by her first husband, who had succumbed to fever when Donal was small. Then, while Ronan had been away at university and thinking himself in love with Mairi, his younger brother William had married her. Despite the shock of it, he managed to accept it. Will was a good father, the only one Donal knew.

Since Will's death, Ronan had done his best to take care of the family. As Glenbrae's laird and owner of Invermorie Castle, he had invited Mairi to live there with her son and her father, Sir Ludovic Brodie, an impoverished knight. Then Ronan had moved to a simple cottage on the distillery grounds.

Invermorie needed a family, not a bachelor. And he needed distance from Mairi Brodie, far enough for his heart to recover, close enough to keep watch over William's family.

Though he thought to marry someday, he was thirty years old now and recently a prisoner; all thoughts of the future felt suspended. Let time tell.

"I help at Strathniven and the distillery too," said Donal, "to bring in coin since Da died, and since you and the others were taken."

"Lad," Ronan murmured, "whatever happens, I will take care of you and your mother and grandfather. Now tell me what you have heard lately."

"When word came in May that the Whisky Lairds were taken, we knew it was you lot. 'Twas said you were taken unfairly by excise."

"More or less."

"Then how is it you are here at Strathniven, Uncle?"

"Liberated on a detail of the law. If Sir Hector Graham and his secretary have their way, it may be only temporary."

"I know them. Sir Hector is decent enough. His clerk is another sort."

Ronan huffed in agreement. "You are appreciated here at Strathniven, I think."

"Aye, they are good to me, give me work now and then. And then MacNie sent word asking if I could work at the house for a while to act as valet to a guest. I had no idea it would be you!"

"It is luck for both of us, then. Do you know how to tie a cravat?"

"Grandda and Mother gave me advice. Will you come to Invermorie soon?"

"If there is time. I suspect you were hired as a guard more than a valet."

"Is it so? But you are free now."

"It is complicated. You had best keep watch over your rascal of an uncle," he drawled. "How goes it at the distillery?"

"The Muir lads are well. We set up a new batch—made three hundred pounds of barley into good mash and sealed a fine barley brew into oak casks and kegs to mature three years, as you prefer."

"Longer if we can. Excellent. You could be a distiller one day too, though you were to go to school soon. You had a letter from Saint Andrews, last I heard."

"Aye, to start next year. But I am needed at home now."

"I am back now. And my brother had set aside the fee for your schooling."

"Aye, but I am undecided. I might study medicine like Lord Linhope. We spoke about it before you all—went to Edinburgh. How is he, and MacInnes? Free as well?"

"Still held. With luck, all will be resolved soon." He gave a flat smile.

"Mother will be pleased. She and Linhope were corresponding about treatments, but his letters stopped. She was worried."

He nodded, aware that he should talk to Mairi, though he had not seen his gifted, stubborn, beautiful sister-in-law for months. His habit of avoiding her stuck; after Will's death, time had begun to heal the gap, but he remained cautious.

He felt he had failed as brother-in-law, uncle, friend, protector. Though a lawyer with a strong sense of justice, he had ventured into smuggling for his family's sake. Frowning, he saw Donal watching him.

"Uncle Ronan, promise you will come to Invermorie soon."

"I will. Call me Glenbrae here at Strathniven, lad. If you are told to call me Darrach, best do so."

"Is there news of the title and estate, then?"

"Not yet. It may never fall to me. But Sir Hector and the others know nothing about that. I must be careful here."

"Is there trouble over it, Unc—Glenbrae?"

Ronan leaned a shoulder against a tree, considering what to reveal. "You know the king is coming to Scotland?"

"Everyone in Scotland knows that!"

"Apparently he likes Glenbrae whisky and wants to meet the distiller. The Scottish government is eager to please him, so I am to be presented."

"To the king!" Donal widened his brown eyes.

"And I must behave myself. You must keep all this close."

"I will. Aught else?"

"Aye." He shifted from foot to foot. "Fetch me my good boots, please."

Donal looked down. "Miss Ellison wanted you to have those. Too tight? The things belonged to her husband. He was tall, but not as big as you. I will fetch your gear from the cottage. Better those than wearing a dead man's things, hey."

"Did know him? Her husband?"

"Colin Leslie? I saw him a few times. A polite man. Young and shy. He always thanked me for what I did. Not everyone thanks a servant," he added. "He fell from a horse when out with friends, they said. Nearly two years now, but Miss Ellison has not yet come out of her mourning."

Ronan frowned to realize the tragedy the girl had endured. He had the sense that she was under her father's thumb as well. Was that why she seemed a bit lost, uncertain? Yet he had seen glimmers of strength and spirit in her, as if she was on the verge of bursting forth if only she would let herself.

"Son of a Lowland viscount," Donal went on. "A poet or some such. Mrs. Barrow said they eloped, and Sir Hector was angry. Miss Ellison is not the same as before, she says. Gone quiet and meek." He shrugged. "Well. How long will you stay?"

"I am not sure. A fortnight or so."

"I will fetch your things today. Aught else?"

"Can you get word to the Muirs? I want to talk with them."

"We may see them today when we ride out. Aleck and Geordie often go up and down the Lealtie Burn that flows through the distillery, checking to be sure the water is clear of debris. Come ahead."

"Ronan! God above, I hardly knew you at first!" Aleck Muir spurred his horse forward, his brother Geordie riding just behind him. Both lads were rangy redheads, easily recognized from a distance. Grinning, Ronan waved.

"Dressed like a city gentleman! We heard you were taken. You were released?" Geordie called. Ronan walked his horse toward them, Donal following as they took the horses into the shelter of a grove of trees near the burnside, dismounting to allow their mounts to graze on sweet grass.

"Good to see you both." Ronan shook hands, patted shoulders. "Donal says you are looking after the distillery in my absence. How is Auld Rabbie?"

"Grandda is well. Getting older," Aleck said. "We were checking the burn today for wild garlic and such and making sure the flow isna blocked where it turns toward the property."

"Some say the water makes no difference to the whisky, but it all goes toward the taste," Ronan said.

"Just as you and Grandda have taught us. For the last batch, we kept the peat fires hot to dry the mash longer than usual, as you prefer, for a good smoky flavor."

"I left the place in good hands." Ronan smiled.

"Sir, while you were gone," Aleck said, "you should know Pitlinnie has taken an interest, coming around with questions, wanting to buy up our kegs. I do not like it."

"How much has he purchased?"

"More than he needs. We canna trust the man," Geordie said.

"How much is in storage? If I want to send kegs to Edinburgh, what is there?"

"Tell us how many and when, and we will see to it," Aleck said.

"There are casks of various sizes at the distillery, many still aging. Our best store is set aside and not at Glenbrae. You know."

"Aye. Still safe where it is?"

"Auld Rabbie checked it recently. Pitlinnie also asked how much we have in store, how many casks in the barn to age, how many elsewhere, how old, and such."

"The longer those casks are undisturbed the better. He is unaware of the other lot? Keep it that way. What does he want?"

The brothers exchanged a grim look. "He is offering to buy all of it."

"The kegs?"

"All of it. The distillery, the property, casks, kegs, and all," Aleck explained.

Ronan glanced at Donal. "Did you know this?"

"Suspected it. We think Pitlinnie wants to merge Glenbrae with his distillery."

"Lord save us. Agree to nothing."

"Aye. He wants something else." Geordie glanced at Donal. "Mairi Brodie."

Startled, Ronan did not show it. "Donal?"

"He comes around and acts the charmer. I find it annoying."

"We think the man is smitten," Geordie said.

"Keep watch over that, all of you." Ronan glanced toward the sky, where rain gathered in high gray clouds. A light drizzle began, and the horses whickered. Time was passing quickly. "I must go."

"Where can we find you?" Aleck asked.

"Strathniven for now. I will find you at the distillery," he added. "We need a count of how many kegs can be sent out."

"To take over the hills by night for a fine profit?" Geordie smiled.

"Not any longer, lads." He lifted a hand in farewell.

CHAPTER 10

In all Strathniven House, Ellison loved the two libraries most. Standing in the expanse of the larger one as she waited for Ronan MacGregor, she inhaled the scents of wood, old paper, and the earthy aroma of the linseed oil polish on the table. The walnut surface was a smooth, dark gloss under her fingertips.

She loved the soaring bookshelves crammed with volumes, the reading nooks set with comfortable chairs, the balcony level and its wrought iron stair. Earlier she had strolled through choosing books suited to etiquette lessons, setting them on a table between two green damask chairs by a tall window. She was ready to begin.

She sat, glancing up at the portrait over the fireplace of Viscount Strathniven, stern and elderly, overlooking his beloved library. Had there been a portrait of Colin Leslie nearby, Ellison thought, she might have avoided it. The wound, the regret, and the conflict still hurt. She had been young, foolish, convinced she was in love, though she had brought only grief to her family and herself.

Hearing a knock, she stood as Ronan MacGregor entered. He looked fine in the black suit that had once belonged to Colin. Amused, she saw he wore his old boots again, buffed but frayed.

"Sir," she said, feeling a flutter in her stomach that no man had roused in her, not even Colin. Yet this brawny stranger stirred excitement in her and an invigorating hint of risk.

"The rain has stopped." He came toward her.

"Yes. Did you have a pleasant ride?"

"We did. Highland air is refreshing in any weather."

"I thought to walk out later with Balor, as long as there is no thunder."

"Where is the wee rascal?" He looked around.

"Banished from the library. He has a taste for carpet fringe. Shall we begin? I have some books on etiquette to look through." She indicated the table and chairs, the stack of books.

"Assigned reading?" He made a wry face and turned to survey the room. "What a grand library. Two collections in one household is a scholar's paradise." He glanced at her. "Is Lady Strathniven so dedicated to studying?"

"She is not overly fond of reading. Books were Lord Strathniven's love."

Nodding, he strolled to examine a tall section of shelves. "Poetry, mythology, literature, sciences—medicine too. And novels," he murmured, pausing here and there to pluck a book, sift through pages, slide it back into place.

Ellison went with him in silence, her gray cotton gown shushing as she moved. In the rainy light, his blue eyes were intent as he looked through books, stroked gilded leather and fluttered pages, his touch tender. She felt a sweet chill of pleasure. His love of books radiated like a current, a yearning that matched her own.

"You appreciate a good library." For a moment she felt she saw the true man. Though he might want others to think him a simple laird, crofter, and smuggler, he was far more. Educated. Thoughtful. Complex.

He touched a green spine. "Percy's *Reliques of Ancient Poetry*. I read this as a boy."

"I loved it too. I still go back to it."

He moved on to matching black and red volumes. "Law books. Erskine's *Institute of the Laws of Scotland,* the set. Burnett's *Criminal Law* . . . excellent."

"You are familiar with them?"

"A rogue must know his legal risk," he drawled. "How many books are here?"

"A count was done for the estate when Lord Strathniven died. Over four thousand books are here." She smiled. "I have added some of my own since, nearly a hundred more, I think."

"You and I have something in common."

Her heart quickened. "Affection for books, yes! I love to read and write too—" She stifled an urge to say more. "Do browse and read as you like in both libraries."

"Thank you. Lady Strathniven mentioned you write poetry?"

"Some." Feeling silly and hopeful all at once, she only shrugged. "But we are here for tutoring. Shall we begin?"

"Aye, or disappoint Mr. Corbie." He waited for her to take a chair, then sat too.

"We can review these." She chose a book. "Most books on manners address what is proper for girls and women. Not many address proper behavior for gentlemen."

"Yet both genders need sensible advice." He took up another book, shifting his chair, too small for a man of his height and build. Her chair felt large, her toes barely touching the floor. Suddenly she felt as if the room was overly fussy and formal. She wanted him to feel relaxed. "Here, let me read a bit. This book discusses how a worthy gentleman must act in social encounters. Ah, here."

She began. "For most social occasions, standing is acceptable and common for a gentleman, except at meals. While standing, it is frowned upon for a gentleman to thrust his hands into his pockets or warm his back at the fire."

"Like this?" He stood, towering over her. A smile teased his lips as he lifted a side flap in the black coat. "This has an actual pocket. Excellent. What is properly kept there? A wee page to remind me what I should say to the king?"

Laughing a little, she stood too. "Do take this seriously, sir."

"I do, madam, for your sake as well as mine."

"All right. No hands in the pockets, then. When sitting, a gentleman never drops down loosely. Especially a tall man. It is most unbecoming, the book says."

"I shall remember." He seemed amused. "Next? Shall we practice going into dinner?" He extended his elbow. "Miss Graham?"

She wrapped her fingers lightly around his offered arm, sensing hard muscle beneath smooth wool. He walked her forward, turned, came back. "Neatly done, sir. A gentleman never jabs out his elbow in case he should hit the unsuspecting lady."

"I would never hurt a lady." His eyes caught hers.

"Just common sense. Most good manners are." She looked away, cheeks burning, for she was too aware of his closeness, his strength. And she was glad of his willingness and droll humor reviewing what he clearly knew well.

"I suppose we only need study protocols relevant to meeting royalty," he said.

"More is expected, I think."

"We can take our time." If Papa and Mr. Corbie knew how easy this was, they might send MacGregor back to prison sooner. She would not be the cause of that.

Seated again, she chose another book. "Lord Chesterfield's letters to his son."

"Ah, the infamous Chesterfield. My father gave me a copy as a boy but said to take only some to heart and reject the rest. The author shows how *not* to behave."

"Oh dear. I have not read it, I confess."

"Nor would you. Though if you have a son someday, be forewarned. May I?" He took the book. "Chesterfield emphasizes hard work, persistence, truth, and honor. Whatever is worth doing is worth doing well, and so on."

"That seems reasonable."

He skimmed his fingers along a page. "A man should keep his eyes open and mouth shut and avoid gossip, also sensible. He then advises gentlemen to impress others of superior rank by copying their dress and mannerisms, even if those are foolish fashions."

"That will not do," she said, surprised.

"His thoughts on women are very interesting," he added, turning pages.

"I can hardly wait."

He chuckled. She loved the sound. "Here—'women are only children of a larger growth; they have an entertaining tattle and sometimes wit; but for solid, reasoning good-sense, I never in my life knew one that had it.'"

"What! You invent that." As she reached for the book, he held up a hand.

"On my honor, madam. Here. 'A man of sense only trifles with women, humors and flatters them. He cannot trust them with serious matters.'"

"Let me see!" Reaching again, her fingers grazed his, feeling a gentle thrill. He held the book close.

"Women love to dabble in business, which they always spoil, he says, and believe they are beautiful even when they are ugly." He glanced up.

"He is a hateful man."

"By the by, none of this applies to you."

"Or anyone." Yet her heart gave a little fillip at the casual compliment.

"I will say I disagree with Lord Chesterfield in most things."

"I should hope so. Give it here, sir." She extended an open palm.

"One last piece of advice from my lord," he said. "'One must be careful never to laugh in company. It is rude and unfashionable.'" He looked up. "Do not dare laugh, Miss Graham—"

Too late, laughter bubbled up even as he waggled his index finger. Lips pinched, he suppressed a smile. "Rude wee lass."

"Give me that awful book." Taking it with two fingers as if it were vermin, she set it aside.

"You would be a revelation to the author," he said. "An exceedingly proper and very capable young woman."

"Not quite, though my father wishes it were so," she said too quickly. "Most of these books state that a woman's chief purpose in life is to make a perfect and comfortable home for fathers, husbands, and children. I am not very good at that."

"You would be if you wanted. But women are capable of far more than that."

"As capable and intelligent as men, but we are not always granted the education or the chance to prove it." She set her chin.

"I learned early watching my mother and sisters that the female is often superior to the male in common sense and consideration. If I have proper manners at all, it is due to the women in my life." His eyes crinkled, the keen blue lights there seeing straight into her somehow.

"Wise man to admit it." She smiled too. But if he knew about her hasty marriage, her dream of writing novels, or her father's low opinion of her, he would not think her very worthy.

"What is this?" He plucked up a slim volume with marbled covers.

"Mr. Scott's pamphlet of protocols for the royal visit. You can borrow that copy. We can review it later."

He nodded. "So we have survived our first lesson in etiquette."

"We have. But before you go, Mr. MacGregor—I had a note from my father this morning when Mr. MacNie fetched the mail in Kinross. Papa says that Lord Darrach is on the invitation list to attend the royal levee. It will be a small gathering for gentlemen who are to be introduced to the king."

He frowned. "Lord Darrach?"

"The royal secretary retrieved the name. My father suggests we should address you as such now."

His curt nod told her he was displeased. "I doubt the events will be small."

"Hundreds of guests, perhaps thousands. Invitations will be delivered a day or two ahead of the levee. The king's secretary needs an address. Do you know where you might be?"

"Hopefully not in the subterranean accommodations of Edinburgh Castle."

"Never that," she said quickly. "But accommodations in the city are filling up quickly. Rooms and houses are being rented for exorbitant fees —a tiny room for a week could cost the same as a year's rent."

"Outrageous," he said. "I will make arrangements."

"The invitation can be delivered to my father's house on George Street."

"Fine. Though we should feel certain of this scheme before we make plans."

"It will succeed. It must."

He stood. "Your father and your suitor may be displeased to know I have not yet mastered forks and dancing."

"He is not my suitor. Mr. MacGregor," she began, standing to look up at him. "I know you are unhappy with the situation. And there is little I can teach you."

"On the contrary, I can learn much from you. And perhaps you can learn a little from me," he murmured. He had a way of focusing intently, of listening closely. She felt noticed. Important, even if it was only an illusion.

She raised her chin. "And what," she said, "would you have me learn?"

"Just this." He leaned down a little. "To straighten your spine just as you are doing now. To know you are strong and intelligent. And to tell your Papa and his clerk that you are not at their beck and call."

"Oh," she breathed. Shivers chased down her spine. "Oh."

"Until later, madam." He strode for the door.

In the half-light after dawn, Ellison tiptoed through the silent, sleepy house, past a maid stoking the fire in the parlor—even in summer, the vast house could be cool—and past the library, where tall windows showed gauzy shawls of mist outside. In the kitchen, bacon crackled on the griddle while Mrs. MacNie chopped fruit into a bowl. Murmuring a greeting, Ellison plucked a fat strawberry to eat as she went to the door. Beside the hearth, Balor jumped up to follow.

Grabbing a straw bonnet and a red and black tartan from wall hooks, she threw the plaid over her gown, the lavender muslin again, clean and pressed. She could leave mourning behind now, but somber colors still felt comfortable to her.

Fastening the dog's leash, she opened the door upon the obscuring mist, but the pleasant summer air promised sun and warmth soon. She hurried her step past the gardens as the dog tugged her along.

Something in her craved freedom this morning. Perhaps the feeling stemmed from Ronan MacGregor's words yesterday. *Know you are strong.* It felt both liberating and unsettling to be seen clearly like that.

Balor pulled ahead and she let him lead her along a path through birches that led to a lochan on the estate. Ahead, the water shone like glass and ducks arrowed through the water as they swam on the mist-draped water. Stepping into the clearing was like entering an enchanted world.

Balor pulled onward, following something earnestly while Ellison kept a tight hold on the leash, recalling the last time she had given him the lead on the day Ronan MacGregor had arrived.

The man was never far from her thoughts. He was a mystery, an educated man, a gentleman of integrity and secrets, contradicting what she had been told to expect.

Balor lurched forward then, barking, dragging her toward the water's edge. Despite his size, he was muscle and determination beneath his long peppery coat, and he was on a mission.

And he caused a commotion as ducks flurried up from the water, quacks echoing in the quiet. The dog jumped, barking furiously, as if he could snatch the birds from the air. Tugging hard against the hold of the leash, his head smaller than the breadth of his neck, he slipped free and ran along the shoreline.

Calling out, Ellison ran close on his heels. The dog slowed, sniffing along the sweep of the water where stones gleamed and reeds thrust upward. He drank a little and trotted along, dancing in and out of the shallows. More ducks flapped up and away, quacking loudly.

"Give up, sir, you cannot catch them," she said, approaching with the leash and slipped collar. Barking wildly, Balor leaped into the water, surging ahead to paddle after more birds. Ellison kicked off her slippers and lifted her skirts to step ankle-deep into the lapping water, gasping at the chill as stockinged feet found purchase on stones and muck.

"Madam," came a deep voice. "Please stay where you are."

Startled, she looked up and around. No one stood on the grassy shore or among the birches. Whirling, she gasped as a man rose out of the sun-sparkled water like a selkie emerging from the sea. Water sluiced off his dark hair and wide bare shoulders—

Ronan MacGregor stood chest-high in the water. "Madam," he said again, holding up a deterring hand, "come no further, if you please."

"Mr. MacGregor!" She stood with skirts bunched and dripping in her hands.

"Go back. I will get your dog." He dipped lower in the water and pushed toward the little dog paddling toward him, reached out, and grabbed him. "Here, lad, aye, there we are." He turned, treading water. "I will send him toward you. Wait there."

She was already surging forward. "I will come to you."

"The water is deeper here than you are tall. And I am not in a state for company, as it were."

"I will not look," she said, moving forward. The water rose to her shoulders, though he stood at mid-chest. Watery reflections danced over his muscled shoulders and chest, lapped at his hair and broad neck.

"That is close enough," he said, while Balor happily licked his chin.

"A man in bathing attire does not frighten me. I was married, sir."

"But it alarms me, if not you. Besides, you will ruin another gown."

"Too late," she said, as she took another step. But the floor dipped away under one foot, and she stopped.

"Go back a bit." He approached, keeping low in the water, holding the dog.

She retreated slightly for balance. The water lapped at her bodice, splashed her chin, and dampened her hair. She waited.

"Now reach for your kelpie." He pushed the dog toward her. Obedient for once, Balor paddled the short length toward her and she caught his wriggling little body.

"Thank you, Mr. MacGregor! You have rescued him once again."

"So it is Mr. MacGregor? Not Lord Darrach?" he teased. She looked away, for her gaze kept dipping from his bearded, stunning face to his wide shoulders, strong collarbones, and chest with its dark, wet mat. Even in cool water, her cheeks heated.

"I can hardly call you Lord Darrach under the circumstances."

He laughed, arms treading. "Ronan, then. Surely after Balor's latest escapade, we can consider each other a friend."

"Friends with a secret," she laughed.

"Many secrets." His eyes cast down, then up.

Glancing down, she saw her bodice and chemise ballooned with water, exposing the tops of her breasts and more. Tugging the cloth up, she pressed the dog close. Still, the tall man had an easy view, though he looked away politely.

He dipped down, the water covering all but his head, his hair floating out in a dark fan, and surged backward in the rippling water. "Take that rascal to the house and get dry. And tighten his leash. He is bent on mischief, that one."

"He is spirited," she agreed, easing backward in the water, holding the dog.

"Go on now." He waved her toward the shore.

"Sir, I apologize. I had no idea you would be out here. Do you often bathe in a loch? Is it a Highland habit?"

"Aye, for some. I came here hoping for a private swim. I am not fond of the beast in the tower."

"The beast? Oh, the shower machine! It can be difficult." She waded backward. "Thank you again, Mr. MacGregor."

"Ronan. We are surely friends by now."

"Ellison," she offered, moving back, water sluicing from her gown.

"Ellison Graham. E. S. G., as in your note. What is the 'S' for?"

"Sophia. My mother's name."

"Ellison Sophia, I enjoy your company, I do. But you cannot be seen here with me. Go on now." He waved again.

As she turned away, Balor struggled to get free, yelping as if insisting on staying with the man. She held him tightly as she surged through the water, walking over slippery stones. One foot found an uneven dip and she stumbled, going under for an instant, holding the dog up, gasping as she tried to regain her balance.

Strong hands grabbed her around the waist and pulled her up. Sputtering, she swirled to face Ronan, who held her arm securely, his arm extended as he tried to keep his distance. Pushing her hair out of her eyes, she coughed, holding the dog closely. "Thank you!"

He let go, hands swirling as he backed away. "Are you steady now?"

"Aye." Sniffling, she stepped back, even as Balor yelped toward the man he adored. "Best no one knows about this."

"Agreed." He surged backward again. "We have had enough compromise for one day." In the morning light, his eyes were even bluer than the water.

She turned to emerge from the water, her gown clinging to her body, and felt him watching as she pulled at the fabric and stooped to attach the dog's collar and leash securely. Finding her shoes, bonnet, and plaid, she glanced back.

He lifted a hand in farewell, far away now, leaning back to boat himself along.

Leaving the plaid on the grass for his use, she hastened toward the house.

～

"My dear, I have some news," Lady Strathniven said when Ellison joined her later for tea in the parlor. "I promised to act as chaperone here, but I will need to be away for a short while. I am sorry."

"What is it?" Ellison asked, just as Ronan MacGregor entered the room. He wore a Highland outfit rather than the ill-fitting black suit—a belted plaid in forest green and wine red with a brown jacket and waist-coat and a creamy shirt and neckcloth, along with tartan stockings and leather brogues. Seeing him, she caught her breath. Not only was he a stirring sight, she felt renewed embarrassment over their encounter that morning.

Beside her, Lady Strathniven gasped a little; Ellison smothered a smile at that, though she tried to dispel the distracting image of MacGregor in the water. This was the first she had seen him since the morning, for he had been out much of the day with Donal and MacNie. She wondered if he had avoided her as she had avoided him. He must think her a silly girl with a silly wee dog.

"I hope I am not late, my lady. Miss Graham," he murmured, taking a seat.

"Not at all. What an excellent costume, if I may say, sir," the viscountess said.

"Thank you, my lady. Donal kindly fetched some of my things."

"Good. We are to call you Darrach now, I hear?"

"I will answer to whatever you choose." His smile seemed tight.

"Lord Darrach quite suits you. Now, I was just telling Ellison as you came in," she continued, "that I had a note from my sister, Mrs. Harold Beaton. She just arrived at Duncraig, her Highland home, for the summer to rest after the stresses of organizing her daughter's wedding last month. Her youngest came up with her—Miss Sorcha Beaton, whom Ellison knows."

"Yes, a lovely girl. She will have her debut later this year in Edinburgh, I think."

"Yes. And my sister's son, Archibald, may come up later but he is a very busy man. A judge, you see, Darrach."

"Ah," he only said, but Ellison saw a muscle bounce in his cheek as if the mention of Judge Beaton gave him pause.

"Beth's wedding in Edinburgh was wonderful. I was good friends with her in school, sir," Ellison told Ronan, "and I feel like an older sister toward Sorcha, who is sixteen now."

"Nearly seventeen, and her Mama is planning the debut—another stress for her. You see, Darrach, I have two nieces and two nephews, the children of my sisters," the lady explained. "My youngest sister was Adam Corbie's mother. Foolish girl eloped with a reprobate. Both she and her husband are gone now, and I shall not speak ill of the dead." She sniffed. "I acted as guardian for Adam, who spent most of his time away at school. One never knows what influences children encounter in those places. Which school did you attend, Darrach?"

"A glen school, and Perth Academy. I lived with my uncle in those years."

"My lady," Ellison said, "how long will Mrs. Beaton and Sorcha be at Duncraig?"

"My sister is undecided, though she hinted that Sorcha could return with me to Edinburgh for the festivities. There will be an exodus from the Highlands to the city soon, mark me. Well, to my point," she went on. "I am asked to visit. My sister has a nervous constitution and I am a calming influence on her. But I gave my word to be here with you, Ellison. So I am torn."

"But you must visit Duncraig, my lady. Mrs. Barrow and the MacNies are here, and the servants too. And Mr. Mac—Darrach and I will be occupied with our work."

Lady Strathniven considered MacGregor for a moment. "Sir, my instinct says you are a true gentleman. But propriety, and Sir Hector, insist on a chaperoning presence. Here is my thought," she said, turning to Ellison. "I will ask Sorcha to come here as your companion. She could be a help to you."

"I would love to see her."

"Good. MacNie will take my note directly to Duncraig today. The post takes so long to go back and forth now," she complained.

"She is welcome, though I do not need a chaperone now."

"Widows trade loss for a little freedom, as you are discovering, dear. But your father insists on propriety while you are here this time."

"Yes," Ellison said, glancing swiftly at MacGregor and away.

"Adam is eager to come up. I could write to him," the lady offered.

"That is not necessary," Ellison said quickly. "You will only be gone a few days."

"Perhaps longer. My sister feels very drained. But when I return, Darrach will be a fine gentleman indeed, and we will be off to the city. Is that not so, sir?"

"I am doing my best to fulfill expectations, my lady."

"Excellent. Dear Ellison is expected to turn a frog into—"

"Oh, here is tea!" Ellison said as Mrs. Barrow entered the room.

Ronan hoped his stomach was not growling audibly. Months of prison fare had grown his appreciation for good food. As Ellison Graham served tea, hot and dark, adding sugar and cream, and then filled dainty plates with cakes or sausages and cold salmon, he smiled, waiting for the ladies to begin.

"Excellent," Lady Strathniven said. "Mrs. Barrow's lemon cake and fresh strawberries too, marvelous! But I shall have a little salmon first."

As Ellison served her, Ronan noticed how petite and wan she looked in gray in marching rows of black lace. Her morning dress had been soaked, he remembered, so that he knew despite lush curves she was thin; she put a little on her plate, while Lady Strathniven's plate rivaled that of a farmer.

She handed him a cup, remembering he took only milk and no sugar in his tea. Had she loaded it with sweetness, he would have sipped it just to see her smile.

"Despite what your father believes, my dear," Lady Strathniven was saying, "He will always think of you as his little girl. But you have earned independence now. It is time he realized it."

Ellison nodded. "Yes, my lady."

"Doing what one pleases is the privilege of widowhood. Sir Hector can hardly protest if you follow my example. I do as I want and interfere with no one."

"It is good advice."

"Though I do wish your husband had left you property without complication. Have the lawyers sorted out the Edinburgh house?"

"Not as yet." Ellison sipped tea.

"It should be yours without question. That house is suitable until you marry again, as I am sure you will do someday."

The girl blushed furiously. Ronan frowned, sipped, listening.

"Mr. Smithson believes the dispute can be solved and I will have the house."

"It is a good house in a desirable area. I just wish the poor fellow had left you more secure, dear. Do prod the lawyer again. Some of them are not worth their salt and so we must continually press them, isn't it so, Lord Darrach?"

Ronan swallowed the hot tea too quickly. "I suppose so."

She spread a scone liberally with butter. "Hearts heal, but property can be lost forever. Colin's cousins need to leave that house now, Ellison."

"It is a problem," the girl murmured.

"Squatters! You see, Darrach," the lady added, "her late husband's relatives insist the house is theirs. They moved in last year and refuse to leave."

"That must be quite distressing," he commented carefully.

"The will was not specific enough about property," Ellison explained. "It stated that his cousins could choose the family items they wanted. So they claimed the house itself. I had moved back to my father's house, you see, and they took up residence without asking, having a key from years before."

"An unfortunate situation," he said.

"Squatters," Lady Strathniven repeated.

"I am sure the lawyers will straighten it out," Ellison said. "Mr. Smithson is here in Edinburgh, and his partner Mr. Cameron has an office in Kinross. Perhaps you know them?"

"I know the names." He was more than familiar with both.

"Do you know much about the law, Lord Darrach?" Lady Strathniven asked.

"Some, madam." He noticed Ellison's sharp glance, knew she was growing more alert to his truths and half-truths.

"Those involved in the whisky business are often well aware of the laws, I imagine," Ellison said.

"Exactly, Miss Graham."

"I sympathize," Lady Strathniven said. "Crofters deserve to earn a livelihood from their barley and whisky. A local distiller gifts us a regular supply of his product, you know."

Ronan lifted his cup in salute. "Pitlinnie? It is a good whisky. I would be happy to send some of our Glenbrae brew here as well."

"Thank you. I enjoy a dram now and then. Do you think they will change the whisky laws, Darrach? I hear it may be so."

"They say the laws may change substantially next year."

"Best you part ways with smuggling and rely on distilling, then," she said.

He smiled. The lady could be bluntly honest at times.

"Ellison, dear, perhaps Darrach has some thoughts regarding your house. What would you do in this instance, sir?"

"I would consult with the lawyer, as Miss Graham has done," he said carefully. "If I can be of assistance—"

"I would not want to bother you with it," she said, standing, her lovely hands flexing, folding. "Here, let me serve the cake." Going to the sideboard, she took up a knife and thrust it into Mrs. Barrow's lemon cake.

"Darrach, perhaps you could visit this lawyer," the viscountess said.

"I could, but Miss Graham may not require my help."

"She may not." Ellison sliced cake, slid it onto a plate, scooped up strawberries from a bowl, and slapped them on top. "She may want to sort it out on her own."

Lady Strathniven frowned. "It is your concern, dear, but a man's influence—"

"Cake, my lady?" Ellison thrust the plate toward her, confection sliding dangerously. Ronan took it quickly and set it before the viscountess.

"Thank you. So, do you have advice for Ellison?"

The girl slapped another helping of cake and strawberries onto a second plate and handed it to Ronan. She also gave him a snapping glare.

"But men have such a good sense of these things."

"Ladies may know these things too," Ellison said, stabbing a strawberry.

"If the will was signed and witnessed in your husband's authentic hand, it should be valid. Vague wording could be the fault of the solicitor but it could still be interpreted to some extent. However, a judge may need to decide it."

"There, you see," Lady Strathniven said. "Darrach knows a good deal."

"Perhaps." Ellison mashed a bit of cake with her spoon and sighed. "I just want to avoid a confrontation. I wish no harm to anyone."

"I understand. But your rights are important too." He had his own legal dilemma and should not entangle himself elsewhere. But oh, this lass, he thought, this strong, fragile, outspoken, soft-spoken lass. She scrambled all his intentions.

Ellison set down her spoon. "Very well. What is your suggestion?"

"Have your lawyer ban them from the property. Until the will is sorted, they have no legal right to be there. The police could be summoned for the task."

"But I would not want to ask that."

"She has a soft heart, you see," the viscountess told Ronan.

"Let the lawyer show the harder heart, Miss Graham. You need not compromise your kind nature." He saw her eyes widen and seek his.

"Could I request the lawyer take a harder approach?"

"Aye. Send a message to your advocate's office, ask him to sort it out and make sure they are gone, and tell you the outcome. May I ask if you have plans to live there yourself?"

"I may someday. Until then, I could rent the place. It is just unfair that the cousins are there when they have no right."

"Squatters," Lady Strathniven emphasized.

"Tell your lawyer what you want. He will handle the details. It is certainly something you can and should do in this case, I think."

"Thank you. I will send him a letter."

"Then it is settled. This cake is delicious," Lady Strathniven said.

Ellison looked at Ronan, her eyes going silver in a sunbeam. She glowed somehow, as encouraged and confident as if she had been lost and saw a light ahead.

Suddenly he felt as if he were the lost one, reaching for a silvery light that shone on all he could ever want. He looked down, dipped a spoon into cake and fruit, sweet and tart, and hardly tasted it.

CHAPTER 11

"Where would you like to go today, Mr. MacGregor?" Ellison smiled as she spoke, savoring the warm afternoon sun on her face and enjoying the fresh breeze that ruffled her bonnet and the skirt of her black riding costume. Shifting the reins of the horse she rode, she looked around at the rugged hills surrounding the green bowl of the glen just ahead. "Likely you know this area well."

Ronan slowed his Highland pony to pull even with her. She too was mounted on one of the stocky, shaggy Highland ponies suited to the steep hills along the day's route. "I do know this region. I thought we might visit the Glenbrae distillery. It is just across this glen."

"I would love to see your property."

"Mine only in a sense. The glen and distillery are part of the Darrach estate and leased to my family for generations. My ancestors once owned much of this region. But I am just a tenant."

"And laird of Glenbrae," she amended. "Is the distillery far?"

"Not far now. Just that way, where the dirt road branches off this one." He pointed to where the military road they followed forked, the wide cobbled way marching north between forested hills, the dirt road heading toward the slope of the glen side.

Donal, who had ridden ahead, came back to join them, riding three abreast on stolid, shaggy Highland ponies. The men outsized the horses, but in their plaids and riding the local breed, they looked a natural part of the Highland scenery.

They left the straight, unforgiving line of the engineered English military road for the old earthen path that followed the slopes and curves of the glen. Ellison wished she had brought a sketchbook and pencil along so that she could capture some of the views that were so inspiring to the spirit—and to her novel. The manuscript, slowly growing, was locked in her writing box at Strathniven. Each day she learned more to benefit her story—and discovered more about Ronan MacGregor. Every slight hint or revelation made her long to understand the mystery that surrounded him.

"We are entering Glenbrae now," he said then. "It is named for that high, steep hill that juts above the slopes, see? Those braes, or *bràighean* in Gaelic, form the bowl of the glen."

"*Gleann Bràigh,*" she said. Noticing the far end of the valley, she saw a small stone castle in the lee of a high hill, an old graystone tower stark against the heathery purple of the hills where goats and sheep grazed.

"What is that castle?" she asked.

"Invermorie," Ronan said.

"Is that your home, as laird of Glenbrae?"

"I lived there as a boy, but I keep a cottage near the distillery now. My kinfolk live in the castle."

"My mother and grandfather," Donal explained.

"Oh?" Surprised, Ellison looked again to see a woman walking outside the castle now. She was slim and dark-haired. "Is that your mother?"

"Aye. This way to the distillery," Donal said.

"Will we stop at Invermorie? I should like to meet them."

"Another day," MacGregor said. "The distillery will take time. I need to determine how much whisky is available to send to Edinburgh."

As he rode ahead, Ellison frowned, wondering at his curt answer.

~

Hearing the burble of water as they neared the distillery, Ronan felt himself relax. The soothing chuckle and shush of the Lealtie Burn could wash troubles away in its flow. But his troubles of late would not rinse away easily.

He guided his pony over the stone bridge spanning the fast burn, Ellison and Donal following. His gaze was transfixed by the sight of his distillery, by the whitewashed walls and slate roofs of its three buildings, by the trees and rumpled hillocks that surrounded his enterprise in a safe and cushioning hand.

He felt infused with pride, with love. Glancing past the main buildings, he saw his stone cottage, thatched roof golden in the sun. Home.

"Beautiful," Ellison said as they halted the ponies in the yard. "So peaceful."

"It is," he agreed. "And a hardworking place as well."

"I will see who is here." Donal dismounted, tied up his pony, and walked to the main building to open its red door and vanish within.

"Only one or two men are needed here most days, depending on the work. Come inside." Ronan dismounted, secured his pony's reins, then turned to help Ellison dismount. Her body slid against his unexpectedly so that he felt a leap and heat within. He set her down and stepped back. She turned away equally quickly.

Donal appeared in the doorway. "Auld Rabbie is here at the spirit safe."

"Spirit safe?" Ellison asked.

"You will see." He led her into the cool, dim interior, a wide, plain room that held three huge copper stills. Sunbeams poured through a narrow window, gleaming over bright metal. Ellison turned around in wonder.

"Are those the stills? And the smell—is it ale? And smoke?"

"Aye, copper stills that we brought here from Perth. That beery smell is given off by malting barley, and the smoke is the peat of the fires in the drying room nearby. The malt house, drying rooms, and still house are all connected by covered passages. Over the years, the odors have permeated the whole place."

"I like it. A comforting sort of smell." She smiled.

He nodded, resting a hand on the warm copper shoulder of one of the stills. Briefly, proudly, he thought of the challenges and the cost, too, in bringing the huge stills here, and in building the place from a cluster of dilapidated cottages. For years, he and his brother Will and their cousin, Viscount Darrach, with the help of others, had worked tirelessly to create what Ronan had been pleased to license as a legal distillery last year.

Soon after, his brother and cousin were killed, and the secrets they had kept from him emerged. The crisis had altered his life and that of his friends.

He had done all he could to right things, but at a cost. Now he needed to reclaim his life and return to Glenbrae to build it into what it could be. But lately, he was beginning to realize that he needed something else as well. He glanced at Ellison.

"Ronan?" She watched him. "You were distracted. Donal called for you."

He took a hand from the copper as if he had been burned and guided her through a doorway to a connecting room, where he saw Donal and an elderly man, ropey thin and swathed in a shabby plaid and bonnet. The man grinned.

They stood beside a metal tank fitted with brass pipes that led to a large glass box banded in brass and set on a pedestal. Streams of liquid channeled and trickled through the pipes into the clear container.

Donal waved. "Good as gold, sir. Auld Rabbie Muir has been watching it."

"Ronan! *Fàilte air ais gu Gleann Bràigh!*" The old man thrust out a hand.

"Rabbie, so good to see you," Ronan continued in English.

"And you! We heard you three were taken."

"Fortunately I am here now, come to see the excellent work you have done while I was away."

"And the others? Linhope and MacInnes?"

"Well enough. We will see them soon, with luck. Miss Graham, this is Robert Muir. He has been making whisky in Glenbrae since my father was a lad. Or was it my grandfather," he added with a chuckle.

Rabbie tipped his cap. "Miss Graham, welcome. I was a lad with Glenbrae's grandda, I was." He winked. "And I taught himself here to make the *uigse beatha,* our water of life. He took to it as a lad and showed a gift for the brewing. Since then, he has made our whisky into a very fine thing that makes all in our glen proud."

"How good to meet you, Mr. Muir." She held out a gloved hand, which he took gallantly. "It is a very nice place and such a bonnie glen."

"Och aye, though not near as bonnie as the lass Glenbrae brings with him today." He grinned impishly, and she laughed.

"Enough of the Muir charm," Ronan said. "Tell me about this lot." He tapped the glass lid.

"We expect fine things from this batch. It goes in the casks soon, Miss Graham," Rabbie explained. "This glass box is a spirit safe. It collects the vapors from the barley mash we ferment in another room. We heat it and stir it again and again. Those vapors you see there are what we call the gift of the spirit. That liquid is stored in casks and then aged to fine whisky. It takes time to make the best water of life," he went on.

"And it takes good barley and good Highland water, the peaty smoke from the fires," Ronan said, "and even uses the flavor of the water that is influenced by rocks and flowers along the burn that runs through here."

"It takes a love of the craft, too," she said.

"Och, aye, Miss," Rabbie said. "Love and care, time and patience are all needed to make the very best whisky. Skilled hands as well. My grandsons work with me. They are out and about," he added to Ronan.

"I saw them recently," he murmured. Rabbie nodded.

"From here the spirit goes into casks?" Ellison asked.

"Aye. The liquid essence captured here," Ronan explained, "is then stored in oak casks. The older the better adds richness, such as casks that have held Spanish sherry. They rest and mature for years."

"Years, aye," Rabbie said. "The longer it rests the finer the whisky. Ronan MacGregor has the patience for it, and the love, as you say, Miss.

Whisky is an ancient brew, and Highland whisky carries the heart and spirit of Scotland in it. Do ye take a sip now and then, Miss? Some ladies will not."

"I do, on occasion. It is invigorating."

He turned to Ronan. "I do not know where the girl was born," he said in rapid Gaelic, "but this one is Highland in her soul."

"And she speaks the Gaelic," Ronan drawled.

"Aha! *Ciamar a tha thu an-duigh?*" Rabbie asked her in a renewed greeting.

"*Tha mi gu math, tapadh leat,*" she responded. Ronan felt a burst of pride as fulsome as if he were her tutor—or something even more meaningful.

"She will do, Glenbrae," Rabbie approved.

"Aye so. Donal, please take Miss Graham around to show her the place, while Rabbie and I catch up on business."

"Miss Ellison, this way." He led her to another door.

"God above, we thought you might not survive prison," Rabbie told Ronan.

"I had a bit of luck and was released. How goes it here?"

"Well enough. Though that scoundrel Pitlinnie comes around with questions, buying kegs and casks. I do not like it."

"So I heard from Aleck and Geordie. How many casks and kegs are in storage? Enough to send a good supply south quickly?"

Rabbie rubbed his chin. "Most of what is here is too young to leave yet. We have a good store set aside. You know where that is."

"Aye. Is it safe?"

"Far as I know though I have not looked myself for a while. My grandsons will go there soon. I tell you, Pitlinnie is too curious. We must be careful."

"Does he know about the hidden stock?"

"I do not think so. Ronan, if aught ever happened to you, what then? We would never sell to Pitlinnie."

"My solicitor has my will. Donal is named my heir," he answered.

"You know Pitlinnie thinks to court Mairi Brodie."

"So I hear." He stepped back. "I am indebted to you and your lads for watching over the place."

"*Tcha.* Let us check the resting casks, now, and find your bonnie lass."

"Not my lass." But his denial did not ring true.

"What a nice luncheon with you and my lady aunt today," Sorcha said, "though she seems eager to leave for Duncraig. Mama will be happy to see her."

"And we are happy to have you here in a sort of exchange." Ellison smiled, taking her friend's arm as they entered Strathniven's main hall after a tour of the house and gardens just as a reminder for Sorcha, who had visited her aunt's home before. As they went about, Ellison had looked around for Ronan MacGregor, until Mrs. Barrow had mentioned that Darrach had gone to the stables with Mr. MacNie.

She was glad to have Sorcha's help, for the girl was gracious and kind, with a sweet enthusiasm that would lend a cheerful note and even charm a smile from MacGregor. He could be dour at times, understandable given his situation, though lately, Ellison treasured his rare smiles and droll humor. She felt as if she was seeing the sincere gentleman in him easily now, his polite and amusing moments and his somber and thoughtful moments too. More and more each day, she looked forward eagerly to seeing him at meals and lessons and times between.

Infatuated, Adam Corbie had once said of her. Perhaps he was right.

He had missed luncheon that day, having gone off with Donal Brodie to exercise the horses and visit some Strathniven tenants. While she was glad that MacGregor found things to do, that took time away from lessons. But the longer it took for his supposed transformation, the better. She dreaded the day they all returned to Edinburgh.

"Lady Strathniven said she is nearly packed and ready to go," Sorcha told Ellison, "and the Duncraig man had lunch in the kitchen and will be ready for the long drive back today. Ah, my lady aunt!" She turned as the viscountess approached.

"There you are! Did Ellison show you the house, dear?" Lady Strathniven asked. "We are so pleased you could come to stay for a bit."

"Thank you for inviting me," Sorcha said, as the lady gave her a quick embrace.

"You are always welcome here."

"My lady, I believe all is ready now for the drive back to Duncraig," Ellison said.

"Yes. I am only waiting on Jeanie to bring the last of my cases down. My goodness, Sorcha dear, you look so grown-up," she added. "So pretty. The image of your Mama."

"Truly you do," Ellison added. Sorcha had a happy, girlish countenance, with large hazel eyes in her oval face, a scattering of freckles on her upturned nose, and soft honey-colored curls. The sunny little girl she remembered from a few years ago had become a graceful young lady. Sorcha remained refreshingly straightforward with a practical nature. She would be delightful company.

"I expect to be gone only a week or two, depending on your Mama," Lady Strathniven said.

"You lift Mama's spirits and make her laugh. When I try to offer solutions, she only wants sympathy. She misses my sister so now that Beth has married."

"Pity, for she has you still at home," the lady said. "She always had a nervous constitution. But she did mention in her letter that she is considering holding a dinner party if she feels strong enough. That would be delightful."

"Perhaps you can inspire her to do so. It would do her good."

"We would all enjoy it. We could bring our guest. Ellison, dear, has Sorcha met Lord Darrach yet?"

"Not yet. He has been riding out and then in the stables, I think."

"I wonder if he would accompany you to Kinross this week on an errand for me," Lady Strathniven said. "The seamstress in town is finishing two dresses, one for me and another for you, Ellison. I asked her to make something new for you to wear in Edinburgh."

"Oh! Thank you, my lady," Ellison said in surprise.

"With all you are doing, you deserve something special. Ellison is such a help here at Strathniven," the lady told Sorcha. "We could not get along without her."

"We would be happy to visit the seamstress for you," Ellison said.

"Good. And Sorcha, dear, you shall have something new for the Edinburgh assemblies too. I will send a note to the seamstress asking her to fit you for something nice and to add it to my account. She may have to work quickly!"

"Oh, my lady aunt, I could not—"

"You certainly could. Something to match your green eyes, perhaps. But be sure to travel into town with Lord Darrach. A gentleman escort is wise. Sometimes there are rogues about in these hills."

And their escort might be as much a rogue as any, Ellison thought wryly.

"Lord Darrach? I know the name," Sorcha mused. "Mama mentioned Viscount Darrach, a neighbor in another glen. He died a year ago, I think. My brother told Mama about it, knowing she enjoys local news. It cheers her out of her doldrums."

"Our guest is another Lord Darrach," Ellison said quickly. "A friend."

"The heir, you see," the lady said blithely, though Ellison winced a little. "The Darrach estate is quite large. It touches Strathniven on our western boundary, with Glenbrae between. Just a few hours' ride from here."

"Oh, I see. Lord Darrach is not staying at his castle, then?"

"Matters are still being settled," Ellison said hastily, realizing they had not thought through all the details of transforming a smuggler to meet the king. *Oh, what a tangled web we weave when first we practice to deceive,* MacGregor had quoted once. This could become a tangle indeed.

"Darrach is with us for a little while until we travel to Edinburgh for the king's arrival," the viscountess was saying. "He is quite an eligible bachelor, with title and lands, and very handsome. I imagine young ladies will be eager to be introduced."

The tangled web just became more snarled. "My lady," Ellison said, "I am sure your carriage awaits."

"Yes. I had hoped to introduce Darrach before I go."

"Perhaps Mama will invite Lord Darrach to supper at Duncraig," Sorcha said.

"A splendid suggestion! Ellison, is that not an excellent idea?"

"Excellent," she replied. Tutoring the man was one thing—introducing him at a country party as Lord Darrach was another. If he was exposed, there would be consequences. Twisting her fingers, she forced a smile.

"A new bachelor in the area—I wonder if Mama would host a country dance as well as a supper," Sorcha said. "We could have fiddlers and dancing and a late supper. Friends in the area will be eager for news from the city and a little society with others before everyone goes to Edinburgh for the king's arrival."

"It sounds perfect," Lady Strathniven said. "Lord Darrach could practice his dancing." She gave Ellison a very bright smile.

"Practice what, my lady?" asked MacGregor. Ellison whirled at the sound of his voice. None of them had noticed him entering the foyer from a side corridor.

"Darrach, there you are!" Lady Strathniven said.

"My lady." MacGregor smiled. His gaze rested on Ellison. "And Miss Graham. And—is this Miss Beaton?" He inclined his head.

"Darrach, this is my niece, Miss Sorcha Beaton, just arrived from Duncraig."

"A pleasure to meet you." He took her offered hand.

Sorcha beamed. "Thank you, my lord. I have heard so much about you."

"Have you?"

"Only that you are a guest at Strathniven," Ellison said. "A friend."

"And grateful for the warm hospitality of friends." He smiled again.

"We were just saying, my lord, that perhaps you would enjoy visiting Duncraig," Sorcha said. "My mother is there now, and my brother, Judge Archibald Beaton, will be coming up from Edinburgh for a brief stay. He is rather fond of Glenbrae whisky. I believe it is associated with Darrach?"

"It is. I am honored," he murmured. "Judge Beaton is your brother?"

"Yes, my oldest brother. Do you know him? He was an advocate and is now a judge of some kind. I cannot sort out all his titles," she added with a laugh.

"I know the name. He is in the Court of Justiciary, I believe. We may have met."

Ellison felt a flutter of fear on his behalf. "How nice," she said.

"Very nice." MacGregor seemed calm and amiable.

"Jeanie! At last," Lady Strathniven said as a tall woman in black appeared carrying what seemed to be a rather heavy valise. "Do give that bag to the Duncraig driver. You should not have to carry it. We should be off soon."

"Yes, my lady."

"Jeanie, let me take that for you. Nonsense," MacGregor said, reaching for the leather bag as she protested. "I do not mind at all. I am just headed outside myself."

Ellison frowned. A lord offering to help a servant could be seen as a *faux pas,* although kind gestures rose above protocol to earn praise and loyalty. She also suspected MacGregor needed an excuse to leave quickly.

"Ellison, I nearly forgot," Lady Strathniven said. "I had a letter from your father this morning when MacNie brought the mail."

"Papa? What did he say?" Ellison dared not glance up as MacGregor paused by the door, valise in one hand.

"He has decided to allow Adam to come up after all."

"Cousin Adam! How delightful," Sorcha said.

"Ah. When?" Ellison asked in a flat tone.

"A week or so. He will send word. I may even be back by then."

"I see." Heart hammering, she felt keenly aware of Ronan's silence.

"Adam looks forward to seeing Lord Darrach," Lady Strathniven went on.

"I am sure he does," MacGregor clipped. "Good day, ladies. I have an errand. Lady Strathniven, I wish you a pleasant visit with your sister." He tipped his head.

Tucking her brows together, feeling worried, Ellison looked at him. "Darrach."

"Miss Graham. Miss Beaton. Good day. I shall see you at supper." He waited, ready to lend a hand to Lady Strathniven at the threshold step.

"Well, I am off!" The viscountess kissed Ellison's cheek, then Sorcha's. "Do not get into mischief while I am away!"

"We promise, my lady," MacGregor said lightly.

CHAPTER 12

*S*eated in the cozy quiet of the tower library, Ellison set down her quill pen and softly read the page aloud, pausing to jot a change here or there. In the late hour, rain shushed against the window glass, and candles flickered as she read.

> Winsome and alone, Lady Isabella returned to her Highland homeland a young widow veiled in black, bringing a small son and a fortune to protect for his sake. In the glen, they said the lady had fled to protect the child, for some in the south were bent on destroying his legacy. She needed a sword arm, they said, a Highland man keen for mischief and danger, a seneschal to hold her castle strong.
> When he heard the news, Alasdair MacAlpin of Garslie sharpened his dirk blade on the whetstone, cleaned and oiled his sheath and targe, unlocked the chest that held his armor, and readied himself to defend the lass he had loved since boyhood.

She glanced at the title page she had created on creamy paper to cover the growing manuscript: *The Highlander's Lament by E. S. Leslie*. Below it, she had added an ink sketch of a castle on a hill.

Waving the quill feather thoughtfully, she considered her story. The hero, a proud warrior descendant of ancient Scottish kings, lived under English rule in the time of Wallace and Bruce, when Scots were hunted and oppressed. A man of heart and loyalty, he nurtured unrequited love for a lass who was unaware how deeply the man loved her, for he had never spoken of it to her, though he would have given up his very life for her sake. Nor did he know that she kept secret her love for him.

Ellison sighed. The story made her hopeful and yet sad. She wanted to find some way to bring the noble Alasdair and vulnerable Isabella together at last. She scribbled another change and wrote on.

Frowning, she tapped her fingers on the tabletop, wondering how to place the hero in yet another pickle. She wanted him to come face to face with his foe, swords drawn, as he protected the lady from harm.

A little clock on the bookshelf chimed softly. By now the entire household would be asleep. Coming here mouse-quiet, she was sure that MacGregor, too, would be asleep in his room one floor above. Through the gap of the partly open door, she could see the dark stair and a bar of moonlight from a narrow window.

She had come here rather than retire to bed herself, for the writing itch was upon her, and the privacy of the tower library was just the place. For nearly two hours now, she had been writing steadily.

Standing, stretching, she glanced through the window at the drizzly summer twilight, which had gone quite dark. Picking up the small drinking glass on the table, she opened a decanter to pour a tiny bit more of the ratafia that Mrs. Barrow had made from a recipe of sherry mixed with a syrup of berries, oranges, cinnamon, and water. The housekeeper, aware that Ellison sometimes worked in the old library, made sure that the drink, a favorite of Lady Strathniven, was available for her.

Sipping the cordial, hoping it would help her sleep later, she had a new idea, and sat to cover another page in fluid writing, pen scratching in the quiet.

Then she froze, hearing the scrape of boots on the stone steps. MacGregor was just now going up to his room for the night, she realized —he may have been reading in the library in the main house. The footsteps paused at the library level, then resumed. Above, a door latched shut. She breathed out.

Dipping the quill, she began a fresh page, but could not focus on her story now. In flickering lamp light, in the silent room, her thoughts slid back to Ronan MacGregor. The very thud of his foot on the stone step had made her heart leap.

Just infatuation, as Corbie had rudely suggested, and it would pass if she ignored it. MacGregor did not return her interest—besides, any attraction would be impossible for them. He was only polite, gentlemanly, and kind to her, and soon he would be gone from Strathniven and her life.

But she wished suddenly that just once he would abandon propriety, express some feeling for her, and return her interest. A long while had passed since a man had cared about her. This widow's existence could seal her off from affection, from love, perhaps isolate her for the rest of her life.

Truly, she ought to go to bed. Tomorrow was one day closer to the day Ronan MacGregor would go to Edinburgh to carry out this risky scheme and depart forever. He would never know how she felt—and she would never say.

Somehow, she realized then, that feeling had entered her story about Alasdair and Isabella. Picking up the pen, she began to write again. Soon, surprising her in the way the writing sometimes did, an impassioned scene began to emerge. She bent over the page, inky nib scratching as she wrote about the girl who was now widowed and desperately needed the help of the Highlander she had rejected years before, hurting him beyond measure . . .

The story poured out, touching her so that tears welled and spilled, blotting the ink. Pausing at last, she slid ink-stained fingers through her hair, its braid falling loose over her shoulder, and then set down the pen.

She glanced outside at the rainy, dark purple night, and saw the reflection on the glass of the candle flames and her face. For an instant, she imagined a face above hers, as if her Highland hero stood behind her, tall, handsome, mysterious. A strong yearning surged through her—

She gasped. Ronan stood in the door, his face reflected above hers.

"Miss Graham," he said as she whirled. "I did not mean to startle you."

"Oh—no, it is fine. Come in." She looked a little dumbstruck to see him. Past midnight, sitting in the library, likely she did not expect to see him or anyone.

He entered, resting a hand on the back of a chair. "I came downstairs to look for something in the library. I did not realize you were here."

"Sometimes I work here late at night. It is so private."

"Or was until I arrived. You are writing letters?" Glancing at the pages on the table, he noticed watery ink blots just as she rested her folded hands over them.

"Not letters. A book," she blurted.

"Ah." Sensing her hesitation, Ronan realized that she felt protective, perhaps fearful, feeling some risk in having dreams and talents. He wondered if her father, perhaps Corbie too, had criticized her efforts, diminishing the shining spirit that he knew was within her. Feeling protective himself, he frowned.

"A book? That is excellent."

"You might think it frivolous." She kept her folded hands over her work.

"If reading is a worthy occupation, then writing books is also worthy."

She raised her brows as if surprised, even pleased. "True! Though writing poetry is considered more suitable for a lady than writing novels."

"I rather enjoy novels. But then some think me a ne'er-do-well," he drawled.

"I do not think so." She spoke with quiet sincerity.

"Thank you. I find much to admire in writers who set to a daunting task and do the work. I shall not interrupt you." He stepped back.

She shook her head. "I am done for now."

"If you come here seeking solitude, be sure that I will keep your secret. You keep enough of mine." He smiled fleetingly and turned to look at the bookshelves. "I only came down to look for a volume that may help my secret work, as it were."

"I have seen you reading in the other library recently. Law books?"

"Aye, puzzling over a legal question that may rely on archaic law. May I?" He turned toward the bookshelves.

"Please do. Lord Strathniven stored some very old books here, so there may be something suitably archaic there to help you. Mr. MacGregor, would you like a nightcap, as Lady Strathniven calls it? If you cannot rest, that sometimes helps."

"Thank you. A dram may improve sleep." Seeing a shelf where decanters and drinking glasses sat neatly arranged, he moved toward it. One glass decanter held an amber whisky. A smaller bottle held a dark liquid. "Is this sherry?"

"A ratafia made with sherry, berries, and spices. Mrs. Barrow makes it herself and keeps bottles filled in the libraries and the parlor."

"The ratafia is more a ladies' drink, I believe. I shall try the whisky." He poured a little into a glass and turned. "Would you care for some?"

"I had the liqueur earlier. But perhaps a little taste of the whisky—I feel a bit restless tonight. Perhaps it is the result of working late. Thank you," she said, as he poured a dram into another glass and handed it to her.

Lifting his glass in gentle salute, he sipped. "A handsome whisky. Pitlinnie again, if I am not mistaken."

"He is a local baronet, I think, who makes whisky and kindly provides it to the household."

"I know him. He has a modest Highland estate and a recent title, which he may have earned in return for a monetary gift to the English government. A gentleman does not gossip," he went on. "Though I am not always a gentleman. To Sir Neill Pitlinnie, who for all that, makes a decent brew." He raised his glass.

"You are not fond of the man."

"Not especially." He set down the drink and turned back to the shelf to look at the books. Finding two that looked promising, he drew them out. "I should leave you to finish your writing session, Miss Graham."

She shrugged. "The inspiration has passed."

"The inspiration—and tears?" He glanced at the pages. "Sorry, I should not have asked. But it must be a very good story to touch its author."

"I do rather like it. But Papa thinks—" She stopped, shook her head.

"Thinks it unsuitable?"

"Worse. Folly." She took a sip of the whisky. "Oh, my. That does warm the throat." A pretty blush crept up from neck to cheeks.

"May I ask what your story is about?"

"It would only sound silly." In the lamplight, her eyes glittered. He had the sense she wanted to tell him despite her denial.

"Perhaps I can offer a fair opinion."

"Thank you for the offer. Perhaps someday."

"I wonder if we will have a someday, Miss Graham," he murmured.

"I would like that," she said, her voice soft.

Something tugged in his chest. He felt the relaxing warmth of the whisky run through him, loosening time and candor. "Tell me about your story."

She took another sip, coughed a little, and finally nodded. "Do sit," she said.

He did, and she began to talk, at first only murmuring, then speaking with more ease and eagerness as she described the story and characters. Listening, Ronan smiled, watching the excitement rise in her.

"And so Alasdair must protect his heart, you see, against hurt. And Isabella is so swept up in what her family needs that she does not—oh, I am sorry," she said.

He lifted a brow. "Sorry about what?"

"I thought you might be bored. You closed your eyes."

"I am listening intently to a charming narrator. Go on. Your Highlander is a man of high morals and proud birth, though he indulges in a bit of cattle-stealing now and then. He loves the daughter of a rival clan chief, but because of an ancient feud, he dares not reveal it. And then her family betroths her to another."

"Yes. Do you think it—just sounds like a romantic indulgence?"

"Not at all. And I like your hero."

"I gave him some of your traits," she said, then blushed again.

"So long as they are the better ones." He tipped his head. "So your Highland lad is in some hot water with the Crown over disputed land. And now his lady love is back and he must defend her. So he offers himself up as her guard at great risk because his enemies may find him."

"Yes. But then I am not sure what to do next."

"We must save him from the gallows and reunite him with his dearest love. He can profess his undying love and she will see—"

"Please do not mock my story."

Sitting forward, he reached across the table and took her wrist gently in his hand. "I am not mocking it. I like it very much. It is just—" He paused. "Sometimes it is easier to make light of one's feelings than be honest about them."

"His feelings? His love for the heroine?"

"Some men have difficulty with such matters." He certainly did. But her expression then—patient, soft, compassionate—touched him. "I feel for your lad Alasdair. I know what it is to love and feel betrayed."

"Do you?" Her little frown of concern was gracious. Caring.

"It was a long time ago. So—they love each other but cannot marry?"

"He thinks her unreachable and does not know she loves him."

He watched her for a moment. "Is she? Unreachable?"

She shook her head. "Not to him. She loves him."

"Then they have only to declare their feelings and be wed."

She laughed, a silver bell in the quiet room. "The story needs complications. Challenges they must overcome. But I am not certain what will suit."

"Magic," he said, surprising himself. "Your Mr. Scott might do it."

"Magic! Interesting. But how?"

"The Highlands are full of stories." He considered for a moment. "There is a small loch that lies between Strathniven and Darrach lands.

Its island is said to be cursed by the fairies. Now and again the fairies take it back to their realm. They say it disappears."

"The entire island? I would love to see that."

"I can take you there, though it may not disappear before our eyes."

"You just need another reason to leave the estate." She laughed softly.

"There is that. I should ride out with my band of smugglers for an illicit whisky run before I meet the king and return to prison where I undoubtedly belong."

"Stop, Mr. MacGregor," she said, half-laughing.

"I will take you fishing there, you and Miss Beaton, and Donal Brodie too. The lad will ensure my good behavior."

"We could make a picnic of it."

"You can teach me picnic etiquette in case we take the king on such an outing."

Again she laughed. He loved the sound and loved the impish curve of her lips and the dimple that emerged in her cheek. "Of course. Tell me more about the fairy legends."

"Well, a cousin of mine makes *uisge-beatha sìthiche.*"

"Fairy whisky?" She tilted her head. "Is there such a thing? Is this it?" She lifted the whisky glass.

"This is only Pitlinnie's passable stuff. Hardly magical. Fairy whisky is very rare, made to an ancient recipe known only to a few. It is a carefully guarded secret in my cousin's family, and he only makes a little each year."

"Does everyone in your family make excellent illicit whisky?"

"Not all of us. His branch of MacGregors keeps the recipe secret. Only a few have even tasted it, and he does not sell or trade it, but gives it away selectively."

"Have you tasted it?"

"I have. My Glenbrae brew does not hold a candle to it."

"Best not let the king know about it, then."

"Ah, the king himself could not obtain this, not from Dougal MacGregor. Only those with Second Sight recognize its power. To most, it is just an excellent whisky."

"What makes it different?"

"Some secret in the process. Legend says my cousin's ancestor once saved the life of a fairy who gave him the recipe in gratitude. When I was a lad, I wished my family had such a legend. We seemed very dull by comparison, just country gentry, titled and—well." He could not tell her that they were sitting in a tower and library that had once belonged to his ancestors. "No romantic fairy legends, alas."

"What about the fairy loch you mentioned?"

"The isle? Not very romantic, that. But you could add a romantic legend to your story that suits your characters."   .

"I could, but how?" She swallowed the last trace of whisky, her throat graceful. Watching, he felt a deep pull inside, and leaned back in the chair as if to distance himself from the yearning that began.

"Complicate their troubles with a legend."

"An intriguing idea. I must think about it. But—" She glanced out the window, then stood, skirts whispering. "It is very late, I am afraid."

He stood as well. "I enjoyed our chat."

"And the magical whisky. I had a bit too much, I think. I am quite tired."

"You will sleep well." As she stretched to blow out the candles, he went to the door to draw it wide. Light from a tiny window in the stairwell cast a beam of moonlight into the darkness.

Then she moved past him, shoulder brushing his chest. Ronan set a hand briefly to her elbow to guide her in the darkness on the wedged stone steps.

She looked up. "Mr. MacGregor, I do not know what will happen after the king's visit," she said. "But if you are ever in need—think of me as a friend."

His heart pounded. "Just a friend, then?"

"More if you like," she whispered.

"Ah." He pressed her elbow, pulling her closer. Taking the chance, he lowered his head to touch his nose lightly to hers and angled his head. Waited.

She tilted toward him, nudged in invitation. He touched his lips to hers gently, questioning, and her lips met his in tender answer. Resting a hand on his chest, she leaned against him, and let the kiss deepen.

He pulled her snug against him then, and feeling her meld willingly to him, he sought a deep, exploring kiss, sinking his fingers into the silky mass of her hair. He felt her sigh, press into him, open her lips to taste more. The feeling that plunged through him was strong, sudden, pulsing. A moment later he pulled back, hand cupping her shoulder.

"Friendship may have to be enough," he breathed. "I should not—"

"Friendship and secrets," she whispered. She did not pull away even when he let go to create a little space between his body and hers.

"Forgive me," he said. "Fairies and whisky have skewed my thinking."

"No apologies." She touched a finger to his lips. "The whisky has skewed me a little as well."

"Neither of us needs a complication, and I should not have—"

"Hush." Her finger touched his lips again. "I am no innocent girl. Ronan MacGregor," she said then, standing so close, tension rising like lightning between them. He felt it and could not, would not allow himself to pursue it. "I trust you. And I—I would be yours, if you wanted. If we agreed. I think we might."

He pulled in a breath. "Go gently, lass. Do not trust me, or this moment."

"But I do. You are not the rogue people think."

"Am I not?" He stepped past the threshold to the stone platform, where the steps led up to his room, or down and away. A precarious place. A precarious decision. He took her elbow. "I will see you to the tower door. These steps are treacherous in the dark."

She took his arm. "Oh, now I must apologize. It was unlike me to say such. It must be the whisky."

"It has a way about it. Come ahead, now." He guided her down a step.

"I made a fool of myself, saying that," she fretted.

"Hush. What you said made me feel like—"

"A viscount?" She half-laughed.

He paused, tipping her chin up. "Like a Highland hero, kissed by a fairy queen."

"Oh," she whispered. In the half-light, he saw her soul shining in her eyes for a moment. It was all he could ever want and could not have. He was like the sorry fellow in her story, filled with unrequited love.

"Best go, lass, before I lose myself utterly and you no longer trust me."

"I think I can always trust you."

"Miss Graham, you are a delicious and idealistic creature." He led her down another step.

"Papa says I am full of dreams and had best wake myself up to the real world."

He frowned. "Listen to me. Hold onto your dreams. Keep them safe."

"I will. Ronan—" She paused on the next step as he went down, making her height closer to his. "Would you—kiss me again, before I go?"

He did, and did again, pressing her so close that she had to know his desire for her. In turn, he felt her response bloom in the curving warmth of her body against his. Moments passed, kisses flowed, until he drew back, made himself surrender a dream that could never be.

"Miss Graham. This way."

"Ellison," she said.

"Elly, my lass. This way." Gently he guided her to the door that connected to the main house, to reality, and tomorrow.

CHAPTER 13

"Such a warm day," Sorcha said, fanning herself with a painted silk fan as she sat in the carriage beside Ellison.

"It should be cooler in Kinross with the breezes off Loch Leven," Ellison said, aware that Ronan MacGregor sat opposite her, a constant reminder of the night before.

"So kind of you to come with us today, Lord Darrach," Sorcha said.

"Of course," he murmured. Ellison noticed his subtle frown at the title. When he returned her glance she looked away in embarrassment, recalling kisses in the tower stair; she had even brazenly asked him to kiss her again. Never again would she follow a nightcap of ratafia with strong whisky.

Oh, such kisses, and his gentleness and caring—she could never forget that.

"We need not be in Kinross for long today," she said, wanting to distract her thoughts. "We only need visit the seamstress and pick up some things for Lady Strathniven as she prepares for Edinburgh."

"It is all so exciting" Sorcha smiled. "My lady aunt offered to include me in her party so I can attend the king's reception for the ladies. Sir, I believe you mentioned you have business in town as well?"

"Aye, my solicitor has an office in Kinross."

Interesting that he meant to see his lawyer, Ellison thought, hoping it did not have to do with smugglers, prisons, or a means of escaping the king's introduction. But she had to trust him, she told herself. Would he feel he could trust her as well—or did he now think her a desperately lonely widow?

Reaching Kinross, MacNie drove the carriage at a leisurely pace along the High Street toward Green's Hotel, close to the shops. She had requested they stop there, thinking it suitable for tea once they had finished their errands. As the vehicle halted and a groom ran up to help with the horses, MacGregor stepped out to help the ladies step down.

Resting her hand in his, she thought he pressed it slightly—apology? Promise? But he only turned away, pulling his black bonnet low over his brow, tugging at the tartan draped over his plain brown coat. Ellison realized he was wary of being recognized; perhaps that was why he chose Highland dress here, where so many men wore tartans and simple jackets. City-tailored clothes might look out of place.

"Where would you like to go first, ladies?" he asked.

"The seamstress's shop is just there along the High Street," Ellison said. "We can easily walk there unescorted. Is your solicitor's office nearby?"

"Next to the town hall." He gestured the other way. "I will meet you at the dress shop if you like. You may have packages to carry."

"Lady Strathniven's errand list will keep us busy for a little while. We could meet you at Green's in time for tea."

"Very good. Will an hour and a half do?"

"Perfect," Ellison said, turning as MacNie approached. She explained the plan to him. "I think you have errands of your own, Mr. MacNie?"

"I do, Miss, collecting the mail and such, and stopping by the blacksmith's, but I will be here whenever you need me."

She nodded, bidding good day and taking Sorcha's arm to head down the High Street. After a moment, she glanced back to see MacGregor walking away, a tall and striking figure in tartan, a man who might capture attention wherever he went, no matter if he tried to merge with the crowd. Yet a sureness in his stride said he belonged, and knew where he was going and what he meant to do.

Once again she had the sense that Ronan MacGregor had more secrets than she could ever guess, or that he would ever reveal.

"Ronan! A surprise to see you in Kinross! I thought you might still be in Edinburgh." Hugh Cameron took his hand in a strong clasp, his hazel eyes warm as he looked at Ronan. Though a handspan shorter, sandy-haired Cameron had the powerful build of his Highland kin. "I recently had an interesting letter from the Provost's office regarding you. A release! Very unexpected, though it said nothing of where you headed after leaving the Castle."

"Unexpected hardly describes it. I will explain. Do you have time now?"

"For you, always. I will not forget how we memorized every law book in the university library between us, matching book for book and then pint for pint. And I cannot tell you how relieved I am to see you safe. Take a seat." Hugh sat in the worn leather chair behind his desk while Ronan took a chair opposite. "So, free! How the devil did you manage it? By quoting the law in dazzling fashion?"

"Just a stroke of luck via the king, if you can believe it."

"I have got to hear this. Are you back in Perthshire to stay?"

"I must return to Edinburgh for the royal visit, and then we will see. First, do you have any word of Linhope and MacInnes? They were transferred to Calton."

"I heard of it from Alan Smithson in our Edinburgh office. He is looking after them. Calton is never a good situation." Cameron shook his head. "But Alan reports that Linhope's medical skills earned some privileges. MacInnes is allowed to assist him, so they are secure for now."

"Good." Ronan felt some relief. "I am searching for a way to get them out."

"Not easy. What do you have in mind?"

"I found a detail that might help lift the charges."

"I see. You were fortunate to obtain a release, but once a trial date is set for those two—well, we must avoid it if we can. Let me know what you need."

"I will. Have you had news about the estate?"

"There is a development. I was about to write to you and thought to send the letter to Smithson in case he could find you. But here you are."

"Here I am. What do you have for me?"

Cameron picked up a sheaf of papers and rifled through them to choose a page. "I do not know how much news you had in the dungeons. Are you aware that old Sir John Murray-MacGregor died last month?"

"I heard. Very sad. Sir Evan would be clan chief now."

"Aye. Then you realize that he will review all clan issues before making any decisions."

"I suspected the Darrach matter might come to him. The chief has the right to absorb forfeited or abandoned lands and titles into his holdings. He may decide to do that and be done with it." He shrugged.

"The matter has gone to the Court of Sessions and the Lyon Court, but it is complicated since your cousin left no will."

"He never completed one that I know of. He did not feel it was pressing—he was young and had other things on his mind."

"The business with William. But anyone messing about with moving whisky should know enough to secure a will."

"True. Nor do we know what he had in mind. He was not yet married, though he hinted he intended to court a fine lass in Perth. It came to naught."

"And no one has come forward in a year. You are the best claimant so far. Now either the court will decide, or they will refer it to Sir Evan as a clan matter." Hugh tapped the pages under his hand.

"The courts will be glad to be quit of the matter with all else going on."

"The king's visit? Aye. But I believe the land and title could still come to you. It will take time. One caveat, Ronan," he continued.

"Sir Evan may be disinclined to grant Darrach to a man accused of criminal activity. I know." He could guess that much, knowing Evan since boyhood.

"But now that you are free according to the documents I saw, you could appeal to Sir Evan yourself. I hear he is in the Highlands now but plans to depart for Edinburgh fairly soon. You could meet him in the city to discuss it."

"I doubt he would welcome that."

"Surely time has softened that old matter. No?" When Ronan shrugged, Hugh sighed. "Aye, well. He will be busy—he will lead the Highland contingent in Edinburgh during the king's visit. Sir Walter Scott and the Lord Provost asked him."

"They could not have a finer man than Evan Murray-MacGregor leading the Highland contingent."

"He will assemble a tail of chieftains to present in full regalia. If you are granted Darrach, you would be a chieftain in Clan Gregor."

Ronan shrugged. He could not allow himself to consider what might —or might not—lie ahead. "All the clan chiefs in attendance will muster men, horses, plaids, and weapons in a great rolling out of Highland chiefs and tails."

"They say all this will cause a shortage of tartan cloth," Hugh huffed.

"We may never see the like of this spectacle again." Reluctant as he was to be part of the ruse in meeting the king, he felt a strong sense of pride within. He wanted to witness the spectacle, feel the excitement in the swell of Scottish strength. It was the rest of the debacle he would just as soon avoid.

"I will write to Sir Evan and inform him of your freedom. As for the charges—and I am sure those were unfairly assigned to you three— Smithson and I are making some headway."

"The charges were unclear, in my opinion."

"Yes. Ronan"—Hugh gave him a severe glance—"would you be willing to speak frankly about all this if it goes to trial?"

"About William and Darrach? I have said nothing and prefer not to reveal their involvement and see them posthumously condemned."

"Your loyalty is commendable, but your stubbornness is to your detriment."

"I will not dishonor my kinsmen. But if you have further word on any of these matters, send me word."

"Can I reach you at Invermorie?"

"For now, send word to Strathniven House up the glen. In Edinburgh," he said, "you could send a message to Miss Ellison Graham at Sir Hector Graham's home. I can trust her to find me, I think."

"The deputy lord provost's daughter? I did not realize you knew the Grahams, or Lady Strathniven either, come to that."

"We met recently. Both have shown kindness and discretion."

"Do they know your history?"

"Not entirely."

"I see. Tell me—how then does the king figure in your release?"

"King George is so fond of Glenbrae whisky that he wants to meet the distiller." Ronan shrugged.

Hugh chuckled, quick and warm. "What a stroke of luck! No wonder Sir Hector hastened to fix your release. Save face, and all, I am thinking."

"Exactly. As it happens, I am to be introduced at the levee."

His friend hooted. "They must be scrambling to hide the truth."

"My situation did present a problem."

"What do they know about Darrach?"

"Not much, but they have decided to elevate the distiller to the local gentry on a chance. A coincidence."

"Is it so? Do not tell me the details. Better for both of us." Hugh's grin faded. "Even more reason to contact Sir Evan to see if he can hasten things in your favor."

"It might just stir trouble."

"Let us have his answer, at any rate." Hugh paused, brow furrowed. "Well. Aught else I can do for you, Ronan?"

"Since you are looking into the charges brought against us, consider this." Ronan reached into a pocket to bring out a note he had written after poring over volumes of law in the Strathniven collection. "They may have overlooked some crucial details."

Hugh studied the paper. "This is accurate? The first of May? Interesting."

"One more favor, if you please. Do you know aught of the will of Colin Leslie? I believe it is in your Edinburgh office. He died less than two years ago."

"Sir Arnold Leslie's lad? Aye. Not my case, but I heard about it. Tragic, that. Drunken fall from a horse, I believe. Young lad, and left a young widow."

"Aye."

"She was the deputy lord provost's daughter—ah, then you know her."

"I do. Miss Graham, as she prefers now, inherited Leslie's house on North Castle Street, but she cannot gain access to it. Leslie's relatives are protesting the will and a few have taken up residence there, claiming it is rightfully theirs."

"That cannot be allowed if the dispute is unresolved. I will ask Smithson to inquire about it. I wonder if he is even aware of the situation."

"Miss Graham will write to him. But if they refuse to vacate, I will go there myself to toss them out."

"You do not need to be arrested for disturbing the peace, man."

"Either way, once they are gone, the place may need cleaning and repair. I will pay for the work. You have access to my account per our agreement before I, ah, became a tenant of Edinburgh Castle." As Hugh quirked a brow, Ronan nodded. "Call it a favor for a friend."

"Quite a favor."

"I owe the young lady a debt."

"Write out a draft, then, if you will." Cameron opened another drawer and drew out a leather wallet of bank drafts, which he slid across the desk surface.

Writing out a generous amount, Ronan handed it back. Hugh glanced at the sum. "It will be done. When you return to Edinburgh, where will you stay?"

"The hotel on Princes Street. My usual place."

"Every available hole is filling fast with the crowds expected. I will be staying with my mother in the Canongate during the king's visit. You are welcome there. She has always been fond of you."

"Thank you, if I need it. How is your mother?"

"Very well, but the royal visit has her at sixes and sevens. She is no fan of the Crown, being born of staunch Jacobites, but she is also insatiably curious. I am to escort her to some of the events. She would be delighted to see you."

"I will let you know my arrangements." He stood. Hugh did as well.

"Take care, Ronan. If the king learns the truth about the Glenbrae distiller, it could go poorly for you. Your young lady's father may regret releasing you."

"She is not my young lady," he protested, earning Hugh's keen glance. "But I know the risks."

"Here we are!" The seamstress carried a gown of sumptuous wine-colored satin draped over her arms. A shop girl followed with a second gown in powdery blue silk. Laying both dresses out on a plump sofa, the girl withdrew, and Mrs. Fowler turned to Ellison and Sorcha. "Lady Strathniven ordered these with headdresses to match, each with nine ostrich feathers, as suggested for the royal assemblies in Edinburgh. And the gowns have the very long trains also specified for ladies at these events."

"It is beautiful," Ellison breathed, reaching out to gently touch the blue silk with its falls of creamy lace at bodice and sleeves and in ruffles around the hem.

"Miss Graham, I am glad you decided on the blue so that you can soon be done with somber colors. Gray can take the roses from the cheeks. The blue silk will flatter your fair complexion quite nicely."

Ellison smiled, the gown's silken train sliding through her fingers like water. Lady Strathniven had chosen the pale blue for her. But was she truly ready to leave mourning colors behind?

"It is time, Elly," Sorcha said, as if knowing her thoughts.

"And for you, Miss Beaton," the seamstress continued, "Lady Strathniven requested that you be fitted for a gown as well. Perhaps a creamy white, which would be demure, with apple green ribbons to compliment your pretty green eyes. Come this way. We will look at fabrics and laces."

While Sorcha went with Mrs. Fowler, Ellison tried on the blue gown with the help of the shop girl. It fit her perfectly, with elegant poufed sleeves and a neckline that showed her slender collarbones. She twirled, spirits soaring to wear something so delightful after hiding in dark and subdued tones for so long.

But she knew that it was time to move on. She had long reconciled to losing Colin—but she had also lost herself, her freedom, relinquished for guilt and loneliness. In a moment of clarity, as the gorgeous blue susurrated around her, she was excited to wear this gown.

And imagined Ronan MacGregor, tall and handsome in Highland finery, extending his arm to her as she draped the long blue silk train over her gloved wrist.

No, she thought, this dream need not rely on a man who would all too soon disappear from her life. This dream was about the freedom and happiness she ached to reclaim somehow. Wearing the blue dress, she would imagine herself an author, living in her own home, writing books, finding her way—

But she did not know if any of her unlikely dreams could prove possible.

"I promised to regale Mama with all the news and gossip when I return from Edinburgh." Sorcha set down her china cup and leaned toward Ellison as they sat with MacGregor in the tea room of Green's Hotel. "I hope I can stay in the city with my lady aunt. I did not think to ask."

"Yes! She mentioned it to me when she left." Ellison took a sip of tea.

"Good! What a delicious tea," Sorcha said. "I do love a Bohea blend with just a hint of orange flavor to it. Mama prefers Chinese green, though I find it bitter. Which do you prefer, Lord Darrach, black or green?"

"Hmm? Oh, a robust black, I suppose." He sounded distracted, even on guard. Stealing a glance toward him, Ellison saw him look toward a table where two young men sat.

Ellison spread strawberry jam on a scone as Sorcha went on talking and Ronan answered politely. She frowned, seeing the two men.

She patted one of the boxes tied with ribbons that sat on the floor beside her. "Shall we leave, Darrach?"

"Soon, aye. You bought something pretty, I trust?"

"Gowns for the ladies' reception in Edinburgh. Very pretty, I hope."

"I know they will be." He smiled, his gaze touching hers, lingering. Then he looked toward the men in the corner, who were rising from their seats.

"Do you know them?" she murmured.

"Rabbie Muir's grandsons." He rose too. "Ladies, forgive me. I see friends there and must speak with them. Enjoy your tea and cakes. I will be back shortly."

What brought Aleck and Geordie Muir to the hotel's tearoom? This was not a usual stop for them. Had something happened? Crossing the room, he saw them leave the hotel and followed them outside. He felt wary, prickly with it.

"There you are, sir." Geordie nodded. "You keep gentle company today."

"I do. Good to see you both. We can talk over here." He led them toward the privacy of a shady beech tree at the edge of the sunny yard.

"We heard you came to the distillery," Aleck said. "We were in Kinross today for supplies and saw Mr. Cameron in the street. He mentioned you might be having luncheon at the inn or the hotel. We have some news."

"Good news, I hope." Sensing tension, Ronan frowned. Their grandfather was loyal as old oak, but he knew that young men might need to do whatever was necessary to make their way and protect kin. These lads were good at heart, but open to temptation.

"Some," Aleck said. "Geordie will be taking over the work on our farm from Grandda. He is to be married, is our Geordie." He clapped his brother on the shoulder. "Mary MacGillie down the way."

"I asked her this week," Geordie said. "She works at Strathniven House."

"I met the lass. Cheerful and capable, and just as ginger-haired as you. We may expect bonny ginger bairns someday." He smiled. "I wish you both well."

"We would be honored if you would come to our wedding in the autumn."

"I will do my best. Is there other news?" he asked as Geordie glanced at Aleck.

"Have you seen Pitlinnie yet?" Geordie asked.

"I have not," Ronan drawled. "What happened?"

"He is making good profit moving goods, and none the wiser but those who keep quiet about it. One of our cousins is working with him, but he is not so discreet a lad as Pitlinnie wants," Geordie said. "He tells us what he hears."

"Interesting. And?"

"Pitlinnie was heard saying he wanted you away and gone, and so it was done," Aleck said. "Something about your arrest, I think."

"He arranged it?" Ronan asked sharply.

"Possibly."

Ronan remembered Dawson, the excise officer who had led the ambush and arrest in Culross. "Is there proof?"

"That might be difficult. He would never admit it outside his own men. He also says you stand to inherit Darrach and will claim the credit and profit for all the whisky-making in these glens. Says you are a wolf among sheep, and dangerous."

"Huh," Ronan said. "You lot are hardly sheep. Keep quiet and stay smart, just as you are doing. And let me know if you hear more."

Geordie cleared his throat. "Sir, we saw him not long ago near Invermorie. He invited Aleck and me to come over to him. Says you are ruined. We can earn money, says he, joining him. Aleck refused straightaway. But I—" He stopped.

"But you will soon be a married man, and someday have a family to support. More funds would help you build a good life."

Geordie looked down. "But I am loyal to you, sir. I would not want to go over to him. But they say his runs are profitable."

"They are. You must do what is best for you, lad. Tell me, how does Pitlinnie know about Darrach?"

"Perhaps from Mairi Brodie and Sir Ludovic," Aleck said. "He acts the good neighbor and treats her well. He makes himself useful, woos her."

"What does he want?" Ronan narrowed his eyes.

"He would marry her if she would," Aleck said. "He wants Glenbrae and Invermorie. Mairi Brodie is one way to get that."

Marrying the widow of Glenbrae's brother would also level a direct blow against the laird of Glenbrae, Ronan thought. "That cannot happen."

"I agree. Do you have work for us, sir?" Aleck asked. "We have not been able to move Glenbrae whisky over the hills for months. We sell through the shops in Kinross and Perth but being legitimate is slow to put coin in our pockets."

"It will grow. When the laws change, illicit trade will bring less profit and harsher penalties."

"What is harsher than hanging?" Geordie asked. "Or being pistolshot on a hillside, like your brother and cousin?" He spat on the ground.

Ronan felt a muscle pump in his cheek. "The free trade is nearly done, lad."

"And just as well." Aleck echoed Ronan's tone like a lad after his father. At times Ronan had felt like an older brother, even a father, to these two. He set a hand on Aleck's shoulder.

"Keep an eye on our goods. Let me know what Pitlinnie does."

"Sir, it might help if I went over to Pitlinnie's crew to learn more," Geordie said.

"I will not send you into the fire. If your cousin seeks you out, that is enough risk. Watch his back and your own." They nodded, both looking a bit relieved.

"We will check the goods stored near Darrach in a day or two," Aleck said.

"Good. I need your help to move goods and arrange shipment to Edinburgh. It must arrive in time for the king's arrival."

"The king!" Aleck said.

"A gift from Scotland." Succinct was best. "The king enjoys Highland whisky."

Geordie grinned. "But any Highland peat-reek the English king drinks surely came to him through smuggling. And that's a fine joke."

"It is." He stepped back raised a hand.

"Glenbrae," Geordie said, "watch your back."

Ellison sipped the last dregs of her tea, smiling as Sorcha chattered on, and tried to quell a thread of fear. The Highlanders talking with MacGregor now had a rough look about them. What if he met with trouble?

What if he was not trustworthy after all, as Mr. Corbie had predicted? What if he ran, never to be seen again? Yet he had promised honesty and had seemed sincere.

Then he was there, just beside her, so close she felt the solid warmth of his being. She glanced up. He looked grim, eyes shadowed and somber. She felt the urge to reach out, offer hope, be a remedy for him.

What came next was not the flash of lightning she would have imagined, nor was it flowery. Rather it was a tender realization as gentle as a kiss. She felt an expansion within, a longing to reach out and touch his hand resting on her chair.

When his gaze met hers, it felt like a caress. But she glanced away before he could tell all her feelings, clear as bells and stars, in her eyes.

"Miss Graham, Miss Beaton. Are you ready to depart? The bill is satisfied and MacNie awaits with the carriage. Let me help." He drew out Sorcha's chair, then Ellison's, and picked up the boxes.

As they walked, he touched her elbow lightly. The sensation lingered. Inside the carriage, she was glad her bonnet shadowed her eyes so that he would not know what she felt in her silly, smitten heart.

Sorcha talked on about the shops, the dresses, the tea and cakes, the plans for Edinburgh, and Ronan murmured politely. His voice sank through Ellison like hot whisky, honey, spice.

"You are quiet, Ellison," Sorcha said.

She avoided Ronan's vivid blue gaze. "I am tired. Just that."

CHAPTER 14

"*I* *have a secret to disclose to you,*" *said he,* "*which cannot be divulged—*"

"Lord Darrach." A soft voice interrupted his reading. "Shall we—"

A secret to divulge—

"Shall we discuss protocols for the royal visit?"

Ronan looked up from the open pages of Jane Porter's *Scottish Chiefs*. "Miss Graham." Setting the book aside, he stood. While reading in the quiet parlor, he had been lulled by the patter of rain and thoughts of his close-kept secrets.

"You are reading Miss Porter's book." She looked pleased.

"And enjoying it. Though I imagine Miss Ellison Graham could write even more brilliantly than Miss Porter," he went on. "While the plot is solid, Miss Porter's prose can be overexcited. I am sure Miss Graham's prose is as subtle and smooth as the lady herself."

"Thank you." She smiled, a tiny dimple emerging. "Practicing flattery and manners? Nor have you read my work, sir."

"Someday I hope to. Did it seem like practice? It was sincere."

She smiled again. "We were to review protocols today." She held up a copy of Scott's leather-bound booklet. "Are you ready?"

"Aye. And here is Miss Beaton," he said as Sorcha entered the parlor carrying a basket of stitchery work.

"Good," Ellison said. "We can review some guidelines together." She sat on a nearby sofa and Sorcha joined her. Ronan was reluctant to sit on the thing himself, its scrolled wood and golden damask giving him pause. He chose a wooden chair covered in red tartan cloth.

"Studying etiquette seems a suitably dull task for a rainy day," he said.

Sorcha giggled while his pretty tutor gave him a scathing look. "We could have gone out today but for the weather," Ellison said primly.

"I thought to ride out later today to look over my lands regardless of the rain." He could not stay cooped up inside for long, not after months in a dungeon cell. He would change first, though, for now he wore trousers and a coat. At least they were his own; Donal had fetched them with plaids, boots, and the rest of his Highland kit.

"Will you tour your Darrach estate, sir? I would love to see it," Sorcha said.

"It is a long distance. He may be too busy." Ellison arrowed a look that warned him not to take the viscount ruse too far. But he needed no reminder.

"If you would both like to tour the countryside, I could show you a pretty loch not far from here. Perhaps Donal would come with us." He noticed Sorcha brighten at the mention of Donal, near her age.

"Is that the one with the fairy isle you spoke of?" Ellison stopped.

"Aye. We might go fishing near there."

"Fishing! I would enjoy that," Sorcha said eagerly. "I have been fishing with my father and my brother. Ellison, have you tried it?"

"Never," she said. "I am not sure I want to catch fish." She wrinkled her nose.

"I will show you the Highland method of fishing. Very authentic. The sort of thing one might read about in a book," he added with a teasing smile.

Her eyes sparkled at the prospect. "Perhaps that would be fun, then."

"We could try tomorrow, if the weather suits," he replied.

"Wonderful!" Sorcha, who he knew by now could radiate enthusiasm for the smallest thing, beamed and clapped her hands.

"Then it is settled. I will speak to Donal Brodie."

"And I will ask Mrs. Barrow to pack a luncheon basket. Now, we have some work to do." Ellison opened the book. "What will be expected in the royal assemblies—let me see." She traced her fingers over the pages. "Here. Sir William Arbuthnot, Lord Provost, will be waiting with magistrates and officials to meet the king and royal party when they disembark at Leith Harbor. The keys of the city will be presented to the king and then all will progress to Holyrood Palace."

"The officials will include your father, Ellison," Sorcha said.

"Likely so. Also, gentlemen welcoming the king are expected to wear a blue coat, white waistcoat, and white or nankeen pantaloons. A handsome costume, so Scott says, in the colors of Scotland's flag."

"Wear the saltire colors? I am glad to miss this occasion," Ronan drawled.

"They say there will be large gatherings of Highlanders in full regalia throughout the city," Sorcha said. "Will you be joining your clan, Lord Darrach?"

"If MacGregor of Clan Gregor summons me, I will answer."

"In plaid, bonnet, feathers and all? So romantical!" Sorcha smiled. "Lord Darrach would be the grandest fellow there, do you not agree, Ellison?"

"Grand," Ellison said, pink rising in her cheeks. "Some may wear Highland dress, though my father says many gentlemen will wear formal black and white."

"Highland gear is a display of the pride and dignity of Scotland," Sorcha said.

"True." Ellison seemed in a prim mood.

Ronan frowned, bemused. "We should return to the protocols. Fire away, Miss Graham." Sorcha giggled again, but their earnest teacher sent him a withering look.

He should not tease her, he thought. She was doing her utmost to fulfill what her father expected of her. He disliked the ruse as much as she did, especially claiming a title he did not own, but his friends' lives might be in the balance. He and Ellison must both endure the scheme.

Yet he had seen how a touch of humor brought a sparkle to her eyes and lifted her mood. And that was worth any sour look she might toss his way.

"Tell us what fancy steps and phrases we backward Scots must learn," he said, unable to help himself.

"Sir," Ellison said, "do take this seriously."

"Madam, I do." He met her eyes directly. She lowered her lashes and looked away.

"You will attend a levee at Holyroodhouse a day after the king arrives. Your invitation will come to Papa's office since you and Mr. Corbie will be in his party."

Sorcha, stitching away, looked up. "Are ladies invited to this as well?"

"A separate assembly will be held for ladies, with gentlemen escorting them. And a ball is planned for another evening."

"It truly is exciting!" Sorcha smiled. "Lord Darrach, will you attend the ladies' assembly? Perhaps you could escort Ellison."

"I would be honored," he said, seeing Ellison's fiery blush. "But I may only be welcome at the levee."

"But you are a Scottish viscount!"

"Papa is taking care of the arrangements," Ellison said quickly. "Darrach will be introduced—Papa will do that, as new guests must be introduced by someone who has previously met the king. Papa will be introduced with the Lord Provost. Also, you must give your card to the Lord-in-Waiting as you approach the king."

"My card?"

"You will need a few. Mr. Corbie will have some printed up for you."

"I see. Ah, Mr. Balor, come to join us!" Glad for the interruption, Ronan patted his knee as the little terrier trotted into the room. Balor came straight to him.

"My father will likely introduce us at the ladies' assembly, Sorcha," Ellison went on. "When a person is introduced," she said, consulting the booklet, "they will approach the royal dais between lines of dignitaries, attendants, and officials. A lady will curtsy deeply to the king. A gentleman will drop the right knee and kiss the king's hand."

"And after an introduction?" Ronan stroked the dog's warm, silky coat, feeling the rapid little heartbeat under his hand.

"The crowd will be enormous, so each person will move on quickly, remembering that one must never turn their back to the king. Sir Walter writes that most introductions take but a half minute or so."

"And then it is done."

"Then it is done," she murmured, watching him.

"Lord Darrach, you must wear full Highland dress," Sorcha said.

"He has a choice," Ellison said, studying the page. "Full dress is advised for gentlemen, although a gentleman with an officer's rank may wear that uniform. Highland gentleman may choose to wear their regalia."

"Lord Darrach, do you have an officer's rank, by chance?" Sorcha asked. "My brother does. Many gentlemen do."

"As it happens, I do." He felt Ellison's quick, curious glance.

"You do?" she asked, her lips a sweet, bewildered moue.

"But I prefer Highland gear," he said simply.

"Oh. Well. Here it says," she went on, cheeks pink, "any Highland chief or chieftain may elect to wear clan costume, but it must be proper Highland gear."

"How does he define that?" Ronan ruffled the dog's ears.

"The plaid, bonnet, sporran, stockings, and such. Highland gentlemen may wear feathers in their bonnets. Three eagle feathers for a clan chief, two for a chieftain, one for a Highland laird."

"A man who carries a grudge wears a single black feather," he said.

"I would not advise that," she said crisply.

"Some might be tempted. Go on."

"Plaid, bonnet, sporran, and weapons. Those who elect to wear Highland dress must be armed in proper Highland fashion, it says here."

Ronan cocked a brow, amused. "Armed how?"

"Steel pistols, broadsword, and dirk." She made a wry face.

He grinned. "Interesting." Ellison scowled, dark as he had ever seen from her.

"Weapons in the king's presence?" Sorcha looked horrified. "How savage!"

"Anyone carrying weapons must be cautious," Ellison said curtly. "Chiefs and chieftains are to attend 'with their tail on'—attended by their gentleman followers."

"Lord Darrach will be attending his chief, then. Exciting!" Sorcha said.

"Very," Ronan murmured. He doubted Sir Evan would welcome him. He rubbed the little dog's head while Ellison turned pages and Sorcha stitched away.

"That dog is very attached to you," Ellison said. "It will break his heart when you leave here."

Ronan looked up. Her eyes, that look of candor, as if all her feelings were there to see—the power of it pushed into his very soul.

"Mine as well," he said.

CHAPTER 15

"*A* beautiful day." Ellison surveyed the blue skies arching over heather-purple hills, then smiled up at Ronan as he strolled beside her along the bank of a calm, winding river.

"Beautiful," he agreed, glancing at her. A breeze stirred through his hair, fluttering his wrapped plaid, shirt, and brown waistcoat, a simple costume suited to a day of fishing. He adjusted the fishing poles he carried over his shoulder as they went, his shoulder bumping hers. She did not move away.

"Yesterday's rain seems to have washed the heat from the air," she said.

"Washed the midges away as well, with luck."

"You were right about the weather and the outing. We need a day out."

"Then perhaps my stern teacher will be pleased with me today."

"We shall see." Smothering a smile, she moved ahead, her gray skirt swishing as she picked her way across the shale rocks that formed a natural pathway above the riverbank. Glancing back, she saw the cart and two sturdy Highland ponies guided by Donal, with Sorcha seated beside him steadying the luncheon basket Mrs. Barrow had provided when the four of them had headed out early that morning. Lady Strathniven's dogcart-style vehicle seated four back-to-back on benches and held their gear and baskets.

They followed a curve alongside the river, heading toward a tributary that in turn would connect to the lochan Ronan had told her about. Tiring of bumping along in the cart, Ellison had decided to walk, and Ronan had offered to accompany her.

Negotiating a rocky incline wet with spray, she felt her straw bonnet slide back, suspended by its ribbons, and felt the breeze lilt through her hair. Freedom, she thought, smiling to herself.

She was glad of her sturdy boots for climbing hills and the simple, unfussy muslin dress, with pantalettes under her chemise, worn at Sorcha's suggestion, should she fall into the water.

But she had no intention of falling into the water that day, having done that recently, to her embarrassment, in front of MacGregor. Instead, she planned to sketch and read while the others splashed and fished to their content. Just being outside on such a glorious day, enjoying fresh air and sunshine and true freedom was enough. Just being near Ronan was enough, too. She smiled.

"Let me teach you how to fish today," Ronan said. "The pole is easier for ladies, but I thought you might find the Highland manner more enjoyable."

"You mean jumping into the water to grab fish? Not me! I will do some sketching, perhaps some writing." She threw out an arm for balance as she picked her way over some tilted rocks. On one shoulder, she carried a linen rucksack with a book, a sketchbook, and graphite pencils.

"It would be a bonny sight to see you jump in after a fish," Ronan said.

"Bonny! But I would be wet all day after that!"

"But feeling free and happy. If I teach you properly, you will not be too wet."

She waved her arms for balance as she walked. "I am enjoying freedom right now, like you. Oh, I am sorry! I did not mean—"

"Free from prison?" He reached out a steadying hand. She took its warm strength. "I am grateful for freedom, lass. And glad to escape my lessons today."

"I should end your lessons entirely," she retorted. "Your English is perfect and your manners would hold up under scrutiny."

"See how much I have learned from you." He supported her as she followed a descending stack of rocks. The rush of the river kept their conversation private, and the brace of his fingers felt good. But too soon he let go.

"You fish with Donal. I will sit in the shade and read. Sorcha might sit with me." She waited as Donal drew the cart along the track near where they walked.

"Miss Beaton! Would you rather fish or sketch?" Ronan called.

"Fish! I like fishing. My father taught me."

"See? But if you would rather read," he told Ellison, "stay nearby." He pointed toward a grove of birches above the spot where the river diverted into a peaceful stream that flowed onward to meet a blue loch in the sunny distance.

Donal drove the cart toward the trees, let the ponies on loose lines to graze, and helped Sorcha down. They joined Ronan and Ellison.

As the others went toward the water, Ellison stayed near the birch trees. From there, she could see the little burn that forked away from the tributary to burble over rocks and cut through meadowland toward the lochan. Beyond an expanse of meadow and rumpled hills lay ranks of high blue-misted slopes.

"Ronan," she said quietly, as he came near to fetch a basket from the cart. "Is it dangerous out here? Do smugglers come over those hills?"

"More at night than in the day. But it is not so common as you may think."

"Rabbie's grandsons," she said then, curious. "Your business seemed important. I hope it did not involve—" She paused, fearing she had stepped too far.

"Smuggling? Relax, Miss Graham. Sir Hector wants a good deal of whisky delivered for the king's visit. I must arrange transport. The lads will help."

She nodded as a gust of wind blew her skirts back, sifted her hair. She set a hand to her bonnet. "You are done with such things, then?"

"It will have to travel by ship, leaving Scottish shores, before it arrives in Leith Harbor. Some might call it smuggling. But the king will have his whisky and your father will have his moment of glory." He sounded terse.

"Papa is not doing this for glory. I only asked because I did not want harm to come to you," she snapped.

"Do not worry about me, lass." He gazed at her, calm and strong.

She lifted her chin. "But I do. And I do not want trouble—for any of us."

"All will be well. Look, those two are down at the water already and will have all the fish if we do not hurry."

"I will stay here," she said, finding a seat on a fallen log.

He stood for a moment, then murmured assent and went down to the water. Ellison settled herself with a book but kept looking up as Sorcha called out, laughing, as Donal splashed into the water, kilted and bare-legged, to grab for a fish, nearly tumbling into the water. Ronan laughed, too.

She tried to read, but their laughter and the sunlit sparkle on the water were too tantalizing to ignore. Setting aside her sketchbook and pencil, she walked toward the bank to watch.

"Hush, you two, or you will scare all the fish away," Ronan told the others.

Sorcha turned. "Ellison! Come into the water!"

Ronan lifted a hand, gesturing to her to come down. She wanted to join him, but hesitated. More and more, she realized how attracted she was to him, how much she enjoyed being with him. More and more, she feared she was falling in love. That above all made her hold back. What she imagined was improbable. And she could not prove herself to be foolish in a love matter again.

She stepped closer but shook her head. Ronan moved deeper into the clear flowing water, its current spinning around his bare, muscular calves. As she watched, she saw a flicker in the water, and he bent, nearly crouching, still as a statue, focused as the water swirled and feathered white over the rocks.

Then he moved slowly, dipping cupped hands into the water. A ripple of brown gold flashed beneath the surface, and Ronan reached down, straightening with a floundering fish in his grasp. He tossed it toward the bank. It landed just at Ellison's feet.

Leaping back, she stumbled, ankle rolling so that she had to step into the water to keep from stumbling. Quickly Ronan was there, hand bracing her arm to keep her balanced. "Here, lass, up to me. Good?"

"Good, thank you." Standing in the water now, the hem of her gown floating around her ankles, she laughed, raising one drenched boot. "Oh, dear. Let me take off my shoes."

"Then you may as well join us," Ronan said, chuckling. He turned away as she sat to remove her boots and stockings quickly and discreetly.

Hearing peals of laughter downstream, Ellison looked over to see Donal knee-deep in the stream. He grabbed for something, missed, and fell with a splash and shout. Laughing, Sorcha surged forward to help, stumbling knee-deep into his arms.

Laughing with the others, Ellison felt hesitation melt away. No one here would criticize her or make her feel less for her choices today. Standing, she walked past Ronan and stepped barefoot into the water with a plunk and splash, shivering at the lovely chill of it. Lifting her gown's wet hem, she moved into the burbling flow. The water felt cool and soft, the rocks smooth and mossy under her feet.

"Good lass," Ronan said behind her.

"It feels wonderful," she admitted. "Very well, Ronan MacGregor. Show me the Highland way to catch a fish."

Once more Ronan glanced toward the hills beyond the trees along the bank. Though he had made light of a smuggling threat with Ellison, he was vigilant in keeping watch. He knew too well what could happen out here.

"Now I know why Highland men wear the plaid and go barelegged," Ellison was saying. "It is much better for the fishing."

"It is. Careful now, the rocks are slippery." He extended a hand behind her, ready to catch her if she stumbled.

"It is not easy to keep my gown out of the way." She bunched her skirts in one hand, fabric trailing and floating around her.

"Highland women hitch their skirts higher than that."

"Like this?" Leaning down, she pulled the back of her dress forward between her legs, drawing it up and tucking it into the cinching ribbon above her waist to form bulky trousers that exposed part of her lacy underthings and the trim shape of her calves and ankles. Her feet were slim, pale, toes darling somehow under the clear water. Ronan smiled.

"Aye, like that." His mind conjured images best not pursued. Her straw bonnet slid back, nearly lost but for its dangling ribbons about her throat.

She bent forward, waving her hands about. "Those fish best look out now," she muttered. He laughed, but she was intent, training her gaze on the water.

Drenched and barelegged, curls wild and loose, she was simply beautiful. Whimsical and joyful, too, for in this moment, she was allowing herself that. He felt a wash of that joy, seeing her, and felt the urge to kiss her, love her, share more easy days like this one with her. He yearned for freedom just as she did. He longed for genuine happiness if such were possible.

"Here comes one," she said softly.

"Hush," he whispered.

As she surged through the water, bending, missing, laughing, and persistent, Ronan walked behind her. He held a hand out protectively, though she did not see it.

An hour or more later, Ronan's attention was caught by some small movement along the hill. He narrowed his eyes, watching—perhaps it was just wind rocking the purple froth of heather at the top of the slope. Earlier he had seen sheep grazing along that hill, so it could be the shepherd. He frowned, seeing nothing more.

Time to return to Strathniven, he thought. They had been out most of the day, fishing, picnicking in the shade, and fishing again. The sun had reached its zenith and would soon sink. Right, then.

"Ellison."

She was splashing through the water, hands out to grapple another fish. A trout, by its rainbow flash. Ronan sloshed toward her. "Here, that rascal will pull you in—let me help—"

"*Ach!* Gone! I nearly had him!" She slapped the water and straightened.

"Is this the wee lass who would not fish today?" He smiled but looked toward the hill again.

"I like it better than I thought. Do you see something up there?"

"'Tis naught. Have you had your fill? We should go. You are adept at giving the fish no quarter and have outfished even Donal."

"It was a wonderful day." Holding her soggy skirts, she came toward him.

"So it was. Donal! Hey!" He waved to his nephew, who reached out to help Sorcha up the bank. The four of them gathered baskets with their catch, and then the girls let down the hems of their tucked skirts and sat to pull on stockings and shoes.

"You are wet and will soon feel the chill. Here." Ronan picked up Ellison's plaid shawl from the grass and wrapped it about her shoulders. Settling her bonnet on her head, she tied the ribbons and fluffed her hair, loose of its plaiting. The straw weave cast a sunny glow over her lightly sunburned nose and cheeks.

"Your nose is pink," he said. She smiled, looking joyful and beautiful. "It looks fine on you."

She smiled, tying a fat bow under her chin. "I wish we could stay."

"But we cannot." He was reluctant too, wanting to savor more time with her. July had already slipped into August.

Carrying baskets, they trudged toward the grove, where Ronan and

Donal harnessed the ponies to the cart while Ellison and Sorcha set the baskets inside and climbed up to the front-and rear-facing seats.

Ellison shaded her eyes, looking up the hill. "Did you hear a sound? Something moved up there."

Frowning, Ronan studied the slope again. "Could be a sheep."

She climbed down and hurried past him. "I heard a little cry. I must see."

"Stay here," he called, but she left. He waved to Donal and Sorcha to wait and followed her up the long slope, a sea of heather blooms parting as they went through. Ellison ran ahead, damp skirts flapping, bonnet sliding back, hair in loose golden ropes. With his longer stride, he caught up to her on the hill's ridge, where the wind blew cool and free.

She cried out and ran then, dropping to her knees beside a tangle of brush and heather. Following, Ronan heard a bleating sound.

"What's this?" He sank beside her.

"Look, a lamb—a wee one, caught in here." She pushed at a cluster of undergrowth to reveal a small pale lamb, trembling, curled up, its little face poking out.

"Wandered away from your mam, did you?" Ronan murmured as the little creature bleated and struggled to stand. "And fell into heather and gorse, wee rascal. It will take some time to free it," he told Ellison. "The shepherd will be looking for it once he counts his flock, or notices that one of the ewes is upset."

"We cannot leave him here. A wolf could find him."

"Wolves have been gone from Scotland for a hundred years or more, my dear," he said without thinking, though she only smiled. Reaching out, he pulled carefully at the prickly gorse, its branches ripe with wicked thorns and yellow blooms.

She pulled, too, freeing snarls of thorns and branches in the lamb's coat, wincing as she was pricked. "There, little one, we will—*oww!*—have you out soon. Oww! This lamb is not very old, Ronan."

"Maybe two months," he said, judging the solid little body, the new coat, the shape of its head, large eyes, and narrow snout. "Be still now," he told it. "This lady wants you free, and we do what she wants, hey. Ah, this he is a she."

"Sweet lassie, we are nearly done, my darling," Ellison said.

"She is fair calm. Must be used to people." Ronan ran his hand over the animal's head, soothing the ears, patting the little belly.

"She knows we are helping her." Ellison pulled at the thorny bush. "Ow!"

"Gorse is pretty, but has a bite." More branches bounced free, and Ronan scooped up the lamb and stood. Taking off her shawl, Ellison tucked it around the creature.

Glancing down, Ronan saw red streaks on his fingers and drew back the shawl. "She has a gash on one leg."

"What can we do?"

He made a quick decision. "Invermorie is not far from here. Mairi Brodie treats illnesses and wounds. I will take the lamb there while you go back to Strathniven with Donal and Miss Beaton."

She shook her head. "I want to go with you."

"It is three miles or so across the glen. You should go back."

"If you mean we might meet smugglers, I would not mind that—for my book, you see." Her eyes flashed with determination and courage. But he could not risk harm to her. He felt an odd sense of trouble nearby.

"Trust me, madam, you do not want to meet that sort."

"I met you."

"I am a nicer sort."

"Sometimes. But I would be safe with you."

Her faith in him touched him unexpectedly. Yet he wanted to protect her. "Very well. The four of us can take her there together and then go to Strathniven."

"Good." She cooed sweetly to the lamb. Something melted inside him as they turned to head down the slope, the lamb shaking like a sapling in his arms, Ellison keeping pace. After a moment she slipped her hand inside his elbow, walking close.

CHAPTER 16

*B*uilt of fieldstone, Invermorie Castle overlooked a slope thick with heather and gorse to one side, with a rocky incline to the other. Ellison recalled seeing the small, rustic castle at a distance as a woman crossed the yard—Donal's mother.

"Invermorie looks quite old," she said, caressing the lamb's head where it lay in Ronan's arms. "It must have been formidable in its day. Donal's mother and grandfather are here? But Invermorie is yours?"

"Aye," he said. "Mairi is my brother's widow."

Startled, she looked at him. "Your sister-in-law? Then Donal is your nephew? You never mentioned it."

"He was assigned as my valet—and my guard—so it seemed awkward."

"Then my father need not know. Mrs. Barrow mentioned Mrs. Brodie, a healer who helps in the glen. Is that Mairi?"

"She is skilled with herbal remedies and such and helps animals as well. She will know what to do for your ewe lamb."

As the cart approached the castle, Ellison wondered about the laird's family living there when he did not, as he had said he kept a cottage at the distillery. But she sensed something in his voice; he had held back the truth and had not met her curious glance. Did the widow Mairi Brodie mean something to him?

Donal halted the cart before the castle entrance just as an older gentleman came through the arched doorway. He was white-haired, wearing an old, patched frock coat of pale blue with saggy knee-breeches, hose, and red slippers. Grinning, he waved a hand.

"Donal!" He waited as Donal handed Sorcha and then Ellison to the ground, and Ronan stepped out of the cart, the lamb in his arms wrapped in Ellison's plaid. "And—is that Glenbrae?"

Ronan smiled. "Sir Ludo, it is good to see you."

"It is you! Where are my spectacles," Sir Ludo muttered, patting his old-fashioned coat, finding a pair of spectacles to perch on his nose. "This is a surprise! Have you come to stay? And who are the lassies? And is that a child?"

"A lamb." Ronan drew back the plaid. "It is injured. We came to ask Mairi to tend to it. Is she here?"

"She is. And here I was thinking you brought a wife and child home at last." He patted Ronan's shoulder. "You are all wet. Did it rain? I thought it was a fine day." He looked at the sky. "Well, come inside and Mairi will sort you out. First, introduce me to these ladies."

"Sir Ludovic Brodie, meet Miss Ellison Graham and Miss Sorcha Beaton. Sir Ludo is Donal's grandfather."

"Pleased to meet you, sir," Ellison said, and Sorcha murmured the same as the old man took their hands in turn.

"I am pleased to make your acquaintance, ladies," Sir Ludo said. "Graham and Beaton, two fine Scottish names. What part of Scotland are your people from?"

"Sir Ludo is writing a history of Scotland and clans," Ronan explained.

"Fife, I think, sir," Sorcha said. "My grandfather said ours is an ancient line."

"The Bethune line, perhaps. And Miss Graham? There are many branches of Grahams. They came from France. Norman, you see, long ago."

"So I have heard. My ancestors were in Strathearn," Ellison said.

"Who is your father? I know many Grahams. Is he of Strathearn as well?"

"Hector Graham. We are in Edinburgh."

"The Deputy Lord Provost! We are in fine company indeed. I must write this down. I keep a record of Highland families when I can. Where are my journal and my wee pencil?" He scrabbled in a pocket to extract a notebook and pencil stub.

"You will have Miss Graham's heart with your scholarship," Ronan said, as Sir Ludo led them toward the entrance while Donal saw to the cart and ponies.

"Strathniven, and Beatons and Grahams! Fine company, Glenbrae. Donal told us something of your circumstances." Sir Ludo cocked a bushy white brow.

"I will explain more, but first let us get the lamb into Mairi's care. We found it in the hills above the Lealtie Burn where we were fishing."

"So that is why you are all damp! Did you bring fish for supper?"

"Aye, and are happy to share."

"Come through to the great hall," Sir Ludo directed, leading them through a foyer area into a large room with planked floors, a high raftered ceiling, and a huge stone fireplace that had seen centuries. An old sofa and threadbare armchairs clustered in an old patterned rug before the blue flames of a peat fire.

As Ellison settled in a chair, a woman entered the room to glide toward them, slim and graceful and dark-haired. She wore a simple dark green gown covered in a rumpled apron, and her black braids were wrapped around her head, tendrils escaping. Her pale oval face was as perfect as a medieval Madonna, her brown eyes as warm as her smile.

"Ronan!" She ran toward him and he extended one arm to embrace her, holding the bundled lamb in the other.

"Mairi." He kissed her cheek.

"I did not expect you yet, though Donal said you might visit." Resting a hand on his chest, Mairi turned to her son, who entered after her. "Wicked, the pair of you, for not telling me to be ready for you today!"

"Sorry, Mother. It was unplanned, but Glenbrae found a wounded lamb down by the Lealtie Burn and said we must bring it to you."

"Oh, the poor dear," Mairi said, peeking into the blanket while Ronan and Donal explained what had happened. "Of course I will take care of her."

Watching them, sensing the affection and bond between Ronan and Mairi, Ellison felt diminished, disquieted. They were close. They were family. She was glad for Ronan, yet the adoring way Mairi looked at him made her sink a little inwardly. He had history here, people who loved him. Though it brought more perspective on the mystery surrounding him, she knew she was not included.

"Will you be here long?" Mairi asked Ronan. "We heard you were—in Edinburgh. But now you are home, will you stay?"

Home, Ellison thought. He was home. Glad for him, she felt a little sadness to see it, having shared kisses with him and feeling as if they were growing close. But he had not mentioned a family; he might never let her come too close.

"I must return to the city soon. We will talk later. Let me introduce my friends, Miss Ellison Graham and Miss Sorcha Beaton."

Friend. Ellison smiled and came forward. "How good to meet you, Mrs. Brodie."

"Welcome." She took her hand, then Sorcha's. "Do call me Mairi."

"Miss Graham is the daughter of the Deputy Lord Provost," Sir Ludovic supplied proudly. "And Miss Beaton is related to the Bethunes of Fife. We are privileged in our guests."

"It is an honor. But your clothes are damp! You must rest and get dry. Will you have tea? Donal," she directed, "carry the lamb into my work-room. I will be right there after I ask Mrs. MacGill to prepare tea for our guests." She turned back. "Come sit by the hearth and get dry while you wait for tea. Ronan, do bring the sofa closer to the fire if you will for the ladies. There—that will do, thank you."

Watching Mairi, Ellison was surprised to realize that this beautiful woman was old enough to be Donal's mother, and was, like herself, a widow. That Mairi was special to Ronan was all too clear—though he was quiet near her, almost somber, he was attentive; Mairi smiled often at him, though he remained serious.

Yet Ellison liked her very much, warming to her so quickly that she did not even feel a twinge of jealousy. That, too, surprised her.

～

It felt good to be back.

The great hall was as shabby and antique as he remembered—heavy leather-seated chairs, stiff red sofa, a scattering of old rugs on the scarred wood floors, whitewash peeling on the stone walls—and he loved every drafty, crumbling bit of it. Ronan looked around his childhood home while Sir Ludo chatted with Ellison and Sorcha, urging them to take more tea, have a scone, and try Mairi's rowanberry jam. As he also coaxed them to tell him all they knew about their family histories, Ronan leaned back, content to listen and savor the place.

He had grown up at Invermorie, the seat of Glenbrae, spending countless hours in this room and everywhere in the castle. Every stone here, every hill and tree outside, all were dear and familiar.

But he had left Invermorie when he had seen his love, the young widow Mairi Brodie, kissing his younger brother. He had walked out because he had seen how fervently she returned Will's embrace, how desperately they whispered together. Packing his things, he had informed his father that he had decided to leave his apprenticeship in the law to seek travel and adventure. Shortly after that, he joined his cousin Evan MacGregor in the military.

He had not wanted that. He had wanted the law and a life with Mairi.

Years in the Highland Black Watch and military duties eventually took him to India and a change of regiment to follow Evan MacGregor, which led to the one day he would erase from memory: a savage attack, a desperate rescue of Evan as Ronan and the rest just managed to escape alive. Bringing a severely wounded Evan home to Scotland months later, with Evan angrily insisting that Ronan stay with him in India to continue the effort—which would only have resulted in Evan's death—Ronan had resumed his practice of law with his uncle. By then, his father had died and he was the new laird of Glenbrae.

He did his best to avoid his brother and sister-in-law, though he was fond of Mairi's small son of her first marriage. William proved a good husband and father. Ronan would never discount that.

Then his brother died on a rocky slope beside their cousin Darrach, and Ronan stepped up to be there for Will's widow and stepson. He moved them, along with Mairi's father, into Invermorie and moved out himself. And then he and his friends became smugglers to solve a dangerous situation and rectify the accounts.

And he had closed off his heart from what was dear to him, even as he provided them whatever was needed until his arrest interrupted the obligation.

Now he looked up as Donal returned. "We should go soon," the lad said. "The fish are wrapped and cool in a bucket of water, but we must get them to Strathniven. Mrs. Barrow expects to cook fresh fish for supper."

"Best take Miss Beaton and Miss Graham back and leave some fish for their supper here. I will borrow a horse from the stable and follow later."

Nodding, Donal left, while Sir Ludo continued his animated discussion of Highland history, holding Ellison and Sorcha all but hostage. Though Ronan thought Ellison looked rather fascinated.

Mairi entered the hall then, and Ronan approached. "How is the wee beast?"

"Nothing is broken, but the gash is serious. She should stay here for a bit. Donal seems in a rush to leave," she added.

"Aye, it is time we got back to Strathniven. I will ask Donal to find the shepherd who owns the wee lamb. Thank you, Mairi."

She nodded, her dark liquid eyes lingering on his. "Aye. Ronan—" She touched his arm. "It is good to see you."

"And you," he said gruffly.

"Is it the same? You are so distant. I feel we can never quite talk." Her eyes searched his. "Will you never forgive me?"

He sighed, emotions tumbling. Behind him, he heard Ellison replying to Sir Ludo. He was ever alert to her voice, her presence, ever wondering what she thought, how she felt. When had that happened? He frowned.

His feelings for Mairi had been passionate, then ravaged by betrayal like a consuming fire, hurting him deeply. He knew how much she loved his brother and thought of Ronan as an older brother, a friend. Time had tempered his feelings, bringing him to acceptance and true friendship.

Just then, he knew he had let it go. Just then, he knew that what he felt for Ellison Graham was fulsome and wise, more mature. Nothing like the young love of his past. When had this new feeling happened? He had not been aware of it. It was simply there now, very real, and part of him.

Looking at Ellison, he shook his head a little in wonder, bemused.

"Ronan?" Mairi asked.

"Forgiven," he said then. "Do not fret. And I have always loved your lad, always will. He has your heart and intelligence."

"He wants to study medicine, did he tell you?"

"I will find a way to help him do that. My freedom is a bit in question as yet."

"But you are home now."

"Some conditions must be met. When all is resolved, I will be back."

"Good. Ronan, what of the others—Linhope and MacInnes?"

"Still held in Edinburgh." He did not want to elaborate.

"I hope they can be released soon too. Please listen," she said, her hand on his arm. "I know we hurt you. I hurt you," she clarified.

He shook his head. "It is not necessary—"

"It is. You never give me the chance to tell you. I know you avoid me, and I understand it. I made mistakes and I regret them. I should have been honest with you. Yet you were always been good to us, despite all."

"You are my family." Now, as he searched for a remnant of the wild love he had felt for Mairi, and searched for the deep wound she had left, he could not find them. They had faded like a dream, healed over the years. Somehow he had not noticed. "It is I should ask forgiveness of you."

"You always had it. I am telling you now, though you never wanted to hear it."

He nodded, humbled, and glanced at Ellison. She glanced toward him, away.

"You never married," Mairi said, following his glance.

"Not yet." He had never said it that way. *Not yet.*

"I like your Miss Graham. I see how you look at her. How she looks at you."

"She is a bright lass. Kind," he murmured. "She is a friend. I am grateful."

"If you feel more than gratitude and friendship, and I think you might—give it a chance, Ronan. Give it time and attention. Do not turn away from what could be."

He shook his head. "I do not have good prospects at the moment."

"But you might soon. Life surprises us." She drew a breath. "Ronan, you should know—I am thinking of marrying again."

He had dreaded that. He did not want to hear the name. "Aye?"

"I will tell you more when I decide for sure. He asked and then left me to consider it until he—returns for my answer." She was pink, who never blushed.

"What will you say?" he asked.

"I will accept if he sincerely means it. I want him to ask again. To be sure."

"A man does not ask such a thing unless he means it." Or unless he sees some advantage for himself, he thought bitterly, thinking of Pitlinnie.

"Here is Donal." She smiled and turned. "The lamb will stay here for a while."

"Good," Donal said. "Sir, we should go back now. We do not want to travel in these hills at night."

Ronan nodded, seeing Ellison and Sorcha come toward them. "How is the lamb?" Ellison asked, and Mairi explained the lamb's condition. "Thank you for taking care of her."

"I hear you deserve thanks for finding her," Mairi said.

"That little cry in the hills caught at my heartstrings. I had to help her."

"We should always follow our hearts." Mairi looked at Ronan, her whisky-brown eyes telling him to listen. He nodded, wishing he could let his heart lead so easily as some could do.

"We are leaving soon," he told Ellison. "You will go with Donal and Sorcha."

"Oh! I just remembered—I left my books by the burn. When we found the lamb, I simply forgot. Can we fetch them?"

"Perhaps Donal and Miss Beaton could go straight to Strathniven since you must get the fresh fish to Mrs. Barrow," Mairi suggested. "Ronan, you could borrow our gig and take Miss Graham back to find her things." She sent Ronan a twinkling, mischievous look. "Just the two of you."

"I suppose so," he said, though his heart quickened.

"You were sitting under those trees." Ronan gestured toward the cluster of birches overlooking the burn where they had fished. He drew up the reins to slow the gig on the earthen track. Climbing down, he came around to reach up for Ellison. "We will go look."

"I will go. I know just where." As she stepped down, he held her fingers a moment, casting a wary glance around the hills. Only a few goats along the upper ridge—yet he felt uneasy, alert as a taut wire and protective toward the girl.

Since they had left Invermorie, the light had faded from blue to a lavender wash that would deepen through midnight. The clear and moonless evening was perfect for men who might venture over the hills with ponies and loaded carts. He knew better than most the conse-quences if one met free traders in the hills.

"Quickly, then," he told Ellison. "We can get back to Strathniven for

a late supper if we hurry. In this summer darkness, there is enough light
to travel."

"You have been watchful again. What is it?"

"Naught. Better to be wary than surprised."

"Smugglers?"

"Must you sound so eager? An encounter would not be pleasant."

"I encountered you," she pointed out. "So far that has been fairly
pleasant."

"So far?" He chuckled. "Go on, Miss Graham, and find your wee
things."

She ran, lithesome and quick, the breeze lifting her hair and billowing
her skirt. Ronan waited, refreshed by the cool evening air, though he knew
pleasant conditions out here could invite trouble. As Ellison vanished among
the trees, he looked toward the hills where stars began to glint in a violet sky.

"I found them!" she called moments later, emerging with a cloth sack
over her shoulder. "What a lovely evening," she said, joining him. "What
did you and Donal call this stream earlier?"

"The Lealtie Burn."

"Loyalty? Surely there is a story behind that name."

"There is a story at every turn in the Highlands. Long ago, a vow was
made here, they say, between a MacArthur lass and a MacGregor
warrior."

"A vow of loyalty? Or love?"

"Both, I suppose, a marriage pledge between them. The MacGregor
was new to the glen—our clan had been tossed out of the west and our
name proscribed. It was only reclaimed in my grandfather's generation.
This exiled MacGregor tended sheep and cattle for the MacArthur chieftain in exchange for a plot of land near the loch."

"The loch down the way? The fairy loch?"

"The very one. But he fell in love with the MacArthur's daughter and
she with him. They made their pledge just here."

"So romantic. And lived happily ever after?"

"They did not. Her father's men killed him, and she threw herself from the old tower beside the loch. Love stories often end tragically." He said it brusquely.

"Not every love story ends in loss."

"So I hear. We must go."

She poked him in the chest with a finger. "Ronan MacGregor, you are not as sour a lad as you like to think. I see through you."

He huffed. "Do you, now?"

"I do. You are a more romantic soul than you will admit." She lifted her face to the twilight, bathed in its glow. He smiled. "Sometimes on a summer evening, when the light fades and the air cools, the world smells so fresh and sweet." Drawing a breath, she closed her eyes. "What is that scent?"

He sniffed. "Bog myrtle. It grows in the marshy ground between the burn and the loch. The leaves give off that clean and pungent scent."

"That is it. Myrtle. We pack our winter things in it to keep them fresh."

"Ellison." Ronan took her arm, pulling her toward the gig. "We must go. Now."

"What is it?"

"Bog myrtle gives off a stronger scent when the leaves are crushed underfoot," he murmured. "Someone is nearby."

She glanced over her shoulder. "Here? Now?"

"We will not wait to find out. Come on." He tugged her toward the gig, lifted her to the bench, and leaped up to take the reins.

CHAPTER 17

She could not imagine danger in these hills on such a peaceful night, though Ronan drove at a swift pace, intent and tense. But when she saw the glimmer of water ahead and a stone tower thrusting up, she pointed.

"There! Is that the loch and the old tower you spoke of?"

"Aye. Loch Brae, we call it." He slowed the vehicle on the dirt track that now ran parallel to the loch.

"Then if we are still in Glenbrae, this is your loch."

"The loch was in Glenbrae, but borders Strathniven lands and became part of that estate. Things changed over generations."

Curious to know more, she only nodded. "There is the island you mentioned, in the center. It vanishes?"

"A fairy spell, so they say."

"I must see it. Can we stop?" A bump in the track sent her leaning against his solid warmth.

"Briefly. We must get back soon." As he drew the gig to a halt, Ellison fairly leaped out, running down to the lochside, beckoning for him to follow.

"Can we go over to the island? A wee rowing boat is over there, see? We could row to the tower on the other shore."

"Another day perhaps. But that old broch is in ruinous condition, centuries old, they say. Besides, if we set foot on the island it might disappear."

"You do not believe that." She saw the teasing twinkle in his eyes.

"Come down to the shore." He took her hand to lead her over stones and bracken to the water's edge, and she wanted to keep hold, savor the sense of belonging, of rightness she felt. But he let go.

She looked toward the small isle in the middle of the narrow loch, a low spread of turf with a few spindly plants, a low hillock. Scattered wildflowers along its length looked like colored stars.

"Legend claims the island vanishes," he said.

"In fog or darkness? But it would not disappear, just be obscured."

"For a romantic, you are pragmatic as well. According to the legend, it sometimes disappears completely. Probably just an illusion in certain weather," he added. "The old name for it is Eilean à Cheo." *Ee-len-a-kyo*, he said in rapid Gaelic.

"Isle of Mist," she repeated. "There is a fairy spell over it?"

"So they say. My mother was a MacArthur, and she told me the tale when I was a lad. Long ago, a MacArthur met and married a fairy, you see."

"The same couple who pledged at the Lealtie Burn?"

"No, the fairy business on the isle happened before that."

"Truly!" She wrapped her arms around herself, delighted with the story, the moment, and the man beside her. He chuckled softly and set his arm around her, drawing her near. Smiling, sighing, she felt happy in the instant.

"This MacArthur warrior met a fairy woman—some say a princess of that realm—and fell in love. But a marriage between a human and a fairy brings trouble. She could not stay, as it is the nature of fairies to be free. They had a little son, but after a time she left them. The husband came to the shore of the loch every day to look for his missing bride."

She sighed. Ronan pressed her shoulder, the warmth of his body welcome in the cooling summer evening, and wonderful to feel. She leaned against him.

"One day MacArthur came to the shore with his old mother and they played with the child. Then he saw his beautiful bride out on the island, and he left the child with the grandmother to row over and bring her back with him."

"And the isle disappeared?"

"Within moments. He was never seen again. They say fairy magic pulled him into her world forever. Or else he drowned. Either way, he left a wee son behind, my mother's ancestor."

She set a hand to her chest. "Love and magic together is a reckoning force."

"I suppose it would be."

"What about the old tower?"

"Remember the bride who pledged at the Lealtie Burn? She threw herself from it on the day her bridegroom was murdered by her kinsmen."

"That is so tragic. But the fairy isle—does it still disappear?"

"It is a good tale. But it is stuff and nonsense, my girl."

"But if these were your ancestors, you have fairy blood."

"It would be dilute by now, I would think."

"I can see it in you," she murmured, looking up at him in the twilight.

"Can you?" He touched his lips to her hair.

She smiled, feeling as if her heart lifted, soared, with his slightest smile, touch, a whisper of a kiss. She was falling in love with a man who might vanish himself, his future unknown. Or was she falling for an ideal, a romantic hero who did not exist?

"I am no fairy-blood prince, Miss Graham. Come. We have been here too long." Taking her arm, he guided her back to the gig.

"Ellison," she reminded him. "My name is Ellison. And your legend is enchanting."

"It is," he agreed, and helped her into the gig.

∼

He saw men in the distance as he guided horse and gig away from the loch road to follow the wider drover's track that ran through part of a vast meadowland. Far off, under the soft purple glow of the sky, he glimpsed heads and shoulders, then men striding full forward over the meadow—three, six, eight in all.

Their lanterns were golden stars in the lowering light; some led ponies bearing pannier baskets. Narrowing his eyes, he recognized the tall blonde-haired man in the lead. Neill Pitlinnie.

What the devil was Pitlinnie doing out here with men and ponies, likely carrying goods in those panniers? Sir Neill, as the man preferred—though rumor said his knighthood was the result of a large gift to fund the work of Telford and McAdam. New roads in Scotland would benefit all—including the free trade. But Pitlinnie rarely did the work of transport himself. He hired others to take those risks.

Remembering what Aleck and Geordie Muir had said, he looked but did not see either of the Muirs among those who walked ponies alongside tall, rangy Pitlinnie, his pale hair recognizable at a distance, though he was dressed in shabby trousers and jacket as if he were a poor crofter.

Though Ronan urged the aging Invermorie horse and old gig faster, neither were capable of much speed. He glanced at Ellison to see her peering at the troupe of men crossing the far field.

"Do you know them?" she asked.

"They are not fellows we want to meet." The lanterns swung, bright dots rising and falling over the hillocks in the meadowland.

"Whisky smugglers?"

"Possibly. Do not fret."

"I am not afraid, but I do fear for you if we should meet them."

"Worried I might run off and revert to my true ways?"

She bounced on the seat as they hit a rut in the road. "Worried they might harm you if they know the king wants Glenbrae whisky. They might crave that honor for their product." The next divot in the road threw her hard against him. Shifting the reins to one hand, he put an arm around her to steady her.

"They would not care. They only want profit. And I want you safe, so we will avoid them."

Bumping on the seat, Ellison clung to the metal support beside her, bouncing against his side now and then.

"Are they gone? I do not see them."

He glanced around to look for the men with lanterns and ponies. "Gone in another direction, with luck."

Suddenly the gig lurched in a deep gully in the track, and Ronan heard a loud crack as the vehicle pitched sideways. Ellison slid hard against him, and he grabbed her to keep her from flying out as the gig tipped sideways. He held her tightly to him for a moment, breathing hard, then relaxed and sat up. She came up with him.

"Elly, are you hurt?"

"Fine," she managed. "You?"

"Right enough. Come out." He extricated himself from the tilted vehicle and reached to lift her out, her skirt catching on an iron fitting. As she worked it free, he went to the horse, murmuring to the beast as he smoothed his hands over its legs and haunches.

"All is well with him. Now for the wheel." He squatted to examine it, finding the steel tire twisted from the track in the wood of the wheel. He swore under his breath and stood, pushing a hand through his hair.

"What shall we do?" she asked, standing nearby.

"I will have to fix it somehow. Damnation," he said. "These old tracks need attention but have had none for a while since—well, for a long while."

"What do you mean?"

"Since my great-grandfather owned these lands." He dropped to his knees and lay on the ground, half under the cart, tugging and testing the broken wheel.

"Your great-grandfather was laird over Strathniven lands?"

"Just our luck," he muttered, deliberately not satisfying her question. This was no time for that revelation. He stood again, brushing his hands.

"Can it be fixed?"

"Here is the trouble." He kicked the wheel rim to show her. "The wood is split at one of the felloes"—he indicated the wooden rim between two spokes—"and the steel tire has come away. I may be able to pry the band into place. It could hold long enough for us to get to Strathniven House."

"How can I help?"

"Keep an eye out, lass. Tell me if you see anyone. But stay near, do."

Walking a little way along the track, Ellison was glad to be Ronan's helpmeet in this. His capable calm was reassuring. Ahead, the drover's track through the meadow met the foot of a long slope where the road curved out of sight. She glanced back toward the gig, where Ronan crouched on the ground intent on his task.

Squaring her shoulders, she walked on to see what lay ahead on the road. If she caught sight of the men with the ponies, she would run back to Ronan immediately.

But she saw only fields and hills beneath the indigo sky. She stood, folding her arms, a watchful sentinel while Ronan worked a little way behind her. After a few minutes, she ran forward a bit farther, leaving the shadow of the steep hill to follow the drover's track.

Then, hearing the chink and jangle of harness, the thud of boots and hooves, she spun to look for the source of the sounds. Not far from where she stood, the group rose like a vision—men, ponies, glowing lanterns—rising out of a deep hollow where the meadow dipped down not far from where she stood.

She whirled, knowing she was exposed here, aware she was too far from Ronan to reach him, and too close to the strangers to escape him. One of them was running toward her even as she whirled to flee.

Grabbing her wrist roughly, he dragged her toward him, and she stumbled with the force of her effort to run. He pulled on her arm so hard she winced.

"And who are *you*, lassie, hey?"

Swearing under his breath, he pried and pulled at the steel band with a small iron lever he had found in the gig. He worked it under the metal band, trying to coax the thing back into place along the cracked wheel rim; that might pull the fractured wood together for a temporary repair. Casting the clumsy lever aside, he pulled a dirk from his belt and pried the blade under the metal band, praying the blade would not snap. As the band popped into place, he crowed victory and sat up.

Dusting his hands, he looked around but did not see Ellison nearby. He got to his feet, shoving the dirk into his belt, and then saw her in the distance.

And saw the men approaching her—saw one of them grab for her. She spun then—skirt billowing, golden hair flying out as she turned to run. But the fellow had her. In the gathering darkness, he recognized the pale hair, the tall form.

"Pitlinnie!" he shouted, striding forward, then running.

"Ronan!" Ellison cried, hauled close against her captor. The other men clustered near them, some holding pony leads, forming a half circle on the meadow.

"Pitlinnie!" Ronan shouted, pounding nearer. "Let her go!"

The leader said something to his men, and then Ronan saw hands move to dirks and pistols shadowed by plaids and jackets. He slowed, afraid for Ellison's sake, his anger boiling. He strode forward, fists clenched.

"Neill Pitlinnie!"

"Hey, Glenbrae." The man kept a firm hold on the girl. "Stop there."

"Let the lass go," Ronan growled.

"What brings you here this evening?" Pitlinnie held Ellison's forearm in a strong grip; she winced when she tried to twist away. Realizing any threatening move on his part would bring weapons out in force, Ronan slowed, came near, and stood still, calculating distances. He was too far away to reach Ellison and pull her behind him.

"Broken wheel," he answered with a shrug as Pitlinnie looked toward the gig.

"I see. I thought the Whisky Lairds were caught at last." Pitlinnie snorted. "But then I heard you were back."

"Aye, here now. Let the girl go."

"This bonny lass is safe with me. What is your name, Miss? You canna trust that rascal to help you with yon cart." Pitlinnie leaned toward her. "I will see you safely home. Where is it you live? I have not seen you hereabouts before."

"Pitlinnie," Ronan said. One of the men stepped forward, fingers clenching the handle of a dirk. Immediately Ronan put a hand to his own sheathed dirk.

"Let me go," Ellison demanded, pulling on her trapped arm, wincing again in the man's tight grip.

"You do not want to go that rascal," he told her. "Ronan MacGregor is not a man to trust."

"He is. Ronan MacGregor is my fiancé." She yanked against his grip again.

Startled, Ronan nodded. "Aye. Betrothed."

"Is it so? Oh well then. Go on!" Giving a harsh laugh, Pitlinnie released Ellison with a push, so that she stumbled, got to her feet, and rushed toward Ronan. He swept her behind him with one arm, his other hand on the dirk.

"What is it you want on these lands?" Ronan growled.

"We are passing by, and do not need your leave for that. These fields belong to Strathniven, not Glenbrae."

"Then you need my leave," Ellison said, "on behalf of Lady Strathniven."

Ronan frowned. Less said the better, but her impulsive idea of a betrothal had seemed to help. Even Pitlinnie had his limits. "Listen to the lady. She can act on behalf of the viscountess."

"Glenbrae cuddling up to Strathniven! Who would believe it! But is it true what I hear, that you are a peer now? Lord Darrach, begging your pardon, sir." Pitlinnie gave a mocking bow.

"Whatever you heard is only rumor," Ronan said.

"But the estate might not go to you, will it, due to your arrest. Whisky Lairds!" He spat into the grass. "I hoped we were rid of you when you were taken. Does the Strathniven lass know who you are?"

"She knows all," Ronan said. He felt Ellison's hand slip into his. He pressed it tight. No help for it now—he would have to tell her something soon. "I only came back to see to the distillery."

"All according to law?" Pitlinnie looked smug. "The new viscount follows the rules while his lads move goods by devious means."

"Who is being devious tonight?" Ronan tipped his head toward the men, the horses, the panniers filled with goods.

"Neill Pitlinnie," Ellison said then. "Lady Strathniven speaks well of you. She enjoys your whisky. My father is fond of it too."

The man's eyes flickered toward her. "Your father?"

"The Deputy Lord Provost of Edinburgh."

Ronan groaned inwardly. This was too far. "Ellison," he said under his breath.

"You are Graham's lass? So. Lady Strathniven—I see. Her nephew is a man called Corbie. You keep fine company, Glenbrae. Or Darrach, since you are elevated now beyond a mere laird." Pitlinnie laughed cruelly. "Odd that I have heard nothing of your engagement."

"Why should you?"

"From your sister-in-law. I saw her just days ago. She never mentioned you. We are courting, did you know?"

Ronan went cold, squeezing Ellison's fingers tightly. "I heard."

"We hope for your approval as her kinsman."

"Mairi Brodie is twice a widow. You need her permission, not mine."

"I hope to have it soon. Then we would be kinsmen. We should work together."

"I doubt that would happen."

"Hah, not now that you have the claim to Darrach and Graham's pretty daughter too. Well done to find a father-in-law to fix your troubles."

"My father had nothing to do with my fiancé's pardon," Ellison said.

Ronan pressed her hand. "Tell him no more," he growled.

"Ronan MacGregor is a criminal, Miss Graham. You are wise to avoid him."

"It seems you may be the criminal here, sir." She pointed to the men. "What are you transporting across Lady Strathniven's land?"

"Just delivering whisky to some loyal customers," Pitlinnie said. "Lady Strathniven is one of my clients. Love thy neighbor, brother Ronan. Aye?"

"Then give us Strathniven's lot," Ronan said. "We will deliver it for you."

"Can I trust you? I think not." Pitlinnie chuckled. "Unless you want to come away with us and work with me again. There is good money in it. You might need it. Darrach is a crumbling old place in need of repair."

"Be on your way," Ronan said.

"Miss Graham. My lord," Pitlinnie mocked. He waved his men onward, pony harnesses jingling, glinting in the twilight. "My felicitations on your betrothal."

Directing his men to follow the track past the curve in the hillside, Pitlinnie vanished into the shadows with the others. Ronan stood for a moment, breathing hard, gripping Ellison's hand.

"We must go," he said finally, tugging to bring her with him. Helping her into the gig, he climbed up to the bench to sit beside her and take the reins.

"Is it fixed?" she asked. "Will we reach Strathniven?"

"Aye." He guided horse and gig carefully out of the rut in the road, and within moments, the vehicle rolled onward with a wobble, but the tires held.

"Ronan," Ellison said after a moment. "I am sorry."

"Do not," he said. "None of this is your doing."

"If I had not forgotten my things, we would not have come this way, and never would have met those men, or—" She caught back a sob.

"My fault entirely. I drove in haste, and the wheel broke." He set an arm about her to pull her close.

"But I should not have told him we were betrothed."

"It worked. It gave him pause, that news, so he let you go."

"If he tells others—"

"Unlikely. If he does, we will deny it. Just a rumor." He released her.

"Did you—want to go with them? He offered you money."

"I keep clear of him and his lot. I know Pitlinnie too well."

"It puzzles me, your past. I trust you. I do," she explained. "But my father and Mr. Corbie cautioned me strictly against you. And just now I was not sure."

"What a parcel of trouble if you had to tell your father that the fiendish MacGregor ran off to pursue crime and profit as soon as he could. Listen to me, my girl. We have a promise."

"A promise?" She blinked at him.

"You agreed to make me into a gentleman. I agreed to let you try."

"Oh. Yes. But you were not tempted just then to return to smuggling?" She searched his face. "Pitlinnie said 'again.'"

His ruses, previous and current, were in clear conflict. The girl did not know if he was a rogue or a gentleman. That was all due to his secrets, his silence.

He stopped the gig, turned to her, and tipped up her chin. "Whatever I am, lass, I would never have left you there."

She watched him, waited. Invited with a tilt of her head, her gaze lowering to his lips, then up to meet his eyes. He pushed her bonnet away, then kissed her. The warm cushion of her lips under his was willing, tender. He felt her breath catch, felt his heart pounding.

A feeling he had denied too long swept through him like rushing water. As if his soul was a fish in a stream, following the current, he followed his heart, kissed her again, whispered reassurance, and drew her closer into his arms.

Once he had wondered if he would ever find this again. Yet here it was, more powerful, more meaningful than he had ever felt. Kissing her, he knew suddenly that this was meant to be. Felt he could tell her all the truths and mistruths of his life. Kissing her, life made sense. He was where he should be, here and now.

Then cold rational sense surged through him, breaking that spell. He pulled away. Not yet, he told himself. Silence and secrets were essential if he was to protect his friends in Calton—and if he was to protect her.

"Beg pardon," he whispered. "I did not mean to—"

"You did. I meant it too." She kissed his cheek, the corner of his lip, but when he leaned in, this time she pulled away. "But we must go."

"Agreed." The gig creaked and bumped slowly along. The sky turned deep indigo.

Ellison watched the stars as they rode. "Ronan," she said after a while. "Why did Pitlinnie ask if I know who you are?"

He was silent. The wheels rattled unevenly. "I am a MacGregor to my bones."

"A MacGregor with many secrets."

"For the good of others, aye."

"Why smuggle whisky and risk going against the law?"

"So many questions. Strathniven's rooftops are there, see, beyond that hill."

"You will not tell me."

"Not yet. You have to trust me."

"I do. But I fear some secret could undo all our plans."

"Our plans?" He glanced at her.

"The king's visit."

"Oh, that. I thought you meant our betrothal," he drawled.

"I am truly sorry about that. It could cause problems. If my father—"

"Ellison. What you said was well done. You did what you thought was best in the moment. I must do what I think is best too, even if it goes against the law."

"But I would like to know the truth."

"Soon we will lay all our truths out between us. Your secrets too."

"Mine do not endanger anyone."

"Nor do mine. I promise." Chucking to the horse, he leaned to the side to look down. "The wheel is holding, just barely."

They moved on, the gig rolling awkwardly. Ellison bounced along, silent. "I am a prisoner, too," she said after a moment.

"Your father's expectations?"

She shrugged. "I think about freedom too."

He glanced down, nudged his shoulder against hers. Just that. "Almost home," he whispered.

CHAPTER 18

"*W*ill that be all, sir, and Miss Ellison?" The housekeeper set a bowl of strawberries and a plate of hot oatcakes, steam rising from the stack, on the dining table between Ronan and Ellison's places.

"Thank you, Mrs. Barrow, this is more than enough," Ellison said, looking at the generous breakfast spread. "You were thoughtful to prepare a late breakfast."

"And kind to leave supper trays for us last night," Ronan said.

"We did return rather late, but it could not be helped," Ellison said.

"Aye, Miss Beaton was worried last night and thought you might be hungry when you finally arrived.

"I will say, Miss Ellison," Mrs. Barrow said as she set a bowl of strawberries and a plate of oatcakes on the dining room table as part of a late breakfast, "it was a relief to hear from MacNie this morning that you were so late last night because of a wheel needing repair, and no harm done."

"No harm done at all, Mrs. Barrow. Thank you," she answered.

"This all looks delicious, Mrs. Barrow. You are a treasure," Ronan said. The housekeeper beamed as she left the room.

"Nicely done. You have quite charmed Barrow," Ellison murmured. "Sorcha, good morning," she said then as the girl entered the room. "Would you like tea?"

Clutching an embroidered handkerchief to her nose, Sorcha took a chair at the end of the table and sneezed. "Dank you," she mumbled.

"Oh dear, are you feeling poorly?" Ellison poured hot tea into a cup, added sugar as the girl preferred, and brought it to her.

"I bay hab caught a submer cold."

"Perhaps you took a chill yesterday. You were awfully wet! Go straight back to bed. I will have a tray brought up for you."

"Dat would be good, dank you. I only came to tell you the dews."

"News?" Ronan translated. "I do hope you feel better soon, Miss Beaton."

Sorcha set two envelopes on the table. "MacNie fetched the post yesterday but you hab not seed it yet," she managed. "He said a wheel broke."

"Yes, just a mishap," Ronan said.

"So you missed dese." Sorcha held up the envelopes. "This is for you, Elly, and this is for me. Good dews for all of us." She handed one letter to Ellison.

"Good news?" Seeing Sir Hector's spiky, impatient scrawl, Ellison felt only dread. "Tell us your news first, dear."

"Baba sent—*Mama* sent," she managed, trying to speak clearly, "an invitation for us to attend a country supper and dance at Duncraig. Lord Darrach, you are invited too. She insists you be there. My lady aunt told her all about you."

"Indeed, how kind," he said, but Ellison heard the wariness in his voice.

Sorcha handed Ellison the invitation and Mrs. Beaton's accompanying note, which she read quickly. "The dance is to be a *cèilidh* in the Highland style," she summarized. "It is usually a celebration for a harvest or housewarming or a wedding, but Mrs. Beaton and Lady Strathniven think it will be entertaining for some friends who are summering in the

Highlands now and plan to depart for Edinburgh soon. We can expect music and dancing and a late supper."

"When will this be?" Ronan asked.

"Saturday," she said. "Not much notice, but cèilidhs tend to be informal, with locals and gentry mingling together. It will be a wonderful evening, I am sure."

"Have you attended cèilidh dances before, Lord Darrach?" Sorcha asked.

"Oh aye. They can be very lively."

Sorcha giggled, which brought on a cough. "I so look forward to it!"

"You must rest if you are to be well enough," Ellison said.

"I will go up soon. Did your father send good news as well?"

"I wonder." Sliding the letter free, Ellison read her father's brief note, written in his usual terse tone. Though her stomach sank, she looked up with a smile.

"He says the city is already crowded with people arriving from all over. The king is expected in less than two weeks." She paused. "He also says—he is sending Adam Corbie north for a short visit and asks that MacNie meet the coach in Kinross on Friday afternoon."

Sorcha stifled another sneeze. "Wonderful!" she said thickly. "He can come with us to Duncraig. I will write to Mama this afternoon."

"Friday," Ronan said. "Two days." Ellison met his gaze and nodded.

"Perhaps we should hurry to finish the lessons," Ellison said as Ronan joined her in the library later, "considering what will happen all too soon."

"Corbie's arrival?"

His prim tutor pressed her lips together. "Your introduction to the king." Standing by the library table, she set down a book and faced him.

"I can conduct myself well enough. We are done preparing."

Her fingers flexed, graceful yet anxious. "At the royal levee, you will be scrutinized by my father and Corbie."

"I promise you they will see only perfection. If there is little time left, I must attend to collecting and shipping the whisky."

"Even so, we still have time for lessons."

He tipped his head, curious. "You want to continue."

"I enjoy our time together." She traced the pattern on the table's oak surface.

"As do I. Need it involve stodgy books and practicing what we already know?"

"Perhaps not. But it may be good to introduce you at the cèilidh first."

"I would be more visible at a small event than a large one, and so I may be directly questioned if introduced as Darrach."

"Pitlinnie did not question it. He seemed impressed."

"He is easily impressed."

"Truly I dread more that he would mention a betrothal."

"I am not concerned about that."

"Ronan," she said then, "tell me you still mean to see this through."

He blew out a breath. Her question hit the heart of the matter. He had loathed the very idea of the ruse but had to follow through for his friends' sake. Just one day, he told himself. But stepping forth at a small local gathering was different.

Yet he was in the thick of it for his friends. And for Ellison. "I gave my word."

"Then we should finish up. We only have two days."

"You seem to think it all ends when Corbie arrives to examine your student."

"It may. Well then." She tapped a fingertip on her chin thoughtfully. "I suppose we should practice some dancing for the cèilidh. Have you done much dancing?"

"A little." He came toward her and held out his arms, right crooked, left jutting out.

She laughed a little. He was glad of it. "I do love a waltz, but we will not see it at a cèilidh. It may still be frowned upon at royal assemblies too, certainly in Scotland. I rather thought of practicing the steps of a Strath-spey or a reel."

"We can, though a waltz with a beautiful woman in candlelight is a fine thing. I know several Scottish dances, but we can practice, my girl."

She tipped her head. "You have waltzed with beautiful women in candlelight?"

"Aye, though they were not as lovely as a certain lass in daylight just now."

Her cheeks went pink. "Where was that? Not here in Scotland, I think."

He owed her some truth. "England and France both, as an officer."

"You mentioned the military the other day. The Highland Watch?"

"I was in the Black Watch for three years, and then exchanged into the dragoons to accompany my cousin to India. Sir Evan," he explained.

"I remember Papa saying that Sir Evan was severely injured in India and had shown great courage there—as did the men with him. You?" She tilted her head.

"Many of us were with him at the Talnar ambush. Four years ago. It is in the past. You wanted to practice Strathspey steps?" He stepped back as if to face her in a dancing line. "With two people and no fiddle, we may not accomplish much."

"You will not tell me more," she said.

"It is not a pleasant tale," he said, extending both hands to her.

Nodding, she stepped toward him, then back, and hopped lightly to the side. "Cast off left, then right," she said. "We will pretend the other couples are here."

"Aye so." He took her hands in his and circled with her. She stepped and hopped, graceful and light, and began to hum a tune, the notes clear and sweet.

"You have another hidden talent," he said, guiding her around once more.

She laughed. "Singing? My music tutor did not think so. One, two, three," she counted as they broke apart, turned, linked arms, spun, parted, faced, and clasped hands again. She laughed, a little breathless, cheeks flushed.

He pulled her toward him. "We could try a waltz, should the king decide it is appropriate for the ball. And in case"—he drew her closer, setting his right hand to the small of her back, extending his left arm with her hand resting in his—"I am invited to that ball."

"That is up to my father and Mr. Corbie."

"Then this may be my last chance to waltz with you," he murmured, pulling her against him, so that she rested her hand on his right shoulder, her breasts pressing softly against his chest. She angled her head to the side, and he began to turn with her, gliding, swirling around in silence. She was airy, soft, warm, and so close. A feeling surged within him, beyond time and the moment. He wanted to stop, kiss her, savor the feel of her—

A knock sounded on the door, and Ellison jerked away from him as if he were made of fire. Ronan looked around to see Mrs. Barrow peek in the door.

"Oh my, excuse me!" she said.

"Yes, Mrs. Barrow?" Ellison smoothed her skirts, looking flushed. "We were only practicing for the supper dance."

"Aye, Miss. Glenbrae, Mr. Cameron is here to see you."

He frowned, surprised. "Thank you."

"Show him in here," Ellison said, and Mrs. Barrow withdrew. "I will leave you to your meeting. I should look in on Sorcha. Is Mr. Cameron the solicitor in Kinross?"

"Aye. He is doing some work for me."

"Perhaps he has good news. I will leave you to it."

Good news or none, either way, some things must be said and soon. "We must talk, Ellison," he murmured.

She blinked, gray eyes wide, and nodded. "When? Where?"

"Tonight, in the tower library," he whispered. She smiled and swept toward the door, and he heard her greet Hugh Cameron in the corridor.

When Hugh stepped into the library moments later, Ronan nodded and indicated chairs by the window. "Good to see you! There must be news."

"Some, aye. This is a fine place," Hugh said, taking a seat. "I have seen Strathniven but have never visited. I met your Miss Graham in the corridor. Lovely."

"She is. Can I offer you something?"

"This will just take a few minutes. I thought it important enough to find you in person. I have heard from Sir Evan."

As Ronan sat, Hugh took an envelope from the pocket of his brown coat, and removed folded papers covered in ink and scrawl. Ronan recognized Evan's distinctive script, the letters formed stiffly; losing the use of his right hand, Evan had learned to rely on his left, however awkward it was at times.

Hugh handed him the pages, and Ronan read the letter quickly.

I trust you are well and in better circumstances than recently. Though we have not seen each other for a few years, I know of your situation from Hugh Cameron, and am pleased to learn that you are free of the burden of charges. Since you were never one to commit felonies, a clearing of charges may indeed be merited.

I have studied the status of the Darrach inheritance, including its properties, environs, means, and heritable title. The Courts of Session and Lyon Court had the matter and entrusted it to me to decide as Chief in my late father's stead. While the courts will finalize the decision, that declaration will honor my opinion.

Turning to the second page, he read through and glanced up. He felt stunned. "He is recommending that the courts grant Darrach to me."

"Lock, stock, and barrel. You will be—you *are*—Viscount Darrach."

Shaking his head, almost unable to take it in, Ronan read the pages again. "He is ensuring that I will be declared the legitimate heir and awarded the estate and all of its grounds, including villages, crofts, and tenanted properties.'"

He looked up, feeling as if the world had tilted and was slowly righting again.

Hugh nodded. "He submitted his decision to the Session and Lyon Courts. We must wait for the letters patent, but Sir Evan has simplified their task. It is done."

"My God," Ronan breathed. "I did not expect this."

"However, there is a condition. Sir Evan detailed it in a letter to me."

Ronan nodded slowly. He should have known not to believe such luck.

"Sir John, his father, favored you as heir to Darrach after your cousin's death, but his death complicated many issues, including this. Sir Evan had to review all clan matters anew. This you know."

"Aye. Go on. What condition?"

"One thing Sir Evan made sure of. Ronan MacGregor, an accused smuggler, is not named in the inheritance documents. Only John Ronan MacGregor of Glenbrae, lawyer, nearest kin of the deceased, is mentioned. He was careful to do that."

His throat tightened. "I must thank him for that. It simplifies matters."

"It does. Now then, the condition." Hugh sat forward. "Sir Evan has decided with regret that Glenbrae must be sold."

Ronan stared, dumbfounded. "Sold?"

"The Darrach estate is in considerable debt, the result of poor decisions and expenditures over two generations. You may not have known about it. Had to do with your uncle and then your cousin."

"My father hinted that his older brother was not the most practical. But my cousin never said. Go on." He felt cold all over—numb to think of losing Glenbrae.

"Clearing the burden on the estate will avoid forfeiture, especially desirable when it is attached to a peerage title. Sir Evan feels selling Glenbrae will solve it."

"I see." The revelation sat like a stone in his chest. But now some things made sense—his father and his uncle arguing about luxuries and expenses. His father's frustration. His cousin John's inheritance and sudden insistence that they must produce more whisky, the finest possible, and move it fast to fetch the highest price.

Risks were taken too often. John had needed the funds to save Darrach. He saw it now. Thus John and Will had become the notorious "Whisky Lairds," working hard, but finally killed. And to rescue their reputations and that of a good whisky, Ronan had taken it on with the help of the Muirs and Linhope and MacInnes.

None of them had known about the burden of debt on Darrach.

"I see," he repeated woodenly. "What now?"

"You will be Viscount Darrach. But you must relinquish your claim to Glenbrae and Invermorie. I am sorry, Ronan."

"The whole of my glen." Ronan scowled, thinking, still stunned. "The tenanted farms. The castle where my family lives. What of the distillery?"

"All of it."

His whisky. He gripped the arms of the chair. "Sold to whom?"

"He did not say."

"But we can guess." He stood, hands fisted. "We have to stop this."

"If there was some other way to absolve the debts, we might."

"I will find a way. Convince Evan to delay the sale. Give me time."

"He might agree, with the kerfuffle in the city this summer. I will write asking him to wait until after the royal visit. Courts and banks will not operate normally for a while anyway." Hugh stood. "That gives you until the end of August."

"It will have to do. Keep me informed."

"In the meantime, you are now Lord Darrach."

"If I accept the title, I must accept the condition. But I do not agree."

"You have never been afraid of a challenge before. Take what is offered—it is a stroke of luck. Then see what can be done. You could start another distillery."

He could not imagine that. Nodding brusquely, he turned away.

CHAPTER 19

*E*llison stood back as Ronan entered the little library. The hour was very late, the room shadowed and golden in candlelight; the house, the world, seemed filled with a deep hush. She pushed away worry and impatience. She had read her father's letter too often that day, and now pulled it, creased and crumpled, from her pocket.

"You have news?" she whispered as he shut the door. "You were gone much of the day after Mr. Cameron left."

"I rode out. I had much to think about."

"Is there trouble?"

"Not exactly." He looked down at her hand. "You have near shredded that envelope. What is it?"

She shook her head and turned the window. Ronan leaned against the table and folded his arms, patient and quiet. His readiness to listen touched her, shored her up. "Papa is sending Mr. Corbie here."

"Aye, to make sure the frog has become a prince."

"More than that," she said. "Mr. Corbie expects to bring me back to Edinburgh immediately. And they will send a guard to take you back to the city."

"We knew that was coming, Ellison."

"But not so soon. And we have promised to attend the cèilidh."

"With Corbie, no less. I can take you to Edinburgh when we are both ready."

"The dance gives us a reason to stay longer." She met his eyes and lingered in his calm, secure gaze for an instant.

"We will do what you want. You do not need to return with Corbie." He tapped his fingers, arms folded. She sensed now the banked tension within him, only part of it directed at Corbie. "If you want to go to the cèilidh, we will do that too."

"And you will be introduced as Darrach?"

He seemed to hesitate. "About that—"

"You have second thoughts again. I cannot blame you. Adam Corbie coming here to evaluate you as a gentleman just makes me so—so crabbit!"

Ronan huffed a laugh. "What?"

"My granny used to say it. Crabbit." She shrugged. "His arrogance is so frustrating. But if I say aught to him, he will report to Papa and twist my words."

"And I needed lessons in manners? Ellison, listen to me. You have a gentle soul and a forthright nature and you need not suppress one for the other. Let him know your strong opinion. That is my own strong opinion on your behalf."

She turned. "Do you think so?"

"It does not matter what I think. What matters is what you think. You have a lovely fire in your soul, but so far you only douse it."

She felt her cheeks heat, felt a swell of pleasure. "If Corbie heard you say that, there would be even more trouble afoot."

"I quake in my boots."

"They are taking advantage of you for their own ends."

"And I am taking advantage of them." He spread his hands. "I am free, after all."

"But if this goes all wrong, they will give you the blame and say you lied about being Darrach." She rounded, began to pace. "This horrible ruse! I hate it so!"

He stood. "It is not a ruse."

She whirled. "I cannot blame you if you should decide you cannot go through with it, though it would go badly for you and your friends. Could we find a way? We both hate it so." She stopped, looking at him as if pleading.

"Ellison. Listen to me." He came toward her, his voice husky. "It is not a ruse. I am Lord Darrach."

She stared. "You—what?"

He took her hands, faced her as if they were about to dance a wild reel, and drew her toward him. "Hugh Cameron brought the news. I am now Darrach."

"How—how can that be?" She looked up at him, her fingers tightening in his.

"Viscount Darrach was my first cousin. He left no will. It went to the courts."

"Papa said it was in dispute and delayed, but how does it come to you?"

"Through my cousin. I kept some of this from you. I had to," he added.

"You were the heir all along, and never mentioned?" She pulled away.

"I was his closest kin, but inheritance was never certain. I could not speak of it, especially if it was decided otherwise."

"When we suggested you take the title—at all our risk—you knew all this?"

"It was a coincidence when you suggested it. Ironic to present me as Darrach, but I never expected it would come to me. Certainly not so soon."

She turned away, her heart beating hard. Had he betrayed her? She did not know how to feel about this. "I—am happy for you," she managed.

"And angry with me."

"I am not sure yet." She looked at him then.

"Ellison, I had no choice. You must understand that."

"I am trying, but you were not honest with me."

"I could not share this. As soon as I knew today, I wanted to tell you."

She waited in silence for a moment, calming her breath, wrestling with the balance of truth and necessity and a feeling of betrayal. But he had not done that—he had carried the burden of this until now. After a moment, she glanced at him.

He spread his hands. "I know this is a surprise. I know you may be upset."

"Bewildered more than upset. And glad for you. But I just want the truth. I just want to know you, Ronan."

"And I you. Come here."

She turned, a little sob escaping, and went to him. He enclosed her in his arms, safe and secure. "See here, lass," he murmured into her hair. "The ruse is no more. There is no risk. Your father has no risk either. We are free of it."

"Free." Nodding, her face in his sleeve, she looked up. "So it is yours now?"

"The viscountcy. The property. Aye." But he frowned. "The courts gave it to Sir Evan to decide. Under Scots law, a clan chief has the authority to absorb a title and lands into the chiefship or to recommend an heir. He decided in my favor."

Her head was spinning, his embrace like an anchor. "The pretense is done?"

"You can call me a legitimate gentleman now—if you want."

She knocked her fist on his shoulder, then tipped her head to regard him. "Do you have any other revelations that I should know about? Not a smuggler, but an educated gentleman. Not a laird, but a lord. Anything else?"

A shadow seemed to cross his face. "One or two other matters." He nodded half to himself. "Well. You should know that I am not just educated. I am a lawyer."

"A lawyer?" She half laughed. "I am not so surprised, though I should be. What sort of lawyer? Solicitor? Clerk to the Signet?"

"Advocate. I typically defend criminals." A wry smile played over his lips.

"Ironic, that. Just wait until my father and Mr. Corbie learn that."

"They need not," he said. "I like my privacy."

"You have so many secrets, Mr. MacGregor who is now a viscount. But I can call you Darrach and Glenbrae and you need not scowl at me for it."

He shook his head, his eyes gone indigo in the candlelight. "In Scotland, a peer can hold only one title at a time. A wee detail imposed by English law. As Viscount Darrach, I am no longer laird of Glenbrae."

"But it is under Darrach, so it is still yours. I feel like I have discovered you are a prince after all, as in a fairy tale. That sounds foolish, I know."

He huffed, listening to her, all quiet power. "It does not."

"But now that you are Darrach in truth, Mr. Corbie may choke over it. This raises you over him in rank. But he will inherit Strathniven one day and petition for the title. It is not attached to the property and heir now, given only singularly to Lady Strathniven's husband."

"Corbie has a good chance of claiming it, though."

"I suppose. I know how much Glenbrae means to you. I am sorry you will lose that title." His fingers flexed and gripped her shoulder tightly for a moment. "But you will have license over the distillery as Darrach. You love Glenbrae."

"I do." He went still as a stone for a moment. Then he cupped her shoulders. "There is something else."

Then footsteps on the stair, a voice and a knocking, sudden and sharp, on the door. Ellison jumped, stepping away from Ronan.

Mrs. Barrow poked her head in the doorway. "Oh! Again!" she burst out.

"What is it, Mrs. Barrow?" Ellison asked, feeling her cheeks burning.

"Glenbrae, sir, we have been looking high and low for you. There is a man at the door. He says it is very urgent. Aleck Muir is his name."

"What is the trouble?" He went to the door as she stood back.

"He did not say. He is dripping wet in the front hall from the rain."

"Please excuse me," he said. "I will go to him directly. Mrs. Barrow, please send for Donal Brodie to meet us."

"Aye, sir." The housekeeper stood back as Ronan rushed down the steps.

~

"It is Geordie. Wounded sore," Aleck said, breathing hard. In a damp plaid, hair slicked with rain, he radiated alarm and urgency. Ronan gestured to Donal, just running into the room. "Bring the lad a dram. Then go saddle three horses—we may need them. Aleck, what happened?"

"We went to Darrach Castle—to the caves near there. You know why," Aleck said breathlessly. "Geordie was attacked. Grandda and I took him to Invermorie. To Mairi. And I rode here fast as I could." He took the dram from Donal and downed a swallow, wiping his mouth with the back of his hand.

"Is it mortal, the wound? Who attacked him?"

"I do not know. So much blood here," he said, touching his head, "but Mairi Brodie is tending to him. I did not see who did it."

"We will come straight away," he said, as Donal ran from the room to head for the stables.

"Aye, do that. There is another problem. The whisky cache we keep there in those caves near Darrach. By the waterfall. You know where."

"I do." Last year, Ronan and his brother and others had moved a wealth of kegs, crates, and barrels to safety in the Darrach caves. Since then, the Muirs had checked them and accounted for each one.

"We found nothing there. No whisky. All gone. We thought we misremembered which cave, so we split up, Geordie going west and I going east of the main cave."

"There is a honeycomb of caves. One could get confused. What did you find?"

"Nothing. All gone, sir." Aleck gulped the last of the dram. "We found just a few crockery jugs and a broken wooden crate. That was all."

Ronan sucked in a breath. "And Geordie?"

"He had not come back, so I went looking. I heard some sounds, heard running. And I found him lying there, beaten."

"What did you hear?"

"Not much with the noise of the waterfall. He took a bad blow to the head. So I ran for Grandda, who was waiting with the cart to transport the kegs and such. We brought Geordie to Invermorie then."

"You did the right thing."

"Then Rabbie sent me for Tam Comrie, the groundskeeper at Darrach. He and his wife are still there, see. We had to know if Tam had seen anyone. He came to Invermorie with us too. But the whisky is gone." Aleck breathed hard, caught back a sob. Shoved a hand through damp hair. "I am very sorry."

"We will find it. It is not your fault. When was the last time it was seen there?"

"Grandda gave it a count and check not a month ago. There were footprints about tonight and dragging marks. Someone else was there, harming my brother."

"Aye then. With luck, it has not been long and they will not get far. Come then," he said. "We will ride for Invermorie."

Tapping her fingers rhythmically on the old, scarred table, Ellison caught the faint scent of the lemon and oil polish that one of the maids had used recently. The scent stirred her out of thoughts and worries and back to the too-quiet tower library and her unwritten letters, her unfinished novel. But she could not concentrate.

What brought Aleck Muir here so late? By the chime of the clock on the bookshelf, it was past eleven. Was something wrong at the distillery?

Frowning, she dipped her pen in ink again and set it to paper to answer her father's letter but blotted what she wrote. Truly, she wanted to tell him not to send Adam Corbie here. But it would be too late. By the time Sir Hector received the letter, Corbie would be on his way north.

With a heavy sigh, she stood and went to the window. Outside, rain swept down from an eerie dark sky. Then a new rhythm merged with the patter of the rain.

Leaning forward, she saw three horses and riders pounding over the graveled drive that fronted the house, riding from the stables and out toward the open road.

Ronan was in the lead—even in darkness, she knew his long, lean, athletic silhouette. The others must be Donal and Aleck. Where were they heading with such urgency, in such weather?

Worry swept through her, but she breathed its force away, spreading her fingers on the cool window glass, rain sliding down the other side. She felt a new strength and certainty take hold. She would not succumb to fret and fear. She could rise above it. Facing smugglers by the Lealtie Burn had shown her that—the rise in her temper that evening, her fierce need to stand up for Ronan MacGregor, had shown her that she did not need to hide behind meekness any longer.

Straightening her shoulders, summoning resolve as best she could, she left the room. However late it was, she must try to rest. Ronan would be back soon. He would be safe. She trusted him, and now must trust that all would be well.

"The lad gave as good as he got. And I hope they are sore hurting," Rabbie said. "I will watch over him for a while."

Ronan nodded, sitting with Rabbie and the others in Invermorie's great hall. Ludo had scrabbled together ham and oatcakes and Donal made coffee as they discussed the situation while rain pounded the roof and windows and Mairi tended Geordie above stairs.

She had allowed them only a few moments to see him, for the lad was bruised and bandaged, tired but comfortable. He remembered someone leaping on him in the dark of the cave—two men in Highland dress, both speaking English. He fought back, blacked out, and knew no more than that. Then Mairi had pushed them out of the room, saying he would heal, but had taken a hard knock to his head and had a broken hand and a rib or two.

Rabbie shook his head. "The last of our whisky lot went out of Culross with Pitlinnie months ago," he said. "We have new brew at Glenbrae, and had a good bit stored in the Darrach caves, and only sold jugs in shops in towns about, waiting for your word on what to do next, Ronan."

"I am sure 'twas Pitlinnie found that lot in the caves," Aleck said. "No one else would do this."

"He made a good profit off of us in the past, but he cannot move a drop of ours without my consent. And I was away," Ronan added wryly. "And we are done with the free trade."

"So they decided to steal it outright," Rabbie said.

"Why now?" Donal asked. "And how did they find it?"

"It is a wealth of whisky, worth taking if they could. With me gone and you lads distracted at the distillery, he may have been searching about what we had stored."

"And finding it, take it and relabel it as his own," Tam Comrie, the grizzled old Darrach groundskeeper. Ronan had known him since boyhood, knew his integrity and wit and loyalty, still waiting for the new viscount. He wanted to tell Tam, tell all of them—but it was not the time to share his news.

"When you came back to the glen," Sir Ludo said, "Pitlinnie had to act quickly."

"And with the whisky due to the king, you needed that lot yourself."

"They say," Tam said, "that Glenbrae, the glen and distillery and all, has been sold. They say the whisky too will belong to another, or soon will."

"Where did you hear that?" Ronan asked.

"My wife Peggy had it from the kitchen maid, who had it from her mother, who had it from an old man down the glen, who heard it from another. Many have heard the rumor now. Pitlinnie makes no secret that he has offered to buy up all of Glenbrae."

"It will not go to him," Ronan snapped. "Tonight I only want to know who beat Geordie Muir, who stole our whisky, and where they took it."

"Peggy said two men visited the castle one day when I was out," Tam said, "not long ago. Not the Muir lads, she knows them. They asked if there was whisky available to buy from Darrach. It might have been Pitlinnie and another. She does not know Pitlinnie, but I do. I think 'twas him."

"What else did she learn?" Ronan asked.

"They asked if it was true the laird of Glenbrae had been named Viscount Darrach and when he would be home."

"What did she tell them?"

"Said they were wrong and Glenbrae was not there and she had no whisky for sale nor to drink. And she shut the door and locked it. Then she went for my pistol and waited for them to come back. I found her in a fury when I got home. Scared me, it did. Fierce woman."

"Give Peggy Comrie my thanks," Ronan said. "All roads lead to Pitlinnie," Ronan muttered. "But I would not think him a low scoundrel or desperate for goods. So this does not all make sense to me."

"But he wants Glenbrae—the land, the distillery," Rabbie said. "And he thought you would hang. So he thought to take over the business."

"All this cannot be solved now," Sir Ludo said. "What is important now is to find that whisky. The king's every wish must be served."

"Just so," Ronan said, and swallowed what was in his glass, a mellow burn down his throat, a fire in his soul. He would make this right some-how, all of it.

She woke in the dark, startling out of a noisy tilt of a dream into a dim and rainy dawn. Had Ronan returned? She had to know. The dream faded as she pulled on a dressing gown and slippers and slipped out of her room. The dull rumble of thunder sounded as she went downstairs and moved through a dark and silent house. The kitchen was empty too, but for Balor, asleep by the warm hearth. He greeted her with a low woof and went back to dozing as she built up the fire in the grate, warmed the kettle, and prepared a pot of tea.

Minutes later, while tea steeped in a pot on the scrubbed oak table, she listened to the whip of rain and grumble of thunder and wondered if she should go to the tower to knock on his door to see if he had come back. She could bring tea. She began to prepare a tray.

Then she heard a new sound over the storm—horse hooves, shouts, and a distant voice so familiar that she gasped in relief. But she could hardly run outside in her dressing gown. Instead, she hurried to search for scones, rolls, jam, and butter.

He would go to his room soon, and she could bring a tray to him. Plain fare this early would surely be needed, since he had been out much of the night. She only wanted to see him for a moment, just to know he was safe and well.

Soon she carried the tray along the connecting corridor to the old tower and headed up the old, worn steps. A few treads bore wet prints. He had come this way ahead of her.

At his bedchamber door, she hesitated, suddenly wondering if she was too forward, too interfering. She should just leave the tray, knock, and flee. But the teapot clinked against the cup and the silver tray scraped over stone as she crouched to set it down.

The door swung open. She stared at two large bare feet, tracing her gaze upward past bare calves dusted with dark hair, past the folds of a plaid wrapped and belted over a loose linen shirt open at chest and throat to reveal a mat of dark hair. She looked up to his face, his dear face and scruff-bearded jaw, his eyes, dark blue in shadows, his hair wet and curling, all of him haloed in candlelight.

"Why, Ellison," he said, and reached down to her.

Blushing like fire, she set her hand in his as she came to her feet.

CHAPTER 20

She looked flustered, delectable, sleepy, and the most welcome sight he could have imagined. He wanted to keep hold of her slim, cool fingers in his, wanted to pull her into his arms. But he let go.

"I did not mean to disturb you," she said. "It is good to see you safe, and home."

Home. That word from her was everything to him. He picked up the tray and brought it to the table, then gestured to his feet and shirtsleeves. "My apologies. I had a wash and was changing."

"I only came to bring tea, thinking you might need it. I will go." She turned.

"Stay." Reaching over her head, he shut the door. "Will you stay?"

"For a moment. I will pour." She went to the table, her dark blue dressing gown, prim, plain, poufy, enveloping her throat to foot, hem dragging. Pouring tea, she added cream. Her hair fell in a tousled mass, her cheeks were pale, and her eyes shadowed purple. Yet she had made tea for him before dawn. His heart warmed.

"Did you sleep?" His fingers brushed hers as he took the cup.

"Not much." Her eyes were the color of the clouds hiding the dawn.

"I left in a hurry last night. I am sorry." He sipped the hot tea.

She shook her head. "MacNie said you rode to Invermorie with Donal and Aleck. It must have been important for you to do that."

If he wanted her in his life—Lord, he did—he owed her honesty. "Aleck said Geordie went looking for the whisky we had stored away. They found it missing, and then someone attacked Geordie."

She gasped. "Is he hurt?"

"He will recover. Mairi is taking care of him."

"Good. Was the attacker the same who took the whisky?"

"Possibly. We do not know, but I mean to find out."

She nodded, thoughtful, brow tucked in concern. God, he thought, she was so lovely, standing here in the privacy of his bedroom as if it was no breach of protocol. As if she belonged here, a natural part of his life.

"You will go out again?" she asked.

"It must be found." Taking a deeper sip, revived, he set down the cup.

"This is Friday," she reminded him. "Corbie will be here later."

The name sullied the air. "Ah. So he will."

She was butterflying her fingers in that way she had, delicate fingers weaving. He realized she had not done it lately—she had been more certain. But with Corbie's imminent arrival, her anxiousness had returned.

For that reason alone, he had a grudge to settle with Corbie.

"Corbie will want to know that we have done what we promised. We have very little time left."

"To ensure the gentleman passes muster?" he drawled.

"To be together." She stepped toward him.

He opened his arms, pulling her close, wrapping her in warmth better than any voluminous gown could do. Pressing his cheek to her hair, he held her. Just that.

But when she lifted her head, he sensed the invitation, touched his lips to hers gently at first—*you are safe*, he wanted to say, but conveyed it in kisses, in his arms about her. *You are loved.* His body pulsed, his soul surged. *So loved.*

Then she looped her arms around his neck with a little soft cry, pressing close, matching kisses with fervor, inviting, exploring. Morning thunder boomed beyond the window and a fresh torrent of rain drove against the glass panes. Ronan felt as if a storm might break within him, yet still, he held back.

"I was going to leave a note," she whispered against his lips. "With the tea. But you opened the door."

"I did," he murmured, kissing the corner of her lip, her cheek. "What would you have said?"

"Dearest Ronan, here is your tea," she said.

He chuckled. "Dearest girl"—he traced his lips along the delicate curl of her ear—"thank you for the tea."

"Welcome," but the breathy word was lost in a deeper kiss that shook him to his core. Her body pushed against his, and he shifted, else would have no secrets.

The squat little clock on the mantel chimed out four times. So late, yet too near dawn. The sound cleared the fog in his brain. He drew back.

"Ellison, this is not how you should be treated. Not"— she leaned to kiss him, and he surrendered, hungry, then gathered his wits—"this is not gentlemanly."

Drawing back, she looked up at him. "I suppose we could go resume the last of your lessons or take this little bit of time—to be alone."

"Lessons be damned." Snugging her slim waist in his hands, feeling her hips against him, so willing, he felt the pulse in her body and his.

She smiled and kissed him. "You need no lessons from me. You never did."

"Oh I did," he said, and took her mouth in a deep, rich bond of a kiss that plunged through him. "I learned—that I have a heart, after all."

"I know you do," she whispered, and sank a little in his arms with the next kiss.

Lifting her in his arms, he turned toward the bed. "Are you sure?"

"Oh aye. I believe we did claim to be betrothed."

"That we did," he breathed, and set her on the bed. As she shoved the coverlet aside, he leaned over her, keeping his weight on his hands as he kissed her.

Stormy darkness filled the room, the single candle burning like a bright star. Thunder rolled in the distance. Under the canopy of the stout old bed, rounded mattress sinking under his weight, he lay beside her, curving a hand along her jaw, then letting his fingers seek the buttons at the ruffled throat of the shapeless dressing gown. Her trembling fingers went ahead of his hands to find others, to open the folds. Just a nightrail beneath, he found, all gauze and lace, the veil of it sliding away beneath his hands and hers together.

She gave a soft laugh and pulled him down to recline in the cool, deep nest of pillows and linens beside her. He rolled to his side and she turned too, allowing him to sweep his hand down along her bared arm, the skin supple and warm as he kissed her, as she returned it, pulling him toward her, over her. His fingers found her breast, cupped, his breath catching as his heart pounded, his body swelling for her. He nuzzled her ear, the line of her jaw, her throat, sank down, found the pearling center of her breast, heard her gasp, her fingers slipping through the thickness of his hair, still damp from the wash, from the moments before she came back into his life in this profound way, in a way he had not expected, not dared dream.

He tasted her, felt her pull in a breath of deepest pleasure, and she arched to invite him further. She knew where this could lead—he knew that, and as her hands found the wooly fabric of his plaid, sliding upward, he knew she was not surprised, that she had more courage in the moment, helping him breach and break whatever was reserved and formal between them. Love and trust would melt barriers.

Sliding a hand along the smoothness of her thigh, the light shift gathering like flower petals under his hand, he shaped her hip, followed the sweet curve of her abdomen, the delicate mound that made her gasp anew against his lips on hers. Every part of her was exquisite, warm, welcoming, soft and slippery as his fingertips found her, rocked her, took her little cries into his lips, her breath and his breath, in and out again. Then her fingers seeking, shaping him, deft, then softly, then bold again, until he pulsed for her. His body echoed his heart in wanting, yearning. The sweet power of her touch shuddered through him.

In his hands, she was soft, golden, lush, all grace and satin where he was taut and hard with deepening need. Her touch had mischief in it, easing him along just as he eased her, until he could hold back no longer. Now the thunder he felt was the pounding of his heart and hers together.

Breaths, and rest, and too soon she rose, kissed him, and whispered something. Thanks? Love? He heard himself murmur in answer. *Love*, he said. Fatigue swamped him and truth prevailed. He could not hold up falseness like a curtain, a barrier, any longer.

"*Tha gaol agam ort,*" he murmured in Gaelic. My love is upon you; I love you.

"*Mo graidh,*" she whispered. My love.

Before the door closed behind her, he slept.

Long into the day, when she finally saw him, her heart nearly bounded out of her breast as she walked down the front corridor and he stepped out of the main library. She had hoped to be casual and graceful upon seeing him, but a hot blush spilled into her cheeks and she stopped, suddenly wondering what to say.

"You—have been gone nearly all day," she said awkwardly.

"Riding out with Donal." He gave her a crooked, wicked smile. "Come here," and he took her hand, pulling her into the library, shutting the door.

"It is nearly time for tea." She could not hide her smile. "Come to the parlor. You must be hungry."

"Not for food. Come here." He pulled her to him and leaned down to kiss her with a tenderness that melted through her. Hooking a finger under her chin, he smiled, set her hand on his shoulder, and placed a hand at her waist. "Miss Graham, would you care to dance?"

She laughed. "I thought we were done with lessons."

"We still have the afternoon to practice . . . whatever you would like to practice." He swayed with her, turned her about.

"There is not much time. Though Sorcha is resting, Mrs. Barrow is making tea, and the maids are busy getting our things ready."

"For Edinburgh?" He stopped.

"For the dance and supper at Duncraig. And MacNie has gone to Kinross."

"I did not need a reminder." He stepped forward and she moved back and to the side, turning with him in the pattern they both knew. He spun her in a half circle between the library table and soaring bookshelves, the hem of her gown filling out as she turned. She laughed with dizziness and delight.

"So you learned the waltz in London? Did you meet the king there? I would not be surprised, you with all your secrets."

"Never met him. I was only there a week before I went to India." He twirled her, pulled her close, and pressed his cheek to her head.

She tilted back to look at him as they whirled toward the end of the long table and back again. No music, just a natural rhythm of step and breath and agreement, as if they had done this often. "There is so much I do not know about you."

"You know more than most."

"With no time to learn more." As he slowed, she rested her head on his shoulder, feeling his strength as they shared the swaying movement.

"We are not done, my girl," he said. He tipped her chin up. "It is just beginning."

"I wish it was so. Too many secrets. But truth will out. I feel I should confess."

"You what?"

"What would you say if my secret made you disappointed in me?"

"You, my dear, are a guileless and lovely creature. Whatever you may have done in the past would not worry me."

"You might think otherwise."

"Who am I to judge? Listen." Serious, he met her gaze. "I know your innocence and your naivete—aye—and how easily you trust people. I know your temper and your backbone and your dream of writing. I think you understand far more about life and love and loyalty at your age than many in a lifetime. You are delicate, you are strong-willed, and you are not perfect. I would not want you to be. And I do not need anything more to know how I feel about you."

"But if there was something to forgive—"

"I am sure you did whatever you had to do. Lass, you have been living like a mouse in your father's home, meek, obedient, pleasing others instead of yourself. You were married once and widowed. You have been protecting yourself. I see that. But it is past. I have seen you changing and growing stronger each day."

"Because of you."

"Then we are in each other's debt. You do not need anyone's forgiveness. Least of all mine."

"But—do listen. I want you to know. My father never approved of Colin Leslie," she said. "He was a poet, the son of a viscount whose title was not heritable. He had little money of his own but for a house and some valuables. My father thought him a useless lad. But Colin was a good man, intelligent and kind. Mr. Corbie was very disapproving too, told me it would all come to naught and I was foolish and could have married a man far more worthy."

"He wanted you for himself. Go on," Ronan said. He let go of her to lean against the library table, folding his arms, listening.

"Only Lady Strathniven liked Colin though she was convinced I would be unhappy someday. But I loved him, or thought I did. I wanted to be in love, I think. And so we eloped."

He waited, said nothing.

"It caused a terrible rift, embarrassed my father, nearly cost him his reputation, or so he said. He said my mother—" She paused.

"You rarely mention her. What did she think?"

"She was gone long before then. Papa made it clear that Mother would have been sick about it. But she would have approved of choosing love over conflict. After the wedding, Papa did not speak to me for the longest time. And then Colin died," she said. "An accident—he fell from his horse when out riding with friends. Reckless, he could be, but all in good spirits and fun. The shock of it was awful. My father was kind then, insisted I come back to his house."

"You were living in Leslie's house then?"

She nodded. "So I moved back home. But Papa told me I must never take such a risk again, must do only what was proper and appropriate—what pleased him and society, you see. Sewing, music, drawing, reading. No visitors or outings. No poetry. A widow in mourning. For my health and happiness, he said. For my safety."

"For his peace of mind."

"He cares, in his way. And I felt guilty for causing him more unhappiness. He changed so after Mama's death. I wanted him to—well, love me again, I suppose." She shrugged.

"You deserved understanding. Forgiveness from parent to child."

"What Papa gives are lectures. He feels it is his duty. Lessons in life and rules in the house will improve me, more so than my sisters."

He gave a wry huff. "Lessons! I have not heard much about your sisters, but later for that. Ellison, you do not need forgiveness from me—or anyone. Perhaps you need to forgive yourself. Though your father sounds an unfeeling fellow."

"He was not always like that. And Mr. Corbie echoes what my father does."

"As for Corbie, what you do is not his business."

"Papa wants me to marry Mr. Corbie because he will go far in the Scottish government one day and is willing to accept my past behavior. Lady Strathniven would not object, I think, since he is her heir."

"Willing to accept?" He shook his head. "Likely Lady Strathniven realizes that Corbie must marry a woman with common sense and a good heart because he does not possess those himself. But it is too late now."

"Too late?" She frowned, puzzled.

"Too late for Mr. Corbie. You could never marry such a cold fish. Besides, I hear you are betrothed to another." He held out his hands. A welcome. A haven.

With a little sob, she ran to him, felt his arms encircle her. He held her and kissed the top of her head. Closing her eyes, she took in the feeling.

"Ronan MacGregor, I think I love you," she said on impulse. "Just weeks, I know, but I feel sure of it." Her heart pounded. She held her breath, waiting. Hoping.

He kissed her brow. "And I love you, Ellison Graham. I am just beginning to see how much. Keep your secrets. I am not one to judge." He tilted her face, kissed her. "Here is a secret of mine—I dread the day I meet the king. The crowds and the attention, even the honor, hold no appeal for me."

"I dread it too, because it could be the last day we ever see each other."

"It may not be—I cannot say why just yet. You must trust me."

"I do," she said, as it welled up in her. "I do not care if you are a lord, a laird, a farmer, a scoundrel. I love you as you are. If I did not see you again, I would search for you. Wait for you."

"If anything happened, I would find a way back." He kissed her.

"Ronan," she whispered. "I know I can be an idealist, a romantic thinker. But this is no fairytale, between us. It is far more. We found each other for a reason. We want the same in life."

He touched her cheek. "Love and freedom."

She nodded. "Freedom to love who we want, do what we want."

"We may have to fight for it, lass. I have matters to resolve as yet."

"As do I. And so we will."

"The sunset today is brilliant," Sorcha said, looking out the window of the parlor later that evening. "All rose gold and purple. It makes me long to paint. But I left my watercolors at Duncraig."

"You can fetch your painting things when we go there on Saturday," Ellison said. "Unless you decide to stay with your Mama."

"My lady aunt says I can come back with her, and you. Mama will be at Duncraig until September at least."

Ronan listened, sparing a glance for the sunset but watching in the distance where he could just see the road curve up from Kinross. Ben

MacNie would be returning soon with Corbie after meeting the Edinburgh coach.

He fisted a hand at the thought and glanced at Ellison, who sat now with Sorcha, talking about plans for the party. Balor sat with them, content as his mistress stroked his head.

"The flowers will be beautiful after all this rain. My mother has a knack for flower arrangements. You will see. This time tomorrow we will be dancing!"

"Yes," Ellison agreed. "I hope the fiddler plays some of my favorite Scottish tunes, especially Strathspeys and reels."

"And the waltz—do you think we will have that?"

"Unlikely at a country dance, dear."

"Lord Darrach, have you danced the waltz?" Sorcha asked.

"I have. But I am partial to the tunes usually played at a cèilidh.'" He turned away from the window to see Sorcha standing, grasping her skirt as she spun about, humming, her voice still raspy from her cold. Ellison laughed, and as Sorcha sidestepped, she set the dog aside and stood to clasp hands with her friend. The girls whirled lightly, skirts belling out like flowers.

Ronan smiled to see it. When the dog leaped and hopped about, barking as if to join them, he laughed outright. As they spun past Ronan, Sorcha held out a hand.

"Don't be a curmudgeon, Darrach," she said.

He joined hands with them, not quite sharing the elation, but willing enough for a moment. He chuckled—never in his life had he done anything similar. The spontaneous joy of two lightsome girls and an impish dog were new to him.

Ellison stumbled over the little terrier underfoot, and Ronan caught her arm. She looped her arms about his neck and he swirled her around as Sorcha picked up Balor to do the same, laughing like silver chimes.

On the last turnabout, Ronan stopped, seeing a figure in the doorway.

∼

"Mr. Corbie!" Ellison stepped hastily away from Ronan's arms. Heart pounding from the dancing and laughter, she went silent—while beside her, Ronan turned icy still. Balor tensed, feet planted, barking in an irritated rhythm.

"Cousin Adam!" Sorcha went to the door, taking Corbie's arm, drawing him into the parlor, unaware of the tension. "We were expecting you. Have you met Lord Darrach?"

"Miss Ellison. Mr. MacGregor." Corbie nodded a greeting as Balor continued to bark, trotting forward to stare down the newcomer.

"Balor, here," Ellison said; after a moment, the dog reluctantly came to her.

"MacGregor? You must mean Darrach," Sorcha said pleasantly.

"Hmph." Corbie looked tight-lipped and tired. Ellison almost felt sorry for him; his dour presence had stifled a sort of merriment he could not even comprehend.

"Hello, Mr. Corbie," she said. "I hope you had a pleasant journey."

"Not particularly." As he joined Sorcha on the narrow sofa, Ellison took a wing chair and Ronan stood beside her. "MacNie kept me waiting while he finished a pint in the tavern. Unbelievable that I should wait for a servant. What exactly is going on?" He looked sternly at them. "Cat's away, mice will play?"

"We were practicing dancing," Sorcha said. "You are here in time to join us."

"After riding in a coach for hours, I am not in a mood for dancing."

"I meant you can join us tomorrow for my mother's cèilidh at Duncraig," Sorcha said, her joyful mood subdued.

"I am aware. Our lady aunt sent an invitation to Sir Hector, but he is too busy to attend. However, it seemed a good time for me to come up. Other matters require my attention here." He looked pointedly at Ellison, though he did not seem able to meet Ronan's steady, searing gaze. "We should discuss what has been going on at Strathniven."

"Going on?" Sorcha looked bewildered. "We have been enjoying the summer and preparing for the royal visit. We are practicing for introductions and such, and looking forward to tomorrow's party."

"I pray it is as simple as that, Cousin Sorcha. Just now, I must rest. Have I missed supper?"

"We had a light supper a while ago, as we were uncertain when you would arrive," Ellison answered. Mrs. Barrow will see that a tray is sent to your room. She has prepared your usual room."

"Good. It has been a long day. Traveling up here took far longer due to the unusual traffic on the roads—crowds at every stop along the way. And we must return to Edinburgh almost immediately. Your father wants to see you."

"I thought we had more time," she blurted, glancing up at Ronan. He stood, resting an arm on the high back of her chair. "And Lord Darrach?"

"Expected as well. We will arrange a separate escort."

"No need. I will find my way there," Ronan said flatly.

"Why the hurry, Cousin? I had the impression we would all travel to the city together," Sorcha said. "First, though, we have tomorrow's dance at Duncraig. Oh, dear, it is late! We should all get some extra rest. Good night," she said to each, as she left the room.

"Mr. Corbie," Ellison said then. "I plan to travel south with Lady Strathniven when she is ready. I will not be returning to Edinburgh with you. I am sorry if you thought so."

"Miss Ellison, Sir Hector is unhappy that my lady aunt left you unchaperoned."

She lifted her chin. "Sorcha has been my constant companion since Lady Strathniven went to help her sister."

"Sorcha's mother must be healthy enough now, since she is hosting a dance. A pity my aunt did not keep her promise." He looked pointedly at Ronan.

Ellison could not see Ronan's reaction, but his silence was a clear response.

"You must remember, Miss Ellison, that your father's reputation can rise and fall on the behavior of his family, and this is an especially crucial time. We will discuss that later, you and I—and MacGregor," he added.

"You mean Lord Darrach," she said. Ronan's silence began to feel ominous.

"Darrach! I heard the rumor—Sir Evan's request to the courts came to our office for review. The law of succession is not clear in this case, and with the lack of a will, we disagree with granting the title and estate to MacGregor."

"'We?'" Ellison repeated. "That is presumptuous."

"I share your father's considered opinion."

"Yet you would present him as Darrach to the king without batting an eye."

Corbie's nostrils flared. "That is different. Temporarily necessary."

"For whom?" she asked.

"We all know the answer to that." Ronan spoke at last. "How fortunate that the recent decision about the Darrach estate eliminates your risk, Mr. Corbie."

"Even so, we are not prepared to accept the decision as official."

"Traditionally, the law of intestate succession in Scotland," Ronan said, "implies the equal division of goods among a spouse, children, or siblings. But Darrach had no clear inheritors. I am the nearest male relative, so the goods and lands can come to me legally. And will."

"Except that the nearest male relative is a criminal."

"Never convicted, therefore innocent of charges unless proven otherwise. But a peerage title hangs in the balance, not just an estate, with this case. The court deferred the matter to the clan chief, as is their prerogative. He recommended in my favor. And," he went on, "neither Sir Hector's opinion nor yours, sir, holds sway."

Corbie gave a scoffing laugh. "Why the legal parlance? Pretending to be a lawyer as well as a peer now?"

"I am a lawyer," Ronan said calmly, as Corbie gaped at him.

"Did no one mention?" Ellison gave Corbie a cool smile. "He happens to be a very fine lawyer." The smug satisfaction she felt seemed almost wicked.

"That cannot be. He is nothing but a small laird, a smuggling thief, and an imposter taking advantage of us."

"Mr. Corbie," Ronan said bluntly, "I am an advocate, in point of fact."

"Outrageous! You should have said so."

"You never asked," he drawled.

"How does an advocate end up in a dungeon, then?"

"A question I intend to resolve," Ronan said.

"I am going to bed," Corbie snapped, and turned on his heel for the door.

Standing as he left, Ellison faced Ronan, who tipped a brow at her. "A very fine lawyer?" He smiled. "How do you know?"

"I have every faith in the incomparable Lord Darrach."

"Miss Graham," he said, leaning to kiss her brow, her cheek, then her lips, so that her knees nearly gave way. "Best leave me before I think of something two people could do in this room now that they are alone."

She sighed. "I cannot feel alone anywhere now that that man is here."

"Aye so. Off with you, lass. Tomorrow will be a busy day indeed."

CHAPTER 21

*A*s the black Strathniven barouche followed the road northeast to Duncraig, Ellison closed her eyes, listening as Sorcha and Adam Corbie talked quietly about the weather, the landscape, the dance to come. An hour earlier, she had waved from the coach window as Ronan, mounted on a bay stallion, rode out with Donal, both wearing wrapped plaids in the dark red and forest green tartan favored by the MacGregors. She felt warm pride seeing uncle and nephew so handsome, with the singular dignity of Highlanders in full kit. They had promised to arrive at Duncraig later, planning to go to the distillery first. She knew Ronan had no desire to be enclosed in a carriage for the afternoon with Corbie, nor could she blame him.

"Lord Darrach knows the dance begins at seven o'clock?" Sorcha asked.

"He does. He and Donal are visiting kin first."

"Kin? Donal is his valet," Corbie said.

"And Darrach's nephew."

Corbie flapped a hand in exasperation. "There is too much we do not know about the man."

"You do not seem to like him, Cousin Adam," Sorcha said. "But perhaps you have not had a chance to get acquainted. He is such a congenial gentleman and so handsome. Mama is very pleased he will be there this evening. Ladies will be very pleased to meet him, too, I think."

"Indeed? I hope you have not become infatuated, Miss Ellison," he murmured.

Silent, she turned her head to watch a sunny stretch of moorland slip past.

"Even if Elly is not infatuated, I am," Sorcha said brightly.

Duncraig House was a fairytale manor of towers and gardens, a pretty sight against a hillside of tall pines as Ronan and Donal arrived at twilight. As a stable boy led their horses away, they walked toward the entrance as a few other guests climbed the steps to the entrance. The windows twinkled with golden light and fiddle music drifted outward in the purply dusk.

Donal slowed, and Ronan sensed the lad's hesitation. "You are as welcome here as anyone, Donal. Everyone is welcome at a cèilidh."

"I am a stable boy," he said, glancing over his shoulder. "And a valet."

"Aye well, there is something you should know. You may hear it this evening." He stopped, pulling Donal aside. "I have been named Viscount Darrach after all."

Gaping in surprise, Donal began to whoop, but stifled it. "Is it so? Already!"

"Sir Evan decided this week. That makes you the nephew of a viscount. And his heir."

"His what!"

"I have no wife or offspring, so you are my heir. I will put it in writing as soon as the courts confirm the title and inheritance."

"But you will marry one day and have children. One of them would have Darrach."

"Perhaps. None of us know what the future will bring." His was still wildly uncertain—but as soon as all came clear, he meant to ask Ellison to marry him; he could imagine no other course in life now. "But I will secure a good inheritance for you. Rest assured of it. You will have education and an income in addition to intelligence and a handsome face, for luckily you favor your mother."

"I am honored, sir. But we are not blood kin."

"You were my brother's stepson. That makes you my kin. Come ahead." He patted Donal's shoulder and walked with him toward open doors, warm lights, merriment, and the promise that someone waited for him.

The vast hall twinkled with lights and reflections from lamps, candles, crystal, and glass. Beneath a high ceiling and walls festooned in swaths of greenery and summer flowers, Ellison tapped her feet to the music, smiling at the women standing near her—Sorcha, Lady Strathniven, and Sorcha's mother Mrs. Beaton. The room was filled with guests clustered about: women in bright pretty frocks, men in plaids or coats and trews—a busy, colorful crowd talking and swaying to the fiddle music wafting through the room. But she had not seen Ronan among them.

The dancing had not begun yet, though two fiddlers stood on a platform playing tunes. Tapping her foot, she glanced around again for Ronan and Donal—and turned away quickly, too late to avoid Adam Corbie's eye as he approached.

"Miss Ellison, a moment, please. I must speak with you," he murmured.

"Perhaps this is not the time, sir," she said in a cool tone.

"I will not keep you. I have a message from your father but have not had the privacy to share it. Have you seen the terrace? Very pretty. Let me show you."

Overhearing, Lady Strathniven waved toward them. "Go with Adam, my dear, it sounds important. Come find us later."

Dread spinning in her center, Ellison walked away as Corbie guided her through the crowd toward the library, a beautiful room of soaring bookshelves and patterned carpets. She wanted to linger there, but he took her arm to lead her to the French doors that led outside to a walled terrace lined with benches, potted trees, and effusions of red and yellow flowers.

She turned. "What is it?"

"Miss Ellison, I am very concerned," he said, "about you and MacGregor."

She bristled. "Is that why you brought me out here? Just know we have done what was expected. He is prepared to meet the king and will represent Scotland and Glenbrae admirably, just as Papa wanted."

He waved that away. "He fooled all of us, especially you, my dear. Apparently, he speaks English already to have such command. And now he claims to be heir to the Darrach title—and a lawyer as well. True or not, he kept a great deal hidden from us. He has taken advantage of your father, and, I fear, of you."

"What is important here is that my father can confidently sponsor him at the levee. What message did Papa send for me?"

"I can inform your father that I have seen some improvement. But," he said, stepping closer, "there is a greater concern."

She moved back. "What is that?"

"You are very taken with him, which is worrisome. You have had too much freedom at Strathniven and no protection from his influence."

"He has been only a gentleman."

"Are you certain? I hear he is moving illicit goods through the Highlands even as we're hosting him at our expense."

"He is arranging to send whisky to Edinburgh for the king at your request."

"I hear it is more than that. I fear you have been naïve and easily led. Thank God I am here to look after you."

"No need, sir. Go back to the city and tell Papa all is well. And remember that Lord Darrach is the one making you look good before the king. What was my father's message?" She suspected that he had none. "Are you quite finished, Mr. Corbie?"

"One more question." He leaned toward her, taking her gloved wrist in a tight grip. "You are keeping something from me. Have you gone entirely mad, Ellison?"

Stunned, she pulled against his hand. "What do you mean?"

"Betrothed to Ronan MacGregor? What possessed you?"

Hearing his name, Ronan turned to see Lady Strathniven beckoning. She stood with a lady who was her smaller version—surely Mrs. Beaton—and Sorcha was with them. Ellison was nowhere in sight, but would be near them somewhere, he thought.

"Darrach, there you are! Allow me to introduce my sister, Mrs. Harriet Beaton," she said, indicating the smaller woman. "Viscount Darrach, my dear."

"Madam, I am pleased to meet you. Thank you for the invitation. Miss Beaton, it is good to see you." Ronan smiled as Sorcha returned a sweet grin.

"Darrach, you'll want to know who else is here." Lady Strathniven pointed around the room in succession. "There is the Earl of Huntly and his lady, and just there is the Duke of Atholl. His duchess is somewhere nearby. I am sorry to say that Lady Elizabeth and Sir Evan Murray-MacGregor were unable to be here this evening. You know Darrach is cousin to the new chief of the MacGregors," she told her sister, while looking proud as a peacock.

Lady Strathniven continued to point out guests, rattling off familiar names, some he knew from the Scottish parliament, and other names he recognized—MacDonald of Clanranald, Glengarry, Stewart, MacIntosh, Fraser, and more. He was reluctant to be seen, but in the crowded room, might not be noticed. As fiddle music soared and chatter filled the room, he looked but did not see Ellison.

"We are fortunate to have so many guests here, Lord Darrach," Mrs. Beaton said. "Many came up to the Highlands for the summer, and most will be going down to Edinburgh for the celebrations. Will you be going south as well?"

"I will, madam. It is a nice gathering. May I ask if you have seen Miss Graham?"

"Ellison went with Cousin Adam to look at the terrace garden," Sorcha said. "Through the library past the entrance."

"Thank you." Nodding, he turned away as Lady Strathniven tapped his arm with her fan.

"Darrach, do wait. There is someone I want you to meet." She indicated Neill Pitlinnie, who stood in conversation with a few others.

Ronan froze. "We have met. Give him my compliments."

"He is a friend of my nephew as well," the lady went on. "He and Adam met in the Edinburgh High School. Boyhood friends, you see. So he treats us to his whisky free of charge. He is very good to us."

"He is," Ronan said. "My lady, I promised to find Miss Graham when I arrived."

"Do hurry, sir. The dancing will begin soon," Mrs. Beaton said. "The principals will be expected to dance first. The highest ranking," she clarified.

"That would be Atholl and his lady—and the Huntlys, too," Lady Strathniven said.

"You may dance too, my dear, as hostess. I will decline. You will need a partner. And a fourth couple is needed to create a foursome."

"I will ask my nephew to partner me. I believe he is in the garden just now. Darrach, would you agree to dance as the fourth peer with the principals? Perhaps Miss Graham would be your partner." He saw a twinkle in her eye.

"An honor, my lady. Let me fetch your nephew and Miss Graham." Inclining his head, he hurried away.

"Betrothal?" Ellison pulled against Corbie's hold, glancing at the house, its windows bright gold in the violet glaze of dusk. "What do you mean?"

"Do not deny it. I heard of it almost as soon as we arrived. Neill Pitlinnie told me the rumor. Does your father know?"

Her stomach sank. "I did not realize you were acquainted with Sir Neill."

"Of course, long before he brought whisky to Strathniven. I met him in school. He said he heard the news straight from you when he saw you and MacGregor out in the hills together. You were alone together near dark. Why?"

"We were out that day. It is not your concern."

"If you promised to marry that rogue, it is very much my concern as your father's representative and as a man who cares about you. Is it true? How foolish to fall for another rascal who will bring ruin to your family! Your father must be told."

"I will be the one to talk to Papa about this—all of this." She pulled against his grip again, but he held tight.

"So you did promise." He yanked her closer, so that she stubbed the toe of her slipper on a stone and nearly fell into him. "This will ruin your father. He is poised to become Lord Provost in the future."

"Lord Provost!"

"He is in position to take Lord Arbuthnot's place in a year or so. And the Crown may grant him a title and property for his assistance with the royal visit. But you would destroy everything." His grip was bruising.

"I would never do that." She tugged futilely. "Is it Papa you are concerned for, or yourself? Do not worry. You will get something from the Crown too, no doubt."

"MacGregor benefits from this more than anyone. Now he has coerced you."

"I was never coerced. He—"

"Loves you?" Laughing bitterly, Corbie let go for a moment. She stumbled and began to step away, but he pushed her backward toward the low garden wall until the stones struck hard at her waist. "Does he think marrying the daughter of the chief of the constabulary will keep him out of prison? You will have to be extricated from yet another disgrace. But this can be fixed easily. I have a plan."

"Another disgrace?" His cruel words felt like a visceral blow. She had brought scandal to her family once, but that was all in the past. "Extricate me? Did you—have aught to do with—" *With Colin's death.* She pinched her lips together to stop the words, the accusation. Dear God, she thought, was it possible?

"Now that MacGregor is smuggling goods again, we cannot risk a royal introduction. He will be arrested as soon as he reaches the city."

"But he did all you asked. He is innocent of charges, and his inheritance is legitimate."

"And you believe that, foolish girl." He shook his head in disdain. "You can save your father's reputation and your own." He moved closer, taking her arm again to press it between them. "Listen. This is how we will fix it. We will announce our engagement, you and I," he directed. "That will end rumors about you and MacGregor. He will soon be forgotten."

Dread and anxiousness rose like bile. "I would never marry you."

"Your father and my aunt have always hoped we would marry. The story will be that you were nearly compromised by a reprobate, and ran to me for help. So romantic, you see."

"I will not betray Darrach."

"If you want him safe, you will do this."

She felt cold all over. "You would harm him?"

"Not me. The law will do it. His guilty actions will bring a hanging for him and his friends. His lands will be lost. His kin will be evicted."

"No." She felt tears sting her eyes. "You would not—"

"I only want to help you, dear Ellison. You will see the sense in this." He relaxed his fierce hold to lift her hand to his lips to kiss it through her glove. Cringing, she stood still.

"No," she whispered.

"I could not stop your first wedding in time, but I can help you escape this situation. You will make your father proud, and you and I will be elevated in life when we become lord and lady of Strathniven."

"Strathniven! Is that why you want this?"

"You will not regret this."

Even if she agreed, she was sure Corbie would see Ronan suffer, ruining him, ruining their happiness. But if she refused, if she relied on her will and her love for Ronan, she could destroy what she loved most in the world.

But she could not betray Ronan. No matter the cost, she would not. He would expect better from her than Corbie wanted.

"You know this is the right thing to do." He pulled her to him and leaned to kiss her, but she angled away so that his lips smeared awkwardly over her cheek.

"No. I will not betray him for you."

"Is that your answer? A great risk, my dear."

"It is not—" From the corner of her eye, she saw movement as a tall shadow strode across the terrace, and the man reached out to shove Corbie aside.

"Leave her be," Ronan snarled.

"MacGregor!" Recovering his step, Corbie moved forward, changed his mind, and tugged at his coat sleeves. "How dare you interrupt a private conversation."

"Am I unwelcome, Miss Graham?" Ronan demanded. Setting a trembling hand above her lace-ruffled bodice, Ellison shook her head.

"Not at all. Thank you," she said breathlessly.

Taking her arm to bring her closer, Ronan faced Corbie. "The lady does not wish your company."

"This is not your concern. We were discussing a matter to do with her father."

"It did not look that way to me."

Ellison stood close beside Ronan, sensing his banked fury, yet feeling the steadiness in him at the same time. This man was all she could ever dream of, all she could ever want. She knew what she must do.

"Mr. Corbie wonders if the rumor of our betrothal is true," she said.

"Does he? Tell the man what we think about that rumor," Ronan said.

He was leaving it up to her. The very air was thick with tension between the two men, and she was about to add fuel to the fire. "It is true. I will marry Lord Darrach, if he is amenable."

"He is amenable," Ronan said, staring down at Corbie. Ellison felt the warmth of love spinning through her as he spoke. His resolve made her stronger, his composure taught her calmness. She squared her shoulders and stared at Corbie.

"My God, woman." Corbie stepped back. "You will regret this grave error. We will all come to disaster unless you make the right decision, Ellison."

Ronan took a step forward, but Ellison set a hand on his arm. "No," she urged. "Mr. Corbie, perhaps you should take the barouche back to Strathniven now. I will take another vehicle later."

"I will do better than that. I will go to Kinross and arrange to return to Edinburgh." Corbie looked at Ronan. "We gave you every privilege in return for a small favor. And you used all of us to your advantage. For what?"

"Nothing you could comprehend," Ronan said. "Get out or I will see you out." He pointed toward the doors as Corbie stomped past.

Breathing out, Ellison felt as if she trembled all over. Ronan took her hand.

"Lass?"

"I am fine." But her voice was faint. "Thank you. He is leaving."

"This is not over, I think," Ronan murmured, as Corbie crossed through the library and out into the crowd. "What did he want?"

She looked away. "Complaints about my poor judgment."

"Pay no attention. He is small-minded and wants something, though I am not sure what. He will soon be gone, but in Edinburgh, keep your distance from him."

"He is not dangerous, just frustrated that I will not obey him. He thinks I will ruin Papa's chances for honors from the Crown and the city. Ruin his chances too."

"Whatever annoys him, I do not trust him. Are you ready to go inside?"

Nodding, she walked beside him into the library. But she could not shake an awful sense of dread. If Ronan came to harm in Edinburgh, she would feel wholly responsible. Corbie's threats were not empty, but she would make light of it and talk to Corbie when he cooled his ardor. She dared not tell Ronan the whole of it. Not yet.

She did not want to lose the happiness she had begun to feel lately, as if her dreams were coming true—love, contentment, freedom. Corbie could ruin it all.

"Ronan." She paused in the middle of the silent, beautiful library. He looked down at her, attentive, patient, the man she loved dearly. "I cannot tell Lady Strathniven about this. What should we do?"

"Do? Why, Miss Graham," he murmured, "I think we should marry."

Her heart thumped, thrilled. "I want that. I do. But—" Though she had defied Corbie and then Ronan had sent him packing, she felt a lingering fear.

"But?" He leaned down and kissed her gently, drew back.

"I need to speak with Papa as soon as possible. I dread what Corbie will say."

"I will speak with Sir Hector as well. Likely Corbie will reach him first and try to poison the waters. We can undo that," he reassured her. "But for now, we will keep our news private. Let them wonder—is Miss Graham engaged? Is the fellow a rogue or a viscount?"

She smiled a little. "A frog or a prince?"

CHAPTER 22

Corbie had not left when they returned to the hall—and Lady Strathniven had already drawn him into the dance of the principals. Ronan brought Ellison into the obligatory Strathspey, the four couples stepping and swirling and nodding in turn, while Corbie clomped his way along and Lady Strathniven proved a lively if inelegant dancer, waving her arms and hopping with enthusiasm.

Ronan wanted to remove the fellow brusquely and utterly, but he danced with decorum, and then, seeing Ellison's graceful steps, her lightsome beauty, and then her returning smile, he felt love pull and burst within him. Corbie did not matter.

As the dance ended and the fiddlers struck up a fast reel, other couples took the floor, soon dancing, whirling, and laughing. Leading Ellison back into the fray, Ronan was determined to keep her swirling, merry, breathless, and happy.

"Have I told you," he murmured when they came together, hands joined in the set, "how lovely that blue gown is on you? It is not the usual gray you favor." The light blue-gray gown, a fine silky thing with lacy bits all around, made her perfect skin glow and her gray eyes shimmer like silver.

"I thought," she said, "it was time I put away mourning."

"Aye so." He whirled with her, separating to circle the next couple.

From the corner of his eye, he watched Corbie dancing with his aunt, then with Sorcha, then vanish into the crowd to reappear in conversation with a cluster of gentlemen. Ronan had to resist the urge to toss the fellow out on his arse.

Later, as he led Ellison into the supper room, he lost sight of the fellow again. He had little appetite, and she ate sparingly too, an hour quickly passing as guests ate, drank, chatted, then returned in twos and fours to the dancing.

He was glad to see Ellison glowing with happiness again, relieved to see she had moved past the unpleasant incident. Then he caught sight of Corbie standing in a shadowy corner in earnest conversation with Sir Neill Pitlinnie and a couple of bearded Highlanders in full dress. Corbie gestured emphatically, Pitlinnie shook his head, and the others hunched their shoulders and nodded.

What the devil was this? Ronan narrowed his eyes, left Ellison with her young cousin, and made his way across the room. A line of dancers crossed his path, so that he paused to wait—and saw that the men, including Corbie, had gone elsewhere. Feeling distinct unease, he went toward the door, thinking to go outside to look.

"Lord Darrach!" Hearing Sorcha's voice, he turned to see her beckon with happy enthusiasm. She stood with a tall, slender gentleman who looked deucedly familiar. Ronan had seen him in Parliament House. On a bench. In a wig and robes.

His heart sank. As Sorcha waved again, Ronan approached reluctantly.

"Darrach, let me introduce you to my brother, Lord Archibald Beaton."

"Judge Beaton," the man amended, holding out a hand. "Pleased to meet you."

Archie Beaton. Of course. Ronan had walked past him often enough in the halls of the Scottish parliament and had argued more than one case before his bench.

Ronan tipped his head. "Judge Beaton, a pleasure."

"I was just saying how familiar you look, sir, and then it occurred to me—the law! John MacGregor! He is one of our most capable advocates, Sorcha my dear. And to find you are now Viscount Darrach, by God! Excellent."

Nothing for it but to own it, despite Sorcha's surprised stare. "Thank you, sir. I am occasionally in Edinburgh, though generally, I work in Perth."

"Ah, that explains why I have not seen you lately," Beaton said, though his eyes narrowed in curious assessment. Archie Beaton was no fool. Possibly he knew more about John Ronan MacGregor than might be comfortable in conversation and chose discretion.

Ronan turned as Ellison joined them to greet Sorcha and her brother, whom she already knew. She stood beside Ronan, not so close as to capture attention, but enough that he felt buoyed up. And close enough— given their dances and shared supper—that he knew some might talk. So be it.

"I hear you are a cousin of the new chief of the MacGregors," Beaton said.

"Sir Evan Murray-MacGregor, aye."

"I heard something about the Darrach inheritance. You are fortunate in your kinsmen, sir. That sort of thing does not happen often."

"Fortunate indeed." He sensed Ellison beside him, silent and supportive.

"Sir Evan wrote Mama to say he regretted missing her supper dance," Sorcha said, "and that he and his lady hope to see everyone in the city for the festivities."

"Sir Evan owes his life to Darrach," Beaton told the ladies. "Saved his life in India. Word got around about it, sir. Your cousin suffered terrible injuries. But Darrach pulled him from the fray in a brutal ambush. He is hearty today because of your action, sir."

"Many of us fought at his back that day. He was the soul of courage," Ronan said. He hated speaking of it. "His own brother was lost in the battle. We did all we could to help each other survive that day."

"Must have been hellish." Beaton shook his head. "But Sir Evan appreciates what he owes you. His family, indeed your clan, are in your debt."

Ronan was aware of Sorcha and Ellison listening intently. Though Ellison knew little of this part of his life, he felt her compassion, warm as a blanket around him.

"Thank you, my lord," he told Beaton.

"Anything you need, sir. Anything at all," Beaton said gruffly. "And ah, Miss Graham, I nearly forgot. I have some news for you. I spoke with Mr. Smithson recently, who had some information from his associate Mr. Cameron. Regarding a house—Castle Street, I think?"

She raised her brows in surprise. "North Castle, yes. The case came to you?"

"Yes. The previous tenants are gone," he said. "Another tenant has applied and agreed to a generous sum. Rental fees are exorbitant in Edinburgh this summer, fortunately for you. Mr. Smithson will have papers for you to sign as landlady."

"Thank you! That is a relief. It is a lovely house. I hope the new tenants will be happy there." As she spoke, Lady Strathniven approached, hearing what was said.

"Your house is resolved? Wonderful! It is in a very desirable location, and not far from my own house in town," she told the others.

Ellison thanked the judge again, but Beaton shook his head.

"Nonsense, we are friends. Oh, there is Huntly. I must speak with him about plans for the procession. We are both on Sir Walter's Celtic committee, you know. He is a grand fellow, the best. But he has created an enormous amount of work for a few willing friends. Please excuse me." Judge Beaton smiled and departed.

"Ellison, I am so glad you have your house back—and a paying tenant so soon! Excellent! And oh my, Darrach," Lady Strathniven turned to Ronan. "What is this about Sir Evan? I had no idea!"

"He is humble about it and would not have told us himself, my lady." Ellison looked up at him, her eyes limpid gray, searching. Someday he would tell her all of it and more, but that could wait.

Then it occurred to him, standing with these three women, that he owed a truth to all of them, not just Ellison.

"Lady Strathniven," he said, "and Miss Beaton. My lady has been away, and I have not yet found a chance to tell you some news. Miss Graham knows already. I do hope you have not heard it elsewhere." He wondered if Corbie had told his aunt, but her blithe look reassured him. "I am to be confirmed as Lord Darrach."

"Truly?" Lady Strathniven asked, raising her brows. "How wonderful!"

"I thought it was a fact already." Sorcha looked bewildered.

"A little question of legalities, dear," Ellison said.

"Darrach, I am so very pleased," Lady Strathniven said, "for all of us!"

"Aye," he murmured, glancing at Ellison. "All of us."

She was not sure how she would get home to Strathniven.

Ellison stood outside as a line of carriages crawled past Duncraig's entrance and down the graveled drive to the road. Drawing her paisley shawl closer in the chill of the summer night, she searched for Sorcha or Lady Strathniven among the guests waiting for transportation. The viscountess had gone off to ask her sister if they could borrow a carriage for their return—Corbie had taken the Strathniven barouche after all. The viscountess had been miffed, as he had taken MacNie too.

Stifling a yawn, she felt weary to her bones, almost swaying on her feet. All she wanted was to crawl into bed—and find a chance to be alone with Ronan before they all departed in a flurry for Edinburgh.

Ronan had left as well, as he and Donal had ridden to Duncraig and would head out on horseback to return to Strathniven. He mentioned intending to follow Corbie to make sure the fellow headed to Kinross as he had promised.

"But if you would feel better, I will follow your carriage," he had offered.

She had refused, shaking her head. "We are waiting for a Duncraig vehicle and driver, so we would only slow you down." Nodding, he had touched her arm in a gentle way before leaving to find his horse in all the commotion.

Now she turned, hearing Sorcha call. "Mama wants us to stay the night," she said. "She asked the factor to find a carriage, but so far they are all in use. My lady aunt has agreed too. She sent me out to ask if you would stay, or leave if a carriage can be found. It seems you would have to wait for one."

Immediately Ellison thought of Ronan, who would worry if she did not return to Strathniven that night. "I would rather go back, so I will wait," she said. "I appreciate the invitation, and I hope you do not mind if I want to go home. I am exhausted. It was a lovely evening," she added quickly. "And Lord Darrach already left with Donal on horseback. They would wonder what became of us."

"Very well. Let me see what can be found for you." Sorcha hurried away.

Gathering her shawl around her, Ellison waited, glancing up at the stars scattered across the dark sky. Hearing a step behind her, she turned.

"Miss Graham." Sir Neill Pitlinnie nodded his head. "I overheard your conversation. Mr. Corbie took your carriage. Very unfortunate. I wonder if I could offer mine to you."

Startled, she shook her head. He was not one she wanted to speak to, and she sidled away. "Thank you, but I will stay the night here if there is no Duncraig vehicle free to take me back."

"You would not be riding with me. I will loan you my barouche and driver. I intend to ride back with a friend. I brought a horse as well, in case my friends needed transportation."

"No thank you, sir." Wishing he would go away, she looked about for Sorcha.

"I feel I owe it to you, Miss Graham. We did not meet under the best of circumstances. I was—perhaps under the influence of my own drink, I confess. And I may have put you in a difficult position by sharing news that was not mine to tell. With my congratulations and my apologies, allow me to provide a carriage and driver to make up for it."

She had not expected that. But perhaps he had second thoughts about his behavior. Mairi Brodie had mentioned that he could be a charming gentleman.

And she was so very tired. "That is kind," she said. "I do want to go home."

"Here is my driver," he said. "Go on. I will tell Lady Strathniven your plans."

The carriage pulled up, a sleek black barouche with lovely cushioned seats of red velvet. She relented, seeing that comfort.

"Strathniven," Pitlinnie told the driver. He opened the door and assisted her inside, then closed it firmly. "Miss Graham, I hope you will forgive me. Do enjoy your journey home."

"Thank you for the loan of your carriage. I do appreciate it." Sinking on the cushioned bench, she leaned back as the carriage lumbered away toward the road. Lulled by the swaying motion in the dark, she soon felt sleepy.

Sometime later, she woke, realizing she had slept deeply. The rocking motion of the carriage had stopped. Strathniven already? Gathering her shawl, she felt the vehicle lurch as the driver dismounted and came around to open the door.

"Miss," he said, "out the coach."

"Sir?" She began to exit, expecting his hand. Instead, he grabbed her and pulled her outside. Another man stood behind him. "I do not understand—"

"Quiet!" The driver grabbed her arm, then dragged her forward. The second man pulled her hands behind her and tied a prickly rope around her wrists.

"Ow! What are you doing? Where are we?" Panicking, pulling away even as the driver held her in place, she looked around in the darkness. She did not see Strathniven House or any structure—just a wide stretch of bleak, dark moorland with hills to one side and a long gleam of dark water in another direction. The stocky silhouette of a tower thrust up from the bankside.

"Come along. And dinna try to get away." The bearded man dragged her forward. Shoved, she fell to her knees in mucky grass and was hauled to her feet.

Taking a breath, she screamed with all the fervor she could muster, hearing the sound travel over moor and water. Then a brutish hand clapped over her mouth.

"Stop it," one man growled. The driver grabbed her shawl and she heard a ripping sound, then a wad of cloth was forcibly tied around her jaw to gag her.

"Now she'll be quiet," he grunted. "Come along. 'Tisna far to walk. I wouldna drag a wee lassie aboot, but it canna be helped this night. Come."

She could only focus on walking ahead and keeping her balance as they dragged her between them along the upper edge of the bank toward the tower.

Where were they? In the purple half-darkness of the summer night, she saw a small island in the water, then realized they walked along the shore of Loch Brae. Ahead, just yards away now, rose the massive ruin of the old tower, the ancient broch she had wanted to visit.

Pitlinnie, she thought. He had lured her into the coach and sent her here deliberately. But why?

"What was that?" Halting his horse, Donal looked at Ronan. "Did you hear it?"

"I did." Ronan stopped as well, looking about, frowning. The oddly familiar sound had sent a chill down his spine.

"Fox, most like. They shriek something fierce." Donal gathered the reins again.

"Aye," Ronan said, though instinct told him that was no fox. He looked around through the darkness. "I saw a coach heading that direction a while ago. Strange."

"I saw too, but many coaches left Duncraig tonight in various directions."

"Aye. But this one took a drover's track and went out where there are few houses or villages, not the way a carriage would usually take."

The uneasy feeling would not leave him. Riding on, he stopped once more. Donal did the same. "What is it?" the lad asked.

"That way," Ronan said, "lies the Lealtie Burn, Loch Brae, and the old tower. Nothing more for miles."

"Free traders? Pitlinnie's men?"

"I saw Pitlinnie and his lot come through this way one night, and I have been wondering why. The only thing out here is—" A thought flashed like a falling star. "That old broch. Have you been there recently?"

"Not for years. Too dangerous. The walls are collapsing. No one goes there." Donal whistled low. "And no one goes there."

"Exactly. I wonder if we might find whisky hidden there. Come ahead, lad."

Why had he not thought of it before? The old broch. Of course. Logic said the place was ruinous, treacherous. But that might not be a deterrent for some.

They were gone.

Tilting her head in the darkness, hands bound behind her, Ellison waited interminable moments for the men's voices to fade as they walked away from the tower back to the carriage they had left on the moor. The silence inside the old broch felt safer now that she heard only the shush of wind through trees, midnight birdsong, and nearby, the soft lapping of water. She exhaled, breathed, exhaled.

Uncertain how much time had passed, she knew she had to escape before they returned. Struggling against the dry, choking grip of the gag, she pulled at the rope behind her binding her wrists. Her hair shook down in loose tendrils, obscuring her vision. There had to be a way to get free of the ropes; having her hands behind her threw her off balance, and this place was a precarious ruin. If she could find her way out of the broch and back to the road, she could get to Strathniven and Ronan.

Tugging at the rope, she made her way carefully across the floor of the broch, earth and grasses scattered with broken stones; the smell of moss and earth and stone was strong in her nostrils. Somewhere above, night air blew through a gap. Looking up, she could see the night sky, a vast canopy sprinkled with stars.

The ancient tower was a massive stone cylinder wider at the base and open to the sky at the top, a fortified keep impenetrable in its day. She had read about these old Celtic structures—typically the rooms were constructed inside wide hollow walls in a honeycomb of chambers.

But why would they bring her here? Because no one would find her, she realized. Moving along cautiously, she searched for the entrance while also looking for some way to break through her bonds. Frowning as she went, she tried to recall what the men had said, looking for something to help clarify why she was here.

A scrap of conversation came back to her. "He should be here," one of her captors had said to the other. "Shouldhae met us by now."

"He will be here. He wants this, is willing to pay."

"And the other one?"

"Eh, if he finds the place, pity him for stepping into a trap."

She froze with dread. Did they mean Ronan might be lured here, as she was? Had Pitlinnie planned this? She had to get free, find Ronan, and warn him away.

More of their chatting came back to her. "Leave the lass here. We canna wait longer. We must look for him. Likely got lost, the fool."

"Aye. But keep her bound. She will go nowhere. This will all be done soon, and gold in our pockets."

"Aye, but we'd earn more if we took what's hidden here, hey." The other had laughed as they walked away, voices fading.

Moving again, she bumped into something hard and heard the dull thunk of wood rather than stone. In the darkness, she saw a wooden chest. Where the wood had split along one edge, a large nail stuck out.

She sat, maneuvering until the rope caught on the nail. Shifting, rocking, she sawed the rope against the metal. After a while, shoulders aching, she nearly gave up—but felt the fibers weaken a little. Pulling, tugging, she kept at it.

The chest was heavy, hardly shifting as she worked the rope over the nail. In the box, she heard a chinking sound. China? Odd, here in this old ruin, to find such a thing. Then the fibers collapsed around her wrists and she yanked her hands free, wincing, easing her stiff shoulders and rubbing her hands. Tearing off the gag made of her torn shawl, she got to her feet.

Turning to examine the box, she saw it was a crate made of rough wood with a broken lid. The contents had chinked together. Peering inside, using a flat stone to pry the lid open, she spied straw packed around the shoulders of crockery jugs.

The sort used for ale or liquor. Gasping, she reached in to pull a jug free, and saw a pale label glued on the body. In a beam of moonlight, she could just see it.

Glenbrae Distillery, Perthshire, Scotland, Est. 1820. An ink drawing showed the profile of Invermorie Castle.

She had to find Ronan. Making her way cautiously around the floor of the broch, stepping carefully over jumbled stones, she searched for the exit. All the while she listened for hoofbeats or voices, praying she could get away before her captors returned.

The men expected others to arrive too, she remembered. That must mean Pitlinnie—no one else would steal and hide a stock of Glenbrae whisky here. Perhaps he had heard it would be sent to the king. But why would it matter to him?

The broch, very wide at the base, showed deep cracks in the old walls from the pressure and weight of centuries. She could see the double stone walls and the spaces within that would have served as living spaces in the past. Moonlight picked out the uneven shapes and shadows of collapsed rubble.

Yet she noticed regular shapes too, squares and rectangles and regular curves inside the fragmented niches. She moved toward one of the chambers. Even at a distance, she could see the shapes of boxes similar to the one she had found.

The moonlight shifted, showing wooden boxes and barrels stacked high.

Heart pounding, she turned and ran, stumbling, knocking her knee against stone, stifling a cry, running on. Light bloomed ahead, a crack in the immense wall, a brightness that revealed an opening.

Then she was out, grass slick under her running feet in dancing slippers. Overhead stars glinted, and white mist floated over the loch at the foot of the hill.

Stopping, turning, she got her bearings and knew which direction to take for Invermorie—it was closest, even over miles of moor and hill ahead.

Then she stopped quick, hearing shouts, horse hooves, and the dip and splash of oars in the water. Frozen, exposed in the open, she spun on her heel and ran back to the broch, the only shelter she could find.

Drawing up the reins inside the cover of trees, Ronan gave the steadfast bay an appreciative pat, then sat to watch. He studied the old broch through the trees. He would not be satisfied until he checked the place for his stolen whisky casks. He wished he had thought of this sooner—if it was here, all would be well once he and his men removed it.

Hearing the approach of another horse, he saw Donal coming forward. Dismounting, he walked out of the trees and signaled.

"Aleck is bringing a cart," Donal said, riding up. "He will meet us on the other side of the loch near the tower. If the whisky is there, we will carry away what we can and come back for the rest."

"Watch the horses—tie them up. I will check to see if anything is stored in there. There is an old rowing boat down by the shore. Stay here, lad."

Donal held up a hand. "Wait. Horses are coming. Not a cart."

Ronan heard the sounds too. He and Donal stayed still. In the darkness, two men rode toward the loch and dismounted, leaving the horses to graze. Voices floated back toward the trees.

"Where is that wee boat? There is always one here."

"Further down," said the other. "D'ye think the lass is still there?"

"Tied up, fearing for her life, a scrap of a lassie? Aye. She will be there."

"Her betrothed best be here soon, and the other. Our reward better be worth the trouble. Wee bit lass screaming like a banshee—and she bit me!"

Ronan felt anger flame up. "Ellison. Damn them," he murmured.

"What now?" Donal whispered. "There's a mist gathering. Hard to see."

"All to our benefit," Ronan growled. "Scatter their mounts. They'll go after them, and I'll take the boat over. Stay out of sight."

"Go find her. I will do this." Donal mounted his horse, pressed its sides, and soon was flying over the moor toward the grazing horses, sending them cantering up the meadow.

Shouting, the men down by the loch turned to run after their escaping horses. Fast and silent, Donal rounded and vanished into shadows and trees.

Turning for the lochside, Ronan found the boat, leaped in, and took up the oars.

CHAPTER 23

The water was a narrow stretch and he passed the little isle, a bar of green too thin to support more than straggly plants, and oared past it in a few strokes. Reaching the shore quickly, he nudged the boat among reeds in the low, lapping water and stepped out. Wary as he went, he reached to broch, walking around its curving wall to find the entrance. He had not been inside for years, but knew from boyhood to beware falling stones.

Just as soon as he breached the entrance, he saw a missile flying toward him and ducked barely in time as a stone crashed into the wall beside him, followed swiftly by another—not fallen but thrown.

Then a figure flew out of the shadows, a fairy bit of a girl in a pale gown with pale hair, coming at him like a wraith, sobbing out as she ran to him. He folded her into his embrace, relief and love and thankfulness infusing him. "Ellison," he breathed. "You are safe now."

"You came for me, you found me," she said against his chest.

"I did. But what the devil are you doing here? What happened?" As he spoke he was kissing her hair, her brow, her lips, cupping her face in his hands. "Are you hurt? Did those bastards—"

"I am fine. They tied me and took me here. Gagged me, too, when I screamed."

"Ah, it was you we heard on the moor! It brought us here. Sure you are not hurt?" He cupped her shoulders and slid his hands down her arms. "Did they touch you? I will kill them—"

"Only to bind me and gag me."

He swore low. "I thought they might have taken the whisky here, so Donal and I rode out. Then we heard two men down by the loch. They mentioned a lass. I came quick as I could across the water. Who was it?"

"Pitlinnie's men," she said breathlessly. "I saw one of them at the dance, and the other I think was with Pitlinnie the day we met him on the moor. He loaned me his carriage at Duncraig, and I believed him. I am a fool for that. They hauled me out, tied me up, but I got free. And now you are here, and oh Ronan, I must show you—"

"Pitlinnie," he growled. "The whisky."

"Aye, the whisky! Let me show you!" She tugged at his hand. "Go careful. This way."

High overhead, the moon slid out from the clouds, spilling light into the ancient courtyard and through cracks in the walls. Then Ronan saw what was there—fat barrels, small kegs, stacked wooden boxes.

"My God," he said, ducking his head to enter the space. He reached out to touch some of the wooden vessels.

She followed him inside. "Is it all there?"

"Possibly." He kissed her swiftly, hugged her against him, let go. "My lass, you have brought me such luck—you cannot know how much. But I must deal with this later, and get you somewhere safe." He led her over rubble and debris toward the entrance and out into the night.

"We must move the whisky," she said. "How will you do it?"

"Aleck is already on his way with a cart. But I want you to go to Invermorie. Come on." He led her to the loch. "Over the water. My horse is on the other side."

"But I want to help."

He noticed then she was shivering in her thin, torn, muddy gown, the pretty blue-gray that he had admired earlier that evening. So much had happened since then. He removed his jacket and draped it over her shoulders. "You have a warrior's heart and do not even know it, my love. Into the boat with you."

She went without question, and he loved her even more for that. She reached for an oar but he shook his head, rowing silently out over the loch.

When he had met the girl just months ago, she had seemed a delicate, anxious thing, yet even then he had glimpsed her courage, her ability to accept what came without complaint and press quietly ahead. In the last weeks, he had watched her discover her strength, test her voice, and find her wings like a kestrel on the edge of the nest. He wanted her to find more of that in herself. But this night, he wanted above all for her to be safe. Just that.

Mist and darkness obscured the shore; he lapped the oars quietly and watched for movement, listened for sounds of men returning. As they reached the center of the loch, the moon was just a soft blur now, its light diffusing in the gathering mist. He headed for the opposite shore on instinct. Then he heard shouts, men, and horses.

"They are back," Ellison said.

He stilled the oars and floated. A torch gleamed onshore through the fog. More shouts echoed over the water.

"Ellison Graham! Where are ye?" He did not recognize the voice.

Picking up the oars, he pulled, but the motion felt odd, slow, as if the water thickened and the boat went awry. With a thunk, the prow hit an obstacle, the small craft shuddering as if hung up on something. Reaching out to push away, he touched a breadth of earth against the side, moss and rock and green plants thrusting out of black water into the curling pale mist. How could they have reached shore so soon?

"Ellison Graham! We will find ye!"

He pulled again, but the paddles thumped solid earth. "We are stuck on something," he murmured. He arced one oar and set to, but the boat did not move.

"Ronan," Ellison whispered. "The fairy isle!"

"What?" He pushed the oars, reached out, and pushed at solid earth and turf.

"The fairy isle—the one that appears in the mist."

"It feels like a sandbar, but it makes no sense. In this fog, I am not sure which way we've turned. Damnation," he muttered. A thick swath of mist came across the boat so that he could hardly see vessel or oars. An arm's length away, Ellison had a sort of moonlit foggy aura about her.

"The isle that appears out of the mist," she whispered. "It is here."

"Hush. Do you hear that?" Men were yelling again.

"Ellison! Come here—we will save ye!"

"How did she escape? She cannot have gone far."

"Maybe she swam the loch and is drowned."

"If she drowns, we are done for. Ellison Graham! The boat is gone. There is another down this way, I think. Hurry." Ronan heard sounds of splashing, grunting, swearing, and then oars moving through water.

"The island. It is here. We can hide here," Ellison whispered, and stood, stepping out of the rocking boat, so that Ronan dug an oar deep into thick, rich earth to stabilize it. What the devil?

"Come here," he whispered, but she was out, stepping back in the mist. She stood like a waif, a ghost. She did not sink into the black water.

"Ellison Graham! Your father wants you home! Your betrothed wants you home! We can help you!"

"Betrothed? Do they mean you?" Her whisper was disembodied. Her hand came out of the fog, beckoning. "It is a good wee isle. Come up."

"Hush." Betrothed? He stood and stepped cautiously out of the boat. The ground underfoot rocked gently, but held firm.

It could not be, yet it was so. The loch had only a thin, insubstantial bar of floating greenery on this loch that would hold no one. Yet they stood on rich, heavy soil thick with plants. Ellison took his hand and he drew her close.

～

Water licked at her shoes and the hem of her gown, and her limbs trembled, but the ground was sturdy underfoot and Ronan's hand was warm over hers.

"Wait," he whispered. "Hush. They may not see us here."

She could hear the boat's oars plashing louder, the men's voices calling, hooting through the mist, taunting now. A chill went through her. Ronan pressed her fingers tightly.

Mist poured around them in a ring now, as if a cloud descended where they stood to shield them, even covering the rowboat beached on the narrow shore. She stood with Ronan in utter silence, the fog a thick white blanket around them.

Shouts echoed over the water. The boat guided by her captors—she knew their voices—glided so close she could hear the lap and surge of the water against the bow, could hear one of the men cursing low. Any moment now they were sure to strike the same mossy bank where she stood motionless with Ronan.

"I canna see a damn thing," one of the men groused. "Where the devil are we?"

"Go back. We canna go through this soup. It is not like anything I've ever seen."

"What about the lass?"

"Either she drowned in this accursed loch or she is lost on the hills in the fog. We will have to find her."

"Nor has that fool shown up who sent us here," the man said. "This is the devil's night indeed. Why did we agree to this madness?"

"Coin, that was why. Coin."

"There are tales about this loch and that old tower. Get shore quick-like before something rises out of the water and takes us down into the depths."

Ellison heard the long swish of oars as the boat turned. As the sound of oars faded, she breathed out in relief. Ronan stood beside her in utter silence after the watery sounds disappeared, and then long after the sound of men's voices and horses' hooves faded on land.

He drew her close. "I do not understand it. They should have seen us, yet they did not. And this isle! I knew it was here but never knew it was so solid a thing. Then the mist coming in thick and fast—what luck for us, hey."

"The Fey protect their own."

He huffed. "The Fey, is it?"

"You said it yourself when we were here before. The island only appears now and then, but it appeared for us because we needed protection. It saved our lives."

"It is just a legend and is a small spit of land. They just did not notice us."

"The isle and the mist saved us, Ronan. I know it."

He kissed her forehead. "The hour is late, you are exhausted. We need to leave this magical mass of vegetation before we both sink."

"The Fey protect their own. You carry fairy ancestry in your blood."

He shrugged. "It is a lovely tale. You must write about it one day. Watch your step, my love." He guided her back into the boat.

Taking up the oars, Ronan pulled hard, drawing the boat around and away from the narrow shore and out into the loch once again. The mist began to thin to a vapor, lifting away. Looking over her shoulder, Ellison saw that the little isle was only a thin hump of land and scrub. She could hardly see it on the water's surface.

"It is all but gone now. Your fairy ancestors were watching over you."

"And over my love as well, who believes in fairies, much to their delight."

As they reached the shoreline, he nudged the vessel in among the reeds, then sat with her in silence, waiting, listening.

"They are gone," he murmured, and helped her out of the boat.

Moments later, as he released his horse's lead from a tree trunk and boosted Ellison into the saddle, she heard a sound and tapped his shoulder.

"Horses," she said. "And a cart, I think. Is it Donal? And Aleck?"

"So it is. Good lads. Up with you, my dear, and we'll go meet them."

CHAPTER 24

"So," Mairi said, "that was quite the adventure, then. For both of you."

"Aye so," Ronan agreed. He sat back, a cup of hot tea warming his hands, and glanced at the others seated around the table in Invermorie's great hall, that warm, shabby, homey space bathed in soothing candlelight in the hour before dawn. He was silent for a moment, and they waited—Mairi, Ludo, Donal, Aleck, Rabbie, and his love, who nibbled at buttered toast and smiled over at him.

"We cannot stay long," Ellison said. "We should get to Strathniven."

"Of course, but no need to rush. I sent our stable boy there already with a note to say you are safe after a mishap on the road."

"Another one?" Ronan chuckled, glancing at Ellison. "Thank you."

"I am just glad all is well," Mairi said. "Will you be rushing off to Edinburgh when you get back to Strathniven?"

"The viscountess wanted to leave today," Ellison said. "She and Sorcha will return from Duncraig eager to travel and wondering where we are. So we must get back."

"All Scotland is in a mad rush to reach the city," Mairi said. "I am glad we are not going. My father decided the crowds would be too much."

"I did hope to see it, but I do not have the strength I had when a younger man. And every nook and cranny is full, they say. I do want a complete report when you both return," Sir Ludo said. "Will you stay at your usual hotel, Ronan?"

"Generally I stay at the Waterloo, aye, but Hugh Cameron says it is full already. Fifty rooms were reserved in July as soon as the royal visit was confirmed. Now Barrie's, The Crown, Davidson's—all the hotels are full, I hear."

"Then I hope you have a friend with a spare bed," Ludo said, waving the knife with which he was buttering an oatcake.

"You could stay at my father's house, or with Lady Strathniven," Ellison said.

"I have a place. Hugh made arrangements."

"I see." She sipped her tea. "Well, we must get to Strathniven soon or they will be terribly worried, even with Mairi's note. But I do not want to see Mr. Corbie."

"If he is smart, he has gone far ahead. Once I see him, we will have words."

"Your betrothal," Mairi said suddenly. "I could not be happier for you, and I am so glad you shared that with us. But does your family know, Ellison?"

"Not from me. They may have heard the rumor last night, though. Lady Strathniven and Sorcha would be pleased, I think. But my father will not be happy."

"Sir Hector will know that our new viscount is an excellent match for his daughter," Sir Ludo said. "Tell him you have a proud ancestral line that includes the MacGregor chiefs, and the old line of the earls of Strathniven—"

Ronan glanced at Ellison, who smiled as Ludo went on. "I will talk with Sir Hector," Ronan said.

"A daughter's happiness can bring a father great satisfaction in life." Ludo patted his daughter's hand.

"You are both so well suited. One day I hope to be as happy," Mairi said.

"Mairi," Ronan murmured, "I wanted to talk with you about that."

"Now is as good a time as any. I did want to tell you." She smiled.

Ronan flared his nostrils, dreading talk of Pitlinnie just now.

"I had a letter," Mairi said, "from Linhope. From Calton Jail."

"Linhope!" Surprised, he sat up, having expected a different subject. "How?"

"He got a letter out somehow. He and Iain MacInnes were only told you were taken back to the Highlands, and they have been very concerned. Linhope took a chance in sending a letter in case I knew something of where you were."

"That he got it outside Calton's walls is astonishing. How are they?"

"Better than expected. Linhope has been acting as a physician there, so their accommodations improved. MacInnes is helping, and they have made some difference to the prisoners."

"Good. What else did he say?"

"That is what I wanted to tell you," she said. "All of you. He said he still hopes for my good answer." Her dark eyes sparkled, cheeks flushed.

Stunned, he leaned toward her. How had he not seen this? "Linhope?"

She smiled. "Whom did you think?"

Shaking his head, he smiled too. "Well done, my dear. Your son and your father should approve before I say aught about it." Relief flooded him, but guilt remained. Linhope's fate, MacInnes as well, hung in the balance, dependent now on his ability to find some legal means to dismiss the charges.

If he could not save his friends, he would cause Mairi true heartbreak, and he could not live with that. He sat, thoughtful, as the others congratulated her.

"Linhope is a very fine man," Ludo said.

Donal beamed. "Truly, Mother? Linhope is an excellent fellow!"

"What is your answer?" Ronan asked. Beside him, Ellison looked from one to the other, silent, eyes shining as she began to understand.

"Marriage?" she asked. "Mairi, that is wonderful news."

"My answer is yes. I wish I could see him to tell him. I wrote a reply today, but I do not know if he will receive it."

"Give it to me. I will take it to him."

"Thank you! And I hoped you would be happy for me."

"Almost happier than I am for myself and Ellison." Ronan reached out to take Mairi's hand. In that moment, he knew for certain his wounded heart had healed and was coming to life again. He had found love again. So had Mairi, and that made all the difference. She too needed to move on, unfettered by guilt.

"Linhope," he mused, feeling pleased and relieved. "Honestly I feared you were thinking of marrying Pitlinnie."

"Pitlinnie!" Mairi looked horrified.

"We all thought so, Mairi Brodie." Rabbie Muir had been quiet all through the discussion. He had been at Invermorie when they arrived, making sure his grandson Geordie was recovering well. "Pitlinnie made no secret of courting you and hinting you would be his wife soon. We feared you had fallen for that rascal's wiles."

"Wiles?" She gave a bitter laugh. "That fool! I always thought he had something to do with my husband's death, and with your troubles too, Ronan. I only let him visit in case I could learn something to help you."

"I am humbled. And I ask your pardon, *mo cridhe*." My heart. He did still love her, and she would always have a place in his heart and his life. He moved his hand to cover Ellison's then, and she gave him her impish smile.

He knew he belonged here with these people he loved so much. Now Ellison was part of that circle too, part of his life, his heart and soul. He prayed she felt that as surely as he did.

"Excellent," Sir Ludo said. "Our family tree is growing. But I want to know why Pitlinnie lured Ellison into danger, and what can be done about it."

"I have my suspicions, and trust me that I will act on it," Ronan said. "But we must go carefully. I do not want him slipping out of it for lack of evidence."

"I would gladly accuse him without any evidence," Donal said. "And how is Mr. Corbie involved?"

Rabbie Muir cleared his throat. "I may know something of that. I did not realize it until I heard all of this from you. Now I think I know."

"What is it?" Ronan asked sharply.

"Last night I went to the distillery while Geordie was resting to check on something. I wanted a good count of the kegs and bottles there, knowing you must ship your quantity out soon. And it is a good thing—a very good thing—that you and Donal and Aleck found that whisky lot and brought it back tonight."

"Aye. Good indeed. What happened at the distillery?" Ronan asked.

"A man came to the yard. He said he wanted some whisky and would I give him some. Said if it was free, he might know where the lost Glenbrae whisky was. I had a bad feeling. No one would know but the thieves where it was."

"True. Then what?"

"I agreed, see, in case he knew something. A second fellow came then and they took a keg." Rabbie shook his head. "They said it was for a wedding celebration, and if I came with them, I would learn about the missing whisky."

Ellison frowned. "Did they mention Darrach? Did they know he wanted it?"

"They asked if Glenbrae was about. They did not know about Darrach, I think. Then those rascals showed me a pistol, and it were clear I had to go with them."

"All this, and you said nothing?" Ronan asked.

"I came back safely, and there you were with the whisky in the cart, and all the news with Miss Ellison. But now I see how it fits."

"Tell us," Ronan said. "And thank God you came back safe, Rabbie."

"I did, and this is what I will tell you. They wanted to take me to a wedding. That were a puzzle for sure. But now it is clear."

Ronan scowled. "Whose marriage? Did they need you for a witness?"

"No. They wanted me to perform the marriage."

"What?" Ronan sat straighter. "Oh aye. Because you were a pastor."

"A pastor?" Ellison asked.

"Oh, aye," Sir Ludo said. "Years back."

"I was ordained as a young man. Had a parish north of here," Rabbie told her. "But the clearing agents came through that glen and burned my home and church. I had to protect my family. Ronan's father, bless the man, was a friend, newly laird of Glenbrae then. He took us all in at Invermorie, made me his factor, gave me land in his glen. Ronan's uncle was Viscount Darrach then and he helped too. And there is no man more grateful to the MacGregors of Darrach and Glenbrae than Auld Rabbie Muir." He thumped his chest.

"I remember how much my father valued your friendship. But how did these men know you were a pastor? And why did they want you?"

"Some fellow marrying his ladylove quicklike, and no one around but the old one who used to be a pastor." Rabbie shrugged. "But I heard a name, see."

"Who?" Ronan was growing impatient.

"Mr. Corbie. He was to marry his lady love. I was to do it that night."

"Corbie!" Ellison cupped her hands over her mouth, going pale.

"Devil take the man," Ronan growled. "Did you see him?"

"No. He never came."

"Interesting," Ronan drawled. "What did you do then?"

"They took me to Loch Brae. I was confused, I tell you. They told me to wait in the cart. Then—there were horses running about, and the idiots what took our whisky were chasing after them. I did not see Donal then, but it was he scaring the horses. They forgot about me. So I caught one of the horses and left." He shrugged.

Ronan shook his head, half amused, then suddenly burst out laughing. "We did not see you there."

"I came straight back to Invermorie. And later you lot showed up."

"Rabbie, you may not know it, but you helped save Ellison from a terrible fate. It looks as if Corbie meant to force her into marriage. I do not know what happened to delay him—but we have all been lucky this night," Ronan said.

"I feared I did wrong when I heard your tale this morning," Rabbie said.

"Not at all, Mr. Muir," Ellison said. "They mentioned another man coming by, but I never heard a name."

Ronan nodded. "Corbie had a scheme—he and Pitlinnie must have agreed to do something once they knew of our betrothal. They were deep in conversation."

"I noticed that too. But why?" Ellison asked.

"Corbie wants to prevent our marriage, and thought this would do it."

"How did he know about Rabbie Muir?" Sir Ludo asked.

"Some in the glen know," Rabbie said. "And I am glad I ruined his plan."

"Likely he is in Edinburgh. But we will find him." Ronan pounded his fist just once on the table; but within, he was white-hot with anger.

"If I were younger, I'd help you beat the sorry fellow into the ground," Sir Ludo said. "I think Miss Ellison could still be in danger if he was that desperate to marry her. What does he truly want out of this?"

That question puzzled him too. Ronan shook his head. "I am not sure."

"Strathniven," Ellison said. "Lady Strathniven told him he must find a wife that she approves if he expects to inherit the estate." Ronan noticed that her eyes were shadowed with fatigue and fear. Again he felt a powerful need to protect her, to surround her with his strength and keep any threat from her.

"He wants your father's approval badly too," he murmured. "He will take any risk to get that and his aunt's estate."

"With a good marriage and a peer's title, he could rise high in civic office. If he sees Papa before we do, he could convince him that he is the right husband for me. Papa relies on him and listens to him."

"We must get to the city before he causes more damage." Ronan flexed his fist, anger simmering. Ellison rested a gentle hand on his forearm.

"What if there was another way?" Mairi asked. "A way to ensure that Mr. Corbie cannot marry our Ellison?"

Our Ellison. Ronan drew a breath. "What is that?"

"Mr. Muir?" Mairi looked at Rabbie.

"I would be honored to perform a wedding if it is agreeable."

Ellison looked bewildered. "Marry us—now?"

Seeing immediately that this could protect Ellison from Corbie, Ronan also knew how much he wanted to marry her. But she had to want it as well. His heart pounded. "What do you think?" he asked her. "Shall we do this here and now?"

"It is so sudden." She looked a little pale. "I am not ready—"

Mairi stood, beckoning to the others. "Come. They need to talk privately."

"Now or later, I will happily perform your wedding," Rabbie offered as he left. "But if you want to outwit Corbie, this needs to happen quicklike."

"He is right about that," Ronan murmured when the door closed. He stood, and Ellison did as well. Her fingers were working, twisting, anxious and uncertain.

"Do you think Corbie is truly a threat?"

"Very much so, if he meant to abduct you for marriage."

"But last night no one mentioned a wedding. They only spoke of my betrothed coming, and a trap for someone. I thought they meant you."

"And we are both fine now. But we must stay that way."

"Corbie did not show up. He changed his mind."

"Perhaps he knows I would hunt him down." Ronan said it casually.

"If we did this now, it would infuriate him. He would turn on you with a vengeance. He could arrange your arrest or find another way to hurt you."

"If you do not want this, we will not do it now. You said you are not ready."

"I meant," she said, "I am not ready for my wedding. I have no dress or flowers. I look a fright."

He huffed a laugh. "You look beautiful. Whatever you want, love, we will do."

Smiling a little, she nodded. "We did promise to marry." Fluttering her fingers together, she shrugged. "I wanted to talk to my father first before I did this again."

He exhaled, took her moving hands to still them, to breathe a little calm into her. "I may never be your father's choice for you. But I now have something to recommend me in his eyes—a title, lands, someday a good income. And I love his daughter dearly. That should count. However," he said, "I do have legal matters to clear up."

"He will respect you once he knows more about you. But—it should not matter what Papa wants. I must make my own decision." She straightened her shoulders.

"You should." He waited.

"If we do not marry now, what then, Ronan?"

He rubbed a thumb over her hand. "Once you are under your father's roof, you may be pressured to marry Corbie and do what is expected of you."

"I would refuse. I would," she insisted, as he tilted a brow. "I have been meek, and felt trapped. When I tried to be independent, it was a disaster. But no longer."

"Whatever you decide, you have my heart. You know that."

"If I am to have another quick wedding, it must be for the best of reasons." She came closer, resting a hand on his chest. "For love. True love. Shall we do this now?"

He cupped her cheek and kissed her. "Whatever you wish, Lady Darrach."

"I havena done a wedding for years," Rabbie Muir said. "But a pastor does not forget the words that bind two souls together in happiness." He smiled. "Let's begin."

Ellison glanced around where Mairi, Ludo, Donal, and Aleck had gathered in a half-circle to witness what was to happen. Looking up at Ronan, she smiled. They stood together with Rabbie before the hall's tall ancient fireplace, warm with a peat fire just before dawn. Ronan still wore the wrapped plaid and jacket he had worn at the dance, his shirt and neckcloth rumpled now. Smoothing her blue gown, muddied and torn, she was glad of the lacy cream-colored shawl that Mairi had draped over her shoulders. She patted her hair, which Mairi had quickly arranged with tiny bluebell blossoms plucked from the garden. In her hands she held a small bouquet of bluebells, white roses, and heather tucked in a sweet tangle tied with ribbon.

"Well, then," Rabbie began. "We have all we need here—two hearts what love one another and are ready to be joined. Take her hands, John Ronan MacGregor, and take his, Ellison Sophia Graham. Then listen and agree."

Rabbie cleared his throat. Though he had not uttered the words for a long time, he proceeded smoothly. Ellison felt her heart soar with the words and with the infusion of strength from Ronan's hands holding hers, and from the warmth of love in his deep blue eyes. Standing before a glowing hearth as morning light edged the hills beyond the windows, she knew this simple wedding was all she could want.

"I pronounce thee man and wife, Ronan MacGregor and Ellison Graham, now Lord and Lady Darrach. No man may put thee asunder. Kiss your bride," he added. "And I will write up a document for all of us to sign in witness."

A tender kiss, Ronan's lips on hers, his hands at her waist. Tears bloomed in her eyes, slid down her cheeks, and she slipped her arms around his neck, her heart full of as much love and thankfulness and hope as it could hold.

"It is done, love," Ronan whispered.

"For always," she answered.

Within the half-hour, mounted on horses from the Invermorie stable, she rode beside her husband toward whatever lay ahead.

CHAPTER 25

"**Y**our carriage suffered a problem again?" Sorcha asked, as Strathniven's big black barouche rumbled along a glen road. Ellison, seated beside her, nodded.

"Just an unfortunate incident on the road. It was Sir Neill Pitlinnie's carriage, as it happens," Ellison said. "He loaned me the use of his vehicle —and driver."

"These awful roads!" Lady Strathniven, settled on the opposite seat, shook her head. "I order repairs on my estate when needed, but other landholders must do the same if the old glen roads are to be maintained. The Crown seems only interested in their military roads in Scotland, straight as arrows and not very picturesque. But Scottish peers are custodians of the Highland legacy. I try to be aware of that."

"I agree," Ellison said, holding Balor half-asleep in her lap. She stroked his head and shoulders while she watched the road and hills fly past. For a moment, she wondered where Ronan was now, and hoped he would not cross paths with Corbie before they could meet with Sir Hector.

"I hope nothing happens to our carriage today," Sorcha said. "It is such a long way to Edinburgh. You should rest, Ellison. You have been up all night, it seems."

"I will," Ellison said. "I am rather fatigued."

"I am glad all is well and Darrach came to your rescue, my dear. So fortunate you found refuge at Invermorie for the night. Donal Brodie's family are such nice people." Lady Strathniven smiled. "We should have them to tea at Strathniven the next time we are in the north. Perhaps in September," she mused.

"That would be lovely," Ellison said.

"Oh, Elly, I nearly forgot in all the commotion as we were leaving. We heard such a rumor about you at the dance last night!" Sorcha's eyes twinkled.

"Truly? What was that?" Ellison dreaded to hear. She had to tell them the truth of her marriage soon. She had promised Ronan to do just that when he had left Strathniven that morning—just hours after their impromptu wedding. He had left to meet Hugh Cameron to arrange moving the rescued whisky, which was to be transported to Culross to be shipped to Leith Harbor.

Standing with her in the shadows of Strathniven's tower library, he had promised to meet her in Edinburgh as soon as he arrived.

"Do that, Darrach," she had told him. "I will be at my father's house." Rising on her toes, she had kissed him, and he had pulled her into his arms for deep kisses that stirred and melted through her. "Oh—my," she had breathed.

"Wife," he had growled, "we must find a way to be together soon."

"We cannot have our wedding night in Papa's house," she protested.

"I have secured a place of my own in the city. We will go there."

After he had left, she had been pulled into a whirlwind of packing and rushing about, since Lady Strathniven insisted that they travel that day. The return would require two carriages, with the ladies in one, with Jeannie riding in the second coach with the trunks and bags. To Ellison's relief, Adam Corbie had not returned to Strathniven; MacNie reported that he had taken him to Kinross to secure a post-chaise back to the city. "The man seemed in an awful hurry," MacNie had remarked.

"What rumor?" Ellison asked, seeing Sorcha's impish smile.

"Oh dear, it is raining again," Lady Strathniven observed, looking out the window. "MacNie expects to keep a good pace so that we can reach Queen's Ferry before dark, and across to Leith and then Edinburgh. We can stop for high tea in Dunfermline, if my favorite little shop is not too crowded. So many are traveling toward Edinburgh now!"

"I heard last night at the dance that the king's ship is anchored offshore at Leith even now, but because of the storms, they are staying beyond the rough waters until they have clear sailing," Sorcha said.

"The storms have been particularly bad this summer." The viscountess looked at Ellison. "Was Darrach able to arrange for Glenbrae whisky to be delivered to Holyroodhouse in time for the king's arrival?"

"He left this morning to see to it. He and Mr. Cameron will travel by water to make sure the whisky shipment arrives safely."

"Excellent." Lady Strathniven smiled. "He is such a gentleman and a good man. We are all fortunate this has turned out so well."

"What has turned out well?" Sorcha asked.

Ellison felt a hot blush rise. They did not know the whole of it. "Fortunate indeed, my lady. But let me ask again—what rumor did you hear?"

The viscountess smiled. "We heard something about you and Lord Darrach at the dance. I thought it was rather good news, if it is true."

"Yes! Do you have news, Ellison?" Sorcha asked.

"Then you heard we are engaged?" Ellison asked.

"Yes, yes! Is it true? Did he ask you last night?" Sorcha leaned toward her.

"I do have news." In her lap, Balor lifted his head to look at her, tipping his head quizzically as if he, too, was curious. She gave them a tremulous smile. "And I hope you will think it the best of news."

"Ellison!" Sorcha urged.

"Last night—well, just before dawn today, Lord Darrach and I were married."

Silence. Then Balor gave a little yelp as if he understood. Lady Strathniven gasped and set a hand to her bosom, and Sorcha clapped her hands in delight.

"Oh, my dear, married!" The viscountess leaned forward to take Ellison's hand. "I never imagined—how marvelous!"

"Wonderful! He is such a lovely gentleman!" Sorcha hugged her. "This means you are Lady Darrach now."

"I suppose so," she laughed. "Thank you. I was not certain how you might take the news. It was a rather sudden decision."

"I could not be more pleased," Lady Strathniven said. "This morning?"

"Yes, at Invermorie. Mr. Muir, an old friend to Ro—to Darrach, was there. He was a pastor in his younger days. We were planning to marry later—but thought perhaps it was better to fix it now before the madness begins in the city. We might not be able to plan a wedding for a while, given all the commotion just now."

"Oh, how romantic! You fell in love with a handsome Highlander and promised to be together always, and then had a simple Highland wedding with no fuss." Sorcha sighed. "I would love that too someday."

"It was just a small wedding with a few witnesses. I have the certificate. No fuss indeed." Ellison patted her reticule.

"I wonder," the viscountess mused. "Did this come about because you felt compromised last night, being stranded and rescued? Darrach is a perfect gentleman and would not want you to endure a scandal. He has such strength of character, I am convinced."

"Compromise?" Sorcha giggled.

"No. It just seemed the best solution for everyone." A simple explanation was best, Ellison thought.

"I suspected from the first there were feelings between you two," the lady said. "You are so well suited. He is calm and intelligent and has such respect for you. And you have come more into yourself in these last weeks than in years, my dear. You are in love. A person would have to be blind not to see it. Very romantic, despite all."

"Despite all?" Sorcha asked.

"There was some—uncertainty about his inheritance," Ellison said quickly.

"Yes, uncertainty," Lady Strathniven agreed. "Although you may hear a fuss from your father. But you have your proof, and it is done. I will speak to Hector if you wish. You have made an excellent choice this time. Surely he will realize that."

"Thank you, my lady." Ellison exhaled and felt herself relax a little.

"But what an odd little wedding day! We will remedy that," the lady continued. "This fall, we will plan a proper wedding and a beautiful reception. We can hold it at Strathniven." She smiled.

"That would be perfect," Ellison answered. She felt grateful, yet wary of what still lay ahead, problems that she could not disclose, much as she loved these two.

"You must talk to your father as soon as you see him," Lady Strathniven urged.

"I hope he can understand that I have made a good choice." She lifted her chin. "My own choice."

"Ah, there is my sweet Ellison. Her spirited nature has returned!" The lady beamed. "I feared she had vanished altogether. Can we thank Lord Darrach?"

"To some extent." Ellison smiled. "But it was time I stepped out of the shadow of the past."

"True. Though I think my nephew will be heartbroken. He is awfully fond of you. But I will talk to him, and it will be fine. You will see." Lady Strathniven nodded.

She arrived at her father's house just as the mantel clock chimed eleven times. Lewison, the butler, hid his surprise as he welcomed her home at that late hour, and the delighted housekeeper sent a serving maid to bring a tray of tea and scones up to Ellison's bedchamber to revive her. The room was ready, for she had been expected within a day or two.

"Is Papa at home?" she asked.

"Not presently, Miss Graham," Lewison said. "He had a dinner engagement with Sir Walter Scott and the fellows of the Celtic Society.

This is a busy time, as you will know. But he will be pleased to know you are home. Mr. Corbie was here not long ago inquiring after him also."

"Is he gone?" She took a steadying breath.

"Yes. He indicated that he would meet Sir Hector tomorrow."

"Thank you, Lewison. It is good to be home." Climbing the stairs up to her room, she ate a little, changed, and lay down to rest.

Dozing, she woke just after midnight, and made her way downstairs, hoping that her father had returned and might be keeping his usual late hours. When she saw the light edging the door of his study, she went there, heart pounding, and knocked.

"Ellison!" Looking delighted, Sir Hector rose from his desk chair, where he sat with books and papers. "Lewison said you had returned. Did you have a pleasant journey?"

"I came down in the coach with Lady Strathniven and Sorcha Beaton," she said. "It was uneventful."

"And the MacGregor fellow?"

"He will arrive in the city tomorrow or the next day," she said. "He is coming with the shipment of whisky for the king. Papa—"

"You accomplished what you went to Strathniven to do? I have not yet seen Mr. Corbie for a report."

"Lord Darrach," she said, "is a fine gentleman. I think you will be pleased."

"Darrach, is it," he murmured. "I heard something about that."

"Legitimately Darrach, yes. Papa, there is much to explain."

"Yes. Lucky fellow to fall into that. I suppose it is to his credit that he did not boast about it beforehand, as it was apparently uncertain, and instead showed discretion. Well. Soon this will all be over." He smiled faintly.

He looked tired, she noticed. She saw lines in his brow and around his mouth she had not noticed before. Was his hair a little more silver? She sighed. "Papa, I know it is late, and you must be very tired and you have much on your mind. But I want to tell you—"

"Tell me later. It is very late. And you need not tell me how these lessons went. I will see for myself if this fellow has achieved what we hoped."

"He did. But Papa, truly, I have some news."

"It will have to wait. I must finish these rosters and get some sleep. I have an official breakfast tomorrow with the Lord Provost and others. Then we will talk. I promise. Good night, my dear." He smiled and waved her out of the room.

"Good night, Papa." She sighed, relenting, and left. Closing the door, she realized that he had not given her a hug in greeting or kissed her goodnight. But then, she had learned not to expect it.

Sleeping later than she intended, she woke to a gray morning promising even more rain. As she went downstairs, Lewison appeared carrying a silver tray with an empty cup and saucer, a small jug of cream, a bowl of fine sugar, and a rumpled napkin—sure signs that her father had finished his customary early coffee.

"Good morning, Lewison. Is Papa still here?"

"No, Miss. He left a few minutes ago for breakfast with the Lord Provost. He looks forward to seeing you this evening. Ah, a note arrived for you this morning." He handed her a small envelope. "A lad came from Lady Strathniven's house."

Cracking the wax seal, Ellison read it quickly. "I will have breakfast on Charlotte Square. It is not far. No need to summon a carriage. I will walk. If Papa comes home while I am out, do tell him where I am. Can someone see to Balor until I return? Thank you!"

Within minutes she was all but running out the door through the rain. Lady Strathniven's house on Charlotte Square was but two blocks from her father's house on George Street. The route took her across Castle Street, where she glanced for a moment toward her own house, set on the upper slope of that street. Thanks to the lawyers, the previous occupants were gone and the house was newly rented. Wondering if the new tenants were there yet, she hoped they would be happy there.

Perhaps when their lease was done, she and Ronan would decide to live there.

Hope rose in her, though an uneasy feeling lingered like a ghost. Once she had a chance to talk to her father, and once the king's visit was done, then all would be well. Love and happiness would prevail. She would not let the shadows win.

"Heather sprigs," Lady Strathniven said as she sat with Ellison and Sorcha at the dining table, "for our bonnets and headdresses. Jeannie picked some for us before we left the Highlands. The Edinburgh Ladies' Silver Cross Society is giving heather sprigs to all the ladies at the royal events, and Mrs. Siddons is adding heather to the bonnets in her hat shop. We must all tuck bits of heather in our bonnets and our hair to show how proud we are to be Scottish ladies."

"A lovely thought," Ellison said.

"Must the gentlemen wear heather as well?" a man asked.

Whirling, Ellison saw Adam Corbie in the doorway. Suddenly the rainy light seemed even darker. He gave her a tight, mocking smile.

"Why, Miss Graham."

"Adam!" His aunt sounded delighted. "We had breakfast already, but I am sure Cook will prepare something for you."

"Thank you, but I breakfasted this morning with the Lord Provost and Sir Hector." Again he looked directly at Ellison.

Silent, she sucked in a breath. Had he told Papa about the betrothal? If so, he would have twisted the story in his favor.

"It is good to see you," his aunt continued. "Will you be staying here this week? You left Strathniven so quickly we had no time to chat."

"No, my lady, I have my rooms on Princes Street. There is much to be done and I would not want my comings and goings to disturb your household."

"We are busy as well. The girls and I were just going out for a bit of shopping at Mrs. Siddons. She is making wonderful little bonnets decorated with heather blooms, and I want the girls to each have one before they are all sold."

"If you are leaving soon, I would like a word with Miss Ellison first." As he approached, Ellison leaned back in her chair as if to escape.

"It is a very busy day," she protested.

"He only needs a moment, Ellison," Lady Strathniven said blithely. "We will wait in the foyer while MacNie brings the carriage around." They left the room, and Corbie went to the door to close it.

"No," Ellison said. "Leave it open."

"I did not think propriety was important to you." Taking her elbow in a fierce hold, he pulled her into a window niche where they could not be overheard easily.

"And I thought acting the gentleman was important to you," she returned.

"Listen. I have reconsidered what to do about your betrothal."

She raised her brows. "Have you told my father yet?"

"I have not had the opportunity, but I will do so today unless you rectify the situation first."

"It has been rectified." Squaring her shoulders, she knew she must risk telling him the truth now. "Lord Darrach and I were married before we left the Highlands."

"What in blazes," he growled. "Married! How could that—when did it happen?"

"The morning we departed. He found me at the old broch near Loch Brae. You know the place." She tilted her head to give him a cold stare.

He went pale, his dark eyes narrowing. "I do not know it."

"I think you do. When we left the broch, we saw Rabbie Muir. Did you know he was a pastor? A quiet ceremony seemed just the thing to do, so we asked him to marry us. We had a few witnesses at Invermorie. There is always such fuss when an engagement is announced, don't you agree? This way was simple and lovely."

"You little—" He raised a hand as if to hit her, and she leaned away. Then he took a step back, looking shocked, pulling at his neckcloth as if it choked him. "This is impossible. I feared your betrothal would undo everything. This is far worse."

"It seemed a better solution than your plan, which I learned about in the most unfortunate way."

"I only wanted to help you. Help your father. You little fool," he ground out. "That man has manipulated you. But he will be caught smuggling again, and this time he will hang, and his friends with him. Trust me."

"You cannot be trusted for much, Mr. Corbie."

"We cannot possibly introduce him to the king. He should be arrested when he is back in Edinburgh."

"He did all you asked and more."

"Oh, much more," he said in a cruel drawl. "Betrothal is one thing, marriage quite another. A very poor choice on your part, my dear. Your father will be furious. He could find himself in an untenable position. Such a scandal might undo him."

"Do not be absurd. I have married a viscount and cousin to a powerful clan chief. Papa will be proud."

"Not after I inform the excise that MacGregor is transporting whisky by sea. That is considered smuggling."

She gasped. "You would not do that!"

"As secretary to the chief of the constabulary, I am obligated to do so."

"You are despicable." She took a step back. Another.

"There is another solution. You can save him if you want. Here is what you must do." He grabbed her wrist. "Listen."

"I listened to you before. It did not go well."

"Listen, Ellison," he hissed. "When Sir Hector learns about this marriage, it will greatly upset him. But you can still fix the situation."

"Nothing to fix. I am married and you do not like it. But it is done."

"And can be undone. You must apply for an annulment immediately. Your father can press the urgency with a judge to have it reversed quickly."

"No!" She pulled against his hold. "Let go! Why do you do this?"

"To save your father from a terrible disgrace. After an annulment, your MacGregor may be arrested and sentenced, perhaps executed. I cannot help him. But I can help you. We will announce our engagement shortly after and marry soon. Your two-day marriage was an impulsive act and I am gallantly helping you recover from harrowing events."

"You are the fool," she said. "You are forgetting that my father is set on presenting Darrach at the royal levee to represent Glenbrae whisky."

"We will find someone else to represent the whisky." He waved a hand.

"No one knows Glenbrae whisky as well as—" She stopped and gasped as it came together even more clearly. "Pitlinnie! Is that part of this? He wants to buy Glenbrae—and have that honor!"

"The debts attached to the Darrach estate must be resolved. Sir Neill is willing to do that. Then he can be introduced to the king as Glenbrae's owner. It is simple."

"None of that requires my annulment."

"An excise officer in Leith awaits my message. I told him to expect it. Your Darrach," he snarled, "stands between me and what I want."

"You said this was for my father's wellbeing."

"It is. As Sir Hector rises in government, so I rise too. And that is good for you, my dear. You will be sought after in social circles. That will not happen with your unseemly viscount. All the ways you have hurt your father can be mended now. Remember that."

"You have hidden your true character well," she said.

"Am I as tough as your rogue? As desirable?" He pulled her to him with sudden strength, and kissed her with rough force, hurting her mouth. Once she broke free, she slapped him.

"He is a rogue. You are a wretch."

"You know what you must do," he said, rubbing his jaw. "Today." Turning, he went to the door. "Truly, Ellison, you have no choice but to do the right thing."

Ellison a trembling hand to her head. She had to think. Had to find a way to stop Corbie. If she went to court to file an annulment—but she could not bear that thought. Nor could she bear the thought of hurting Ronan—or Papa.

Soon, riding with Lady Strathniven and Sorcha to the hat shop, her mind was racing as fast as her heart. She could not betray Ronan or her father.

She could not betray herself either, she thought. She had found a tenor of strength within in the last weeks—she could not let that go.

Then she knew what to do. As the idea dawned and grew, she nodded to herself. It might work. But Corbie's words echoed and stung.

All the ways you have hurt your father can be mended now. Remember that.

CHAPTER 26

"This is a madhouse," Hugh said, raising his voice over the cacophony on the quay as he rejoined Ronan, who was overseeing the unloading of the barrels and crates. "But I was able to hire a cart to take the whisky to Holyroodhouse, and I found a hackney to take us into Edinburgh."

"Excellent." Ronan nodded. Leith was busier than he had ever seen it, with ships arriving in advance of the royal party expected in a day or two. He moved aside with Hugh as several English gentlemen, hardly glancing at them, pushed past. "Once the whisky reaches the palace, and after the king's levee and that blasted introduction are done, my obligation will end. The king will likely not even notice that he asked to meet the distiller."

"All this for a few seconds of greeting. What then, my friend?"

"First I intend to see a certain legal issue resolved even before the levee."

"We had best act on that today. They say Parliament House and the courts of session and judiciary will close early this afternoon—that almost never happens—and may remain closed for a few days amid this lunacy."

"I see. Can you meet me there in a short while? I want to stop at my house."

"Aye. First I must visit my mother. I promised to go straight there when I arrived. Will you come along? She would be glad to see you."

"Later, but please give her my regards. We can open one of these crates, so you can bring jugs of Glenbrae for your family. I will keep some as well."

"After this legal matter is done and the grand spectacle is over, I am eager to get back to Kinross. The countryside has spoiled my taste for city life. And there is a lady I would like to call on—well. What for you, lad?"

"I will go to Darrach, and perhaps build a new distillery. I have not given up on retaining Glenbrae yet, but—" Ronan shrugged.

"Either way, a second distillery would be a boon. Is your bride agreeable?" Hugh grinned. "I am still stunned by your most excellent news."

Ronan smiled. "I hope she is agreeable. But I hope to practice law in the north as well as in Edinburgh, so she may see her family as often as she wants."

"If you are interested, I think our firm can give you plenty of clients."

"Thank you. I appreciate that."

"You could not have found a finer lady than Ellison Graham. I hope to be as lucky someday."

"Aye. Though there is still the dragon to confront in his den."

"Sir Hector? He is more bluster than malice in my experience. The real threat comes from his secretary, from the sound of things."

"Another matter I mean to address. Is that our cart? And the hackney with it?"

Riding into the city a short while later, Ronan recalled the last time he rode through these streets, wrists bound, not knowing where he was being taken or what would become of him.

And he realized he was a changed man in some ways, more firm of purpose, lighter of heart, walking an unexpected path that seemed nothing less than a miracle. Ellison Graham was a gift in his life and he would be forever grateful. Whatever she needed, he would provide;

whatever she desired, he would find. He wanted her to feel more cherished, loved, and valued than she had ever known.

The buoyant feeling sobered as he reminded himself of the serious matters yet to be resolved. He would need luck to outlast the trying days ahead.

"I have never seen so many Highlanders in such full, fierce gear in my life," Hugh remarked. "The gathering of the Highland clans will be a massive showing. Will you be part of the procession that moves the royal regalia of Scotland from the Castle down to Holyrood for the monarch's stay?"

"I will. Sir Evan wrote that he expects to see me there, now that I am a MacGregor chieftain. I brought my gear to join the march of the clans—bonnet and feathers and all. And may the king appreciate authentic Scottish strength, hey."

"The grand spectacle begins." As the carriage halted on the Canongate before Mrs. Cameron's house, Hugh exited and looked up at the sky. "More rain to come. The king will certainly experience miserably authentic Scottish weather. Oh by the way—you will find the key under an urn and the place in good repair. Driver," Hugh called, as the man unloaded bags and the crate. "North Castle Street for this gentleman."

The hackney coach progressed up the long slope of the High Street and turned toward Princes Street and beyond to North Castle, while Ronan watched throngs of people walking, chattering, a noisy mass of color and activity, with bright tartan patterns more in evidence than he had ever seen here. Bagpipes skirled on another street, perhaps Highland units practicing for the procession. Over it all, the bells of Saint Giles' cathedral rang out the hour.

Reaching into a jacket pocket, he pulled out one of the visiting cards Ellison had given him that Corbie had ordered: *John Ronan MacGregor, 6th Viscount Darrach, Darrach Castle, Glen Darrach, Perthshire.* The image beside the title and address depicted the arms of Clan Gregor, a crowned lion circled by a buckled belt. The motto read *S'rioghal mo dhream*—royal is my blood.

The scheme that led to these cards had brought him a pardon, a return to home and family—and had led him to a love he never thought to find.

"Driver," he called. "George Street, if you please."

The ride through the crowded streets took several minutes, longer than usual. Asking the driver to wait, Ronan went to the door and pulled on the bell.

The butler, answering the door, studied the card. "Ah, Lord Darrach. We understood you might call."

"I am here to see Miss Graham, if she has arrived home from the Highlands."

"Miss Graham is not at home at present."

"I see. May I ask if Sir Hector is at home and perhaps available?"

"The Deputy Lord Provost has gone to his offices for the day. It is a very busy time, sir."

"Of course. Please give Miss Graham my card." Keenly disappointed, he returned to the hackney. Above all, he had hoped to see Ellison today.

Minutes later, the coach pulled up in front of a house on North Castle Street.

The tall narrow townhouse sat high on the incline of the cobbled street, an elegant structure with a castle-like façade. Number Forty-five's front was curved like a castle tower, set with a tall door in bright red and a wide bowed window. Beneath a stone urn filled with red flowers, he found the key.

Stepping inside Ellison Graham's newly empty, newly repaired house, he found a hallway dividing the house with a parlor to the left, dining room to the right, and a kitchen at the back. Upstairs he saw two bedrooms and a bathing room, while the uppermost floor held three small rooms.

A simple but handsome house, he thought, pleased as he went back to the parlor. Its rooms were freshly painted, wood floors scrubbed and polished. It was nicely suited for a happily married couple and a small family someday.

But the place was nearly bare of furnishings, with a single chair and table in the kitchen, one chair and a table in the parlor, and upstairs one bed and a chest in one room, the others empty.

Ellison could furnish it as she liked. She might decide to keep it, rent it, or sell it altogether. If she wanted, he would buy her a different house with no memories of the past. Up in the Highlands, they would have Darrach Castle, someday other properties. Whatever she desired, she would have. He would see to it.

Sitting in the parlor's single chair, he stretched out his long legs. The wide curved front window overlooked streets and houses, with Edinburgh Castle in the distance, a commanding presence high on its dark cliff. Rainclouds gathered overhead.

An odd feeling swirled through him. Ronan frowned, trying to define it. Not weariness, though he was tired. Not dread, for he and Ellison had made the right choice, and the legal solution he had discovered would help solve all. Hurdles lay ahead, aye—Corbie, Pitlinnie. Sir Hector too. But he felt hopeful.

Happiness, he realized. That was what he felt. For the first time in years, he felt content. He had love, and a vision of the future again.

Later, he left the house to walk toward the bridge and over to the High Street and Parliament House. The city teemed with a commotion of people of all ages, shapes, origins, and ranks, bumping shoulders, skirting others, and making their way along. Tantalizing smells, bread baking, meats roasting, oranges piled high, ale spilled here and there—all of it was good. Shops and street carts offered treats and toys and thigmaleeries, and everywhere he looked he saw swaths of tartan, heather in bunches, flags of lions rampant and the blue-and-white saltire. Scottish pride had consumed and inspired the city. Sir Walter's vision of a magnificent Celtic spectacle infused and exhilarated the very air.

Walking along, shouldering here, begging pardon there, Ronan smiled. He was just another tall gentleman, just another Highlander heading up the High Street.

～

"Oh, do stop, I've lost my slipper," Sorcha said. "You are in such a hurry!"

Ellison paused in the crowd to offer her hand in support while Sorcha retrieved her slipper and hopped to pull it on again. Around them, pedestrians strolled, pushed, bumped past. Bells pealed overhead, and the haunting skirl of bagpipes filled the air.

"Another warm and rainy day," Sorcha said, pulling her shawl higher on her shoulders against the drizzle. "Look, Saint Giles! May we go inside?"

"Later. We must rush," Ellison said, locking elbows with Sorcha as they crossed the wide street, avoiding a constant stream of horses, carts, and people as they walked past the cathedral and across the wide square formed by Saint Giles and the enormous Parliament building.

She wondered if Papa was in his office here, or somewhere else in the city. No matter—she had another purpose here and must hurry before the courts closed. Brushing her dark blue skirts, adjusting her bonnet with its heather sprig and big blue bow, she tugged at her snug blue-and-green tartan jacket. She needed to look like a lady of merit today.

Taking Sorcha's arm, she forged ahead, past the tall pedestal with its bronze equestrian statue of King Charles II—the only other English monarch to visit Scotland under peaceful circumstances—and pushed open one of the great doors. They stepped into the soaring marble lobby of Parliament House.

"Thank you for coming with me," she said. "I did not want to do this alone."

"I would not miss this, after what you explained when we set out to come here," Sorcha said. "What a kerfuffle!"

"This way." Ellison paused, then turned about. "Or is it this way?"

Sorcha peered at a brass plaque. "Court of Session is in here. Court of Justiciary is over there."

"Justiciary." Ellison marched to a huge polished door and pushed her way inside, Sorcha following. In a reception area with several chairs and tables, a few men stood about speaking quietly. A young clerk sat behind a desk. Ellison went toward him.

"Yes, Miss—?"

"Miss Graham," she said. "And I wish to file a complaint."

He raised a brow. "You want the constable's office. I can direct you."

"I have spoken to the chief of the constabulary." Partly true—she had spoken to her father, but he did not know about this. "I wish to speak with a judge."

"I see. Well, since you have seen the constabulary chief, I suppose I could refer you to an advocate who can review the matter. It would be unusual to see a judge right away."

"But I am in such a hurry, Mr. Robertson." She smiled sweetly, reading the name plaque on his desk. "Did I mention that I am Sir Hector Graham's daughter? And I truly need to see a judge today."

"Oh! Well! You will need to provide your name and address and the reason for your visit." He handed her a paper. "You will find an inkstand on that table. But I cannot guarantee one of the judges will be free to see you. May I ask the nature of your complaint, Miss Graham?"

"Kidnapping," she said, taking the page and whirling away.

Crossing the huge expanse of the Parliament lobby, Ronan headed for the great oak and brass doors leading to the justice courts. As the bells of nearby Saint Giles echoed through the vast space, he turned to Hugh.

"Half two," he said. "We have time." Hugh nodded. Nearby, another door opened and three men walked into the lobby, deep in conversation. Ronan stopped, hand on the door.

"Blast," Hugh muttered. "Of all the luck."

Steeling his spine, Ronan watched Sir Hector, Adam Corbie, and Sir Neill Pitlinnie walk toward them, so focused on their discussion that they did not look up.

When they did, Ronan would have given any amount for an ink sketch of Corbie's expression. The man was stunned, alarmed, and then frightened in order. He stumbled back as Graham and Pitlinnie turned to follow his shocked gaze.

"Lord Darrach," Sir Hector said in a voice that boomed across the space.

Ronan inclined his head and waited. "Sir Hector, good to see you. And Mr. Corbie and Sir Neill. What a surprise," he drawled.

"Darrach," Pitlinnie muttered. Corbie gaped like a fish.

"I believe you know Mr. Cameron, my solicitor," Ronan said.

"Yes. What brings you here today?" Sir Hector asked.

"A judiciary matter, sir."

"Ah. I heard only recently that you are an advocate, in fact," Sir Hector said. "Wish I had known that sooner. Mr. Corbie has filled me in on some events of the past weeks. You have been—persevering, sir." He pinched his lips together.

"I have," Ronan drawled. "Has Mr. Corbie told you about what he and Pitlinnie have been up to in the Highlands lately?"

"This is not the time, MacGregor," Corbie muttered.

"Darrach," Ronan corrected him, fixing him with a flat gaze.

"That is enough, sir," Pitlinnie said.

"Sir Hector, we must hurry. The courts will close soon and Sir Neill wishes to sign the documents." Corbie gave Ronan a smug smile. "To do with Glenbrae."

"That can wait." Sir Hector waved a hand. "What is your business, Darrach?"

"It will come across your desk soon, sir. We are here to submit a warrant for the release of two men in Calton Jail."

"Unlikely," Corbie said.

"Actually, quite possible," Hugh returned.

"On what grounds?" Sir Hector demanded.

"We cannot disclose that here in a public space," Hugh said. "You understand."

"Sir Hector, you are welcome to accompany us to learn more," Ronan said.

"Yes. I want to hear this," Graham growled. As Ronan opened the door to the judiciary area, the deputy lord provost and then Hugh went through before him. He shut the door just as Corbie and Pitlinnie began to enter. He heard them swear.

"Go easy," Hugh warned him. "This is neither the time nor place."

"I know that," Ronan clipped.

In the small waiting area, Ronan hardly glanced at the few people in room, a few men, a couple of women, and a clerk. Behind him, he heard the doors open again—likely Corbie and Pitlinnie. Without glancing back, he approached the clerk, but Sir Hector spoke first.

"Mr. Robertson, which judges are still here today?" Graham demanded.

"Sir, uh, Jameson and Beaton. We close at half three, sir."

"I am aware. This way," Sir Hector told Ronan as he cut around the clerk's desk and opened a door beyond the waiting area.

Ronan did not glance back as he and Hugh followed. But he was sure he heard a woman gasp somewhere in the room behind him.

What was this? Ellison rushed to the clerk's desk as her father, her husband, and Hugh walked through a side door. Sorcha hurried with her. "Ellison, wait!"

"I do not know what this is, but I mean to find out," Ellison said. She turned. "Oh! Mr. Corbie!"

"Why, Miss Graham," he said. "You cannot follow them without authority, you know. What brings you to Parliament Hall today?"

"I am submitting papers," she said, handing the papers she had just completed to the clerk. She had also completed a copy, which she folded hastily and slid into her little mesh reticule.

"Papers? Good! You will remember Sir Neill Pitlinnie."

"Miss Graham," Pitlinnie said. "And young Miss Beaton. A pleasure. You are both looking well."

"Despite all," Ellison said, stepping toward the door where Ronan and the others had gone. Pitlinnie merely smiled at her answer, while Corbie scowled.

"I hope you came here to see to the matter we discussed," he said.

"That has been on my mind," she said, and turned to the clerk. "Sir, why did my father go back there?"

"They have some business, Miss," he answered. "I will take these papers back to one of the judges." He rose from his seat and went to the side door.

"I must know what is going on," Ellison said, and took Sorcha's arm to pull her along in Robertson's wake. Corbie and Pitlinnie followed her through the door.

"Miss Graham! I cannot allow you back here! Any of you!" the clerk said.

"It is urgent that I see my father. And my friend is Judge Beaton's sister. We will only be a minute!" She dragged Sorcha past the protesting clerk to hurry down a corridor lined with closed doors featuring brass plates.

"Mr. Robertson, I will take care of this," Corbie said, and he and Pitlinnie and the clerk rushed down the same corridor.

Ignoring them, Ellison walked swiftly along with Sorcha, scanning the name plaques rapidly, looking for Beaton or Jameson. Hearing muffled voices behind the door marked with Jameson's name, she raised a gloved fist to knock and entered.

CHAPTER 27

"This better be important, Sir Hector. Mr. Cameron, I know you—but who is this? You look familiar, sir." Seated behind a large mahogany desk, Judge Jameson peered over his spectacles at the men standing before him. He offered no one a chair.

"This is John Ronan MacGregor, an advocate," Hugh explained. "Lord Darrach now."

"Ah, heard about that. What do you want? It is late. I will allow you in here only because the deputy lord provost is with you. Even so, I want my tea, so be quick."

"Lord Jameson, thank you for seeing us," Sir Hector said. "Darrach has a matter to submit to the court. Perhaps you could entertain a brief preliminary discussion."

"Is this matter in your bailiwick, Sir Hector?" he demanded.

"Under the constabulary, yes."

"Proceed. Quickly."

"My lord," Ronan said, "Mr. Cameron and I wish to submit an application for a warrant of liberation."

"For whom? You? Now that I think of it, I have heard of you, sir. But you look liberated to me." Jameson folded large, pudgy fingers and frowned at him.

"My lord, Darrach was incarcerated briefly," Sir Hector said. "He was pardoned several weeks ago. I oversaw the matter personally."

"A misunderstanding, something of that order? Fine. Go on, tell me why I should listen to you today. I vow your office is just as busy as mine at the moment."

"It is, my lord. I do not know what Darrach and Cameron wish to present today. But I will vouch for them, if not for the matter of concern."

Ronan lifted a brow in surprise. "Thank you, sir." Graham nodded curtly.

"Let me see it." The judge held out a hand.

Hugh produced a packet of papers from his pocket and gave them to the judge. "We have prepared a petition for a warrant of liberation under the Habeas Corpus Act of Scotland of 1701."

"Whom do you want to liberate and why?" Jameson opened the packet.

"Arthur Stewart and Iain MacInnes," Ronan answered. "They were arrested with me under irregular circumstances. Currently, they are in Calton Jail."

"So you are petitioning for two writs of habeas corpus today, not one."

"Yes, my lord," Ronan said.

"Why should we release them? This could be a ploy by one cohort to free the others." Jameson turned pages and glanced up as a knock sounded on the door. "What is it!" he bellowed.

Ronan looked around as the door opened and a young man peered inside. "Pardon, Lord Jameson, sir. These people insist on seeing you."

"I am not to be disturbed. And I have already been disturbed."

"Uh, sir, one says he is Sir Hector's secretary. The other says she is his daughter. And Judge Beaton's sister is here. And someone else. They insist."

"Damned circus," Jameson muttered. "Damned gypsy fair, the whole blasted city! Let them in. Let them all in! Open the windows and let the whole noisy horse fair in here! Damned pipers too! Where is the king? Send him in here too!"

"Sir, sorry, sir," the clerk said, standing back as the others filed into the room.

What on earth—Ronan huffed in surprise to see Ellison and Sorcha followed by Corbie and Pitlinnie. Hugh shook his head, equally bewildered. Beside them, Sir Hector had turned an interesting shade of puce.

"Do you know these people, Sir Hector?" Jameson demanded.

"Yes, my lord. My daughter, Miss Ellison Graham, and her friend, Miss Beaton—Judge Beaton's sister. The other is my secretary, Mr. Corbie, whom you may know. And Sir Neill Pitlinnie, an honored donor to city expenses of late."

"Sit over there and be quiet, all of you," Jameson barked, pointing the newcomers toward chairs at the back of the room.

Ronan caught Ellison's gaze. She glanced away, shaking her head slightly. Beautiful in dark blue plaid, she looked delicate, determined—and worried. He narrowed his eyes, fisting a hand surreptitiously as Corbie sat beside her.

Outside, the constant noise in the streets was drowned by the peals of the great bronze bells of the cathedral, followed by booming strikes.

"Three already! I see I will have no blasted tea today," Jameson grumbled.

Feeling pulled toward what was happening at the judge's desk, Ellison leaned forward, ignoring Corbie beside her, while Sorcha leaned with her to listen.

"Your Honor, we are petitioning due to the length of time these two men have been incarcerated without trial," Ronan said.

"Sixty days?" The judge turned one page after another. "Ah. I see it. Since the first of May?" He looked up. "When was the sixty-day mark?"

"A letter of intimation was issued as required on the day after the arrest," Hugh Cameron said. "I notified the constable's office, which would have sent it on to the Court of Justiciary as well. The prisoners reached Edinburgh that same week. The indictment was a preliminary issue, but since no murder was involved, it did not go to the high court, but was referred elsewhere. It seems the final papers were not signed, as is noted in our petition."

Jameson glanced up. "You are certain of this?"

"Yes, my lord. The law requires indictment or trial within sixty days, which would have fallen on the twenty-ninth of June. Trial should have been set within a subsequent forty days. That time expired without a trial date on eight August, as you will see there. Today," he said, "is eleven August, as you know. One hundred and three days, my lord."

"So it seems," Jameson grunted, reading. "Interesting. And no signature."

"Yes, my lord," Ronan said. "The Scots Habeas Corpus Act of 1701 expanded a law established in 1695 and has not been altered under English rule. It holds that any prisoner incarcerated in Scotland for one hundred days without a trial may apply, or his advocate may do so, for a warrant of liberation."

"You are acting as advocate on behalf of your fellow prisoners?" Jameson rustled through the pages.

"Mr. Cameron and myself, aye, sir."

Listening, Ellison felt a thrill as she began to understand what Ronan was doing—what he had been doing all along. She recalled many nights that he sat late in the library at Strathniven, poring over law books, making notes. All that time, he had been making certain of the law, counting days, shoring up an argument.

In all this time, he had not forgotten the plight of his friends. Although taking the matter to a judge could expose him to dangerous scrutiny, he stood here today arguing for their freedom and risking his own.

Corbie snorted. "Much false information is in those papers, no doubt."

She rolled her eyes. "Be quiet."

"Issued in Culross, approved in Edinburgh," Jameson said, studying more pages. "Sir Hector, as constabulary chief, what do you know of this?"

Graham cleared his throat. "Sir, the case came through my office as a routine case of accused smuggling."

"Hardly routine. These were the Whisky Lairds, as I recall. Notorious and highly annoying, with crowds eager to see them. A spectacle. Now we have another spectacle in our streets," he muttered. "Go on."

"My lord, if there was a lapse in dates or part of a process was missed, as these men claim, it was never brought to my attention. Such things are stamped and approved routinely by my secretary and passed along as necessary. All should be in order."

"Humph. One of these men was released and the other two were moved to Calton early in July." The judge looked up.

"Lord Darrach—MacGregor in the documents—was released due to a confusion in the dates," Hugh said. "That should have applied to the others too. One hundred and three days have passed since the initial arrest. After one hundred days without a trial, a prisoner may petition for liberation."

"True. Sir Hector—how was this missed?"

"I, uh, cannot explain it, sir. My office is exacting with details. Yet we have seen a flood of matters needing our attention in the last few months."

Ellison frowned, glancing at silent Corbie beside her. A mistake had been made that traced back to him. Had it been innocent—or deliberate? She glanced at Pitlinnie, too, who had wanted to acquire Glenbrae distillery at any cost.

Jameson tapped his fingers. The men standing near him waited. *Tap, tap, tap,* then *thud* as the judge slapped a hand flat on the papers.

"We have all been sorely burdened with nonsense from the Crown," he said. "The city's civic and legal offices have been inundated with requests and decisions and tasks well beyond the norm. The royal visit was only confirmed weeks ago, giving us just a few weeks to prepare."

"That is true, my lord. Some details may have been overlooked."

Tap, tap. The judge looked from one man to the other.

Ellison breathed deeply, spine straight as pride filled her. Ronan had shown only integrity, following his principles, even to personal risk. Yet she feared he might face unfair scrutiny with Corbie so determined to take him down.

Sliding a glance at her father's secretary, the gleam in his narrowed eyes made her feel ill. He wanted to destroy Ronan. He would turn this bid for justice sour if he could. Though she had known him most of her life, she had not seen the darker side of his character lurking beneath ordinary arrogance and obstinance.

"Well," Jameson said, "I will read the petition and study the question."

"If I may remind Your Honor," Hugh said, "the law of 1701 holds that a warrant of liberation must be issued within twenty-four hours of a petition for freedom."

"I know damn well what the law requires, Mr. Cameron! But this court is closed tomorrow. Any day the court is closed means an extension of twenty-four hours. You will have an answer when we reopen. Return then."

"My lord," Hugh said, bowing his head.

"Thank you, my lord," Ronan said.

"Darrach, remind me of your status. Explain your arrest and pardon."

Ellison felt as if her heart sank. Beside her, Corbie gave a dry chuckle.

"Now it will be known," he muttered. She wanted to kick him.

"My lord," Ronan answered, "my friends and I were arrested at a tavern in Culross one evening. Excise officers took us by force and accused us of something we had not done. I sent word to Hugh Cameron before we were taken to Edinburgh."

"I have copies of those papers as well." Hugh handed a second packet to the judge, who ripped it open to sift through the contents.

"As I recall, the prisoners were displayed like animals and people lined up to see them. The decision came from the Captain of the Castle and Lord Provost, not directly from the court. Revenue was involved, I believe."

"Sir, it provided useful income for city expenses," Sir Hector explained.

The room went silent as the judge studied the pages. After a moment, Sir Hector looked over his shoulder, saw Ellison, and smiled. Surprised by that tentative, almost apologetic, show of affection, she nodded.

"You are a lawyer, yet that is not noted in these documents," Jameson said.

"I was not asked to explain my background, sir."

"Is there false information here?" Jameson snapped.

"No, my lord. We gave our birth names. Some details were never asked."

"Arrested for a crime but being an advocate is irrelevant? Hah!" Jameson shook his head. "And your friends? Lawyers too?"

"Sir, both are educated gentlemen. Arthur Hay-Stewart, Viscount Linhope, is a physician. Sir Iain MacInnes is a respected engineer."

"Then why in hell," Jameson growled, "were you all smuggling whisky?"

"Sir," Hugh said. "That has not been established or proven."

"Aye. *If* you were—why in hell did you do it? This nonsense surrounding the Whisky Lairds belongs to you, after all."

Seeing the judge's frustration, Ellison clenched her gloved hands and bit her lip. Beside her, Sorcha looked distressed. But Corbie huffed in amusement.

For a moment, Ronan was silent. Then he cleared his throat. "My lord, if it will save two men who do not deserve to be jailed and accused, I will explain."

"No promises," Jameson barked.

"My compatriots and I are not the ones the public has been calling the Whisky Lairds. We never were."

Ellison gasped. Ronan, not a Whisky Laird? He had never said any such thing to her. She saw Cameron's frown as if he was unsure what Ronan might say.

"Lord Darrach, while you are not under oath here in this room, you are well advised to speak the truth," Jameson reminded him.

"My lord, I had a brother, William MacGregor, and a cousin, Viscount Darrach. Both were killed by excise men. They were called the Whisky Lairds by the journals. I believe Sir Walter Scott named them. My kinsmen felt forced to move whisky out of the Highlands, as it was the only way to make a profit to help the people of our glen. The clearances have devastated many Highland glens and countless families over generations. My kinsmen did what they could for their kin and their tenants."

"Forced to smuggle? Good intentions cannot justify a crime."

"It is a dilemma for Highlanders, my lord, as you are no doubt aware. Land is sold, tenants are evicted or their herds and livelihoods are greatly reduced. Severe limits and high taxes are imposed on whisky production. Too many glen folk have few means left. But Highland whisky is a highly valuable product. Selling it keeps people from starving. Keeps them in their homes if their lands have not been sold off to wealthy men for hunting lodges and the like."

"Did you help your kinsmen build this noble enterprise, thus being part of their notoriety?" Jameson asked with more than a hint of sarcasm.

"I was in India much of that time, sir, with the dragoons under Sir Evan MacGregor. When I returned home, I set up a legal distillery with my brother's help. I helped with the whisky making, though I spent much of my time practicing law in Perth and Edinburgh."

"Were you part of the smuggling transport?"

"He was not, my lord," Cameron said. "Any transportation was arranged and run by others. That information was verified by witnesses but overlooked by the excise."

"Huh. I have seen you in these halls and before my bench, I think. Remind me what you do."

"Most often I act as a defending advocate on behalf of Highlanders accused of smuggling or charged with violence due to circumstances such as forced eviction."

"So you claim you were never a Whisky Laird?"

Ronan hesitated. "I was not, my lord. But after my brother's death, I did my best to complete business arrangements in his name."

"What the devil, Darrach? I am running out of patience."

"Sir, when my brother and cousin were killed by excise, my brother left a widow and a son, and tenants in need. Some business agreements were not met. My friends and I took on those obligations to prevent threats against innocents."

"By whom?"

"I prefer not to say, my lord," Ronan said.

"So you did not let this go when you could have," the judge grunted. "You saved their lives at risk of your own. Some would call it noble, some foolish."

"Aye," Ronan said. "But I could not let kinfolk suffer or let my distillery be destroyed by rivals. Glenbrae whisky is excellent in part due to my brother. I could not let everything he worked for be lost."

"Excellent? A bold claim. Most Highland whisky is superior."

"Lord Jameson, there is a unique testament to the quality of Glenbrae whisky," Sir Hector said. "The king favors Glenbrae so much that he requested to meet its distiller. Lord Darrach is to be introduced soon."

"Indeed? This is all very interesting." Jameson tapped the pages again.

Ellison set a hand over her chest, waiting. So much of this she had not known, had not realized that Ronan's actions and motivations stemmed from respect and integrity. From love. He was not driven by greed or disdain for the law.

She looked at Corbie, feeling a sense of triumph, wanting him to see it. But he did not look toward her.

Tap, tap, tap. "When were you named Viscount Darrach?"

"My lord, if I may," Hugh said, "MacGregor was recently named Viscount Darrach with the approval of Sir Evan Murray-MacGregor, chief of Clan Gregor. It is currently in the Lyon Court to be certified."

Thud. Jameson slapped the desk, folded the papers, crammed them in a drawer, and slammed it shut. "I heard about that. It all comes together now. Return here at noon on the first day we reopen. You in the back there! What do you bring? Quick!"

Corbie stood immediately. "My lord, I believe we should revisit the charge of smuggling. MacGregor, who calls himself Darrach, recently transported illicit whisky by sea. Yesterday he arrived in Leith with goods smuggled out of Perthshire." He walked toward the desk. "I ask that the court renew the charges against him."

"Lord Darrach comes by his title decently, and you will respect that, sir. But this is a serious allegation." The judge scowled and turned. "Darrach, is it true?"

"I brought Glenbrae whisky into Leith Harbor this morning, aye. Two barrels, three smaller kegs, and three crates of crockery jugs."

"That is a good deal more than is allowed for personal use."

"The kegs and barrels were delivered to Holyroodhouse today as a gift for the king from the city."

"The king!" Jameson stared. "Very well. What about the rest of it? If those are sold, you have endangered yourself."

"I had it sent up to the Castle for the Highland contingency. Thousands of Highlanders are in Edinburgh for the parades and to act as honor guards for the royal party. The cost of provisions for them is considerable. The casks went to the attention of Sir Evan and Sir Walter Scott to be dispersed among the clans."

Jameson looked at Sir Hector. "Did you know about this?"

"I did not. Lord Darrach is to be thanked for such a generous gift."

"Indeed. But what use does the king have for so much whisky?" Jameson swiveled toward Ronan. "He will be in Scotland a fortnight at most."

"My lord, it is a gift to be sent to England for his personal cellars."

Jameson nodded, chuckled—then guffawed. He laughed so heartily that others smiled and laughed too, somewhat uncertainly. "So the king favors smuggled whisky, does he? And if he ships this lot home to England—that makes him a smuggler in the letter of the law."

"It may, Your Honor." Ronan smiled.

"A lawyer of your caliber would not miss that detail." As Ronan shrugged a shoulder, Jameson guffawed again, then pointed. "You! Secretary, what is your name?"

"Adam Corbie, my lord."

"Your request is denied. Darrach will not be charged. But the king, a smuggler! It suits this travesty of a Scottish spectacle. Worth missing my tea."

A knock at the door interrupted him. The clerk peeked in. "My lord, you asked to be told when Judge Beaton was available. He is here now." He stepped aside.

Archibald Beaton entered the room, dressed in black robes and a wig. He lifted a hand toward Jameson, then turned. "Sorcha! I was told you were here!" He took her hands. "What a surprise."

"I came with Ellison, and we saw the others here too."

"What is going on?" Beaton went to Jameson, leaning forward to confer quietly. "I see," he murmured more than once. "Astonishing. I see."

Jameson rose from his desk. "I leave you in good hands," he told the group. "My tea awaits. Lord Beaton will hear Miss Graham's plea. Come forward, Miss."

She stood, feeling doubt flutter through her. "My lord, thank you, but it can wait."

"Nonsense. We are here and may as well continue," Beaton said as Jameson left. "As a courtesy to your father, I will consider your request."

She quailed, began to demur, but caught Ronan's steady glance, though he did not know what she intended to do here. She nodded stiffly and came forward.

"Bring your petition here, Miss Graham. I have already seen the papers that Robertson had. Come closer." Beaton waved her toward him.

Crossing the room, feeling everyone's gaze, she saw Ronan and her father watching her, concern and puzzlement in their expressions. All the while she could feel Corbie's piercing glare like a knife blade. Handing the pages to Lord Beaton, she hoped he would not ask her to explain the matter before this company. Still, she had to do this. She stood waiting, twisting her fingers back and forth while he read.

Beaton cocked a brow, then looked up. "Everyone but Miss Graham and her father may leave the room. The rest wait outside. Do not leave the building. This will not take long. Robertson!" he called. "Lead them out. Ask one of the regiment officers out there to ensure they stay."

"Ellison," Ronan murmured as he walked past. His gaze caught and held hers. Ellison felt her heart gallop, hands shaking. This was something she must do on her own. When she was near Ronan, she felt calmer, more certain. But her nature was to doubt herself, a demon that resurfaced as her father approached her.

"Ellison," Sir Hector said in a stern voice. "What is this?"

Again she wondered what Corbie had told her father. But her happiness, her future, would be determined by what she did here and now. She would have her say.

"Lord Beaton," Sir Hector said, "allow me a word with my daughter."

"Of course." Beaton went to a tall bookshelf to extract a volume and flip through its pages. Sir Hector took Ellison's elbow and led her away.

"What is all this about?" Her father faced her, glowering.

"I wanted to tell you, Papa, but you did not have time to listen." She looked up into gray eyes so like her own, but his gaze was hard, cool, and concerned.

CHAPTER 28

Through the windows high in the wall of the Parliament façade, Ronan saw lead-colored clouds heavy with rain. The bells of the cathedral that shadowed the square rang out again, drowning the chatter, the drone and skirl and rat-a-tat of distant pipes and drums. Half three, the bells tolled.

He ought to be practicing there, he thought, with Sir Evan. He would have to forego that. He and Cameron had another appointment too, a pressing one that Hugh had arranged earlier. He paced, glancing at Hugh, growing anxious.

But this was where he needed to be, here waiting for Ellison. He stood in silence beside Hugh, who chatted with Sorcha. A few feet away, Corbie and Pitlinnie stood looking annoyed and impatient. Nearby, Lord Jameson lingered with some colleagues for a few moments.

Wondering what Ellison, her father, and Beaton were discussing, Ronan exhaled heavily, tapping a foot. What did she want in the judiciary court? Had she had the chance to speak to her father yet about their marriage?

He should be with her—but then he realized she might need to do this herself. Whatever it was, he would support her. He had committed his heart and life to her.

"Darrach." Corbie approached. Turning stiffly, Ronan saw the sneer on the man's face. He wanted to wipe it off but caught Hugh's warning glare. "If I were you, I would not wait long for Miss Graham. They have much to discuss in there."

"I am sure they do," Ronan murmured. He flexed a hand, fisting it behind him.

"Let me give you some advice." Hands in his pockets, Corbie looked smug. Though not a tall man, he had a knack for radiating arrogance. "Leave Miss Graham be."

Ronan took a breath. Two. Three regimental soldiers stood within twenty feet, talking idly. Jameson stood not ten steps away. Outside, thunderclouds gathered overhead, rumbling, echoing his rising temper. But this was no time to heave Corbie by his neckcloth and fling him through a window, much as he ached to do it.

"Why do you say that, sir?" he finally asked. "Do you know her mind?"

"The papers Miss Graham delivered today, and which she is discussing with her father and a judge this very moment, comprise an application for annulment."

"Oh?" Ronan flared his nostrils.

"She confided in me. Quite upset, feeling she had made a mistake. You understand."

"Ah." Ronan turned away, sucking in a breath, wrestling with his temper. Then he whirled back, fingers clamped in a hard ball, reared back, and slammed a punch to Corbie's jaw.

Thrown back, Corbie stumbled, caught under his arms by Pitlinnie. "What the devil!" he groaned, nursing his jaw. The soldiers came running, footsteps hard.

"What the hell, MacGregor!" Pitlinnie shouted. Ronan opened his fist, closed and balled it again, and hit Pitlinnie with a bull's force, knocking both men down like wooden pins in lawn bowling.

Spinning on his heel, he walked away. Hugh followed, Sorcha

running after them. Two soldiers veered to chase him the length of the huge hall.

Jameson stepped into his path. "Darrach!"

Ronan stopped mid-stride. "Sir," he growled, simmering with residual anger. Let them arrest him. He hardly cared.

"I read Miss Graham's petition," the judge growled. "I would have done the same. Bastards. You earned the privilege. That is my private thought, not my legal opinion. Guards!" he called. "Leave this man to me. Take those two and hold them for Judge Beaton's decision when he finishes his current meeting."

"My lord?" Ronan ran a hand through his hair. His thoughts were in a jumble. A petition for annulment? And yet those two were being held when he had been the aggressor. "I do not understand."

"Take a walk. Cool your head," Jameson said. "Then find her."

"Sir," Ronan said, anger, relief, and gratitude mixing within. He pushed out through the doors into a light rain. Hugh followed, Sorcha hurrying beside him.

"Ronan! What in blazes was that?" Hugh asked. "You could be arrested."

"It was only what they deserved." He turned. "Miss Beaton, my apologies. Can we take you to Lady Strathniven's house?"

"No, I will wait for Ellison. Lord Darrach, what you did was magnificent! I know something of it, you see."

He opened his aching hand, closed it. Smiled bitterly. "It did not feel magnificent. Go to Ellison. She will need you."

"Are you coming back inside?"

"I have a meeting, lass. I will see Ellison later. Hugh—with me."

"Where to?"

"Calton Jail." His stride, long and fierce, cleft through the horde in the square. He went out to the High Street and turned to follow the downward slope without waiting for Hugh. He knew the man would catch up.

～

Her chance was here and now. Mustering courage as her father spoke, she nodded. Much of what Corbie had told him was slanted, just as she expected.

"But Adam tells me," her father added low, "that you agreed to take steps to correct this impulsive marriage. And so you are here."

"Papa, I am sorry Mr. Corbie told you before I could. It was not his place. If we had time to speak at home, I would have explained the whole of it. He left out some details."

"Best forgotten. I have the essentials. He said you were compromised, so at least, we can assume Darrach recognized his obligation."

"I was not compromised. I owe him my life." *My heart.*

"I do not consider myself a poor judge of character, so I was surprised by what Corbie told me. MacGregor, er, Darrach, seemed a solid enough fellow to me from all that I heard. But you are making amends. Though I allow that I may owe Darrach an apology."

"He is more a gentleman than most, Papa."

"And fortunately he is heir to the Darrach estate after all—rather a miracle, that. And today I thought he proved himself a gentleman in spirit as well as manners."

"Truly so. Papa—"

"Soon this unpleasant situation will be over, and we can all move on from the Highland spectacle—and the little scheme we had planned. Luckily we do not need to continue that ruse." Speaking in a low tone, he smiled flatly.

"Please listen. I am not filing for an annulment."

"You submitted the papers. I expect I am here to witness them."

"No, Papa. I prepared a complaint against Mr. Corbie and Pitlinnie for conspiring to kidnap me and endanger my life. Darrach did not compromise me that night. He saved me."

"What madness is this?" His thick silvery eyebrows snapped together.

"Corbie had a scheme with Pitlinnie to abduct me for marriage. If that had worked, trust that I would be seeking annulment against Corbie. Instead, Darrach found me. And we decided to marry that night—

because it was the only way to prevent Mr. Corbie's hateful plan to marry me and harm Darrach."

He stared at her. "I do not understand."

"It is the truth, I swear. I will tell you more later when there is time. But yes, I am married. And I am happy, Papa. I chose to do this. I love him," she said, leaning toward him. "Please listen."

"Ellison, I am astonished."

"You need to know what sort of man Adam Corbie is. Apparently he schemed with Pitlinnie to destroy Ronan and take over Glenbrae's whisky business. They schemed for Corbie to marry me so Lady Strathniven would make him her heir. She is undecided and thought he should have a good wife before he could inherit. I think she realizes the truth about Corbie more than she admits."

"She has always been of two minds with that lad." Creasing his brow, he shook his head slowly. "Corbie tells all this quite differently."

"I am sure he does. I am sorry you must learn it this way. But it is true, Papa."

"I must think about this. Possibly I have not paid enough attention."

"You have been so busy, Papa. You have much on your mind, and daughters to raise. You have always done what you thought was right. I know that."

"Dear girl. Perhaps too busy. Perhaps I owe you an apology too. But let us see what Beaton has to say. I need to read your account." He led her back to the desk.

Reading the documents and discussing them did not take as long as Ellison expected. Judge Beaton and Sir Hector were of shared mind— terse, efficient, and quick to see that Ellison's claims were warranted, serious, and deserved legal action.

"This is all very disturbing," Sir Hector said.

"At the least, you may need to employ a new secretary," Beaton said.

"Whatever comes of it, my lord, I cannot give the man the benefit of the doubt where my daughter's honor and safety are concerned. As for Pitlinnie, I only know his whisky, and little of him otherwise."

"He makes donations to pander for privilege. The Scots are not impressed, but he has some favor among English peers. I do not know what he wants with this unseemly involvement, however."

"He wants Glenbrae," Ellison supplied. "He wants credit for the finest whisky. If he purchases Glenbrae and Corbie inherits Strathniven, in the future they could make a huge profit together. They could even rise in power in the government."

"Huh," Beaton grunted. "Your daughter has a keen mind, sir. I believe she may be correct."

"She has a very keen intelligence, my lord. She is a writer, I should add. And if her—husband holds Darrach and Glenbrae both, that would be well done."

"Indeed. Pitlinnie's bid for the land and distillery should be reconsidered. For now, this particular situation needs investigation—and restitution for the lady."

While they spoke, Ellison felt her heart lift, felt burdens leaving. Thinking of Ronan waiting outside, she wished he was here with her. But she would be patient. All would be well.

"I must say, I believe I have misjudged Lord Darrach," her father said.

"Many have been misjudged here, but we will do our best to rectify it," Beaton said. "Well, Miss Graham—Lady Darrach," he amended, "I will take this matter further. For now, Mr. Corbie and Pitlinnie will be detained. A little time in Calton Jail until this comes to trial, as I believe it should, will give them time to think."

"Thank you, my lord. I did not want to cause trouble, but I thought this should be brought to light."

"You did the right thing. They will have a chance to defend themselves and the outcome remains to be seen. They will need a good advocate. These are very serious charges. But we shall see."

"Thank you, Judge Beaton."

"Of course." He stood. "I am glad to assist Lord Darrach as well, particularly considering his bravery in India—and his integrity today. A worthy man."

Walking out with her father later, Ellison glanced around the hall, but did not see Ronan. "They must be waiting outside," she said, as they went into the square.

"Ellison," her father said, holding her back with a hand on her arm. "I wanted to tell you that I saw Sir Evan MacGregor earlier today. Another meeting about this royal visit, and we are plagued with rain again," he added, looking up at the drizzly sky. "Sir Evan spoke highly of Darrach. A man of golden character and courage, he said. And he ought to know."

"Yes. Darrach will be glad to hear your improved opinion of him."

"I have been wrong about him. I see it now. He possesses the composure and values of a true gentleman. What he did to help his friends is singular."

"He would do anything for friends and kinsmen, and his family."

"And you, I think. But what finally changed my mind was you," he continued. "I saw it in your face. You love this man. And I saw he loves you. He has the character and the means to make you happy. That is all I want. If there are legal issues yet to be cleared, let me help."

"Oh, Papa, thank you."

"I am seeing a change in you too. You are a strong young woman. Confident, standing up for what you know is right, and standing up for those you love." He smiled. "I thought I could make you stronger and happier through discipline and pushing you to improve. Perhaps it was not the best course. It is not criticism that improves, I think, but love. I am seeing that now."

"Oh!" Ellison said through tears. Rising on tiptoe, she kissed his bristly cheek.

"We will talk more, you and I, your husband too. We must welcome him into the family." He looked around. "But I do not see him here."

She turned. "I thought he would wait."

"He will find you. It is raining in earnest now. Go back to the house—take my carriage. I will send it around. I have some work to finish, and dinner with another committee. I will see you later."

"Thank you, Papa." Ellison smiled, wiping away tears. Seeing Sorcha on the other side of the square, she went toward her.

"Darrach had an appointment," Sorcha told her. "He promised to see you later."

"The king a smuggler?" Linhope hooted. "I wish I had been there to hear it!"

"Wish we had both been there, and out of here," Iain said. "By God, it is good to see you, Glenbrae. Cameron, you too."

"Darrach," Linhope reminded him, for Ronan had told them the news, or most of it, from lessons in manners to missing whisky to the legal petition to free them.

"It is time we were done with the past," Ronan said. "We could not stop William and Darrach from doing what they did, and I do not regret our efforts to finish their work. But we are fortunate to have an avenue of escape from the risks we took."

Cameron leaned a shoulder against the cell door. "I agree with Darrach."

"Aye well, we did think we would never be caught," Linhope said.

"If this warrant for liberation holds, we will be released?" MacInnes asked.

"If it holds, aye," Ronan said.

"And then?" Linhope asked.

"Behave," Cameron said. "That is my best advice for all of you."

"I plan on it." Iain scratched his beard. "Next we need a barber and a tailor."

"I will send a barber tomorrow," Ronan said. "A tailor as well. We have no guarantee in the court matter, you do understand that. But I want you to be prepared to walk out of here with your heads high. And if this petition does not work, I will find another way. I will never give up."

"You have both been of service while you are here," Hugh said. "That will count for something too."

"So, no longer Highland heathens?" Iain asked.

"No longer. You can be the gentlemen you are."

"I do not feel much like a gentleman just now," Iain said, scratching his beard.

"One hundred and three days? You are certain?" Linhope asked.

"By all counts, aye." Hugh said. "Some steps in setting up a trial were missed."

"For which we may thank the king and the chaos around his visit," Ronan said.

"This means freedom," Hugh said. "It also means you are done with free trade."

"What! We were never involved in that," Iain said blithely. The others laughed.

"If this is resolved quickly, you may be free to enjoy the festivities in the city," Ronan said. "And I want to introduce you to some friends who have helped me. Lady Strathniven, for one. And Miss Graham."

"The angel who visited here, the one who gave you some unnecessary lessons in etiquette? Lovely lass, that," Iain said.

"Aye. And she is Lady Darrach now," Ronan said. He had held that back until the rest was told. The possibility that she had filed for annulment hurt deeply—he would have to deal with that. But his friends deserved the news, and later the truth.

They stood, clapped shoulders, and laughed, while Ronan smiled faintly. Hugh said nothing, watching them.

"Will you go back to the Highlands?" Ronan asked. The others nodded. "Well, someone will be very happy to see you when you do—especially you, Arthur."

Linhope regarded him for a moment. "And who is that?"

"I have a letter here for you somewhere." He patted his jacket and found a crumpled envelope. "Here. From Mairi Brodie."

Sliding the note inside his rumpled shirt, Linhope shoved a hand through tangled blond hair and gave a wry smile. "Darrach, when you send fresh clothes here, remember the royal Stewart sett is my right and honor as Viscount Linhope. And send a good deal of soap. I need to look my best when we head north at last."

~

Alasdair MacAlpin saw her in the moonlight, standing at the parapet. Never had he seen a lovelier sight than Lady Isabella studying the moon. The light cast a glow over her hair, burnished it to bronze, and turned the walls of the castle to pewter. She sighed, leaned her chin on her hands, sighed again.

But he held back. He was only her loyal guard and seneschal, not a man privileged to approach a lady except for matters to do with her castle. A widow now, she was elevated to the lady of this stronghold. To her, he just was her seneschal. Yet she would always be sweet Isabella to him.

All he could do was protect her. Love her. Keep her safe. It would have to be enough—

Ellison set down the quill, frowning in thought—but she could hardly concentrate on her novel just now, though she had tried. Looking around her bedchamber, the room where she had spent so much of her life, she sighed. Beyond the window, clouds made the sky a plum color, though it was barely past high tea. She had hoped Ronan would come to her father's house, but he had not arrived so far. But it was only six.

If he did not come soon, she would find him tomorrow. Perhaps like her father, he had duties—the procession of the clans was set for morning, with the king's levee in a couple of days. She must be patient.

Finding courage for the larger things, she had learned, she was finding it for the smaller things too. She had finally stepped beyond her timidity with her father. She truly was stronger now, and grateful to Ronan for helping her realize that.

She was reclaiming her bolder self, the girl she had always been, but wiser now, sure of herself. She might still plummet into worry and feel anxious. But she need not shrink and concede; she could stand strong, knowing she was loved.

She wanted desperately to see him. But she had to wait. Standing, she stretched, glanced out the window, and dearly wanted a long walk to clear her head.

Then a thought occurred. Earlier she had intended to visit her tenants and had even prepared a gift basket of treats, flowers, ribbons, oatcakes, even a small notebook. Was it too late to deliver it? She would drop it on the step and hasten away. She just wanted to get some fresh air.

Tossing on a shawl, she slipped out of the house into the street. Gas lamps, newly set throughout the city, twinkled like stars overhead, likely turned on early by city workers due to the rainy gloom and the crowds. She hurried along George Street toward North Castle Street.

All was quieter here on this residential street; the cacophony of the city was confined for the most part near the High Street between the Castle and Holyrood. The sky still held a lavender glow despite rain clouds. She would hurry and could be home again in a quarter of an hour.

Passing Scott's own house on North Castle, she paused for a moment, seeing lamplight through the windows. Voices floated out as men talked inside. She wondered if her father was there—perhaps Ronan was there, too. She moved on.

Ahead, she saw a coach depart from the houses higher on North Castle. And ahead, she saw the curved front window of her townhouse. It looked dark.

Perhaps the tenants were not there after all. She would leave the basket and slip away, back to her father's house, glad for an outing on a soft, pretty evening.

Ronan sat in his single chair in his empty house, swirling the glass in his hand, watching the amber liquid flash and swirl. He looked up at Hugh.

"There is a little food in the kitchen if you are hungry," he told Hugh. "I bought bread and cheese in the market earlier, and plums. It is all I can offer. That, and another dram of this excellent Glenbrae. The king's favorite, by the way." He sipped.

"I ate enough at Sir Walter's table this evening," Hugh said, leaning against the door jamb. "I suspect you have had a good bit of that fine Glenbrae by now and should have the bread and cheese yourself. You are a bit fou, lad."

"Not yet. There is not enough whisky to erase what I learned this day. Though I should save some to drown my sorrows tomorrow." Ronan set the glass on the floor. "I need a maid," he said, glancing around. His jacket lay on the floor beside his valise and his folded dress plaid meant for the next day, topped by a bonnet fixed with the two feathers allotted a chieftain. He would wear the gear tomorrow as part of Sir Evan's retinue. "I need a maid, and furniture for a maid to dust. And food. And a cook to cook some food."

"Settling in, I see."

"And I need my wife who has annulled me. Thrown me over on the advice of a fellow half my worth. Half my size," Ronan groused.

"Nowhere near your worth. Feeling sorry for yourself is useless. It will be sorted out."

"Will it? She's annulled our wee wedding."

"So you believe Corbie, who is no friend to you. Or her."

"Why would he invent that?"

"Perhaps she will change her mind."

"She changed her mind about the wee wedding. She seemed happy," he added. "I thought we were happy."

"Her father is a strong influence. It cannot be easy to be his daughter."

Rubbing a hand over his face, Ronan shook his head to clear it. "One good thing about this damnable royal visit—with all the chaos around it, Corbie forgot to count the days of our arrest."

"There is that. Brilliant of you to notice it."

"I am a bit fou," Ronan admitted, setting down the glass. "No dinner, you see."

"You should rest. I have a carriage waiting to take me back to my mother's house. I have stayed away. The house is overrun with people and good cheer."

"Tomorrow is an important day for many, I suppose. Not for me."

"Riding beside Sir Evan at the head of the Highland contingent is an honor."

"Huh," Ronan said bitterly. "Until tomorrow, sir."

Hugh left the house, and Ronan heard the vehicle creak, heard hoofbeats. He upended his glass on the floor. He was not so very drunk as such things went, but he would have no more. He was tired and irritated. Miserable was the better word.

Miserable without her.

But with or without her, he would be fine. If he had to live without Ellison, by God he would. He would try to forget her, or at least pretend to do so.

For now, best seek his bed and sleep all of this off. He stood.

Hearing footsteps, a sound at the door, he shook his head. "What did you forget? Come back in, lad." He opened the door.

A woman stood there, slight and graceful in a sweep of dark skirts and a plaid shawl. She stared up at him, her delicate face shadowed by a bonnet stuck with heather. She looked like an angel to him.

"Ah," he drawled. "My little landlady."

CHAPTER 29

"*R*onan!" She stared at him, astonished. "You—are here?"

"I," he said, "am your tenant, madam. Is that for me?" He took the basket and stood back to allow her to enter.

Heart pounding, thoughts racing, she stepped inside and looked up at him. He was in shirtsleeves, no neckcloth, the flat collar open to his strong throat. His dark hair was curled and mussed; his blue eyes glittered. So very blue, even in lamplight. He did not look glad to see her.

"Are you drunk?"

"A bit. Not a usual state for me, I assure you. Fine stuff, that Glenbrae whisky. What can I do for you?" He swept an arm toward the parlor. "Would you care to sit?"

"There is just one chair." She walked into the room. He followed. She noticed the chair, the upended glass in a puddle on the floor, the stack of tartan clothing.

"Fortunately, I am gentleman enough to offer the chair to the lady."

She whirled. "How is it you are here? I thought I had tenants here."

"A tenant. Me. Hugh and I conspired, you see," he said, setting down the basket and leaning a shoulder against the doorjamb, "to release you from an untenable position in this house, and provide a trustworthy renter."

"You did say you had a place, but never said it was here."

"Meant to surprise you. Do not fear. I will not stay where I am not wanted."

She frowned, puzzled by his words, his manner, feeling they spoke at cross-purposes. "I waited at my father's house. I thought you might call there. Then I recalled the new tenant, so I thought to—just leave a basket on the step."

"A kind welcome. I have been busy. No time to visit."

"You did not wait for me at Parliament Hall."

"Should I have?" He leaned in the doorway.

She continued to stand, hands tightly folded. "I hoped you might."

"Ah, but she is independent now. She needs no one. Has found her backbone. Came here alone. Drove a gig?"

"Walked. Only to find her husband drunk."

"Sorry." He inclined his head. "Please sit. Or have you come to inspect the house? Your property, after all."

She stifled a surprised sob in the face of his anger, sharp, hurtful, and bewildering. "What is wrong?"

"Why are you here without Mr. Corbie at your heels?"

"Mr. Corbie is in jail with Mr. Pitlinnie."

"Jail! Justice is served. I punched him," he told her. "Both of them."

"I did not know. You were not there when I came outside. I hoped to see you tonight." *So much,* she wanted to say, but his scowl discouraged it.

"For what? Ah, you need a signature on your paperwork."

"If you want to speak as a witness, you may."

"That is cold, madam."

"I do not understand." She felt so confused. Tearing off her gloves, she wove her fingers together. "I am at a loss."

"He is the one at a loss. She is the one who knows what she wants."

"I thought we were—" *In love.* But she hesitated, feeling his coldness. Love was strong, love was fragile—which had the upper hand now? "I thought you were fond of me."

"Fond!" A bitter laugh. "Oh aye. Perhaps we can be friends."

Her thoughts tumbled, fractured. a sob rose again. "Please—"

"Shall I call you a hackney, my lady? They are all about for hire these days."

"No! I thought—since you are here, I might stay."

"Stay the night? Have your cake, is that it?"

"Truly, I am confused. What happened?"

"A great deal. I am told you applied for an annulment."

She felt the blood drain from her head so quickly that she felt dizzy, set a hand on the back of the chair. "Is that it? Who told you?"

"Corbie said you brought the papers to court to see a judge."

"But I never meant—"

"Never meant to hurt me? It slipped your mind to tell me about this?" He sounded bitter, crossing his arms, a ferocious guardian of his anger. And like her father, he was not listening, just assuming, plowing ahead.

Her temper gathered too. "You are very wrong right now. And very drunk."

"I am not so drunk. I am a gentleman, my dear. A lawyer, a distiller. A viscount, as it happens." He moved toward her. "I speak perfect English, Gaelic too. I can tie a damned cravat and polish my boots and use the proper blasted fork."

"Ronan—"

He took another step. "And I would give you every part of me, pledge my life to you. Because I love you beyond life—"

"Do listen—" Hearing his words just then, tears filled her eyes.

"And I am repaid with a paper that releases you from this marriage. But freedom is what both of us wanted. We did agree on that."

"We did. But stop this. You—you are being beastly!"

He nodded, pushed a hand through his hair. "Then best go before I say something I cannot undo." A wince flashed across his face.

"Sit and listen."

"A gentleman does not sit while a lady stands."

"Do you know," she said, "even when you are angry, you are still a gentleman. And still the finest man that I have ever known."

Fingers raking his messy hair, he sent her a sidelong glance. "Say what you want to say, then."

"I did not submit an annulment, you beast."

A quick look of surprise. "What?"

"I brought an accusation of kidnapping against Corbie and Pitlinnie. That is why they are in Calton tonight."

He stared. "I thought otherwise."

"Yes you did." Her tone was cool, deliberate.

"That accusation took courage. Not many would listen to a lass bringing it."

"I did what you said. Stood up for myself and accused them of wrongdoing."

"So—not an annulment?" He tipped a brow, looking mollified.

"Of course not. Why would I obey Mr. Corbie? That was what he wanted me to do."

"Huh." He watched her for a moment. "You are beautiful, you know."

"And you," she said, coming closer, "usually have perfect manners. You dance well, you choose the right fork, you catch fish in your bare hands. You make the best whisky in the world, you defend others with your very life. And you made a lonely widow feel heard and seen and so good—" She drew a ragged breath.

"Ellison—"

"—And I love you with all my heart and soul. Madly so, even now. Beast."

"I was. I am sorry."

"I do not care a whit what title you have or do not have. I do not care if you live in a cave or a castle. Or in this house." She gestured with a flailing hand. Tears ran freely down her cheeks. "The house is so clean. You made it so nice. When did you do that?"

"It has a chair," he said. "And a bed."

He opened his arms then, and she sobbed out and ran into his embrace, knocking into him, feeling his warmth and strength close around her as he caught his balance and drew her deep into his arms and set his cheek against her bonnet, crushing it.

"Silly damn thing," he said, and with deft fingers, loosened the bow and tore the hat away, tossing it aside. "Fetching, though."

She pressed against him, inhaling his scent, male and musky, laced with whisky, and felt the warmth and power of his body against hers. "I do so love you."

"I love you dearly," he whispered. "I was very wrong."

"Yes you were. And so was I, for not telling you what I planned to do."

"Well done for taking them down. They deserved it. Did I ever tell you," he went on, "that I fell in love with you the day you walked into that dungeon? Angel. The one who changed me, changed my life." He cupped her cheek, tilted her face up, kissed her so gently she felt as if she melted there in his arms and had to clench her toes to make sure she was whole.

"You did not need changing. But I did. I am better for it."

"You were always fine, lass. You just did not know it." He kissed her again, lingering, so that she felt it run through her body like fire and honey.

"Oh," she said, sinking against him. "Oh! There is one other thing."

"Later," he murmured, deepening another kiss, pulling her hard against him.

"My father—I told my father"—she kissed him—"that we were married, and he said—"

"Later, love." He pressed his lips to her hair. "No talk of that now. But I am glad you told him."

"He says he may have been wrong about you," she went on.

"Good." Ronan chuckled and tipped her face up to kiss her again. She renewed the next one and the next, each touch and taste hungrier and more fervent.

"But it does not matter to me what he thinks," she said.

"It does, for you will feel better knowing he is content, love." His lips on hers took her reply. Her limbs were dissolving so that she nearly

sagged in his arms. "Hush now. Shall we go upstairs? Aye? Darling girl."
He lifted her in his arms as if she weighed nothing at all and headed for
the stairs.

"Wait—the lock."

"The lock." He swung, carrying her as he latched the door. "Happy?"

"So very," she whispered against his neck.

Ronan adjusted his plaid, patterned in MacGregor blood red and forest
green, smoothing the drape over his left shoulder, pulling at the sleeves of
his jacket of the same tartan. The weather was warm, though the air was
humid and heavy, iron-gray skies threatening yet another bout of rain. He
tugged at his flat black bonnet with its fir sprig and the two feathers that
declared him a chieftain of the Gregorach.

With a twitch of his shoulders, he balanced the painted wooden targe
looped over one arm and checked again the sheathed sword and pistol at
his waist. He was part of a Highland army, ranks of them replete with
colorful plaids, gleaming weapons, and feathered and sprigged bonnets.
They were everything Sir Walter Scott had envisioned for this day.

All done up, Ronan thought, even to his stockings in a MacArthur
tartan in honor of his mother, who would have enjoyed this day; his
father would have been thrilled by it too. Over a decade had passed
without them, and so much had happened. They would have been proud
of what he had achieved—and pleased with his bride as well.

Smiling to himself, aware deep in his core of his great good fortune,
he leaned forward to smooth a gloved hand over his horse's neck. The
mount was a docile rented bay like most of those in the procession that
morning. The enormous gathering along Queen Street was comprised of
over a thousand Highlanders on foot and horsed, along with dignitaries in
carriages, accompanied by bagpipes, drums, and flags. Soon they would
be escorting and guarding the royal regalia of Scotland. And to a man,
they were restless to begin the march.

"Darrach!" Sir Evan MacGregor rode back toward him. Beside him on a pony was his eldest son, just twelve, a beautiful lad dressed in Highland kit like his father, complete with targe and sword. "Will you come up front?"

"I will—but others are more deserving to ride beside you."

"Nonsense. You belong there," his chief, his cousin, answered. Sir Evan's smile puckered with the deep scar that ran from his brow along his nose to his mouth. His right arm lay still on the reins, limp fingers protected in a thick leather glove. The man was known for leadership, kindness, and pragmatism—and for surviving devastating injuries and coming back to lead his clan.

He was also renowned for a singular physical beauty that even the deepest scars could not dim. The handsomest man in Scotland, they called Sir Evan Murray-MacGregor. And among the most respected and admired, Ronan thought.

"Thank you, then." Ronan smiled and glanced over his shoulder at more than fifty MacGregor Highlanders handpicked by the chief to form his tail and guard. In those ranks, Ronan glimpsed Donal Brodie, proud in his Highland finest, ready to march on foot with the others. The lad waved and grinned, seeing Ronan.

"Did you know I have a younger lad too, just three, also named Evan?" His cousin smiled again as they rode to the front and took their places. "He is watching the parade today with his mother. Ronan," he said then. "That wee lad would not be here if not for what you did in India. You saved my life and I will not forget it."

"I am honored. I—when I did not hear from you for years, I thought some memories were too difficult. I thought—you still resented what happened."

"I was angry at you, I admit, for dragging me back to Scotland when I insisted on staying. I was bitter about—what happened. I still have nightmares, I confess. But I never blamed you for my brother's death."

"I felt responsible for it, all the same. I left his side that day when you fell—and then he was taken down. I thought you avoided me because of it."

"Nothing can diminish what you did for me. I owe you more than I can ever say. I mean it sincerely. I am sorry you felt—otherwise. I should have said."

His cousin's resonant voice, so familiar from their younger days, was kind and warm. Ronan nodded, relieved and reassured. "Thank you."

"And I understand you are to be congratulated. Sir Hector's daughter, indeed! My wife wants to meet her. We shall have dinner soon."

"That would be excellent. We owe part of our happiness to you. Her father likes me better as a viscount."

Evan laughed, then glanced up. "Rain soon. This poor weather is cursing the king's visit. Well," he said, "shall we get moving?"

"If you are ready, sir."

"Let us show everyone the strength and majesty of the Scottish Highlanders." Riding forward with his young son and Ronan flanking him, Sir Evan paused to draw his sword and raise it high. He looked over his shoulder.

"*An Griogarach!*" he shouted.

A rousing clamor of voices echoed his cry as the Highlanders stepped forward.

EPILOGUE

$\mathcal{E}$llison sat in the carriage, twisting her gloves in her hand. "Do you see them?"

"Oh, do relax, Elly," Sorcha said. "You are so nervous today."

"Unnecessarily so," the viscountess agreed. "He will do well. And be patient. This will take time."

"I know. I just wish ladies were invited too. It is not easy to wait in the carriages while the introductions go on and on." Looking through the carriage window and across the courtyard of Holyroodhouse, she saw countless carriages gathered in the graveled drive fronting the palace. In each vehicle, ladies waited for their gentlemen. Some of them strolled around the grounds, skirts billowing, bonnet ribbons flying on that windy afternoon.

Inside the old palace, the levee was taking place exclusively for gentlemen, and the event was proving interminable. Ellison sighed.

"If the Duchess of Atholl and Huntly's countess and all the rest must wait, we are content to wait too," Lady Strathniven said. "Your Lord Darrach will be praised as an absolute gentleman. This day will lead to good things for both of you. Wait and see."

~

Sir Hector stood in front of Ronan, the two of them moving slowly ahead, step by step part of a long, crowded line of gentlemen waiting to be admitted to the inner room. Beyond the open doors on the other side of the hall, Ronan caught glimpses of King George, tall and flushed and decidedly portly, rushing through introductions.

"Our names will be called soon, I think," Sir Hector told Ronan. "We are moving ahead. Only a dozen or so men ahead of us now, and hundreds behind us. You are prepared. This will go well."

"Very well, thanks to your daughter, sir."

Sir Hector gave him a rare smile. "This whole thing has turned out better than I could have hoped. I owe you for this. And I owe you an apology."

"No sir, as we discussed earlier. All is well and will be well, once this is over and done."

"And once Corbie and Pitlinnie have had their comeuppance," Graham muttered. "By the way, you should know that when Lord Arbuthnot and I dined with King George last night—in a group with Sir Walter and some others—your name was mentioned."

"Was it?" Ronan tipped a brow, not sure what might follow. Sir Hector often leaned toward lecture and was rarely praiseful. Ronan was getting used to it.

"The king heard something of the scandal surrounding my secretary. Sir Walter filled him in on some details and your name came up. The king asked if this was the same Darrach who was responsible for the Glenbrae whisky he enjoys. I took the opportunity to say yes, the same, and my son-in-law. His Majesty seemed intrigued. Though very busy and hearing all manner of things that may not interest him, he—oh," he said. "We are moving ahead again. There is the dais."

Ronan peered ahead as they entered the inner room, shuffling along in the queue. At the other end of the room, he saw the dais, draped regally, and the king, tall and red-faced and rather large, with a booming voice and a rapid, abrupt manner of greeting and waving people along all at once. "Aye, sir. Continue."

"Then, you see, the king remembered seeing a petition recently to do with restoring an earldom that included Glen Darrach. His Majesty asked if it could be that whisky fellow. I confirmed it was so. And then— here, you need to show your calling card."

"I have it. And?" Ronan glanced toward the Lord-in-Waiting, who was accepting calling cards from a group of gentlemen in front of them.

"He seemed disposed to be helpful. I would say"—Sir Hector stepped forward, as did Ronan—"even pleased to be helpful. He very much likes your whisky—here we go," he murmured, surrendering his card. Ronan did the same. "And he likes being associated with heroic men. You saved Sir Evan MacGregor, who impresses him greatly, and my daughter as well in a chivalrous way. Acknowledging you makes the king look good. And that pleases him."

"Thank you for speaking up for me, sir."

"Another thing," Graham said. "I told Sir Walter that my daughter is an exceptional writer who I now understand is working on a very good story. He expressed interest in reading it when she has finished her manuscript."

Ronan grinned. "Excellent news, sir. She will be thrilled. If I may ask, sir, what is this petition that concerns the Darrach estate? I am unaware of it."

"It is new, but your lawyer may have heard of it by now. There he is, waiting for you. He is not being introduced but is here to cheer you on. Mr. Cameron!"

Hugh waved and made his way through the densely crowded room. With him was Judge Beaton. As greetings went around, they shuffled forward together as the line carved through the crowd.

"Darrach, have you heard the latest? Murder is afoot," Beaton said.

"Murder!" Ronan lifted a brow.

"Corbie seems eager to paint Pitlinnie with tar. He says Sir Neill was involved in setting up your arrest, wanting to be rid of you. And it seems he may have arranged for the deaths of your brother and cousin too. This is all according to Corbie, you understand."

Ronan shook his head. "My God. But I cannot say I am surprised."

"We need evidence, of course," Beaton said. "But those two are determined to undo each other now. Corbie claims Pitlinnie schemed to have all of Glenbrae eventually. And Pitlinnie claims Corbie wanted to marry Miss Graham—pardon, Lady Darrach—and bring harm to you. He was not going to inherit Strathniven, you see. His aunt did not favor him. She had decided to name Lady Darrach heiress."

"What! She never told us that. What a tangle indeed." Ronan wondered if Ellison suspected it. "But the murder of my kinsmen—I did wonder about Pitlinnie. The excise men were the ones that carried it out."

"Paid by Pitlinnie, says Corbie. It will take a while to sort through this unsavory mess. We are indebted to your wife for bringing these rascals to our attention."

"Mr. Corbie," Sir Hector said, "was not what I thought, I am humbled to say."

"Your daughter was in real danger. We see that now," Beaton said. "But we must wait on what a jury decides. All sides will be heard. Darrach, you have agreed to be a witness. And your wife could act as a witness too, sir," he added, "if you will allow it."

"My lord, that is her decision, not mine."

"The line is moving quickly now," Beaton said. "Who is next? Ah, Sir Willie Collins. People mistook him for the king yesterday due to his size. Got quite the laugh. Sir Willie enjoyed it. We will see if the king finds it amusing."

Hugh pulled Ronan aside as the others talked. "You know Pitlinnie was offering to buy Glenbrae. Sir Evan has refused the offer now."

"What! I thought it was signed and done."

"It was only under discussion. Pitlinnie never had the chance to sign. And now Sir Evan will not consider him. He has had another offer that will cover the debts owed on the property."

"Ah. Good." But he felt a new twist of grief at the thought of losing Glenbrae to anyone.

"The matter is not settled and is private. But I can tell you the arrangement would give you full rights to the glen and the distillery."

"Is that possible? But this party would still own Glenbrae."

"I believe it will be gifted back to the Darrach estate."

Ronan narrowed his eyes at a sudden thought. "Is this—coming from a certain viscountess, a neighbor of Darrach?"

"I did not say that." Hugh smiled.

"Truly, I am honored. My God. Does this have anything to do with a new petition?"

"Concerning the earldom of Strathniven? Could be."

"But the earldom is extinct. Well, dormant, specifically. Strathniven lands were split into Darrach, Glenbrae, and Strathniven when my great-grandfather lost all after the rebellion."

"Lady Strathniven wants to reinstate it. She is petitioning the king."

Ronan blinked, astonished. "She said nothing of that either."

"Everyone has their secrets," Hugh said, smiling. "The Crown owns the land legally, so it must be released. The Lyon Court would also need to approve the restoration of the earldom. But it seems the king is inclined to be generous. Sir Hector may have mentioned it."

"He did, just now." Ronan said. "But this is beyond anything I ever hoped. I never thought this could come back to my family."

"It is not guaranteed, but it could happen. You would have to give up the title of viscount in favor of earl. Scottish peers may hold only one title at a time."

"I understand. Restoring the original estate would benefit many. But what of Lady Strathniven?"

"She confided to me that she would be perfectly happy to rent from you."

"I could never take anything from her."

"Peppercorn rent, lad. A token. She would like that."

Ronan laughed. "A bunch of heather every summer?"

"It could be written into the lease. But we must wait for all this to develop."

"I am in no hurry. I am still getting used to being Lord Darrach. And a married man. And a free man."

"More than enough at the moment, sir," Hugh drawled.

"Listen for your name," Sir Hector advised, turning. "We are next."

"John Ronan MacGregor, Viscount Darrach," the Lord-in-Waiting called out. "Maker of Glenbrae whisky. Introduced by The Right Honorable Deputy Lord Provost of Edinburgh, Sir Hector Graham."

Ronan stepped forward.

When Ellison saw him walking between carriages just as a fresh downpour began, she leaned to fling open the carriage door and gathered her skirts.

"It is raining buckets!" Lady Strathniven protested. "Get back in here! You will ruin your gown!"

"It will dry!" Ellison called back, stepping down. "Ronan! Over here!"

He saw her then and ran toward her, rain pummeling his plaid and the dark bonnet, its feathers sagging wet. She ran toward him, laughing, the rain pouring over her, slicking her satin gown against her, dipping her bonnet's rim.

Grabbing her by the waist, he picked her up and spun her about, then set her down and kissed her thoroughly, lingering, a public display that brought forth laughter, even applause from some of the carriages.

Laughing, Ellison looped her arms around his neck, the next kiss hidden under the dripping brim of her bonnet and his flat cap, rain soaking them both.

"Not very proper behavior, sir," she said, leaning back to regard him.

"Hang proper. Though if you wish to tutor me further, I would not object."

"You know all you need to know, sir. How was it in there? You are in a rare mood."

He tipped up her chin and kissed her. "I heard some excellent news."

"Tell me!"

"Later, my lass. You are wet as can be. And we must wait—this news will take time if it is to come about."

"Can we wait in the Highlands? I am weary of being in the city."

"We can. But I can tell you that the king wishes to meet you at the ladies' assembly next week."

"A personal request?" Eyes wide, she looked up, hand to her hat in the rain.

"A quick kiss on your cheek and done, they say—after you wait hours in stifling heat in a crowd. But," he said, guiding her toward the carriage, "that one moment could change your life."

"One moment! I know what you mean. I met a Highland smuggler once, and my life has never been the same since."

"Nor has his." Laughing, he opened the door to the vehicle.

"Come in out of the rain—hurry!" Lady Strathniven beckoned as he handed Ellison into the carriage, then entered with a long step to sit beside her. Ellison smoothed her damp skirts while Ronan, still chuckling, removed his bonnet to ruffle his wet hair. "Ladies! Good to see you."

"Darrach, you seem cheerful," the viscountess said. "What did the king say?"

"His Majesty likes our whisky, my lady." He gave her a quirking smile.

"He is right! It is excellent stuff. We may all need a dram after this long wait in such miserable weather. You are thoroughly wet, the pair of you. But I vow you look happy as puppies."

"Happy? Oh, yes." Ellison smiled as Ronan lifted her gloved hand to kiss it. His blue eyes twinkled with some secret he held close, which she hoped he would share once they were completely, deliciously alone.

"Indeed," he said, weaving his fingers in hers, strong and warm through her lightweight glove. "Shall we go home to North Castle, my dear?"

"For a bit. But we must run to the Highlands as soon as we can." She leaned her head on his shoulder while Sorcha giggled and the viscountess beamed. "That is where we are truly home, and truly free."

"Now," Lady Strathniven said, "about our plans for your wedding at Strathniven. I was thinking—"

"Later, please, my lady," Ellison said. "We have plenty of time to plan the wedding."

"It will be a lovely affair," the lady continued. "I was thinking we could ask Sir Walter Scott to help us plan the perfect Scottish wedding—"

"No!" Ellison and Ronan said together, laughing. "He is surely exhausted after orchestrating this elaborate celebration of Scotland for the king's benefit," Ellison added.

"Well, I suppose. But it does no harm to ask," Lady Strathniven said, chatting on as the carriage lurched forward and rolled out of the courtyard.

Leaning in the circle of Ronan's arm, Ellison smiled. Indeed, it would do no harm to ask.

ABOUT THE AUTHOR

Susan King is the bestselling, award-winning author of 22 historical novels and novellas praised for historical accuracy, master storytelling, and lyricism. As Susan King and Sarah Gabriel, she has written several historical romances for Penguin Putnam and Avon; as Susan Fraser King, she writes historical fiction, including Lady Macbeth: A Novel, and Queen Hereafter: A Novel of Margaret of Scotland, from Random House. A former college lecturer and founding member of the popular Word Wenches blog, Susan holds graduate degrees in art history and lives in Maryland with her family.

susankingbooks.com
www.wordwenches.com

www.ingramcontent.com/pod-product-compliance
Lightning Source LLC
Chambersburg PA
CBHW030242030726
47493CB00023B/517